Ripping

Ripping Publishing
PO Box 286
Epsom, Surrey,
England KT19 9YG

The Author asserts the moral right to be identified
as the author of this work.

ISBN 1 899884 18 1

Printed by Cox & Wyman Ltd, Reading

The Author

Simon Shinerock was born on the 15th April 1957 in Tooting London. It was whilst studying for his degree at the University of London that he became engaged to Mary-Anne. They married in 1980 and together have built a successful real estate business in the UK. Simon is a keen sportsman, continuing to compete in veteran athletics and off-road motorcycle racing. In the future he would like to learn to Paraglide.

Throughout his business career he has maintained a strong interest in reading, being particularly fond of the work of Stephen King. He always intended to try his hand at writing a novel and the publication of the Dark Lagoon marks the realisation of a longtime ambition.

Whether there are any more books to come depends a lot on how this first novel is received and the pressures of business life.

Simon lives with his wife and three children in Coulsdon, Surrey.

Acknowledgements

For my wife Mary-Anne without whom I would not have been able to complete Dark Lagoon. For my children Charlotte, Catherine and Joshua. Thanks for listening to all those early chapters and being interested. For everyone at Choices for not making me feel guilty about the time I spent writing the book at work.

A word from the publisher...

It is with great pleasure that I introduce a new author to you the reader, from the growing *Ripping* library.

Dark Lagoon is a real *'Dark Fantasy'* and a compelling read. Simon Shinerock and myself go back many years now; so it is with particular pleasure that I am able to offer his work to you the reader. I know that he has been working on Dark Lagoon for many years. Certainly, long before the creation of Ripping Publishing.

In truth, I was concerned about publishing the work of a colleague and friend. However, now that *Dark Lagoon* is complete, any concern has evaporated. It is undoubtedly, a *Ripping* read!

I hardly dreamed that when I wrote *'Minds of the Empire'* in 1995 I would, just two years later, be publishing works from other authors. Authors with a taste for adventure and an understanding of the *Ripping Yarn* genre. It is a great thrill and pleasure to give others a chance to stick their central digit firmly up at the stale book-world!

In traditional fashion, grab a beer, put your feet up and enjoy!

Cheers

Warren James Palmer
Ripping@compuserve.com
WWW. Ripping-pub.co.uk

The
Dark Lagoon

by Simon M Shinerock

Prologue

Indigestion

I

By the time the service ended and Herbert returned to his car it was 10.30 p.m. As usual he hung around for a while, talking to the priest and other notaries about church business. Even though it was a week night the car park was stuffed full of cars, vans and ambulances. It was the same after every monthly healing mass; there was mayhem, as friends, relatives and nurses loaded up their sick and disabled charges ready for the drive back home (or back to the Home as was often the case).

This made leaving a hazardous and frustrating procedure, giving Herbert an excellent opportunity to indulge in one of his favourite pastimes; helping other "less worthy" people than himself to learn the gentle art of patience.

After making certain he hadn't forgotten to talk to anyone important, he said goodnight to Father Kennedy and slowly walked back to his car. He got in and made himself comfortable before starting her up and carefully, deliberately, manoeuvring his pride and joy out of its parking space and into the main thoroughfare where he stopped dead, blocking everyone's exit.

Once in position he collected himself together and went through all his usual pre-journey checks, oblivious to the inconvenience he was causing to the other churchgoers. While this was going on some of the less Christian worshippers started sounding their horns impatiently. This didn't worry him though, far from it, he found the sound gratifying, a sign of how necessary his little lesson really was.

No, these protests didn't concern or bother Herbert, after all the Lord taught patience and he was a patient man. If others were less so than he then perhaps they would benefit from his example; praise be the Lord.

When he was finally satisfied everything was in order, he eased the white Pinto into drive and moved gently towards the exit. As he snuggled comfortably into the fleece lining of his car coat, he thought how dark and unusually cold for the time of year it was. The thought of all the poor unfortunates in the world who didn't have a nice warm car coat, or a nice warm car for that matter, added considerably to the smug self-satisfaction he already felt, which he always felt, after one of these services.

It had indeed been most uplifting. He particularly liked going to healing masses, there were so many unworthy people to feel sorry for. Many were ill, only returning to the church in desperation but Herbert knew these people weren't true believers and could expect no help from the Lord. In spite of this belief, he always made sure he was among the worthy who stood and helped catch the souls "struck by the spirit" at the end of the service.

He would stand there waiting as the minister first prayed over them, then touched their foreheads lightly, (or sometimes not so lightly if the case demanded). Over backwards they would go, "struck by the spirit", into his waiting arms or the arms of one of the other good people of the parish. It never ceased to amaze him how most of them had the gall to come to church in the first place, some weren't even Christian and there they were expecting to be healed, no questions asked; fat chance. But he would smile comfortingly anyway and do his duty like he always did. Yes, he'd been going to the church and doing his duty rain or shine, three times a week minimum, for the last twenty three years. Twenty three years of service guaranteed a few favours when you needed them; oh yes, when he needed the Lord's help he got it and he always would, no question.

It was true, the Lord had been kind to him. He'd never needed to call on too many favours though, his life had been mostly uneventful, shielded by the Lord's mercy he liked to think and he was grateful for it. As he drove home that night he let his mind wander through the past, counting his many blessings until, as always, he ended up thinking about "the incident"; the one blot on his otherwise unblemished copybook, the one thing he most wanted to forget.

He'd moved twice since coming to the city. The first time was for the right reasons, he was doing well at work and there was no longer any need to stay in the little rented apartment in James Street. He still remembered the thrill of buying, of going into the Realtors' office to give the agent his requirements. No doubt they charged a small fortune in commission but as it wasn't him paying, it was worth every penny. He really made them work for their pieces of silver, going to see at least fifty properties before making up his mind (for the third time that is) and nearly driving the agent mad in the process.

In the end, he chose a modest neat little house in a good neighbourhood within easy reach of the museum where he worked as a curator, it was perfect, just perfect. The previous owners had no children or pets and the place was in truly lovely order, they'd really looked after it. He gave them hell when it came to working out the price though; he heard they were in financial difficulties, the man had lost his job and the bank was about to foreclose on the mortgage. Well that was their problem not his, he had certainly never seen *them* at the church and he doubted they attended any other, so few did these days, more's the pity.

Buying that house was a real milestone, after fifteen years at the museum he'd finally arrived. He was a respected member of the community, he earned a decent five figure salary in a respectable job, and owned a respectable but modest house in the suburbs. Yup, he had it made all right, he had everything he wanted to satisfy his needs.

Well, most of his needs anyway.

Never a particularly sexual person, some people didn't even hide the fact they thought he was gay, but he wasn't. Men, or women for that matter never really interested him, not like that anyway. Throughout his teens the other kids were obsessed with sex whereas he could never really see what all the fuss was about. Then one day he found out there were *things* that could turn him on, harmless *things*, though as he was to discover, others didn't share his view.

It had been in order to pursue these harmless fantasies that he signed up to help out at the local Children's Theatre. Being an English Lit major, it was easy to convince the Principal of his earnest intentions *and his intentions were after all very earnest indeed*; even if they weren't the same ones he talked about at his interview.

Despite never having acted or directed in his life he threw himself into his role in the group, quickly establishing his status as a stalwart member of the behind the scenes crew. Nothing was too much for him, he worked tirelessly, putting everything on the line for those kids.

And what thanks did he get for all his hard work,

huh? That was a joke; thanks! Even the thought of what happened made him feel sick to his stomach.

Who'd always been out there backstage making sure the props were put out (and put away) on time?

Who would sit there for hours listening to them recite their lines over and over again till they were right?

Who was always there at every first night and most performances?

Herbert Miller, that was who! And what good did it do him in the end? No good at all. The reverse actually, if it hadn't been for the Lord's help after the unfortunate incident, he would have had to do more than just move house. The mere thought of the possibilities sent shivers down his spine, partly out of fear but mostly out of righteous indignation at the way he was pilloried after all he'd done for those kids.

The incident itself was unplanned and to his mind totally harmless, he would never hurt anyone, much less a child and it was shameful for anyone to think that he could. Even now he could feel his cheeks flush red with temper as he remembered what happened and the brutal way he was treated.

It was early September, they'd been rehearsing for six weeks. The kids, mainly aged between ten and thirteen, were going to put on a showing of Peer Gynt. It was by far the most ambitious production ever undertaken by the youth theatre and it needed a lot of organisation. There were a lot of people who said the idea was a stupid one, saying that if it went ahead it would be an embarrassing disaster. He and a few others dug their heels in though, insisting it could and should be done.

Maggie Weismuller was especially insistent that the

show go ahead as she was keen to do all the costumes. She knew it would be a bit much for the kids but just couldn't resist the opportunity to indulge her passion for dressmaking and design. This hobby of hers was quite surprising considering the way she looked. She was a big woman, at least a hundred and eighty pounds and to say she wasn't very glamorous was like saying Attila the Hun wasn't very friendly. Her shoulder-length hair was usually dirty and unkempt looking, she bought all her dresses in the outsize department at K Mart and they were invariably too small, failing to disguise the fat hanging from her midsection in great blubbery rolls. But the two things that made Maggie particularly unattractive were her heavy facial hair, which had become so bad lately she'd been forced to take up shaving, and the fact that she constantly smelt like a lumberjack on a hot day. Designing and making beautiful clothes had become a fantasy outlet for Maggie and one she loved to indulge at every possible opportunity.

Her voice on the other hand was a revelation, it was warm and melodious with perfect pitch, it was a voice that caused many men to make suggestions on the telephone that they would soon forget if they ever were to meet her face to face.

But she and Herbert had developed a kind of understanding; it was unspoken, they simply recognised each other as kindred spirits, different from others, "special". He never socialised with her away from the theatre but he knew that if she was around he was safe to indulge himself and his little fantasies in the dressing rooms without fear of being interrupted unexpectedly, or of things being misunderstood by one of the meddling busybodies who passed for helpers.

On the day of his "mishap" rehearsal had gone badly, the children were disorganised, none of the links came off right and there was a disruptive element in the show that needed to be dealt with. This disruptive element went by the name of Gregory Fisher. Gregory was twelve years old and small for his age, he had dark curly hair and a cheeky smile which he quite often relied upon to get him out of the trouble he had a habit of getting himself into.

Maybe it was the long summer evening that was responsible for the restless atmosphere but whatever it was, Gregory took every opportunity to ambush the rehearsal by distracting other members of the cast. He made rude remarks about the girls' costumes, he made cracks whenever someone fluffed their lines and generally orchestrated the kind of havoc likely to drive a grown man to tears.

Now everyone knew that you couldn't put on a half decent production without *discipline*. If he'd said it once, he'd said it a million times, these kids needed a strong hand from time to time if the best was going to be got out of them. Although he was never actually asked to do the job, after a while it had become accepted that when a child played up, he would deal with it.

It was certainly true that after he'd spoken to a child they rarely gave any further trouble; a few of the more sensitive creatures had even chosen to leave the group as a result, but if that was the price that had to be paid to maintain *discipline*, then so be it.

He always handled these situations the same way, never scolding or chiding in public; he would simply ask the offending child to see him after rehearsal. These meetings would invariably take place in the *Props Room* that doubled as a kind of administration office. *The Props Room* was a place where he could be very *stern* indeed, often reducing the child to tears but always making sure they had dry eyes before their parents arrived. For that same reason he always kept a few packets of sweets and the kind of small junky trinkets that children liked in the *Props Room*; you never knew when they might come in handy.

A couple of times, when he may have been a little over zealous, a small bribe made sure there was never any come back. If he was honest, he'd had a few scares in the early days before he worked out how far he could go without attracting unwelcome attention. What particularly appealed to him about Gregory was the fact that his foster parents had hit hard times and were recently forced to give him up, so for a while he'd been living in a Home. From experience he knew he could afford to go a lot further with a Home boy without fear of repercussions, so Gregory's antics that day received his *special* attention.

Nevertheless the child was given fair warning; he fixed him with a deliberate stare at least three times before informing the young man that he required to see him after rehearsal in the *Props Room*. He remembered how Maggie had thrown him a knowing look which reassured him they wouldn't be interrupted. At the time he felt very happy at the prospect of administering the naughty boy with some much needed *discipline*, he was confident that it would do the lad good (*and he was sure as hell it would do him good as well*).

The rest of the rehearsal seemed to drag on endlessly, there were several more total breakdowns before it was finally over. The youngsters' already short attention spans had been further reduced by the prospect of playing outside in the warm evening sun. They knew if they carried on playing up eventually the adults would give up and let them go early. Unusually, given his predicament, Gregory was as annoying as ever, perhaps even more so. Kids who were asked to see him after rehearsal normally had the good sense to keep their heads down afterwards lest they incur his greater wrath.

Gregory however appeared to be totally unconcerned at the prospect, if anything he was playing to the crowd who found his antics even funnier because of their disrespectful implications. He remembered thinking how that type of behaviour could not be tolerated, it really incensed him. He felt like his entire authority and reputation was being undermined by a kid and he wasn't about to overlook it. No siree, he was going to teach that kid a lesson he wouldn't forget in a hurry he surely was.

He remembered the bittersweet feelings of anticipation that built up inside him that day, and how when the time finally came for the kids to pack up and go, he could hardly contain his eagerness to get on with it. Then there was a despairing moment when he looked around and there was only Maggie and a couple of stragglers left behind, no sign of Gregory Fisher. Surely the little tike didn't have the temerity to leave without seeing him? The thought burned him even more, he started to entertain *bad thoughts* about the boy, much worse than in the past and those *bad thoughts* made him feel stronger and more powerful than he could ever remember.

By the time Gregory finally appeared he'd worked himself up into a bit of a frenzy which he found difficult to conceal. His top lip was shaking, small beads of sweat had broken out on his forehead and even better, he had one of his rare erections. The boy, who had merely gone to the men's room, probably because he was scared and needed to relieve himself, stood before him looking hopeful. He'd changed back into his everyday clothes and carried his bag over one shoulder as if he were about to leave.

His expression was easy to read. It said, "Do I have to stay behind? If you let me go this time I promise to be good in future". That's what the expression said but the eyes, those eyes, they said something different. They said *"I've been bad today, very bad and if you let me go I'm going to be bad tomorrow and the day after and there's nothing you dare do about it"*. Nothing he, Herbert Miller dared do about it? *Well they were going to see exactly what he did dare do about it and Gregory Fisher was going to learn never to mess with him again.*

He gave one final glance at Mary who was still clearing the stage, she nodded in understanding and he motioned the boy in the direction of the *Props Room*. They arrived at the door with Gregory slightly in front which further irritated him as he was forced to shuffle the boy out of the way in order to get the key in the lock to open up. Once he'd unlocked the door, he stood back and stuck out his arm indicating that Gregory should go in first.

There was still that teasing look in the boy's eyes, he'd been wrong about the fear, there was no fear, just an insolent cockiness. It suddenly struck him that this boy wasn't taking matters seriously enough. In the past all the children he'd *disciplined* had been vulnerable and supplicant. This had somehow always taken the edge off the experience because deep down he *wanted* them to put up a fight so he could demonstrate how truly powerful and dominant he really was.

This one on the other hand was more challenging than the others, his teasing attitude goaded Herbert to go further than he ever had before. At first things went as usual. He sat the boy down on the stool at the back of the room where he'd made a clearing between the rows of costumes and boxes full of props. This measure was designed to ensure his little interviews were well screened should some busybody decide to poke their nose in where it wasn't wanted at an inappropriate moment. There was also a chair for him but at first he chose to stand, he always started off this way, it showed the child who was the boss and made Herbert feel more masterful, more in control of what was happening.

Even once he was seated the boy still wouldn't show any signs of nerves or apprehension. He didn't smile or laugh outwardly but there was a smirk in those eyes, a smirk which seemed to imply they knew something that gave the boy power over *him*. All through the lecture that followed he kept that same look in his eyes, refusing to show due respect, or take things seriously, never mind be intimidated.

Finally Herbert really began to lose his temper (*get excited*) his cheeks had flushed and his body began to shake slightly. He sat down on the chair in front of the boy, who seemed to find his reaction amusing, and steadied himself.

'Gregory,' he said in the most menacing tone he could manage 'I can see that nothing I say is going to have any effect on you, so I'm afraid you are forcing me to resort to more extreme measures, I am going to have to administer *corporal punishment*.'

Now that got the boy's attention at last; it was amazing the way the look in his eyes turned so rapidly from insolence to fear, he started to squeak in protest but by now Herbert was all out of patience, he wanted some action. He made a grab for the boy who was too frightened to move or cry for help, his jaw just moving up and down soundlessly. This reaction filled Herbert with excitement, he was finally in control, now they would see who the real boss was around here.

He twisted him over his knee bringing one arm down on his back so he couldn't move. He remembered being surprised at how little he struggled, all his previous cockiness gone, like a cornered deer, frozen as the lion prepares to move in for the kill.

Like a lion, he felt the need to toy with his prey a little; surprising himself at how deftly he managed to slide the boy's trousers and pants round his ankles. He started to spank those bare buttocks with exquisitely light strokes which were almost (but not quite) caresses. Suddenly and violently the boy did start to struggle, catching him unawares, making him lose his grip for a moment, enabling him to wriggle free and shout out loudly.

Almost instantly the door to the *Props Room* was flung open without warning and two cleaners burst into his inner sanctum.

It all happened far too quickly to have been in response to Gregory's call for help although it may as well have been, the outcome was the same. The cleaners took one look at the scene, the adult seated, red faced and out of breath, the minor semi-clothed and now crying with relief and confusion. They knew what'd been happening and given the rumours about Mr. Miller, they weren't surprised, or so it seemed, particularly concerned. There was something else on their minds, something important enough to override their natural outrage, for a while at least.

It was a cruel irony that it was Maggie, his soul sister who was responsible, at least indirectly for his disgrace. In another way though it was only the melodrama surrounding her death that enabled him to escape without losing his job, gaining a criminal record and quite possibly a jail sentence as well.

They said it was Maggie's weight that was responsible for the heart attack that killed her. She didn't die straight away, but at the state hospital a few days later. The stupid woman had forgotten to take her medication and her blood pressure had soared out of control popping the major artery in her head. Even if she'd survived, she would never have been able to walk or talk again.

As far as he was concerned, the only tragedy about her death was it meant she didn't have to pay for what she'd done to him, the fat bitch. He could feel the bile coming up in his throat, the feeling he always had whenever he recalled those events, it always put him in such a bad mood, something he didn't deserve, especially coming back from doing good work at the church; life could be just so unfair.

II

He was so engrossed in his own thoughts, he almost didn't see the man standing in the middle of the road until it was too late. He could have sworn he came out of nowhere, one second the road was clear, the next there was this crazy guy trying to commit suicide in front of him. There could be no doubt that he was trying to do away with himself either, he wasn't scuttling across the road having misjudged the oncoming traffic, in fact he wasn't moving at all. He just stood there facing the oncoming car, looking him directly in the eyes, challenging him to drive on and run him down.

Herbert wasn't a violent man, he abhorred violence, he was also very squeamish, the thought of all that blood and the damage the impact would do to his beloved car was too much for his gentle nature. It was therefore a knee jerk reaction that caused him to swerve to avoid the man, for all he knew he could have been turning into a brick wall. Although he was only doing thirty, the effect of hitting a brick wall head on would have been the same as if he were going eighty. His car was old and somehow he never had got the habit of wearing a seat belt, very out of character given how cautious he was in most other things.

He was never to know that it wasn't the impact of a collision that killed him, his last memories would have ended as he entered the side road. It was possible, though unlikely, that he may have regained consciousness for a moment later on. If he did, the thought would probably have crossed his mind that he was wrong again, when it came to the crunch God wasn't there to protect the righteous, all his good works were for nothing, it just wasn't fair.

III

Wilbur had no difficulty dragging Herbert's limp body from the car and carrying it to his own. Ever since he met Proctor his strength seemed to have multiplied, giving him a power that belied his size and age, never mind the amount he smoked and drank.

This was a routine affair for him, he found the whole thing quite ordinary, after all Proctor needed a constant supply of bodies, correction, live bodies and it was his job to find them.

They say honesty and fairness is its own reward, well he wasn't sure about that, but he did find his work rewarding, Proctor was good to work for, he made him feel important, part of something bigger than himself of something extraordinary.

Before he met Proctor he'd been at rock bottom, involved with the mob spending his life on the make, hustling, pushing and sometimes killing to get what he wanted. He'd controlled one of the biggest Italian restaurants in Miami, a front for drug dealing and a particularly vile human trade. They would ship in young girls from South America, usually Costa Rica and use the rooms above the restaurant as a kind of halfway house before finding profitable homes for them in the specialist paedophile brothels of Miami.

Judged in dollars business was going well; he was amassing a fair sized fortune, he had a young wife and all the material things he could ever want but it wasn't enough, nothing was enough to fill the empty void inside him. The only thing he had that could touch that void was hate, he hated the people he did business with, he hated the people he met in bars, in supermarkets, he hated everything and almost everyone, even his wife.

The only person he didn't hate was his only son Ronnie, and of course Ronnie had hated him. It didn't seem to matter what he did, that boy wouldn't give him a break. He'd sent him to the finest private schools, given him a generous allowance, bought him a new car every year but it hadn't mattered. Ronnie didn't like the way his old man spoke, didn't like the people he associated with, didn't like the way he treated women and above all didn't like the business he was in. Of course these finer feelings never stopped him taking the money but they did lead to fights.

Eventually, they had one fight too many and Ronnie had gone away taking his mother with him. At least that was what Wilbur told everyone and what everyone had come to believe. The truth was more bitter, the truth was he'd murdered them both.

Wilbur always had a terrible temper and the boy knew it, what he never knew was when to back off for his own good. Oh no, he'd just keep on pushing... push, push, push; the day it happened he just pushed too far. He was twenty one years old and they'd been at home arguing as usual about something or other, Wilbur couldn't even remember what it was. Oh yeah; it was coming back to him now.

It was all caused by Margarita not being able to account for the housekeeping money. It wasn't the first time either, the dumb bitch was always running out of cash halfway through the week and it drove him mad. That day he'd had enough and he was going to teach her a lesson she'd never forget.

Of course Ronnie had to get involved, taking her side like he always did, accusing him of having double standards, of taking out his gambling losses on his family. He'd been drinking heavily all day and wasn't in the mood to be lectured by anyone, least of all his son. The bottom line was he ended up losing his temper and working him over pretty bad. Even then the boy wouldn't leave it alone, he kept needling and needling, saying anything he could think of to make him madder; accusing him of being an impotent psychopath, a sadist, a homosexual, anything to get a reaction.

What made him pull the gun he still wasn't sure, it might have been an automatic response to being pushed so hard, all he could remember was feeling disappointed, let down, all he wanted to do was to shut him up. Here was his only son, the only person on earth he had ever loved and he was just like everyone else, just as weak, disloyal and pathetic. He had to kill him, he had no choice and even after he did it he felt no remorse, just more emptiness, more disappointment and more hate. Then of course Margarita came running in screaming and crying and he shot her as well, although that was no great loss really.

The feelings of being empty, unfulfilled and disappointed didn't go away after Ronnie's death, just the reverse, they grew and grew. No matter how much he drank or gambled, or how many people he killed, there was nothing that would make those feelings go away. It

The Dark Lagoon

would only have been a matter of time before he got careless and either ended up in some stinking jail, or just like his father before him, the cell of some sanatorium for the criminally insane. Even more likely, he'd be taken out by one of his business partners, if the hate and bitterness in his heart didn't totally consume him first.

He went through three women before he married his second wife, a Costa Rican beauty less than half his age called Maria. The first had survived but the second wasn't so lucky, he sometimes thought about the first woman and wondered where she was, what she was doing. There was even the thought that he may one day hunt her down and kill her, or pay someone else to do the job.

Then one day something happened, which although he didn't understand it fully gave him back the meaning to his life in spades. He was given a second chance, a reason to live.

He'd been at the restaurant, a place he tried to avoid these days. Too many people, too much noise, too much life. The reason he was there was simple, he had a deal to do, a big deal, the biggest he'd ever done and it involved a lot of money. There were always going to be risks, the kind of business partners he was involved with weren't above avoiding a debt by eliminating their creditor, if they thought they could get away with it. As with all things though there are degrees of risk and levels of craziness. That night he descended to level zero, the lowest level around, the one where the craziest characters lived and the chances of escaping with your life were slimmest.

Life really didn't matter to him any more, he already felt dead and he wasn't going to be worried by a few drugged out grease-balls no matter how well connected they were. *It even occurred to him that he might be the craziest cuckoo in the nest, and it was the grease-balls not him who needed to watch their backs if they wanted to see the dawn of another day.*

The *stuff* he was buying was uncut heroin. The price was too cheap and there was a reason for it. The grease-balls had already sold it to his biggest rival. His information came from an unimpeachable source, one of his own people on the inside of their organisation, so he knew if he made the buy it was liable to start a war. Now ordinarily he wouldn't necessarily be put off by a little conflict, provided he could see himself coming out on top at the end of it. But over the past months he'd let things slip in his own organisation, if there was a showdown now he would almost certainly lose and end up dead in the process. Somehow though, the prospect of death made him even more determined to go ahead; the way he looked at it, if he was going down it might as well be sooner rather than later and it might as well be in flames.

After the deal was done and the money and drugs safely exchanged, he decided to go outside for a walk. This was possibly the stupidest thing he could do. There was a good chance that someone would be out there waiting for him in an unmarked sedan, ready to put a few bullets into him as soon as he put a foot onto the side walk. So what? he thought, what the hell! Perhaps after killing him they'd raid the place and steal back the drugs. Who knew? Who cared? Not Wilbur Kohn that was for sure.

Once he got outside the night air was colder than expected, there was no black limo waiting for him, no rat tat tat of machine gun fire to finally put him to sleep. The street was empty and quiet; uncannily so. In addition, the cityscape was blurred by a mist that seemed to be erupting from across the street in front of him. The whole scene kind of reminded him of a magic show he'd seen when he was a kid, when the magician appeared on stage in a puff of smoke.

He reached into his jacket pocket and pulled out a pack of cheroots; there was one left, so he removed it and cast the empty packet onto the sidewalk. As he lit the cheroot, in the flame of the match he caught a glimpse of a dark figure standing across the street. The mist made it hard to make the figure out but it vaguely crossed his mind that this could be it.

He could have just seen his killer waiting patiently to do the job he'd been paid to do. The match burned out but he could still see the figure, perhaps even a little more clearly now. He looked up at the sky and noticed a bright crescent moon shining through the mist. Slowly reaching into his jacket he gently withdrew his Beretta part way out of its holster, thinking, if this was to be his encounter with death, then the least he could do was to make it an interesting one.

He spat the cheroot into the street and started to walk slowly towards the figure. As he got closer he could see it was a tall man dressed in a heavy black coat (any amount of weaponry could have been hiding in that coat). What did he have to worry about though? One cap from his little B and it wouldn't matter if the fucker was carrying an anti-tank gun under there for all the good it'd do him.

He stepped off the sidewalk and onto the empty highway, this was a commercial part of town and most of the buildings were run down, in any event at this time of night they were deserted. The stranger hadn't moved from his spot, he stood about twenty five metres away, between two old monolithic factories dating from before the war. They weren't tall but their tops were hidden by the mist which seemed to be getting thicker by the second, threatening to obscure or absorb everything around it.

As he approached, the man made a movement with his left hand, reaching deliberately inside that heavy coat, finally confirming his mission that night. Wilbur knew what would be in that hand when it emerged and whose name it was that would be written on the bullet that would follow. Well he was real sorry to ruin the plan and everything but he was going to have to end the party before it began. He withdrew his own gun, taking the time to notice how the Beretta felt natural, comforting before he opened fire. He hesitated for a moment when the stranger didn't react at all, the thought even occurred to him that he may have got it wrong, that he may be about to shoot an innocent man. Then the thought evaporated, there *were* no innocent men, just hunters and their prey, killers and their victims. Then he realised that although the stranger's expression hadn't changed nor his movements speeded up, they hadn't stopped either, if he didn't stop thinking and act he would pay the price for his indecision.

The gunshot crashed through the night, it was a comforting noise, something you could always rely on, the flash momentarily forcing back the mist and bringing the skyline into sharp relief.. He didn't fire again, why waste the bullets? He was a great shot and he'd aimed carefully, the guy was dead, end of story. Slowly though, it dawned on him that *the man in black* wasn't doubling up in pain or recoiling with the force of the impact. He wasn't writhing around on the ground and dying like a good little fuck; nope, he wasn't even reacting, he just kept on reaching for whatever he was reaching for as if nothing had happened at all.

He felt a little put out by this behaviour, it threatened his perception and shook his faith in the fundamentals of life. There was only one thing for it, he had to re-establish the order of things and to do this was going to be simple.

The Dark Lagoon

He raised his aim away from the man's body up to his unprotected head. There was no more holding back either, no more Mr. Nice Guy as he unloaded the remains of the clip right into the stranger's face.

The explosions seemed to go on forever and with every one he felt a little better. When the clip was empty he carried on pulling the trigger oblivious to the impotent sound of the hammer falling onto empty chambers.. When the smoke finally cleared and he saw the man was standing holding out his hand towards him, he stopped firing and dropped the gun. It was impossible, he should've been lying on the floor without a head, not standing there for all the world as if he was greeting a long lost friend.

The thought struck him that perhaps he'd finally crossed the frontier between sanity and insanity. I mean here he was standing in the street, having just unloaded his Beretta into a man who seemed not to have noticed. Yup, the men in white coats couldn't be far away now.

'*Wilbur, come to me. I have something for you.*'

He wheeled round when he heard the voice, he'd been watching the man carefully and the sound definitely hadn't come from his mouth, there had to be someone else in on this, an accomplice who was watching the whole farce and laughing at him.

'*Come to me now Wilbur, don't keep me waiting.*'

Eventually he accepted that there was no-one else around, which left only two other possibilities, either *the man in black* was some kind of *magician*, or the voice was coming from inside his own head.

Somehow, without being aware of it, he'd crossed the distance between himself and *the* man in black and stood before him holding out his hand ready to accept the gift.

'*Wilbur,*' said the voice. '*I am not your master and you are not my slave, do you accept this gift willing?*'

He shouldn't have known what the voice was talking about but somehow it all made sense. This man *was* his master and he *was* his slave, he didn't need to be coerced into accepting the gift, he wanted it, he wanted it so bad it hurt. The man in black smiled and withdrew his hand, watching the expression on Wilbur's face change from wonder to despair as he realised the offer was being withdrawn.

'*I see*' said the voice, as if confirming whether or not it had made the right choice.

Wilbur was sure he'd been rejected and for some reason the thought was too much to bear, the emptiness had finally won, there was no longer any point in living. If his Beretta hadn't been empty he would have finished it right there in the street in front of the man in black.

'*Don't be sad,*' said the voice. '*I mean to redeem you*'

Redemption; the word had no meaning to him but the sound of that voice put his despair on hold, he realised he needed that voice now more than he needed life itself. If that voice had commanded him to jump off a bridge he would do it, if it asked him to save his own life, he would even do that too.

'*Take this gift and wear it as a sign of our friendship.*'

The hand was outstretched again and now he could see that it held a silver ring. The ring was simple in design but a closer look revealed the emblem forged on to its surface, was in the shape of a crescent moon.

He extended his hand to receive the gift and the man in black took hold of his wrist and slipped the ring onto his left forefinger. There was a moment of searing pain as it seemed the ring was welding itself to him, becoming part of his body. He smelt the burning flesh and imagined the smoke curling up from around the edges of the ring, then the pain was gone and his head was clear, clearer that it had ever been. More to the point, the emptiness had gone and since that day it had never returned.

He had a new mission and meaning to his life, one that he pursued with enthusiasm and carried out proficiently. His job was to make sure the man in black was supplied with a steady stream of .... of, he didn't know how to describe them, victims, sacrifices, or just fuel he would use in his own unique way. Herbert was just the latest in a long line and he wouldn't be the last.

IV

It didn't matter how many times he went out to the Island, he always felt the same feeling of awe as he entered the mist, knowing that just before him lay a land other mortals would never know, could barely even comprehend. The thrum of the twin engines of the motor launch took on a deeper note as if the mist was harder to ingest than normal air. He felt sorry for his quiet passenger who couldn't appreciate the honour that was being bestowed upon him. He looked across at Herbert sitting beside him looking straight ahead, vacant, the lights were on but no-one was home. It was a look he'd seen many times before and one with which he'd become only too familiar.

'So old buddy; enjoying the ride?' He paused as if he was really waiting for a reply. 'Cat got your tongue huh? Never mind, you just relax and let me do the talking for both of us, after all this is your day.

You see, I've seen all this before, whereas you....you

need a chance to take it all in. Just one thing old buddy, don't take too long getting used to things because you may not have as much time as you think.'

He laughed out loud at his private joke, and gunned the launch towards the Island's shore.

As they emerged from the mist that surrounded it, the south side of the Island was revealed. It didn't matter how many times he made this trip, Wilbur was always filled with wonder at the sight of it. If there is a heaven on earth, then it would probably look like Proctor's Island. Even from five hundred metres offshore it was easy to see that here was a very special piece of terra firma.

The Island didn't conform to any natural laws. By rights it should have looked much like all the other Islands in the region, Key Largo for instance which was a long thin piece of land, its shape determined over millions of years by the sometimes tiny, sometimes catastrophic movements of massive continental plates. There was no high ground, no forest, and the tallest tree was the palm. Proctor's Island should have been much the same but it wasn't.

As the launch drew nearer, it became clear just how impossible the Island really was. A perfect sandy beach was flanked by white cliffs rising a hundred feet above the ocean. Along the tops of the cliffs you could clearly make out the edge of a rain forest. At various points waterfalls cascaded into unseen pools sending up great spumes of spray; sunlight turning the droplets into shimmering rainbows which danced in the air, making the Island look as if it were set within some fantastic precious stone.

Wilbur felt his breathing quicken with excitement as it always did every time he saw the Island. For a few moments he just gazed at it, totally enraptured until his eyes could take no more of its excruciating beauty.

The Dark Lagoon

He aimed the launch straight at the entrance to the cove, throttling back at the last minute and letting the vessel coast silently towards the shore. As they moved in closer he headed towards a small jetty, bringing the launch up alongside and making her fast before turning to his prisoner who had given no sign of having registered anything at all.

'OK old buddy, this is your stop,' he said taking Herbert by the left hand and guiding him out of his seat, up the ladder and onto the jetty. Even the smell of the Island was different from any other place on earth, There were hints of cinnamon, lime, and vanilla in the breeze, overlaid with the scent of exotic flowers, as if someone had spent hours choosing exactly how they wanted the Island to smell.

Underneath the fragrant facade though there was something else, something disturbing lurking beneath the surface speaking of secrets dark and dangerous.

Often Wilbur would go up onto the beach and wait for his master. When he came they would talk and Proctor would let him know anything special he wanted him to do. Over the years their interests on the mainland had increased although it seemed they didn't really interest Proctor at all. Gradually he also lost interest in these mundane pursuits, delegating the everyday running of their operation to well paid underlings, becoming more and more captivated by the Island and its development. When he thought back to the first time he set foot on these shores, it was hard to believe they weren't completely different places. There was hardly a trip he would make when he didn't notice some new feature and there was no doubt about it the Island had grown, it was a lot bigger these days. He took great pride in these changes, maybe he wasn't the architect of them but at least he could claim to be his main assistant.

Today however he didn't stop, he was pre-occupied with something else, a search that was taking up more and more of his time lately, a search important enough to make him impatient to return to the Keys as soon as possible.

He walked down the jetty, Herbert needing only a little encouragement to trot along in front, seeing nothing, feeling nothing, totally unaware of his fantastic surroundings. One of the things that tickled him the most was the way he could take a person and make them like Herbert. It was one of the things he learned from Proctor early on. Not everyone was susceptible to the influence but he quickly established how to choose his subjects wisely and he hadn't made a mistake in years. Sometimes he wondered whether the effect would eventually wear off, he didn't know because he'd never seen anyone he'd brought to the Island ever again. He left his latest victim sitting on the white coral sand and turned around without a backward glance. A few moments later he was powering back to the mainland leaving Herbert to await his doom.

V

Herbert didn't have long to wait, within seconds of the launch disappearing over the horizon and into the mist Proctor appeared to claim his prize. Herbert found himself being led through the impossible Island a silent witness to all its miracles and follies. Of course he could appreciate none of it, nor would he ever understand the contribution he would make to its destiny.

Proctor had made this journey innumerable times before, the fact that he still personally guided each of his new guests to their destination was out of ritual not necessity. If he desired it his victims could have been delivered to him wherever he wanted but that would be to deny himself the symbolic transition from light into darkness.

He would walk with them through the Island appreciating as he went all the wondrous marvels he'd created. It helped to remind him of the inestimable value of his work and the enormous privilege he was bestowing on the one who accompanied him. If he had spoken to Herbert at all, it would have been to tell him how greatly honoured he was to be allowed to make his small contribution towards such a wondrous place. Of course there was no point in talking to Herbert so he saved his breath, instead hurrying onwards towards the Island's centre where it hid its blackened heart.

The moonlit walk took about half an hour during which the strange pair travelled through a land of many marvels. It was as if someone had gone round the world shopping for the right animals and plants to complement the habitat and where none could be found made them up to suit. But as they started to approach the centre of the Island, things started to change. At first it was hardly noticeable, the odd tree infected with some wasting disease, a dead bird lying untouched by predators, a small patch of land where nothing grew. The further they walked the more evidence there was of decay and rot until it became clear something was drastically wrong.

From a paradise on earth, the surroundings had gradually metamorphosed into an earthly hell in which all living things were either dying or dead. The smell which had up to now lurked beneath the fragrant air leapt unbounded to the fore, finally revealing itself for what it was, the stench of evil decay and death. At the centre of the dead plain like an open sore on the landscape lay a sinister oasis, a Dark Lagoon, towards which Proctor led Herbert Miller. It was to be by its blackened shores that he would meet his destiny.

When they arrived at its edge, Proctor stood absolutely still and looked across the oily surface of the waters. His expression was one of intense meditation, as if he were in communion with a monstrous deity lurking beneath the depths. After a time the waters seemed to sense their presence and began to send small waves rippling slowly to the shore. He seemed happy with this and turned to Herbert who was still waiting patiently by his side, looking quite dishevelled now, his clothes crumpled and torn. It was many hours since his abduction, hours during which he'd had nothing to either eat or drink, although from the stain on his pants it seemed his body's desire to relieve itself remained intact. His face was tired and drawn and he stood with a pronounced stoop, only the forces controlling him keeping him on his feet at all.

Proctor looked across at this sorry looking individual and allowed himself to indulge in a brief moment of sentimental reminiscence. He could remember in the old days how these human offerings were so much more robust, spiritually as well as physically. There was a time when the positive life force he drained from a simple peasant would satisfy him completely, leaving little to add to the waters. Over the years though things had changed. Man was becoming more civilised, more sophisticated. In a way, these changes made his job easier as his victims became less wary of him and his servants but they also brought with them an unwelcome side effect. People seemed to contain less and less goodness and more and more badness. Lately he could almost see the level of the dark waters rising after every new sacrifice and often he would be left feeling unnourished and unsatisfied. He cut short his lament for the good old days, knowing the time for the

The Dark Lagoon

transformation was approaching.

He felt Herbert's mind opening to him, the night darkened, blotting out the stars, the only thing saving them from inky oblivion was the half light of the silver crescent moon.

He tilted his face skywards, acknowledging the moon extending his arms upwards and outwards in a gesture of welcome. The diffused moonlight began to waver and break up, patches of darkness appeared, hanging in the air eating the light, rendering the world putrid and rotten. But the light was itself gathering together, light with light, concentrating its strength as if preparing to launch some unimaginable counter-attack against the invading darkness.

Finally the remains of the light, surrounded and under siege made a last ditch bid for freedom towards the moon. The beam became a flood lasting less than a second, then it was over and the only thing that prevented the land being overcome totally by the darkness was the faintest of glows from the crescent moon.

Herbert's body had begun to shake and contort struggling vainly with an unseen force, the struggle didn't last long, his already weak spirit had no stomach for the contest. When it was over his facial muscles relaxed and his jaw fell open in surrender. A luminous glow appeared in the centre of his chest, brightening first to burnt umber, then red; orange, yellow and finally to a dazzling white which threatened to consume his body, leaving it a charred sacrifice on the banks of the dark lagoon. No human could have stood that light, yet the brightness intensified still, until within the incandescence there could be seen the seeds of unborn stars, the furnace of creation revealed in all its awful glory.

The place where they'd been standing had turned supernova, the nucleus which started in Herbert's chest now rose and spread out to hang like the sun above the dark lagoon. Just as it seemed the whole Island would be consumed by this cosmic inferno, the light began to wane. Whereas it started in Herbert it ended in Proctor, the fading glow disappearing into his chest with a symbolic finality that left no doubt as to the fate of its prior owner. The moonlight had returned, perhaps a little brighter, revealing the two figures standing as before but no longer the same, no subtle transformation this but a terrible change leaving one stronger and one drained of all that saves a man from damnation. Around them the Island had grown a little stronger, a little larger, perhaps a few new features had been added, or a strange new species would be found flourishing in a newly created habitat.

Herbert, though still standing and breathing had changed. He was a charred and blackened shadow of his former self, a hulk whose life force had been stolen leaving him only with the unspeakable part of his nature for which Proctor had no use. No use, true, but a place certainly. Yes there was a place for him, a cold place where he could share his fall with the others who had gone before him. That place even now sensing his changed nature, beckoned to him. Proctor watched dispassionately as the latest source of his increasing strength and power turned sightlessly and walked on guided feet towards the edge of the dark lagoon where he paused and looked down. But the look became a stoop and the stoop a fall. There was no splash as his body hit the water, no splash and no sound.

Proctor looked deeply into the blackness for a long moment after Herbert disappeared, contemplating his own doom. In over a thousand years he'd witnessed countless endings such as this and after each there was always the shadow of insecurity, a feeling he only ever felt at these times. Insecurity because he didn't know the price of his ascension or how it must be paid. Insecurity because as his power grew and the Island flourished, so too did the dark lagoon. Even now its banks groaned under the weight of the swollen waters. There must come a day when it could hold no more; he couldn't help thinking about that day, how soon it would come and what its consequences would be.

The Dark Lagoon

For a thousand years he'd watched it grow as he grew wondering when it would try to consume him. He turned to walk away, knowing that when he returned it would be just a little bit deeper, just a little more swollen, just a little closer to breaking point.

VI

He had less time to wait than he thought. At first the vibration was hardly noticeable, a trembling emanating from deep down in the earth's centre, gathering strength, working its way slowly but inexorably towards the surface, seeking the lines of least resistance, always returning to its chosen course. He made no attempt to run or find cover, for this was the long awaited moment. Soon he would see if his nightmare or his dreams would be realised.

The ground started to shake, in the silver light of the crescent moon the still black waters began to dance and jump in tune with the vibration. Ripples were forming, ripples that grew quickly into small waves. The waves travelled in all directions, colliding into one another and sending great splashes into the air which fell back to the surface in a fetid stinking rain.

The trembling in the ground developed into a full blown quake, one which would go unregistered by any Richter scale. The ground was rocking and rolling like an enraged bull trying to dislodge an impudent rider and trample him underfoot. Proctor though was not to be dispatched so easily, he stood his ground, moving fluidly with each new convulsion as if he were part of the fabric of the Island itself. As the shaking grew to its climax, the air responded also, the elements had decided to have a party and all were welcome. The wind came suddenly and violently, whipping the waters into a frenzy of foam and dark spume which rose up in a doom-laden mushroom cloud to be carried away on the infected air.

Then the pain started. In a thousand years he'd never experienced pain but now he experienced a thousand years of pain compressed into a single second. Every poisonous drop of rain that fell to earth, felt like acid burning his flesh. Everywhere the waters dealt out decay, corruption and death. He was the Island and the Island was him as they suffered their destruction together.

Confirming his despair a giant geyser erupted from the centre of the lagoon. It rose over three hundred feet above the Island in a dark column forty feet across and hung there in defiance of nature. His vision was blurring but in his mind's eye the column had become a monstrous hand, reaching out for him. It was a hand made up of all the hate, revenge and evil that lurked within the dark lagoon, put there by him... and now coming to destroy him.

He could see the waters bursting through their banks, rivulets were forming, taking the gushing black waters out through the Island to destroy everything they touched until there was nothing left to destroy. The acid rain burned the flesh from his upturned face. The crescent moon stared down, mocking the grinning porcelain whiteness of his skull as it reflected moonbeams over the boiling waters. He could feel himself disintegrating with the Island, all his power unable to save him, until finally he succumbed and with a cry of despair dissolved into the screaming earth.

More suddenly than it began, the holocaust ended. The winds died, the ground was still again and the dark lagoon returned to flat oily blackness. All was quiet on the Island, all was still, there was only the silent emptiness of the dead.

It was a long time before Proctor awoke once more. He didn't yet know how much time had passed since his downfall. At first there was no thought, no understanding, just agony; an agony that reminded him that he still existed, that he had survived. Then came understanding of what happened and the knowledge of his vulnerability.

Proctor contemplated his ruined domain, considered the countless years of toil taken to build the Island, how all his works had been snuffed out as if they were meaningless, insignificant. He considered these things and he brooded.

VII

Time was suspended, what were in reality merely the fleeting hours of a single day became aeons during which he searched for an answer. When it came the answer stood out amongst the lies and false trails, so obvious as to be hidden by its own simplicity. He had to find a soul of absolute purity and persuade them to enter the dark lagoon of their own free will. Only such an act of selfless sacrifice could redeem him, give him back all that was lost and more, so much more. The thought of redemption washed through his mind like the cooling waters of a mountain stream, stinging him into action.

He stretched out into the world, scanning countless minds, forever searching for the one to save him. But no-one would serve, all were too blemished by life. There was no priest, or holy man, no child or peasant in all creation who wasn't in some way rendered imperfect for his purpose. Eventually he gave up his wanderings, sinking into a deep dark despair. Then, as all seemed lost, the answer revealed itself.

A deal would have to be done, a pact made and a favour granted. That was all right though; he was used to granting favours and there was always a price to be demanded in return. He would have to be patient though, the planning would need to be meticulous and the timing perfect. That was all right as well, time he had, and patience he could learn. The game had begun and soon the first move would be made. To confirm this last thought in the distance the sound of twin engines could be heard and soon the shape of the launch could be seen coming through the early morning mist.

Book One

Chapter One

Storms

I

Ever since they left London, Jack Simons had been in torment. Nothing had gone right and the way he felt now nothing ever would until he sorted Tom out on a permanent basis. Tom Kidman had been a pain in the ass from day one, disagreeing with everything, moaning and complaining all the time, making his life a misery. The worst of it was that he felt guilty, after all he did have a secret agenda he hadn't discussed and it was as if Tom was punishing him for his duplicity.

This sort of thinking was paranoid though and he knew it. They had always argued, about just about anything, both wanting to be the leader, it was childish and stupid but it had always been like that. Now though things had changed for good and neither of them had come out and admitted it. Whereas in the past they were best friends, partners, with no-one and nothing to come between them, now their relationship was complicated by the fact that he had gone and fallen in love.

It was ridiculous really, the last thing he'd planned was to fall in love at the age of twenty one. Exactly the opposite really, before he met Ruth he had everything planned out very differently. He was going to be as slippery as quicksilver, a real playboy, no woman was going to tie him down until he was good and ready and that wasn't going to be for a long time. Nice daydream, except that wasn't the way things had turned out, one look at Ruth and he'd fallen head over heels in love.

That wasn't the problem though. Tom was the problem, his erstwhile best friend and bosom buddy, the one he'd come away with to have a good time, the one he was letting down on a daily basis. So here he was on his post college dream trip to the States; it was ten in the morning on his day off and he was wandering around a Win Dixie like a love sick schoolboy, the great adventure totally lost and wasted on him. Added to that things hadn't exactly been exciting since they'd arrived either. Apart from all the arguments, it was all turning out to be hard work; especially as he was fighting to hold down two jobs, never mind about having time for any adventures at all.

What made things worse was that his fiancee arrived in three weeks and he still hadn't booked a hotel; if he wasn't careful the three of them would end up sleeping in the damn tent.

'Hey you!'

The voice came from towards the exit and immediately grabbed his attention it was as if it were definitely meant for him. The tone was pleasant enough, even charming in a gruff sort of way, yet behind the friendliness there was something else, something demanding, disturbing, hard to resist. If he'd listened carefully he may have just heard another voice waking inside him, his own internal voice, if he'd have listened really hard he may just have heard that voice telling him to run.

The man looked at him directly in the eyes, his expression one of authority and confidence.

'Hey you, kid, come over here I need your help.'

For some reason Jack wasn't surprised that the voice was directed at him. Its owner, a smallish man in his late fifties, was standing by a photocopying machine waving a fist full of papers in his direction in a purposeful sort of way.

He hesitated, natural suspicion holding him back. *'Run Jack, run while you still can,'* the voice was a mere tinkling in his head, not loud enough to make itself heard. The man looked harmless enough but who could be sure? There must have been a hundred reasons why he should have steered clear of the stranger even without the warning voice, but he was bored, he was overworked, he needed more money, he needed a break. What the hell, he thought, what harm can it do to talk?

'Are you talking to me?' he said. 'Can I help you?'

He walked confidently towards the man, ego saying there wasn't anything to worry about here. After all, he thought, what was the downside? Maybe the old guy was a queer looking for a cheap thrill, or maybe he wanted money, it didn't matter, there was no way he was getting either and you just never knew what the upside could be unless you went along a little way now did you? In the mean time the man started to walk towards him, his expression changing as he came closer from authority to affable familiarity.

'Last chance to run you stupid bastard,' the voice tried one final time before it was too late.

'Hey kid!' he addressed Jack like they were already good friends. 'Know how to play racket ball?'

Jack had a vague idea that racket ball was a bit like squash but with a bigger racket and different rules.

'I can play squash.' he offered

The man looked at him hard, maybe caught off guard by the English accent which contradicted his appearance.

The Dark Lagoon

Jack was slim, well muscled, about five eight with dark curly hair and a clear olive complexion. He was wearing blue jeans, trainers, and a white T shirt with "Ocean Pacific" emblazoned across the front. Asked to guess, eight out of ten people would have said he was from the southern Mediterranean. Wilbur's expression remained open and friendly during this scrutiny but his eyes changed, it was as if a plan was forming in those eyes, a plan in which Jack would feature whether he liked it or not.

'My name's Wilbur, Wilbur Kohn,' he finally announced. 'You're a limey aren't you?'

Jack wasn't sure if being called a limey amounted to an insult or not but the tone wasn't offensive so he tried to sound open and friendly himself. 'I'm from England if that's what you mean,' he replied, still weighing up the eccentric looking old American.

At the same time his situation came home to him; here he was carrying out a very public conversation with a perfect stranger in the middle of a busy Winn Dixie. He wasn't worried but he *was* starting to get embarrassed. It was embarrassment rather than caution that made him decide to walk away, silly really considering nobody he knew was anywhere around.

Wilbur noticed the change immediately and before Jack could brush him off took control of the situation.

'Listen kid, I'm about finished here,' he said waving the sheaf of papers around purposefully. 'Why don't you and me go and have us a game of racket ball and get to know one another. By the way, what's your name or do I keep calling you Kid?'

Embarrassment gave way to curiosity, it just didn't seem likely that this old man really wanted to play racket ball with him, on the other hand unless he went along he would never know what the man's motives really were. Anyway he had sweet nothing better to do so what the hell!

'*Tosser,*' yelled the voice petulantly, this time Jack heard it clearly but chose to ignore it.

'OK, my name's Jack. Where do we go?'

Their eyes met and Wilbur's expression became almost fatherly, possessive; he nodded, motioning towards the door.

'Follow me,' he said.

They walked in silence towards the exit, Wilbur leading the way, then across the huge car park until they reached a rather shabby looking Chevrolet sedan. At one time it was probably close to top of the range but that was many years ago. Now it was just an old car and a gas guzzler at that. The paint-work, originally a lustrous green, had faded to a non-descript dullness. Wilbur balanced his sheaf of papers in one hand and with the other extracted the car keys from the pocket of his long shorts, opened the car, put the papers on the back seat and got in.

Jack hesitated for a second outside the car. He had no idea where this guy was going to take him but although the voice inside him knew that getting into that car would be a very bad move, somehow his curiosity got the better of him, he opened the passenger door and eased himself inside. The interior had once been plush, the seats were covered in heavy grade velvet, the dash was adorned with an impressive array of chrome knobs, there was even an eight track cassette set in to the centre console and a healthy looking collection of tapes. He noticed the ashtray was open and overflowing with small cigar butts partly explaining the car's stale smell. The rest of the odour was made up of sweat, ozone from the air conditioning and something else which he didn't recognise, something sickly, rancid.

'*I don't like this,*' squeaked the voice. '*This old wreck smells spooky to me, are you sure you want to be doing this Jack?*'

Wilbur turned the ignition key, the engine caught and he gunned the throttle, unexpectedly it settled down quickly to a reassuringly rattle free V8 burble. He unconsciously took a cheroot from a pack on the dash, simultaneously depressing the cigar lighter. The lighter popped back out and he offered the red glow to the cigar, inhaling deeply as he did so. Jack found the button that controlled the electric windows, just in time to avoid the full blast of his exhaust.

'Sorry kid, I should have asked, habit I guess,' He said as he moved the column change into drive and started to move off towards the car park exit.

'Where are we going exactly?' asked Jack as the big Chevy darted forward to join the highway.

'*So now you ask, you putz,*' said the voice sulkily.

Wilbur didn't take his eye off the road. 'To a local high school, there are no kids, it's the vacation and we can use the racket ball courts without being disturbed.'

Only now they were under way did a cold shiver of warning run down Jack's spine. He sank back into the generous front seat, designed for well fed Americans, and started to ponder his fate.

He had always had a keen sense of adventure. As a boy he was the one who would always end up balancing on the flimsiest, highest branch of the tallest tree. Except the older he got the more he glimpsed his own vulnerability. One day he was in a tree, as usual perched in the highest branches, when the unthinkable happened, one of the branches snapped. Before he could even react he was falling helplessly out of control towards the ground thirty feet below. By some miracle he landed full square against a large hedge which simply spat him back on to his feet. It was as if someone or something was issuing him with a warning.

'There now that's a lesson for you smart boy, next time I might not be here to save you.'

Now, a long way from his back garden, on the highway through Key Largo, he remembered that warning and wondered if there would be a friendly hedge to catch his fall this time.

'Where are you staying?'

The question startled him back to the present. The Chevy was slowing down, as Wilbur turned off the highway into a suburban back road.

'So, did you hear me, where are you staying?'

He looked out the window over the ocean, the late morning sunlight was reflected brightly off the still water giving the impression of a golden highway ending in a mist, probably created by the heat, but at that moment that mist seemed to be concealing dark secrets.

'I'm staying with a friend, I mean I'm here with a friend and we're staying at the Bella Vista park,' He said at last.

'That's right putz, tell him where you live, why not give him all your money as well, do the job properly.' The admonishing voice sounded so self righteous, so pompous and so very right.

They'd only travelled about a mile and a half from the Winn Dixie but it could just as easily have been one and a half thousand. Gone were the modern landscape, the well kept asphalt and modern air conditioned buildings, it was like they'd entered another country. Either side of the road, if you could call it a road, it was so neglected and riddled with pot holes, there was a series of broken-down shacks which had presumably at some time been inhabited. Now though, they looked abandoned, deserted, of humans at least. The only life in evidence were a lot of small black birds, perched in the bare looking trees which lined the road. There was something disturbing about the way they followed the car with their eyes, something knowing in their hard lifeless stares that freaked him out and had the voice chiming in with choruses of '*I told you so.*'

Despite the fact they were travelling at over thirty he had a crazy urge to open the car door and fling himself out onto the road. Luckily before he could do or say anything, Wilbur who was clearly in a good mood if his tuneless humming was anything to go by, was turning through the gates of St Heliers High School and on up the long drive towards the school building itself. Jack managed with some difficulty to fight back the irrational fear threatening to send him into a blind panic. He closed his eyes, breathing slowly and deeply, the pounding in his head gradually getting softer until by the time the Chevy drew to a halt he felt reasonably calm once more.

When he opened his eyes what he saw was an empty yard in which dust devils danced and teased in front of him, rising up mockingly as if to say, '*you too will be like us soon, just like we used to be like you*'.

He was starting to wish he'd taken notice of the voice's warnings, it was ridiculous but there was something wrong with this place, something *very wrong*.

The school was a shabby sixties affair, arranged on two floors, slab sided and ugly, made mainly of aluminium reinforced concrete it was showing visible signs of advanced decay. Once an architect's vision for a low cost Utopia, an alpha child ruined by a recessive gene, suffering from premature senility, dying of cancer. Also and more to the point as far as he was concerned it too was totally deserted. At least that's what he thought until out of the corner of his eye he noticed someone standing at a first floor window directly above the front entrance. They were transfixed, staring silently out over the yard. As the Chevy came to a halt the figure at the window raised its hands as if it were conducting an orchestra, at the same moment the dust devils which had been appearing sporadically rose up in unison, forming across the yard like soldiers guarding a castle.

Acting on instinct he went for the door handle with only one thought in his mind, to get the hell out of there. He pushed hard against the heavy door and felt immense relief as it gave way, spilling out onto the ground expecting to be confronted by one of the dust devils, turned to flesh. All he saw though was an empty expanse of decaying tarmac, no bogey men, nothing.

Wilbur had by now joined him outside and was rummaging around in the boot of the car. He turned towards him holding two rackets and a bag of balls. When he saw his face he stopped for a moment.

'What's the matter kid? You look like you saw a ghost or something'.

Jack looked around the empty yard, no ghosts: he looked up at the first floor window but there was no one there either. He began to feel pretty stupid and more than a little bit disorientated. Maybe he was overreacting, maybe there was nothing here to be frightened of, regaining his composure he answered in the most confident voice he could muster.

'I thought we came here to play racket ball, let's get on with it.'

The Dark Lagoon

They played the game outside on a quadrangle similar to a squash court but open at one end. At first Jack found the pace of the ball hard to judge and the older man scored a few points. After a few minutes though he found his rhythm and the tables quickly turned, he clawed back the points he'd lost and took the lead. The physical exertion was helping him to relax, calm down, get a perspective on the situation. Just as he was beginning to enjoy himself Wilbur dropped his racket and walked off the court.

Jack couldn't believe the older man's behaviour, OK so no-one likes a pasting but there was no excuse for this kind of petulance. He decided to cut his losses and ask to be driven back.

Wilbur turned around and eyed him up like a fisherman with a box of lure's, trying to decide which one he should use to land a particularly prized fish. He eventually decided to use the biggest, bluntest one he could find.

'What's the matter kid, have I done something to upset you?' his tone was sarcastic, cutting 'Look if you don't mind me saying so you've got better things to be thinking about than a game of racket ball. You're in a real mess, you don't have any transportation, you're living in a tent and you have a crap job, you need to get your act together boy.'

He paused to let the effect of his words really sink in.

Irritated as he was by the unexpected ticking off, in a way Jack was relieved, being told he was screwing things up wasn't so bad, it was true. Before he could reply Wilbur continued.

'The first thing you need is some transport, round here you're nothing without transport. How much money have you got?'

Jack decided impulsively that he was no longer bothered what he told this old guy, perhaps he was a nutter, even a dangerous one but for now he seemed as good a bet as any other.

'I've got about five hundred dollars spare, do you know where I can get a decent car for that?' he asked, trying to sound as sarcastic as Wilbur.

'I give up, from here on in whatever you get you deserve, you listening to me, heh I'm talking to you' but he wasn't listening to the voice, for the moment at least he'd tuned it right out of his head.

Wilbur looked really pleased, he could see Jack's guard lowering and wasted no time pressing home the advantage.

'As a matter of fact, I know just the place,' He said.

Without further discussion he started to gather together the balls they'd scattered round the yard. Jack, dragged along by the situation joined in the hunt, remembering he hit one of the balls right over the back of the court, set off around the side to find it. As he turned the corner in front of him was a service path which meandered its way unobtrusively round the school. *He was about to cross the path and look for the lost ball in the bushes beyond, when he noticed something glinting on the floor. He bent down to see what it was. To his surprise it was a pendant on a silver chain, the pendant was in the shape of a crescent moon.*

'Hey Jack, what are you doing back there?'

Wilbur's tone was gruff and impatient, He looked up from his find.

'I'm coming, just hang on a second,' He replied looking down at the path, sure there was something there, something important. But there wasn't anything and as he stared at the empty space he even forgot why.

Without wasting any more time he pushed his way into the bushes and found the lost ball. He put it in his pocket and ran back to where Wilbur was already walking towards the car. *As he ran the pendant swayed unnoticed around his neck, the sunlight glinting off its silver crescent moon.*

II

They loaded up quickly and Wilbur headed back out towards the highway. As they drove out of the school gates the strangeness of the place seemed to have disappeared, there were no eerie blackbirds in the trees lining the road, even the shabby slums no longer looked as deserted and forlorn as before. Nevertheless Jack felt restless, there was something he was trying to remember, something he knew was important but it remained stubbornly out of reach, just beyond the edge of his consciousness. He was therefore relieved when after only a few minutes they rolled to a halt on the forecourt of a grubby used car dealership and he could apply his mind to other more tangible matters.

Wilbur parked on the dealer's forecourt and showing a certain amount of enthusiasm jumped out of the car. Within seconds he was wandering around the junkers inquisitively prodding and poking at them as if by doing so he'd be able to tell if they were any good or not. Jack got out the car and joined him, he was the first to admit that his knowledge of cars was strictly limited so he was content to watch and learn, although to him the sorry collection of old heaps scattered round the lot looked more than a bit dubious.

'I don't know about this Wilbur,' he said after examining a Chevy Impala of indeterminate age. It was a huge car with a no doubt equally huge gas guzzling engine. The sticker price said $500 so it was in his price range. Outside the body-work was missing various bits of trim. The paint, originally a lustrous if distasteful metallic brown had faded to an unpleasant matt finish. There was more than the odd speck of rust worming its way to the surface and no doubt the chassis was riddled with the stuff. More worrying still the suspension seemed to have settled at the back, the tyres were bald and the "optional extra" vinyl roof had all but peeled completely off.

Wilbur just grunted his disapproval at Jack's condescending tone and walked off to look at an old Ford station wagon at the far side of the lot.

In the meantime a salesman, if you could have called him that, had sidled over. Even he didn't seem to hold out much hope that anyone would actually buy this car. By his gait you could tell this was a call of duty, not opportunity. Jack stopped examining the wreck and gave his attention to the salesman who wasn't a bad reflection of the car itself. No sharp suit and electronic calculator here, no sir, what he saw before him was a middle-aged man who'd let himself prematurely go to seed. Dressed in a loud short-sleeved Hawaiian shirt, shorts and sandals, he was carrying a fair sized paunch, and he looked like he could use a wash and a shave. His hair was parted on the right side down almost as far as his ear, the resulting frizzy crop distributed across the barren top in an attempt to disguise the baldness, the red-rimmed eyes, florid complexion, and bulbous nose confirmed that his was the face of a heavy drinker.

'This here is a classic. Yup, a real classic,' he said with forced bonhomie. 'Up in New York they restore these beauties and sell them for ten thousand dollars you know.'

The salesman, whose name was Vince was having a

bad day, in fact it was a bad month and a bad year so any prospect no matter how unpromising had to be pursued. He produced the keys from a chain he kept round his waist and without enquiring further proceeded to start her up.

The sad old Impala coughed and spluttered into life, like a senile demented old man suddenly asked to sprint the hundred metres. The exhaust belched smoke and the mill rattled pitifully but Vince didn't seem to notice. He just gunned the throttle and mumbled on about how 'they don't make 'em like they used to.' As the old engine started to warm up some semblance of smoothness and life seemed to return to it. Jack started to imagine what it must have been like to drive the car across the States in its prime. The interior was in even worse condition than the exterior but nonetheless he accepted Vince's invitation to sit behind the wheel. The dash was a disgrace, sun-split and peeling in several places. For such a physically huge car there was surprisingly little space inside, the back seats were cosmetic buckets, suitable only for small children on short journeys. The rear parcel shelf was almost entirely missing and there were the remains of some ancient speakers hanging down onto the seats.

He gunned the throttle hard. There was still some power in there somewhere though. The sound of the V8 combined with his own faded daydreams were starting to work a spell on him, he'd heard parts were really cheap in America, a few dollars and a little tender loving care, who knew maybe the thing was viable after all?

'Want to take her for a spin?'

Vince read his mind like an open book, clearly he knew a sucker when he saw one. Fingers crossed the old piece of shit wouldn't break down on the test and he was home and dry, home and dry. Maybe his luck was changing, maybe he could get back on a roll. He made a mental note to go to Sam's that night and show those bastards how to play poker.

They had their respective daydreams shattered by the same rude outburst.

'Look, maybe you have the time to waste messing about with this piece of shit but I don't, let's get out of here.'

Although it was Wilbur's idea to come to the broken down lot, he was once again showing just how fickle and unpredictable he could be. The effect of his intervention was to instantly burst Jack's bubble and allow him to see the hopeless old wreck for what it was, Vince on the other hand wasn't happy about it, no sir; he wasn't happy about it at all. This craggy old bastard was shoving his nose where he had no business shoving it, where if he wasn't careful he'd get the damn ugly thing bitten off. His best prospect of the day wasn't going to be ripped away that easily, or his dream of poker winnings at tonight's game. He wasn't about to take that kind of interference lying down, no siree bob he wasn't.

'Just one cotton picking moment, who the hell are you?' he demanded.

Clearly he hadn't noticed the pair arriving together and was desperate enough to make an issue of it. He was a large man, much larger than Wilbur and he was set on intimidation, walking up to within a foot of where the smaller older man stood and staring at him belligerently.

'I'm the boy's father if it's anything to you pal.'

Jack listened incredulously as the words spilled out of Wilbur's mouth as naturally as if they were true. Vince seemed taken aback by the reply but he wasn't ready to give up yet.

'He's over eighteen ain't he?' he said, then turning to Jack. 'Do you always let your old man make your decisions for you?'

Seeing he was getting nowhere fast he quickly gave up and resorted to abuse. It was what he always ended up doing these days, it didn't pay any bills but somehow it made him feel a little better, not so empty. Lately he'd even crossed the line a couple of times into actual violence, he picked his subjects carefully though so there were never any comebacks and this pair looked over ripe for a good lesson Vince style

'I bet he still changes your diaper for you,' He barked at Jack who was out the car by now and standing there dumbfounded at the sudden change in the salesman's character.

'Well who needs you? Get out of here before I set the dog on you.'

As if to emphasise this last point, a large black dog could be heard growling loudly from where it was chained up by the caravan at the far end of the site. The dog was about thirty metres away and he still looked big. Closer up, Charlie, for that was its name, looked like some kind of freak mutation he was so big. Bred from a full blooded Irish Wolf Hound mother and a Rottweiler father, he'd inherited his mother's size and his father's disposition. He'd been watching carefully since the intruders arrived and was quick to sense the change in atmosphere. His hackles were rising as he readied himself straining mightily against the heavy chain. For a moment the rusty railings creaked ominously threatening to give way, they held and Charlie settled reluctantly on the ground while continuing to observe the proceedings with keen interest.

Wilbur listened to the threat with apparent disinterest,

far from appearing intimidated his expression changed to one of sympathetic concern.

'What's the matter, Vince, something wrong, finding it hard to catch your breath are you?' he spoke the words with a note of genuine worry in his voice as if he were addressing an old friend who suddenly wasn't looking so good.

Vince was nonplussed for a second. "Was this little old guy pulling his chain?" he thought, because if he was it would be the last chain he pulled for a long time, if he wasn't careful he'd never pull another chain again, not once Charlie had torn off his arms anyway.

But before he could reply or do anything, he felt a sudden tightening in his chest so sharp it made him double over in agony. Sure enough he was finding it hard to breath. He didn't know how but he was sure the old guy had something to do with it too. The pain was increasing, like someone attached a vice to his heart and was gradually turning the screw. His head began to spin as he sank to one knee, no longer concerned about the pair in front of him, all he was concerned about now was survival.

'Help me,' he croaked painfully.

'What was that?' said Wilbur who seemed to be enjoying the man's distress.

'What was that? We can't hear you, speak up man!'

It was the use of the word "we" that galvanised Jack into action. Up to now he had been a passive observer but now he'd been pulled into the crisis he wasn't about to stand around and watch while this man died in front of him.

'For pity's sake, get a doctor.' The voice was fainter now, there was a trail of spittle running down from the corner of his mouth, dripping from his chin in long strands as his chest rattled like the old Impala.

While all this was going on old Charlie was working himself up into a state of uncontrollable anxiety. Although aggressive when roused he was basically slow and lazy by nature. This was fortunate because it meant he really didn't know his own strength. If he had then he would long ago have known that he could break free from his chains any time he wanted. As it was he didn't think like that. Freedom wasn't a concept he could understand, all he wanted was a dry bed, plenty of food and a purpose in life, which was to protect Vince and guard the lot. Seeing both under attack galvanised him into action, using every ounce of his considerable body weight and muscle power he launched himself against his bonds. There was no contest, the only question was where the weakest link would be. As it happened it turned out not to be at the railings but about three quarters of the way down the chain. This lent extra momentum to the dog's charge as he covered the ground between himself and his master. Except Vince wasn't the object of his attention, it was the small man standing in front of him that he wanted, the small man was obviously responsible for his master's pain and he was going to tear him to pieces.

Wilbur seemed unaware of the two hundred pounds of enraged carnivore bearing down on him. The sight wasn't lost on Jack though. Whatever he intended to do he stopped as he realised what was about to happen. He couldn't believe how the day was turning out, first he allowed himself to be picked up by this weird old guy and now he was about to witness the mysterious death of a car salesman and the same weird old guy being ripped to pieces by some sort of avenging canine monster.

At the second before Charlie's jaws could close around his throat, Wilbur turned towards the dog. He didn't raise his hand or utter a sound but it was as if the mutt had hit a brick wall. It collapsed in front of him yelping in pain and confusion. It didn't even attempt to get back to its feet, it just lay there whining pathetically like a gigantic lost puppy.

III

'So what's happening Jack? Are we going or what?'

Wilbur spoke as if nothing out of the ordinary was happening at all, Somehow Jack knew there was something going on, something he had to do but it was as if the thought of what that thing could be was draining out of his mind like sand through a leaky sieve.

The feeling was infuriating, like having something on the tip of your tongue, something interesting and important only to feel it disappearing no matter how hard you tried to hang on to it. Vince, the huge dog, the old car, they were all just melting away like a snowflakes on a spring morning. All that was left was Wilbur's demanding voice and he had no power in him to resist it, so he followed him meekly back to the car. By the time he settled into the passenger seat he was feeling unbelievably sleepy, there was no harm in catching a few zeds he thought, whatever it was niggling in the back of his mind could wait till later, he could ask all the questions he wanted later.

Wilbur looked across at the young man curled up fast asleep on the seat and smiled. Satisfied he gave his attention back to the road and to the long journey ahead.

Vince watched the Chevy move off. His sight was beginning to dim; the pain in his chest no longer seemed too important and his recent rage had gone. He was on both knees now. Anyone who came upon him would think he was engaged in some sort of religious ritual. The way his eyes stared almost peacefully ahead, he could have been experiencing a vision. Charlie was aware of his master's pain but could do nothing about it. Even when Vince finally fell forward on his face Charlie didn't have the strength to move.

Later when their bodies were found there was endless speculation about how they met their end. The post mortem revealed that Charlie had suffered sudden and massive internal injuries, as if he'd been hit by a truck. Vince had died of a heart attack which surprised no-one except the coroner. There was no doubt that the victim had a heart condition, indeed he'd already undergone extensive surgery, however the heart disease wasn't what killed him. It was the pacemaker Vince was wearing which was cause of death; in all his years of cutting up corpses the coroner had seen nothing like it, the device had melted right into the man's heart.

Jack slept and as he slept he dreamed. In his dream he was floating over the ocean. No, he wasn't floating, he was flying. He could see for miles around and there was nothing but bright water. He swooped and soared intoxicated by the sense of freedom. No-one confined to a physical body could possibly experience such elation. He considered the possibility that he was dead and to his surprise the thought didn't bother him too much. If this was death then it was OK by him, it redefined the meaning of life.

Without a body to cloud his senses he could see, hear and feel more sharply than ever before. He was aware of life teeming beneath the ocean, of the elements working rhythmically to an unseen plan. All tragedy, all comedy fell into place, for the first time he thought he understood.

His heightened senses perceived every slight change to the

balance of nature, every birth, every death, contributing towards a harmony; terrible in its simplicity; awesome in its magnitude.

But what secrets are contained within the earth? Dark things that nature would perhaps prefer to forget, buried for vast ages, confined by rock. This thought occurred to him at the same time as he became aware of something appearing on the far horizon. Something out of place, something that didn't belong.

At first he wasn't sure if he could see anything at all, it was more a tangible feeling of disquiet nagging at his subconscious, eating at his new found equilibrium. Instead of swooping and soaring where it pleased, his spirit was drawn irresistibly towards that far point by an unseen force. As he drew closer the sunlight no longer reflected off the ocean and yet it wasn't yet night. There was a mist rising from the waters, a foul unnatural cloud, seeping up through cracks in the ancient rock of the sea bed, bubbling and hissing its way to the surface, pulling him in closer as a cold dread gripped his heart.

Well before he reached the outer edge of the mist, he became aware of an absence of life in his new surroundings. The ocean around him was deserted, the skies were empty, except for a crescent moon, which seemed to be leering down at him, delighting in his discomfort.

His eyes were torn from the sky back towards the mist. Now he was closer he could see there was something else up ahead; there was an island beyond the swirling vapours, he could just make out its grey shores giving way to craggy rocks, rising into sheer cliffs resembling the battlements of some ancient pagan fortress.

He made a superhuman effort to turn his face from the island. He knew that something worse than death awaited him there. He managed to look briefly behind and saw the sunlight disappearing on the horizon. He thought of Ruth, he thought of his family and wondered what they were doing now. Finally he thought of Tom Kidman and his blood ran cold.

His power drained again, he felt the malevolent force regain control, as out of the mist came a dark hand, gigantically grotesque reaching out to take him. Terror and despair crystallised in his heart as the awful hand reached out its greedy black maw impatient to engulf him. As all hope threatened to vanish from his heart something in him fought back. He thought of Ruth waiting for him back in England, and he fought so hard his mind felt like it would burst inside his head but instead, miraculously, the hand dissolved in front of him.

IV

Then there was pain, not the supernatural kind but a more down to earth variety. As he awoke the first thing he saw was Wilbur's face staring down at him as the old bastard alternately shook and slapped him back into the real world.

'Hey kid wake up.' The voice was brusque but not unkind, it was the fatherly tone again, only this time it contained more than a hint of possessiveness as well. He wasn't in the mood to notice these subtle changes though, he was just glad to be awake and for the nightmare to be over.

He put his hands up defensively. 'It's OK, I'm OK, you can stop hitting me now,' He shouted.

Wilbur stopped somewhat reluctantly and sank back into his seat. There was a moment's silence before he turned to Jack.

'You shouldn't do things like that to me kid, you should watch what your dreaming.'

It was obvious to Jack that the older man was very flustered, there were beads of sweat on his forehead and he'd gone a pallid greenish grey colour. It was almost as if he knew what he'd been dreaming, almost as if he'd been there in the dream with him. At the same time he became aware of his own condition, he was soaking wet and not just from sweat either, whatever it was he had dreamed caused him to do something he hadn't done since he was nine and there was no mum around to discreetly clean up the mess.

In the meantime Wilbur lit a cheroot while Jack looked out the window of the Chevy and saw they were parked outside a large bungalow on a quiet residential street.

'What are we doing here?' Jack demanded, for once glad of the smoke, the acrid smell effectively disguising his embarrassment. Wilbur took a deep drag from the cheroot and held the smoke down for a long time before he exhaled slowly and deliberately.

'We're here to collect something which I think you're gonna like, come on let's get out and take a look.'

They got out of the car and stretched their legs, Jack was acutely aware that the wetness round his crotch was slightly visible through his jeans. He didn't know how long the journey had taken but it must have been a fair while if the stiffness in his joints was anything to go by. Wilbur wasn't paying him any attention though, he had started to walk briskly towards the house, puffing earnestly on his cheroot as he went.

Jack looked around him. The road was lined with trees, he didn't know which kind but they were tall and thin with sparsely covered branches, the greenery such as it was looked parched and grey. Perched in many of the trees black crows watched them with dead disinterested eyes, they reminded him of the birds he'd seen near the school only these ones were bigger, better fed perhaps. Beyond the trees there were rows of houses, some on one level like the one they were visiting and some on two and three levels. They were all quite big and were set in wide plots but somehow none of them seemed very attractive, as if the same visionless architect had designed them all.

He looked skywards, the sun was high and hot, there were no clouds but a smog laden heat haze lent a dullness even to the sunlight. He sighed, sometimes you just have to go with the flow he thought. He didn't believe Wilbur meant him harm any more, if anything the old guy seemed strangely besotted with him. You never knew, he thought, maybe these omens weren't all bad after all.

With this thought still dying in his mind he turned towards the house and started out for the front door. The property didn't look very special even from the road but as he got closer he could see that there were other problems. The gardens had been sadly neglected. The scorched lawns were almost totally brown. He could see the hose pipe was still connected and lay uselessly across the grass, obviously unused for many months. There was a fair amount of rubbish and debris strewn around the front lawn, mostly gardening items like an old wheelbarrow and some heavy canvas gloves, but there were also the tattered remains of what looked like women's clothes and expensive ones at that.

The house was a sixties design born out of the then fashion for the modern and practical, it had been built down to a budget rather than up to a standard and it showed. Whoever ordered this house was more interested in superficial opulence than lasting quality, it had a used up consumerist feel to it seeming far older than its years. At first he thought it just looked a little sad, tatty and neglected but there was something else as well. The house looked empty; of course lots of houses are empty, there's nothing strange about that, the owners are away, or for any number of other reasons, but it wasn't that kind of empty this house looked. *This house looked like the empty husk of a snake-skin after the owner had moved on.*

He shook his head, he was spooking himself again and he had to stop it, if he wasn't careful, pretty soon he'd be seeing ghosts as well. This was a house like any other, it was just that he was far from home, with a man he hardly knew and he was nervous. It was self preservation and that was good but he wasn't about to let sensible caution turn to paranoia.

'You've been abducted only you're too stupid to know it,' said the voice petulantly. *'If you go into that house you won't come out alive but what the hell do I know.'* He hesitated for a moment unsure of himself again but the voice was like a weak radio signal blinking in and out, never allowing the listener to quite recognise the tune it was playing.

The house had a wooden veranda, the kind on which you expected to see a rocking chair occupied by an old man wearing dungarees, wearing a straw hat and smoking a pipe. There was however no such warm hearted caricature waiting here to greet him. The veranda was almost bare save for a couple of large pots, the kind you pick up cheap at a garden sale because they're too big to put anywhere else, the plants they once contained had died long ago and were draped unrecognisably over the painted wooden boards.

The front door itself was an insubstantial frame half of which was filled with mosquito netting. There was no chance of it keeping any mosquitoes out though, it was badly ripped and a large flap hung down revealing a hole big enough for a crow to fly through never mind a mosquito. This outer door gave way to the main front door which was already partially open.

He noticed the smell even before he reached the door. An acrid glutinous stench leaching from the house and blending reluctantly into the outside air.

He stopped at the entrance. There was no need to go inside, he could wait where he was, even investigate the other side of the house and the grounds if he wanted. In the end it was curiosity that got the better of him again, he wanted to see inside the house, he needed to see inside the house. Somehow he knew that inside the house there would be important signs and clues to help him understand his new found benefactor and the strange situation he found himself in. He needed to understand the people around him and their motives for doing things. He was used to being one step ahead, used to being able to second guess what other people were thinking and predict what they would do next. Now though he was at a loss, what he needed was some kind of insight, he needed to get a perspective on things and the house could give him that.

V

He'd assumed the smell was a result of a blocked drain or an overflowing toilet but immediately he stepped into the house he realised this wasn't the case. There was no entrance hall as such, rather you walked into a large open plan area which was the house's main living room. It contained all the usual people paraphernalia, strewn around in a messy abandoned sort of way but what caught his eye wasn't the mess or the contents, it was the glass panelling at the end of the room that overlooked an indoor pool.

It seemed unlikely that this house should have such an excessive amenity but apparently it did. Not that the pool in any way added to the charm of the house, far from it. Rather its presence dominated the property physically and aurally. If the house was abandoned several months ago then the pool looked like it had been abandoned several years before that. Even from where he stood, he could see its dark waters and imagine the rancid vapours rising from their surface.

The pool was clearly the source of the disgusting smell which he realised was increasing in intensity with every step he took towards its door. There was something irresistibly attractive about the repulsive odour, he found himself navigating his way across the room, around the upturned furniture and assorted debris towards the pool room door. He was beginning to get light-headed, stumbling into a large metal framed coffee table, grazing his shin, the pain briefly clearing his head. He turned back towards the front door, the bright sunlight filtering in through the hole in the mosquito netting beckoned to him, almost beseeching him to leave the house before it was too late.

He almost broke away, but in the end the thought of the pool and its dark waters reared up in his mind its power drawing him in. The room meanwhile had grown, it was no longer a room but a plain, a plain on which he stood lost and alone, staring into the distance at shining cliffs overlooking the ocean. Far out amidst the foaming waters a mist was rising and through the mist he glimpsed the shores of a dark island.

'Jack are you in there? Hey Jack, where the hell are you?'

For the second time since they met Wilbur gruffly interrupted his dreams, only this time it was a waking dream and all the more disturbing for it. His voice was coming from the backyard, he must have made his way outside while Jack was occupied by the pool.

'Hold on a sec, I'm coming,' he said thickly before Wilbur had a chance to bellow at him again.

He walked briskly towards the kitchen trying to ignore the pool room pretending he had no interest in what lay behind its glass barrier. For a minute he thought he'd made it, he was nearly past when something caught his eye, a hint of movement almost too small to notice coming from inside the pool room. He stopped and listened but there was no sound, he looked directly through the glass at the pool and into the murky waters, his hand creeping unbidden towards the door handle.

He already knew the pool had been neglected and that the noxious smell was coming from its polluted waters but the full impact of just how bad things looked close up, not to mention smelled still caught him off guard. The smell was so strong it was almost palpable, it had a sweet sickly theme reminding him of the smell of gangrene in his grandmother's room before she died only twenty times as powerful.

Scattered round the pool lay a variety of bathing towels which he guessed must have once been of the brightly coloured variety, probably with large pictures of sea creatures emblazoned across their fronts. Any colour had long since disappeared, now they were covered with a grey fungus of a type he'd never seen before. Whatever it was, it was certainly voracious because it'd infected everything, even the plastic sun loungers were covered with the stuff. Here and there the fungus gave way to a translucent dark blue ooze, the same colour that dominated the waters of the pool.

As if they somehow realised they were being watched

the waters suddenly ended their slumber. They erupted in a great spume of black liquid, leaping into the air, becoming an evil demented creature which reached out to grab the impudent young man who had strayed into its domain. Jack stood frozen as the creature's black maw reached out, sure it would pluck him from where he stood and drag him into itself. Instead there was a loud crash as it hit the glass barrier between them and disintegrated before his eyes. The sight rocked him back on his heels and broke the spell that held him, he released the door handle and ran for his life.

VI

The sunlight made him squint as Jack burst into the backyard, he was shaking and covered in sweat but being outside again made him feel better straight away. He took a few slow deep breaths feeling his racing pulse returning to normal.

Jack was starting to feel a little bit silly. After all what had really spooked him? A dingy house with a filthy disused poolroom? Nothing had happened he told himself, there was no black creature lurking in the foul waters of the pool, that was simply his own imagination playing tricks on him again, it was probably so polluted large amounts of methane were bubbling to the surface every so often and creating the side-show that'd sent him running from the house like a scared rabbit.

But no matter how rational his explanation sounded there was a part of him that wasn't convinced, the part where his internal voice still struggled uselessly to make itself heard.

The Dark Lagoon

There would be more time to speculate later, for now his attention was diverted by an old Ford Van which stood in front of him up to its axles in the soil of the garden. Wilbur stood beside it fiddling with a fat metal cylinder the purpose for which he couldn't guess, upside-down and bolted to its roof was an old rowing boat. The sight of the ridiculous looking Van was enough to take his mind off the pool room. He had a very strong urge to burst into hysterical laugher and if it hadn't been for the serious look on Wilbur's face, he probably would have done.

'What are you staring at? Get over here and give me a hand will you?' Wilbur growled.

The cylinder looked quite heavy and if Wilbur had carried it all the way from the Chevy he must have been stronger than he looked. Nevertheless the exertion had left him red faced and slightly wheezy, this made Jack feel a bit guilty so he wasted no time in going over to lend a hand. As he arrived Wilbur flung him a set of keys.

'Go round the back and open up the doors,' he barked.

He was never very good at following orders, only responding positively to people he respected. At this moment he hadn't made up his mind about Wilbur and he didn't like the tone he was using, he sounded like an impatient father dealing with an incompetent child. Despite his irritation he decided to obey, partly because they were a long way from the keys and he needed a lift back and partly because he was curious to see what was inside the Van.

'What are you trying to do?' he said as he caught the bunch of keys easily in his left hand.

'Can't you see? I'm about to go scuba diving! What does it look like?' came the sarcastic reply; although to be honest, the day had been so weird up to now he was almost prepared to go along with scuba diving as well.

Deciding not to take the bait, he walked around the back of the Van to find that even the back doors were odd. Stuck through one of them where the window should have been was a large box, which he later found out was an air conditioning unit. Ignoring it he located the lock and after one failed attempt found the correct key which he pushed carefully into the slot.

There was a little resistance in the lock, though not as much as he'd imagined there would be after what must have been years of disuse. Consequently he used more force than necessary to turn the key while at the same time pulling hard on the door handle. The result was predictable. He reeled backwards as the doors flung open, landing in a heap on his rear end. This was rendered more uncomfortable for two reasons, firstly the wetness in his pants reminding him of his previous accident, secondly Wilbur had chosen the precise moment to come up for air and having witnessed the whole thing was laughing like a drain at his expense.

Jack felt his cheeks flush and his muscles tense, ready for action. They had reached a cross-roads in their relationship. Humour or anger, what was it to be? He looked deep into Wilbur's eyes and started to laugh, once he started he couldn't stop, it was like uncorking a bottle of warm champagne, the laughter bursting out of him in great uncontrollable guffaws. Even after the pain in his stomach began to feel serious he still couldn't stop, he was starting to lose his breath when a movement coming from the back of the Van caught his eye. Something was in there and whatever it was he had woken it up. The distraction had at least one good effect though, it enabled him to get control of himself before he suffocated.

The Dark Lagoon

He felt much better now, the laughing fit actually did him good, except his unhealthy curiosity had been aroused again, this time by the movement in the Van. Ignoring Wilbur who hadn't noticed anything and was still chortling away, he got to his feet and stepped towards the Van.

With the doors open it was possible to see right inside and get an impression of the interior layout. The sun was almost directly behind him his shadow cast into the Van creating an unusual contrast of intense light and utter darkness mixed with a fine cloud of dust reminding him, for some reason he couldn't explain, of a thick sea mist. Looking upwards he could see that the interior of the rowing boat had given the Van a ceiling high enough for a tall adult to walk around in comfort. The sides of the boat had been decked out with shelving and the spaces had been filled with a dirty gold coloured shag pile carpet.

Either side of the cabin were long upholstered benches with built in storage space underneath, the gangway was strewn with various articles of debris entangled with the sodden remains of more of the gold shag pile. Draped across the left hand bench was what looked like an old tarpaulin; it hung down to the floor creating a kind of tent, a perfect home for something, probably whatever he'd seen moving.

He peered into the entrance of the makeshift tent but he couldn't make out anything in the gloom. Feeling confident after the laughing fit, he grasped the old tarp firmly in both hands and gave it a mighty tug. The effect was dramatic as the tarp rose bat-like into the air sending up great clouds of dust before landing in a dishevelled heap on the opposite side of the cabin.

The sight that met his eyes made all the other weird happenings of the day fade into nothingness, they were mere daydreams, flights of fancy cooked up by an overactive imagination.

But here was real horror made flesh, no spooky pool, no nightmare, just the demonic red eyes, long yellow fangs and wicked looking claws of the largest rat he'd ever seen. It didn't take much to figure out what was making the rat so aggressive, it stood before a nest full of its revolting eyeless offspring. He could see their grey hairless bodies heaving like a living swamp, he could hear their mewling cries and smell their acrid slightly sweet odour. The mother rat's upper lips were curled back, revealing wicked yellow incisors, needle sharp and over an inch long. It smelled danger immediately the doors opened but now it saw the source of the danger, what it smelled was fear.

VII

Stark fear gripped his heart and froze him to the spot. He wanted to move but his legs wouldn't obey his brain's commands, he wanted to cry out but his voice all but deserted him. The best he could manage was a pathetic barely audible cry for help.

The rat recognising a pushover when it saw one, lowered its head slightly as it took aim at his throat, moving its weight back onto its hind legs ready to spring forward with maximum force. He could see the sinews in its thighs tighten as it prepared to attack, yet he was still transfixed. He could imagine the rat in the air, flying toward him and then hanging from his throat by its teeth as the warm blood flowed down his shirt.

The giant rat launched itself, fangs barred, saliva drooling behind it in long strands, eager for the kill. Something inside of him turned solid as without thought he leapt to meet it, hands outstretched, looking for its throat, just as it was seeking his. At the moment of truth he'd come good; for the first time in his life he'd had to face a situation where he couldn't run away or talk his way out, and he'd found out the real Jack Simons was a fighter to the core. But neither predator were ever to find out what would have been the outcome of this strange confrontation. Before either could make contact it was all over and the rat lay dead.

Wilbur didn't stop to inspect the corpse but brought the heavy cylinder down again and again on the carcass until it was barely recognisable as a rat at all. When it was over for a moment Jack thought he was going to start on him, such was the look of blood lust in Wilbur's eyes. At the last second though he turned his attention to the nest and to the brood of newly orphaned vermin now mewling pathetically for their dead parent.

He didn't do as Jack expected and set to work on the defenceless infants with the cylinder. Instead he grabbed hold of the tarpaulin and scooped up the nest, kits and all. He dragged the makeshift sack out of the Van and without a word began walking back with it towards the house.

Jack looked at the remains of the rat. Even in its present condition it was possible to see how big it was; a passer-by, asked to identify the remains would never guess its species. The bloody carcass passively lying there in some way made him feel cheated, it was ludicrous, if Wilbur hadn't intervened, chances were it would be him lying on the ground with his throat missing but there was still some part of him that missed the fight he'd been denied. The whole experience left him feeling in some way different, changed, for good, (or for evil), he wasn't yet sure.

Wilbur had already disappeared into the house. Jack wanted to know what he was going to do with the rat's offspring. Although the thought of the pool made him feel sick to his stomach, in the end his curiosity won out and he followed him back inside.

As he walked through the kitchen it struck him that something didn't add up. The kitchen was fully equipped with all the necessities of living, including stale and rotten bread on the table and milk in the open freezer. Whoever the last occupants had been they had left in a hurry. No time to tidy up, or even collect their belongings, they'd left in a hurry all right, as if the devil himself was pursuing them.

He reached the door to the main living area and stopped. There was no need to go any further, from this vantage point he could survey the whole room. A quick glance confirmed it was empty and his eyes were drawn slowly to the glass screen dividing the pool room from the rest of the house. Sure enough, there was Wilbur standing before the pool with his arms outstretched. It wasn't immediately clear what he was doing but then the sack was floating through the air above the dark waters, he was drowning the rat's babies in the pool.

As the sack hit the water there was no large splash, rather it seemed to rise up and take the offering, swallowing it whole and receding in one fluid movement. Wilbur remained where he was, arms still outstretched chanting some ancient magic rite, hoping the dark god that inhabited the waters was happy with the sacrifice. As if to show its appreciation the waters answered by putting on a show similar to the one that frightened Jack earlier on, only this time it was even more spectacular. The waters went crazy consuming their devotee as well as the sacrifice itself. When the display was over and the pool settled down to its dark but quiet state Wilbur was still standing there, bone dry and unharmed.

Whatever ritual he had been performing over, he turned and began to walk towards the door. As he emerged his face

The Dark Lagoon

was perhaps a little more pallid than usual, it was hard to tell in the dim, otherwise he seemed none the worse for having paid homage to the dark spirit that lurked in the waters of the pool.

Jack wanted to say something, but nothing came to mind so he followed him back outside where once again the rational side of his brain convinced him that what he was experiencing was some form of hallucination, nothing more. He thought about talking to Wilbur about what happened but decided against it, he'd already made a fool of himself, he didn't need to convince him he was a lunatic as well.

Chapter Two

I

Wilbur was clearly determined to get the old Van running and return with it to the Keys. The metal cylinder was full of compressed air and he used it to inflate the van's tyres which though flat were unholed. It was an odd sight, watching the old Van rising up out of the garden like the hulk of some ancient warship. Having exhumed it from the garden and dealt with the rat infested interior, Wilbur climbed into the driver's seat and pulled the bonnet latch.

'You don't really expect to start this thing do you?' said Jack in amazement.

'Listen kid, there's nothing wrong with this Van that a little patience won't see right. When I laid it up eight years ago I did the job properly, that means I disconnected the battery, drained down the fuel system and just to make sure, poured a whole tin of Reddex into the carb. Chances are when she gets going she'll be better than new.'

Jack looked at the scabby vehicle with more than a little scepticism while Wilbur busied himself refitting the battery and making a whole load of adjustments under the bonnet. Tightening the fan belt, checking the radiator hoses, removing the worst of eight years of detritus from the places where they could foul moving parts. When he'd finished he got inside the Van and checked to see if the electric's were working, which apart from an errant horn they were.

The Dark Lagoon

The steering wheel was made entirely of chrome plated chain links with a chrome plated boss, Wilbur removed the boss and replaced some wires which had come adrift. He refitted the boss and gave it a sharp push and was rewarded by a loud blaring from the now fully functioning horn. Wilbur smiled in satisfaction and flipped a cheap looking after market switch on the dash and pushed the horn again. This time instead of the startling blare of the klaxon, the horn played a tune which Jack thought he recognised from the fairground. Wilbur flipped the switch to a new position and pushed the horn again. This time it made yet another sound, this one reminding Jack of a chain smoking opera singer clearing his throat first thing in the morning.

'I had the horn fitted specially, triple klaxons and its own separate power supply. You should see how it gets the locals scuttling in Costa Rica, damn thing nearly gives them a heart attack.' Wilbur was speaking quietly, almost as if he was talking to himself.

'So you had a few adventures in the Van then?' asked Jack interrupting his reverie.

Wilbur was so lost in his reminiscences he was quite startled by the interruption, turning to Jack with misty eyes as if he'd forgotten he was still there. In a second though his eyes cleared and he replied.

'You betcha kid, when you drive through a place like Costa Rica the last thing you want is to look like you've got money. That's why I had the Van look the way it does. Sure I could have bought a fancy flip top with a classy paint job and a V8 but it wouldn't have lasted ten minutes. This baby did just fine I can tell you, just fine.'

Jack wanted to know what Wilbur did in Costa Rica and was a little disappointed when he didn't continue. Instead, there was silence for a few moments while he got on with his checks on the Van. When he was satisfied that nothing vital was amiss he turned his attention to the huge plastic cover between the front seats.

'Hey Jack, get the catches your side will ya,? We're going to open this baby up.'

Not being familiar with engines Jack had no idea what he was talking about, nevertheless he watched the older man bend forward and flip two large metal catches on the floor of the driver's side. Jack could see and feel the cover give, like the stomach of a fat man loosening his belt after a good meal, he lent forward and tried to flip the catches his side but was surprised at how firmly they were held in place. It took him both hands and all his strength to flip the first catch, the second though was beyond him, no matter how hard he tried it wouldn't budge.

'Having a little trouble there are we Jack?'

The question was rhetorical, the tone fatherly, although not in a benign way. More the voice of a father who doesn't give his children a chance to learn things for themselves, who criticises eagerly but forgets to praise.

'I'm doing fine, this last catch is stuck that's all, hang on I'm going to get some leverage on it,' Jack sounded exasperated as he pushed open the door of the Van and twisted round till his legs slid down onto the running board.

He gripped the catch in both hands so he could use his back muscles and body weight as well as his arms and wrists. Nevertheless, it still took virtually everything he had before the catch finally gave up. When it did let go, it did so spectacularly and, not for the first time that day he ended up on his back in the dirt listening to the sound of Wilbur's rattling laughter.

Jack suddenly realised that he was starting to get used

to the teasing it was as if he had known Wilbur all his life instead of just a few hours, the thought rattled him. He got to his feet noticing the sun beginning to set and the thought occurred to him that Tom would be wondering where he was. He knew the journey back would take at least an hour and a half and there was the faint possibility that Tom would be worried.

'Wilbur, is this going to take much longer?' he enquired. 'I have to be getting back soon.'

Without needing to be told the reason for his sudden need to get back, Wilbur picked up on his concern straight away.

'So this guy Tom, he's your sitter or something huh?' he replied coldly, the overt sarcasm concealing a growing possessiveness that made Jack feel uncomfortable again.

He decided that discretion was the better part of valour and to let the issue drop, he could wait and Tom would have to wait too. Wilbur wasn't waiting though, the engine cover was already lying in the back exposing a lot of mechanical stuff which he was in the process of dismantling, trying to get to the Van's carburettor.

'See this baby here,' he lectured, pointing triumphantly to a flat metal disc, if she sticks open the engine'll blow itself to pieces, if she sticks shut it won't run at all.'

Wilbur started waggling the butterfly back and forwards vigorously, after a while an expression of dissatisfaction came over his face and he began muttering profanities under his breath. He moved upright and got out of the Van. Jack looked in bewilderment into the engine compartment, sure in his own mind that "This Baby" as Wilbur called it would never run again.

When he returned he was carrying a can of something

called Winn's carburettor treatment: "a carb overhaul in a can".

'Problem is, over the years a lot of varnish builds up and makes the carb stick, this stuff dissolves it,' Wilbur said sagely.

Jack nodded encouragingly and said nothing. Anything he did say was only likely to invite further abuse so he decided to keep quiet and see what happened.

Wilbur tipped the contents of the can into the carb throat and waggled the butterfly around some more. This time he appeared to be happy and turned his attention to a spring loaded screw at the side of the carb. He pumped the screw up and down a few times and Jack could see fuel starting to trickle into the bowel of the carb.

'We have to prime her before we start her, this way the pump won't have to work as hard and neither will the battery,' muttered Wilbur as if to himself.

'Great,' said Jack perversely, aware that the older man wasn't listening. Wilbur seemed to have finally finished whatever it was he had been doing and was refitting the cover. The whole process had only taken twenty minutes but it seemed like a lot longer to Jack, by now he was actually getting quite excited about the prospect of the old Van firing up. He still felt it wouldn't run but the thought that it might conjured up possibilities, freedom, independence, escape from the claustrophobic tent he shared with Tom. Wilbur again left the Van, when he returned he'd re-parked the Chevy off the road. Jack wondered how many years would pass this time before he returned to the house to collect the car. Somehow he felt it would be a long time.

When Wilbur got back into the Van he was really animated, he'd stowed his things from the car in the back and he was holding a silver ignition key in his right hand, like a child with a new toy. He placed the key carefully into its slot, checked the transmission was in neutral, and turned it fully to the right. There was a clicking noise from the solenoid which started fast and gradually slowed to a stop but the engine didn't fire. Wilbur swore under his breath and tried again, this time there were only a few clicks in response and again the engine failed to fire.

'Come on Baby,' he said the words gently, almost cajolingly, as he twisted the key for the third time. He was rewarded by a heavy whirring and clattering followed by a metallic coughing as the starter motor fully engaged. The old motor turned over, needing only a little encouragement to burst into asthmatic life, valves and pistons shaking off the dust and grime of the years, cylinders welcoming life giving fuel to their parched surfaces. After a few seconds the engine note changed character, starting to sound more powerful and a lot healthier than either of them expected. Wilbur blipped the throttle a couple of times to clear out its passages and it settled down to a steady idle. Behind them a great cloud of thick white smoke was clearing, the job was done and after all the time it had spent interred at the house the Van was going back on the road.

'It's time to hit the road Jack,' Wilbur spoke the words with the rhythm of the song.

Jack feeling generous joined in. 'And don't you come back no more no more.'

Wilbur finished 'And don't you come back no more.'

They both laughed out loud, Wilbur's laugh sounded like it came from a bellows that'd seen one too many fires, Jack's hid a serious thought. He never did intend returning to that house with its dark pool..... never in a million years.

II

As he guessed, the journey back to the Keys took about an hour and a half. By the time they got to the twenty mile bridge it was gone nine thirty and his thoughts returned to Tom. He didn't think for a minute Tom would be worried, he'd be fed up though fed up and even more suspicious than usual, which would make persuading him that they should buy the Van virtually impossible and buying the Van was exactly what Jack had decided they had to do.

The Van was performing better than he could have hoped and even though it was noisy and smelly, he was starting to get quite fond of it. The irony was, when he and Tom planned the trip the big objective was to get together enough money to buy a Van and drive across the States, preferably getting laid in every town along the way. Although they'd never actually revised the plan officially, with Ruth on his mind the whole time there was no way it would ever come to fruition. *Oh well he thought, sometimes you have to make difficult choices and live with the consequences.* As sensible as this rationale sounded, it didn't make him feel any better, he still felt like a heel.

Thankfully Wilbur had been silent for most of the journey back, lost in his own, no doubt twisted little world. Whatever; Jack was glad of a chance to think things through again, continuing his futile search to find a way of keeping everyone happy.

As they approached Key Largo and silence still reigned, he started to get anxious. He was angry with himself because he couldn't make up his mind about what to do, he was angry with Tom for making things so difficult but more than anything he was missing Ruth. He couldn't stop thinking about her, how she looked, what she was doing, who she was seeing and above all he kept wondering if she was missing him as much as he was missing her. It was as if a vital part of himself was missing and he couldn't function properly without it. Maybe, he thought, it would be best if he went back home, called it a day. At least that way he could stop pretending to himself and Tom that things were going to be like they'd planned. Even as the thought traced across his mind he knew he couldn't do it, he was no quitter, he would stick things out no matter how hard they got.

On top of everything else on his mind, Jack couldn't get rid of the feeling of foreboding that was growing in him like the seed of some poisonous tree. Below the level of logic a voice kept telling him to stop revelling in his own self pity and to keep his eye on the ball. The voice was saying that he'd fallen in with bad company, that he was lucky to be alive, that he should get the hell out of there while he still could. He suddenly realised he'd broken out in a cold sweat, his hands were gripping the arm rests as if they were stopping him from falling over a cliff and his heart was racing out of control.

Wilbur meanwhile had started humming the tune to Uretha Franklin's "Killing Me Softly With Your Love", the melody rattling and bubbling out of him like it came from an old music box with a faulty spring.

Jack recognised where they were, they were passing Pennycamp park, a state nature reserve containing a lot of crocodiles, snakes and bugs; the locals thought it was a waste of money, plenty of bugs and crocs to go round without spending taxes protecting them. He didn't care at this point what lived in the everglade swamps of the park but seeing it meant Henry's bar was only a mile away. Henry's was right on top of the Bella Vista which meant they were nearly back. It was nearly ten and he was sure he would find Tom in Henry's, probably sucking on a tuna and ham sub, already the worse for a few beers. He would be pissed off for sure but somehow right now Jack didn't care, Henry's seemed like home right now, whereas the Van felt like......*fear*. He became conscious of the stale air in the Van and of its source still humming gently to himself, the fumes coming out of him like some kind of hoary coal fired power station.

'You can drop me anywhere round here,' Jack spoke the words unbidden as if the voice in his head had made the decision for him. *'Best to play it safe'*, the voice was saying reasonably, better to get out here and walk the rest of the way to Henry's than ask any more favours of this man whose strangeness seemed to be increasing with the night.

Wilbur didn't brake or even slow down, instead he broke his long silence. 'We got business to discuss first Jack. I didn't drive all the way to Miami and back for my health.'

The reply was just what he would have expected yet coming as it did, without so much as a pause for thought it confirmed to Jack what the unheard voice had been telling him, he was in over his head...... probably way over his head. He tried to reply but suddenly felt too tired to think straight. He looked ahead at the road, trying to focus his thoughts but the unvarying speed of the Van, the relentless drone of the engine and the lights of the oncoming vehicles only served to cloud his mind even further.

'You went out for the steak dinner and now he wants to take you back to his place' the voice was back on form, it had lost its reasonableness sounding high pitched, mad.

'Wilbur.' He spoke the name only with great effort, looking directly across at him as he did so. Wilbur sensing he was being looked at took his eyes off the road, turning to meet the stare. The eyes that regarded Jack were black and dead, they were inhuman, betraying nothing of their owner's inner thoughts, instead they bored into him, worming their way into his mind.

The spell was broken by the violent sound of a trucker's horn. Without anyone to pilot it the Van had strayed onto the wrong side of the carriageway. The truck's horn bellowed out like an enraged bull but it seemed like Wilbur either didn't hear it, or wasn't bothered. Perhaps he thought the Van was surrounded by some kind of force field, that at the moment of impact, it would dematerialise like Dr Who's Tardis and transport them to another *(hellish)* world.

Jack reacted instinctively, throwing himself forward, elbows down, head between his knees bracing himself uselessly for the inevitable impact. An impact that would see his body hurled forward into the footwell where it would be met by the engine block, leaving him an unrecognisable cocktail of twisted metal and bloody mush.

He huddled there braced for the inevitable collision but it didn't come. His internal clock flipped a cog, he didn't know how much time passed before he tentatively uncurled himself from the foetal position. For some reason his hands slipped down to his crotch, maybe subconsciously he was checking to see if his equipment was still intact, it was. The experience had cleared his mind leaving him wide awake and well aware of how close to death they must have come.

What he didn't see when he ducked below the dash was how Wilbur finally responded to the situation. He faced the truck, staring into the dazzling light of its head-lamps, seeking out the driver like a predator stalking its prey. For a moment it seemed as if neither driver was prepared to give way, then at the decisive moment before a collision became unavoidable the truck driver chickened out and turned his wheel. The truck had no chance, it simply ploughed across the road, through the flimsy barrier separating the highway from the ocean and like some kind of monstrous phantom disappeared into the night. Jack didn't even hear the splash as it crashed into the bay.

'Where's the truck Wilbur, what the fuck happened?' He demanded, cheeks burning with anger and relief.

Again Wilbur croaked his mirthless laugh, as if the question revealed Jack to be both stupid and weak.

'Relax Jack. Nothing happened, that truck's long gone, never even came close.'

There was a long pregnant pause during which Jack fought back the urge to grab the wheel off the old man, stop the truck and punch him out. Wilbur sensed how near Jack was to losing his temper and immediately changed his tune.

'Listen kid, sorry if I scared you, no hard feelings huh?'

There was an unmistakable note of concern in Wilbur's voice, no, it was even deeper than concern, like Jack meant more to him than he had a right to. Listening to that voice left Jack feeling more uncomfortable than ever.

'Listen Wilbur, unless I'm a prisoner or something, I'd like to be let out here. Any business we have to discuss can wait till tomorrow, I've had about as much excitement as I can take for one day OK?'

Wilbur heard the near panic in Jack's voice and hesitated for a second before taking his foot off the gas pedal. He stamped brutally on the brakes, bringing the Van to a halt in a dirt packed lay-by at the side of the road, brake drums squealing in protest as it came to rest. When he switched the engine off Jack was immediately aware of the high pitched rhythmic sound of a million crickets chirruping endlessly in the background. The sound seemed to have ambushed the night, infecting it with some leprous disease that had it pulsating, bloated and full to the point of eruption.

'Gonna be a storm tonight Jack, hope that tent of yours is tied down tight.'

Wilbur wore a forced smile as he made the comment, a smile that sat uneasily on his craggy face like a rictus on the newly dead. Jack looked out the window and saw a crescent moon hanging in a clear sky, its less than half light framing Wilbur's head with a pale aura which reminded him of the haloes around the heads of the saints in Renaissance paintings.

'Thanks for the advice,' He said while at the same time reaching for the door handle. He couldn't believe he was going to get off this easily but he had no intention of tempting fate by opening up the conversation any further. Meeting Wilbur had been an experience..... he just wanted to leave it at that. He stuck out his left hand and forced himself to look calm and confident.

'See you around,' he said, the words echoing round the interior of the Van.

'Yeah kid, see you around.'

No mention of the Van or the trouble he'd gone to on Jack's behalf, he really was going to let him off the hook. Jack wanted to open the door but something was stopping him, he felt compelled to say something else to Wilbur. He felt unsure, maybe he was wrong to run away from this man, maybe he was just acting like a child, frightened of unseen goblins, afraid of the dark. Also there was the question of the Van, he had become curiously attached to it and the thought of giving it up forever made him feel bad.

'Look Wilbur,' he said wearily. 'It's been a long day and I'm tired, we'll talk tomorrow OK'

The atmosphere between them had somehow changed, for some reason he was no longer the focus of Wilbur's attention, when he did reply, he sounded vacant and distracted, as if something far more important and serious had just come up, something he couldn't ignore.

' Sure thing kid, whatever you say, I'll be seeing yuh.'

Well if that's the way he wanted it thought Jack, it was fine by him, at least he'd tried to be civil. The power came back into his arm and the door handle gave way sharply sending him cascading out of the Van and into the dirt. He was almost getting used to the experience even managing to laugh at his own clumsiness. He got back to his feet, the sound of the crickets almost climactic now, the air thick and humid. He dusted himself down and slammed the door, then in a gesture of friendly dismissal he confidently banged the roof twice. He wasn't even rewarded by a blast from the klaxons, just the roar of the engine as Wilbur fired her back up followed by the screech of tyres as the Van headed off into the suddenly storm laden night. A few seconds later it disappeared and Jack was alone on the highway.

Chapter Three

I

Jack felt tired, confused and dirty. The events of the day were a jumble, Wilbur, the house, the pool and the school-yard all mingled to form a hideously deformed collage in his head.

In the meantime he was standing by the side of the road on a night that was fast turning to shit. Flashes of lightning were splitting the sky with increasing frequency revealing an angry-looking thunderhead that was getting nearer with every minute that passed. All he really wanted to do was go back to the tent and sleep; yet he knew if he did that and Tom wasn't there, his guilt at not having told him where he was going would prevent him from getting any rest.

The truth was, part of the reason it had been so easy for Wilbur to suck him in was that he needed some space away from Tom to think. Life had become more oppressive with each passing day, Tom took every opportunity he could to pick an argument or make a complaint. He'd needed time on his own to get his mind together, work out a strategy for fixing things between them before they got out of hand.

Of course he wasn't expecting, couldn't have anticipated what happened, not that this fact made him feel better, to the contrary it only served to make him feel even more insecure. After all if he couldn't even control his own destiny how could he hope to resolve his relationship with Tom. He trudged the six hundred metres to Henry's bar deep in thought. He didn't even notice the wind beginning to rise or the spots of brackish rain carried on the breeze. His feet barely cleared the scrub grass, his head hung low, he walked with the gait of a man weighed down by an unknown foe in some nameless war.

He crossed the road to get to Henry's, barely looking for traffic as he did so. Somehow it was obvious that the roads would be deserted, only a fool or a lunatic would be out without good reason on a night like this and right now he felt like he qualified on both counts.

Henry's was a long low building probably constructed in the mid sixties on a budget. There was never a "Henry" to give the place real character, the name was cynically chosen to attract the sort of clientele at which the bar was aimed. They were the respectable working men who shunned the fashionable and expensive night-spots of the wealthy tourists, the bread and butter Joe's who wanted a comfortable place where they could regularly consume their wages and all at reasonable prices. Of course in reality these people hardly existed, where they did, they were too hard pressed paying off their mortgages and bringing up their families to be out drinking. Too many folks in the Keys had to live off minimum wage, a trade off they were told that had to be made by anyone who didn't work in the city.

As far as Henry's bar was concerned this left a slightly less lugubrious clientele as its mainstay. Mainly composed of heavy drinking single men, women who weren't attractive enough to compete for anything better and an element that was well represented by the group of six Harley Davidsons that now stood at all angles outside the front entrance. Of course you also had guys like Jack and Tom, not street-wise enough to avoid the place because it just happened to be the closest watering hole to the Bella Vista Park.

The Dark Lagoon

Normally he would have been wary of the collection of radical looking Hogs that blocked his way to the door. He'd heard about the indigenous gangs of Hell's Angels in the area and had already been warned to avoid them. The way he felt though it just didn't seem to matter. He hardly looked at the scoots as he walked by, even pushing the handlebars of one of them out of his way. When he got to the door he caught a whiff of himself and smiled ruefully, thinking if there was any undesirables in the bar tonight he should feel right at home with them.

As he walked into the bar there was virtually no change in brightness, Joe the barman didn't believe in putting on too many lights, it just burnt electricity and showed up the shabby decor and even shabbier patrons. Illumination was mainly confined to the bar itself, and the pool table that lay at the far end of the room to the right. Joe clocked Jack right away and glared at him even more than usual. Perhaps the glare was a friendly warning to get out of there, come back some other time when it was safe. In any event the look was lost on him, he hardly registered it and even if he had would have ignored it anyway.

He could see Tom wasn't there, the bar was almost empty. There were just two regulars in, one was an enormously fat man whose name he didn't know and the other his girl friend, one of the ugliest women he'd ever seen, they were sitting on stools at the bar talking in low secretive tones.

At first he noticed no-one else until he registered the group of dark clothed bikers by the pool table. They either hunched over the table or were seated round it smoking and drinking. He gave them no mind and strode directly to the bar where Joe was methodically polishing a beer mug as if it was some sort of prize exhibit in a museum. Joe was a tall swarthy man who looked as if somewhere in his ancestral line at least one Spaniard had crept in. He was unshaven and his overalls didn't reflect the same cleanliness standards he appeared to be applying to the glass. He was never the most friendly person, having the opinion that all foreigners were "limeys" and probably only there to work illegally stealing jobs from local people. He conveniently forgot that without this source of cheap labour, he along with a lot of other local businesses would have to close down.

Tonight however was different, the look in his eyes had progressed from cool indifference to positive hostility. Jack's first thought was that he would be thrown out without even being allowed to make his enquiry.

He had in fact misjudged the look completely. Joe was never friendly to anyone since his wife ran off with the kids and that commie musician from out west. He had no friends of his own, seeing no use for them, they only sponged off you and when it came to the crunch let you down. But he noticed this kid coming into the bar a lot over the past few weeks and he liked what he saw, he brightened the place up, though he never gave him any indication of the favour he had found. The look was his version of a show of concern, he didn't want the kid to get hurt. Also, he didn't need any trouble in his bar and trouble was exactly what this kid spelled with a group of Heathens in the place with nothing better to do than to cause it and no better person to pick on than a young limey like Jack.

'Has Tom been in here this evening Joe?'

Jack's voice was flat and jaded, it said "don't fuck with me tonight, I've had a bad day". Joe got the message and his feeling of concern went into overdrive.

'Sure, he's been in but he went about an hour ago,

best you go look for him kid,' Joe lowered his voice and his eyes moved sideways to the group of Heathens by the pool table. *'If you know what's good for you if you know what I mean.'* Most warnings go unheeded, come too late or are misunderstood, there wasn't time to see if this one would qualify on more than one count. The tight group by the pool table had started to break up, one member in particular peeled away from the rest and was walking slowly towards the bar.

II

His name was Onyx and he was the leader of the local chapter of the Heathens, reputed to be the most depraved and violent of the Hell's Angel gangs that prowled this part of Florida State. He'd earned his name from the green tattoo that covered his bald pate. Originally he hated the tattoo, it was performed by a rival gang after a dispute over a drugs deal. They abducted him, shot him full of cocaine, shaved his head and tattooed it green, then threw him off the back of a motorcycle on the highway at fifty miles per hour. It was a miracle he survived and it took him six months to get out of hospital. By the time the hair on his head grew back you could still see the green border like a creeping disease spilling over the edges of his hair line.

After a while he found he got more respect by keeping his head shaved, it kind of enhanced his image. Since the incident his stock had really risen in the gang. Always a cruel violent man, the tattooed head spurred him on to even greater atrocities. He became an even heavier user of the white powder than before and showed great delight in the humiliation and torture of the many victims the gang picked on, innocent and otherwise. He got the name

Onyx because one day during a fight he used his head to batter a man to death. Afterwards someone said it must be made of solid Onyx, everyone laughed but the name stuck and Onyx he had become, he also became known as one bad hombre, an rep in which he took great pride.

Jack regarded the biker sidling towards him with bitter resignation. It now became obvious what Joe was trying to do, warn him to get the hell out of there before there was trouble. It was so clear what this thug was after, you could tell by the casual arrogance of his walk, by the way he was staring him down and by the way his cronies were beginning to follow like jackals.

There was no denying the menace, or the danger he was in but for some reason he couldn't turn away, he was held by those snake charmer eyes and the body now bobbing to and fro to some silent rhythm. The biker was about five ten, with a medium but heavily muscled build, weighing out at maybe one eighty, one eighty five pounds. It was difficult to tell his age by the face but looking at the muscle tone of the exposed arms, Jack guessed about thirty. He was wearing a biker's black leather waistcoat with tassels with white ends hanging from it, the white ends were sharks' teeth. His jeans were tight and straight with several tears, although not in fashionable places. It was clear even in the gloom that they were soiled, probably never been washed since new. Poking out the end of the jeans were the bottom of a pair of heavy black leather boots with thick soles and silver metal sides which trailed behind, Jack didn't know it but they ended in two wicked looking spurs.

The thing that captivated his attention though wasn't his menacing appearance, or the threat of violence, or the way he was dressed, or even the semi hypnotic way in which he was weaving and bobbing towards him. What prevented him from turning away and staring down meekly into the cheap wooden veneer of the bar was the sight of the man's head. He was clearly bald as a coot but the surface of his scalp looked like it had been polished to a mirror finish and painted green, like a human billiard ball.

'See something funny do you limey?' Onyx spat the question directly at Jack, pleased it was going to be so easy to pick the fight, it was never as much fun when they turned away and went all sheepish right from the start. This one looked like he had some fight in him and Onyx liked that, weekday evenings could get so boring otherwise.

Jack was taken aback at the directness of the question, at the relaxed way this punk was going about his business, as if he'd done this sort of thing many times before. The voice in Jack's head which had been silent since he left Wilbur started chattering away again. It was telling him if he didn't do some fast talking he was dead meat.

'Nothing funny, friend, I'm new round here that's all, let me buy you a drink, what're you having?' It wasn't much but under the circumstances Jack was reasonably happy with his response, most important of all his voice came out even, there was no hesitation, nothing to give away how threatened he was feeling.

By the expression on his face Jack could see the human billiard ball wasn't buying it, far from disarming this snake with his British accent and the offer of a free beer, he'd given him dangerous information. The look on his face said everything, this kid was new round here, no-one to protect him, no-one to miss him, Onyx's plans took a bolder, more sinister turn.

'Buy us all a drink huh limey?' he said turning towards the advancing gang, 'Got a lot of money have you? Don't you know it's dangerous to carry a lot of money in these parts?'

Onyx paused for a minute to allow the tension to build, then with an evil looking smirk on his face he moved in for the kill.

'Yeah, it's dangerous for a limey like you to carry a lot of money, no telling what kind of trouble you could end up in. Lucky for you we met; here give it all to me, I'll look after it for you.'

The smirk on Onyx's face broke out into a crooked smile which said "Yeah first give us your money and then we're going to jump you anyway".

Jack knew what the score was here, he knew the danger he was in, he could smell it in the stale air of the bar, feel it in the quiet tension that had descended on the place. He tried to keep his cool, throwing in a smile of his own, trying to seem like a dumb harmless kid. Nevertheless he could feel his hackles rising, hot blood rushing to his head, his cheeks burning as his muscles tightened in readiness for a fight.

'Listen, I'm only here for a quiet drink,' he said calmly. 'I don't want trouble and I'm sure you don't want any either so why don't I just buy you that drink and we can leave it at that?'

This time Onyx laughed out loud and there was real amusement in the sound, all pretence about his motives peeling away with the laughter. The group of Heathens were closer now and Jack could hear them jeering in the background, getting ready to join in once Onyx got started on the limey.

Jack was starting to sweat now, his face burned red hot and his muscles felt wound to breaking point. Running away was not an option, he had seen one of them go to the exit and lock the door.

'Hey, boys, this punk wants to be our friend.'

Onyx was unashamedly playing to the crowd now, deliberately building up the tension. 'We can all be peace loving pukes together, maybe he wants to get us drunk and butt fuck us.' He turned back to Jack

'What do you say faggot is that what you want to do, get me drunk and butt fuck me huh?'

Onyx could see he was getting to the kid now and he always liked the sound of his own voice when he was terrorising someone, if he really tried maybe he could get him to piss his pants and cry.

He continued. 'Well I've got news for you, me and the boys here have got a mission in life' and here his voice became low and conspiratorial, as if he was about to take the kid into his confidence. 'Our mission in life is to rid this world of sorry arsed queer-boys like you and you know what?' here his voice took on a happy booming quality, his lips pulled back across his face exposing yellowed broken teeth.

'We like our work, we really do.'

Joe had ducked down under the bar, Jack assumed to get out of the crossfire when it started but he was wrong again. When he emerged he was carrying a blackjack, the illegal kind, the kind designed with only one purpose, to put a man down hard enough with one blow so he would never get up.

Joe's voice was thick with fear but there was also a grim determined quality in it that said he meant business. 'OK boys, that's enough, show's over, you've had your fun now leave the kid alone.' There was no 'or else', no need to say more, the blackjack spoke for itself.

Onyx turned briefly away from Jack and looked at the barman, considering this new development. The barman was big but he was scared and flabby looking, even if he could handle the cosh it was no problem, he and the boys had a few equalisers of their own if needs be, including some guns just in case things really started to deteriorate. Nope if Joe wanted to be a hero it was fine by him, the more the merrier; let the party begin. His right hand moved to his side with practised speed, reappearing with a flourish holding a short bladed combat knife, the blade twinkling in the light from the red tinged lamps.

Jack was once again caught in a waking dream, everything was happening in slow motion, time stood still as he listened to the voice in his head telling him that soon he would have to meet that blade. This time though he heard the voice and listened to it too, it spoke the truth after all. If this was to be his destiny then the least he could do was to meet it head on and if he had to go down, then he would go down fighting.

Then suddenly Onyx froze in mid step, a look of recognition and surprise on his face. The hand that held the knife, instead of darting forward to strike, reached skyward with its twin in an unexpected gesture of surrender.

'Hey man, no need to flip your spool, we were only kidding, see'

Onyx dropped the knife to the floor where it hit the filthy carpet with a silent clatter. 'A little fun, too many beers tonight, hey boys: time to go.'

His hands dropped from above his head but his arms remained wide, he started to take small backward steps towards the door, shepherding the jackals back with him. They didn't demur, being content to follow their leader in

The Dark Lagoon

whatever direction he chose to go. As they reached the door Onyx first straightened up, then gave a small bow as if he were a great actor leaving the stage after one of his finest performances. When they were all gone, Joe and Jack were left praying they wouldn't return for an encore.

After the Heathens departed there was silence between as the two men stared at one another across the bar, neither able to find the appropriate words, eventually it was Jack who broke the silence.

He let out a long whistle and said 'Were those guys high or something?' The question was a rhetorical one, needing no reply.

'Yeah, they're as ugly a bunch of mother fuckers as you could wish to meet and if God hadn't stepped in to save us I guess they'd be scraping our remains off the floor in the morning.'

Jack suddenly felt the urge to embrace this sweaty swarthy man who had saved him from a severe beating, if not from death itself. Luckily the urge evaporated before he could do anything embarrassing, instead he was struck by tiredness.

No, it was more than simple tiredness, he was totally exhausted mentally and physically. During the confrontation with the Heathens he'd felt full of energy, almost supercharged, now the effects of the day had caught him up big time. He felt like an inflatable toy after someone had removed the stopper, he was sinking fast and he knew if he didn't leave soon he would collapse exhausted where he stood.

Although Joe congratulated himself for his heroism on many occasions after that evening, often dining out on the tale as it grew like the size of a prize fish, it wasn't his intervention that saved them but the presence of a talisman that even Jack wasn't aware of.

What Onyx had seen reflected in the light from his blade was the silver crescent moon around the boy's neck. It was a sign he ignored at his peril. This boy was under the protection of his own master. To hurt him would be to invite a retribution so terrible, even the thought of it had him sweating as he rode away into the storm, rain lashing against his bare chest, wind rushing past his smooth green pate.

III

It was only a half mile walk back to the campsite, though it seemed a lot longer as Jack nodded his goodbyes to Joe and headed for the door. He was slightly stooped and he dragged his feet, every so often his head would swim and he began to wonder if he would even make it back. Walking out into the night air was like receiving a high powered electric shock directly to the brain.

It was one of those nights when Heaven and Hell fought for domination in some age old elemental conflict. The sky was ablaze with a lightning induced afterglow which highlighted the monstrous thunderhead dominating the night in livid tones of crimson and scarlet.

He was immediately awake and alert, his first thought drowned by an explosion so loud it seemed to shake the ground beneath his feet and threatened to send the whole Island crashing into the sea. This was the monster the lightening had heralded except it wasn't alone, before the last vestiges of noise had rolled into the distance, the world turned supernova. A white

The Dark Lagoon

light too bright to behold split the sky, forcing his eyes to close instinctively and his hands to fly up in front of his face. He saw the lightening etched into the air, a fat pillar of light coming out of the clouds and reaching out for the land. Reaching out was exactly what it seemed to be doing because at the end of the pillar was the same dark hand he had seen in his dream. The rain was increasing in intensity, immediately drenching him, the drops large and warm smelled of swamp water and stagnant pools.

He put his head down and strode into the storm. He had walked no more than fifty yards when he was struck in the face by something hard and sharp, a few feet further and he felt something else hit him in the chest. Something strange was being carried by the storm, small pebbles perhaps or even hail. Then he realised it was neither of these things. Where he felt the last impact there was a squirming in the folds of his shirt, he reached inside and his fingers were met by something alien and alive.

The sensation of something crawling over his skin, something that could bite sent him into a cold panic. He clawed at his own flesh in an effort to capture the interloper, but it seemed to know his intention and had somehow wriggled just out of reach. He couldn't think straight any more, he tore at his T shirt, ripping the fabric as if it were tissue, flinging the shredded remains, together with whatever it was had invaded him, into the dark.

All self control left him, he picked up his heels and bolted, never fully remembering that final half mile or how he ended up back at the Bella Vista in his bag beside Tom, who was lying there in a coma-like sleep, unaware of the chaos going on around him.

Chapter Four

I

Wilbur had gone silent for a reason and it wasn't because he wanted to let Jack off the hook either.

Something had come up to distract him from the game he was playing with the boy, at least something had entered his mind anyway. He was suddenly filled with a feeling of dread foreboding, it was all he could do to stop himself from crying out. He could feel the bile in his stomach rising up into his throat, like some kind of spontaneous volcanic eruption burning the soft tissues and threatening to send him into a paroxysm of coughing. With difficulty he fought the urge to gag and tried to refocus his mind. His first thought was that his duodenal ulcer had burst again, he remembered the quack doctor with the goatee beard telling him if he didn't moderate his habits it would be the death of him, one more flare up and that was it; untreatable. Well that had been nine years ago and there had been nothing since. Maybe now was pay-back time. The thought was killed at birth; Even as it died he knew the ulcer wasn't to blame. Something had happened outside himself, something so catastrophic it sent ripples out to reach him, ripples that felt like tidal waves although what created them he couldn't imagine.

Looking back, his unplanned duel with the truck was the precursor to this premonition, a sort of curtain raiser, a way of making him participate in some other greater crisis. It was as if someone had switched off a great neon light in his head, a light that had been on ever since he'd met Proctor, he had used that light to restore himself, without it he was nothing again, he knew he could no longer survive in the dark.

It was ironic really, for this to happen on this night of all nights. He had finally come across someone who he felt could give his life back real meaning and compensate him for the loss of his son. Jack didn't know it yet but Wilbur had big plans for the boy, plans that were now threatened with extinction before they were even given a voice. Jack would now have to wait, whatever happened in his direction in the future was now bound up in whatever had happened to cause the light to go out in his head.

Wilbur knew there was only one place he would find the answers he needed and only one person who could give them to him. He had to return to the island and speak to Proctor. Proctor would know what was happening, he always did.

Wilbur hardly noticed Jack getting out of the Van or what took place between them in those last few minutes. He was preoccupied with the journey back to the island. When he heard the door slam, he involuntarily slammed the transmission into drive and headed out to the quay where the launch was waiting. Although it was only a five minute drive, the roads were narrow, unmade and windy. It was therefore amazing that he managed the journey without incident. It hadn't anything to do with the weather, although there were ominous looking thunderheads gathering to the east. It hadn't anything to do with the Van's lights, they continued to send out their constant beam into the night air, highlighting the bugs and flying things in their path. It had everything to do with the fact that during that journey he was completely blind.

At least he was blind in the sense that he had no awareness of the road ahead. He must have been aware of it unconsciously or the Van would have ended up in a ditch or even the ocean instead of parked neatly in its bay beside the launch at the quayside.

During that five minutes Wilbur Kohn was lost to the world, his mind cut adrift from normality, spiralling out of control in another universe. A universe full of black images, of stars turned supernova where monsters from the nether-world reached out with blood-soaked fangs to devour anyone daring to trespass into their domain.

By the time he resurfaced he was in the launch with the engines running, casting off from the quayside. At first he had no idea how he had got there, it was as if time had skipped and the last five minutes had simply ceased to be. The pain in his stomach from the awakening ulcer combined with the burning in his throat served to remind him of where he'd come from, why he was there and where he was going.

The launch was a powerful one, fitted out as an offshore pursuit vehicle to coast-guard standards and then some. When her twin 1000 hp Mercuries were at full chat she could outrun anything the law enforcement agencies had to offer, performance which had been used on many past occasions and not just for recreation. It was power that he now used to the full, wheeling her round viciously, almost capsizing her so steep was the angle of the turn. Once straight he slammed the throttle forward to its stop and headed out of the bay as if he was being pursued by the devil himself. As he left the shore behind, the white flanks of the launch reflected the moon light onto the uncannily still waters in a pattern like white fire.

He reached the mist which always encircled Proctor's Island in record time. The sea remained calm all the way assisting his passage, urging him on to make even greater haste. At first he didn't notice the change to the swirling vapours but once the launch was fully enclosed in the mist he couldn't help seeing how there was a greenish tinge in the air that had never been there before. Worse there was a smell of decay, the kind of smell you get from a disturbed grave. His head was starting to clear, so in spite of this new contamination, when the Island finally came into view he was able to take in the full horrific extent of its destruction.

At first he thought there was something wrong with his eyes. It was as if he had gone colour-blind, everything he saw was in grey-scale. The once luxuriant landscape of the Island had changed completely. What was in its place now was more like the aftermath of a nuclear attack. Even the sand had lost its lustre lying still and unreflective along the shore. As the launch got in closer he could see no sign of any living thing. The cove was still there although the jetty was now charred and blackened, he drew alongside anyway, tied the boat off and stepped onto the weakened timbers.

Wilbur regarded this scene with a casual detachment that surprised him. Here was the island he had helped to build, the brightest jewel in an otherwise dull world, utterly destroyed, yet he felt nothing at its passing. His mind was still full of other things, feelings awoken by events on the mainland, feelings which he thought he would never have again and which he needed to share with Proctor before they faded away. But where was Proctor? Was it possible he too had perished in whatever cataclysm had befallen the island? Somehow this thought brought home what the devastation of the Island couldn't, this was a tragedy that affected him and he wouldn't be immune from its consequences.

He knew that over the years he had come to rely on Proctor to give his life a purpose. It was only now he considered the prospect of life without Proctor that the full extent of his dependency became clear. If Proctor was dead then there wasn't anything left. He may as well douse himself with paraffin and set light to himself as go back to the mainland and live out an empty meaningless existence on his own. Even the thought of Jack..... *his new son*.... was pushed out by the thought that Proctor could be dead.

Wilbur stood on the beach and surveyed the scene. the devastation appeared to be total, he wanted to take a look at the rest of the island but then realised he had no strength to do so. Whatever it was that gave him the energy to make the journey with such speed and focus was now gone. His body seemed to be infected by whatever dark force had destroyed the island. His legs felt like the turned to rubber, a rubber not strong enough to support his weight.

Wilbur swayed drunkenly from side to side before falling to his knees, his face pressing into the polluted sand, the grains filling his nose and mouth, choking him with their tainted touch. So it wouldn't be necessary to take matters into his own hands then. It seemed the island itself would see to his demise. How ironic that he should die at the hand of that which he had striven so diligently to build. In that moment he realised he didn't fear death but welcomed it, in most practical ways he had been dead for years, dying now would just make things official.

II

'*Wilbur.*'

The sound of his name being spoken jolted him back to consciousness. Had he died for a moment? He thought so and being dead had felt good, peaceful. Now he had been brought back by the insistent sound of his own name being uttered by a voice he knew only too well and yet it seemed not at all. For the voice of Proctor had changed, it no longer sounded even vaguely human, it was the disembodied voice of a phantom and it came from all around him, it emanated from the land itself.

'Wilbur. Get up, you have news for me Wilbur. Get up and give me your news.'

What was the voice talking about, news? Here he was lying on the sand as nearly dead as any man had ever been and he was being asked about news. Why couldn't the voice just leave him alone let him return to the peaceful death that had enfolded him. He started to drift off, knowing this time there would be no return.

The hand on his shoulder touched him only lightly, yet with sufficient power to raise him to his knees and then to his feet, his eyes were blinded by the sand, his nose and mouth were full of the stuff. He couldn't have replied even if he had wanted to.

'We are reborn you and I.'

The voice was coming from straight in front of him and sounded more like the Proctor he had known. More like him but not exactly the same, there was a difference, the voice was harder, stronger than it had been.

'Yes Wilbur, we are reborn and out of this wasteland we will build something so fabulous it will fill the world with its beauty. You and I Wilbur, we have been charged with an awful task but I need you to tell me what you know.'

Wilbur felt himself being guided along, his feet unsteady, his breathing coming in sand-filled rasps. Then he was going down, toppling over like a felled tree in an infected forest. He waited for oblivion but all he got was the shock of cold sea water as he was plunged into the waters of the cove. The sea water stung the small abrasions on his face made by the sand, it also cleared his eyes and mouth. Before the water could fully replace the sand and find its way into his lungs, he was pulled out and found himself once again standing on the beach. This time though there was no disembodied phantom voice to haunt him but the figure and form of Rex Proctor still holding him by the shoulder.

'What happened?'

The question came unbidden from Wilbur' slips but the sound he heard was 'warch habhnd'.

The effort of trying to speak sent him off into a paroxysm of coughing which went on for what seemed like forever. He felt like he was going to cough his lungs right out of his body and into Proctor's face; now wouldn't that be a thing to see. Eventually though the coughing subsided, leaving a thin trail of bloody sputum around his mouth, dropping down in thin strands onto the front of his shirt. In a queer way he felt better than he had before, as if the sand had purged his lungs of the congested by-products of thousands of tar-laden cheroots, leaving him cleaner and stronger than before.

Proctor was staring at him the way a python stares at a billy goat. It was a look Wilbur had seen before, it was the look he wore when he first regarded a new victim.

'*Wilbur. Tell me your news.*'

The usually clean air of the island smelt sulphurous and insipid in the moonlight. *Like the drains of Miami had run unchecked into the pits of hell and their smoking fumes were being carried on the breeze.*

He thought the repeated question had a rhetorical quality. He felt sure Proctor already knew the reason for his unscheduled visit, had been waiting for him on the devastated beach, it was all part of some incomprehensible

The Dark Lagoon

plan that he would never be completely party to.

Wilbur had to know what had happened. For once his curiosity overcame his natural urge to obey.

'First tell me what happened here, I need to know.'

He was impressed at the surety of his own voice. Maybe it was knowing that Proctor wanted something from him that gave him the resolve to stand firm, or maybe it was the feeling that his news was somehow connected to the disaster that made him hold back.

Instead of punishing Wilbur for his impudence, Proctor appeared to be considering his request seriously, he was silent for some time turning over the possibilities in his mind. Eventually he reached a decision, fixed Wilbur with that predatory stare and began.

'Very well, I will tell you what you want to know, though you may have cause to regret your impudent curiosity.'

As he recounted his story of endless atrocities against man and nature his form started to change. The moonlight though dim highlighted these changes lending ghastly shadows of emphasis to the caricature of evil that he was becoming. The features of his face elongated in a way that would have been absurd had the cheeks not sunk into deep hollows and the lips not drawn back to reveal overlong incisors that were yellow, pitted and ravenous. Proctor's eyes became black caverns shadowed by a monstrous forehead, his nose flared and curved into the hook of a witches Halloween mask.

As the tale concluded his body changed also, the torso growing, the back arching and the arms stretching down until they almost touched the sand. Finally when he had finished he stood, faced the moon and stretched out a claw tipped by talons such as no mortal beast ever possessed. Proctor had become what he had always been, a creature of darkness born in the Stygian depths *but somehow free to roam the waking world.*

As if to add emphasis a bolt of dry lightening tore open the moonlight like Gentleman Jack tearing open the stomach of one of his whorish victims. In that fleeting flash of blue Wilbur saw what no living man was meant to see, the face of..........(Satan? Beelzebub? the Devil? or something far worse?)..and then it was gone, he was unconscious on the sand his mind screaming in silent agony. If he ever had any doubt about who he worked for, or more accurately to whom he belonged, that doubt was now gone, extinguished as easily as a candle flame in a hurricane.

When he awoke Wilbur felt curiously better, calm and at peace with himself. While he was asleep Proctor had returned to his old self and was sitting on the sand in front of him waiting patiently for his news. Proctor must have cleaned him up while he was out because he felt refreshed, almost scrubbed. Strangely his clothes which should have been stiff and high with sea water were also fresh, they even looked as if they'd been pressed. Sitting comfortably facing Proctor, still not knowing what was so important about his news, or why Proctor needed to hear it so badly, he told him about Jack and Tom and his hopes to replace his lost son,. After he'd told him everything Proctor leaned forward conspiratorially and placed his hand (*claw*) on Wilbur's shoulder.

'This is what I want you to do,' the Demon whispered.

III

Though Wilbur was uneasy about Proctor's instructions he was nevertheless prepared to carry them out. After all had he not delivered countless offerings to him in the past without so much as a second thought? So why could he feel his stomach burning with acid from an ulcer he knew wasn't there? Why could he not obey the command with his usual casual detachment from the victims fate?

He knew that no-one but he had ever visited the island and returned to the waking world unharmed. They all dwelt forever in the inky blackness of the dark lagoon, doomed to eternal non-existence, part of an ever growing accumulation of evil.

He had an unbidden urge to protect Jack from that fate, a possessive paternalism perhaps as dangerous for Jack as anything Proctor had in mind.

'You won't harm the boy will you?' The words escaped his lips sounding more strident, aggressive even than he had anticipated. Proctor's now straight cut features darkened instantly, a shadow of the demon crossed his face, filling Wilbur with instant dread and regret at his insolence.

'You needn't worry about the boy, about either of them,' stated Proctor. 'I mean them no harm, quite the contrary actually, I have a deal to offer one, a deal which could make him rich and the other.... well the other will live at least. Now I tire of this talk, I have much to do and everything must be just right, go now and do what I have asked.'

Somewhere over the eastern everglades the thunderhead finally burst. The rain was being driven westwards by a wind of abnormal strength although not as yet at its strongest. On its wings it bore a vast army of flying things hijacked from the swamps. The first drops of tepid rain began to fall in large droplets around the two figures on the beach, making a distinct plink plink sound as they hit the still waters of the cove, shattering its glassy smoothness. The clouds black and sullen obscured the moon throwing the island into pitch dark.

Wilbur didn't see Proctor raise his right hand to the skies. If he had he would no doubt have noticed how much like a claw it had become, though he may not have seen something less obvious but more significant. A mosquito had settled on the demon's index finger; it rested there after its long journey, wings folded, body pulsating rhythmically as if it couldn't make up its mind if it wanted to taste the blood of its new found host. Eventually it made its decision and punctured the flesh drinking deeply, tasting an unfamiliar brew, one which managed to chill its tiny soul. Then Imbued with new purpose it flew from its perch to the launch to join Wilbur as a second messenger, perhaps more deadly even than he.

Book Two

Chapter One

Corruption

I

Who knows how the Devil corrupts a man's soul? He probably starts with little things, something innocent, innocuous, something that just sucks you in gradually; like a harmless drink to relax the nerves, a little wager to excite the blood, a short term loan to tide you over, but who really knows? Of course that could be quite wrong, maybe he just bowls right on up when you least expect it, your heart's desire in one hand and a contract in the other, it seems unlikely that's all. Nope, the odds are he's a lot more subtle than that.

Greed, Lust, Envy, Jealousy, Gluttony, Pride, Sloth, the seven deadly sins. From the beginning of creation even the purest have been susceptible to one or all of these cunning deceivers. So, what makes them different and more powerful than other lesser sins like incest, theft, and murder?

Is it their unique ability to mimic virtues and cause their victims to commit those other crimes? Sloth can masquerade as socialism, pride as self esteem, greed as ambition, envy as motivation, jealousy as concern, lust as love, gluttony as hedonism. Maybe it's in this way they gradually work their way into a person, growing slowly like a malignant tumour until their victim is totally consumed.

Some will be more easily fooled than others, giving in

The Dark Lagoon

readily to their baser desires. Most will hold back, either through moral fortitude or, more often than not, the threat of retribution in this life or the next, should they give themselves over to their weakness.

It is often said that if the Devil didn't exist the church would have to invent him in order to give itself meaning. Gamblers Anonymous, Alcoholics Anonymous, Marriage Guidance, the Samaritans and even the Church itself, all fine institutions existing because of our susceptibility to evil. Without evil, corruption, temptation, they wouldn't even exist. It is also said that the Devil's finest achievement has been to convince mankind he is only a fairy tale.

Whatever. Neither Jack Simons nor Tom Kidman were saints, they were susceptible to temptation like anyone else and like anyone else there was one area where they were weakest. In Jack's case it was probably *pride* that held the upper hand, but it was *jealousy* that gnawed at Tom's insides, *jealousy*, waiting for the opportunity to turn cancerous like a bad mole in the sunlight.

Left to nature Tom probably would have learned to control and direct his desires, use them to achieve his goals of riches and power without the need for outside help. He would never have allowed himself to be consumed by *jealousy* or made its slave. But nature wasn't to be allowed to take its course. His destiny was to be given a nudge by a force beyond nature, a clever cocktail of deceit and lies injected directly into the bloodstream while he slept fitfully under a storm troubled sky.

There are times when even the strongest man becomes weak and susceptible, drops his guard or through ill fortune attracts the attention of forces beyond normal understanding. Forces which once awoken don't rest until they have their prize. Once the game begins there are no lengths to which they will not go to claim victory, no price too high, no time too long, no lie too big.

Even if Proctor could have guaranteed the defeat of his victim, he probably wouldn't have, a guarantee of victory with no element of chance would be but a Pyrrhic victory with no taste or meaning. What's more it would have spoiled the fun, taken away the challenge and there wasn't anything he enjoyed more than a good challenge. If this one resisted then there would be other candidates along in time and time and patience were commodities Proctor had in abundance.

Proctor's small but potent messenger delivered its package intact and on time. It could have been luck that led the mosquito to alight on Tom's cheek and not Jack's, or it could have been design. Either way the subtle changes it worked were decisive and the die was cast.

Like all good cheats Proctor had turned the odds in his favour, given himself an edge. In the games that were to come he would have a secret weapon working for him, one that would set the scene for his ambitious plan and help him to perform his immoral sleight of hand. Of course there was no guarantee that the serum he so cleverly concealed in the innocuous insect would do its job, it had to first find fertile ground. *In Tom, it was to find a soft and rotting place deep inside in which it could take root and grow.*

II

During that long and troubled night Tom was tortured by dreams that invaded his sleep and prevented him from finding rest.

He already felt ambiguous about the trip before they set out but since arriving in the States his relationship with Jack was like a missile set on self-destruct.

He told himself it was Jack's duplicity that was at the bottom of the conflict. That the reason he was seizing, or even manufacturing, every opportunity to argue or oppose him was to teach him a lesson for being disloyal and betraying their friendship for a woman. Even though he was a past master at self deception, he couldn't entirely hide the truth from himself. When that truth shone through like the sun coming out from behind a clouded sky, it hurt his eyes and pricked his conscience.

The truth of course was that he was *jealous* of Ruth. Instead of being pleased his best friend had found a wonderful girl, probably his perfect match so early on in his life, he was bitter, resentful and *jealous*. She was taking Jack away from him, had already taken him away and into the bargain soured what should have been a great adventure. It was only subconsciously that he acknowledged that what he was doing was wrong. On the surface he felt fully justified in expressing his outrage and disappointment by making Jack's life as much a misery as he could.

The only problem was he was also making his own life a misery at the same time. It made matters worse that Jack seemed to be accepting the treatment so meekly, as if by doing so he was vindicating himself and putting Tom in the wrong.

What a bastard, he couldn't win whatever he did.

So lately he'd been sleeping badly, rehearsing the moral argument in spite of himself and waking up exhausted from the conflict. The answer was of course staring at him in the face. Only a fool or a martyr stands in the way of the inevitable. If he valued his friendship then he should rise above his own selfish considerations, make it easy on the guy.

If nature had been allowed to take its course eventually it was likely that this side of the argument would have prevailed. With the debate so finely balanced, just a hair's weight stood between right and wrong. So it wasn't difficult for Proctor's intervention to help him fall into a waiting sea of jealous self pity.

In his dreams that night Tom was floating over a magnificent garden, like the one in Hampton Court Palace in London, a place he remembered being taken as a boy and marvelling at its perfect symmetry.

As he floated downwards he noticed a couple of young lovers nestling close, sitting on a love seat under a rose arbour. He felt warm feelings towards them, although he didn't know who they were. When he was close enough to make out their features he saw it was Jack and Ruth. He felt no surprise and called out to them but they didn't respond. They were right there in front of him, so caught up in their private little world, they didn't even notice he was there. The feeling of being ignored was ten times as painful as any physical hurt could be, it stirred something in him, something at once cold and terrible, warming him with the heat of its power.

As he drew closer still he started to make out some of what they were whispering to one another. To his horror it wasn't words of love they were exchanging but jokes and cruel jibes at his expense. He wanted to reach out his hands and shake them, tell them to stop but he was powerless to move. As his frustration increased so the intensity of their teasing mockery also amplified. He was a fool in their eyes, a clumsy jester to be used for amusement only and then when he became too tiresome, to be discarded without a second's thought. They found the funniest thing of all was how stupid he was for not guessing what was

The Dark Lagoon

going on. How could anyone be that stupid?

A white hot lava of rage ignited in his chest. A fire that demanded revenge to douse its hungry flames. Suddenly it was as if he had materialised in front of the mocking lovers, his false friends.

Far from appearing perturbed or ashamed at their treachery, they laughed all the louder to his face, their eyes glowing red with pure evil, eyes that spoke of mischief and of murder. As their hands closed around his throat choking the life out of him he couldn't move or even cry out, he could do nothing. He lost consciousness thinking what a fool he'd been to have allowed himself to have be deceived so easily.

'Give me another chance' his soul screamed out the words.

'Give me another chance and I won't be such a fool again.'

He awoke with a start, his body covered in a cold sweat, his red hair plastered against his head, the inside of his sleeping bag smelling as rank as a fish shop on a Monday morning. He could feel something crawling around in the bag with him and to his disgust put his hands on the crustaceous squirming body of the largest cockroach he'd ever seen. It was all he could do to remove the beast without screaming blue murder to the early morning mist.

As it was he lent over Jack's still sleeping body and opened the zipped flap that acted as the small tent's front door. After he hurled the creature out into the open he rubbed his tired bloodshot eyes and surveyed the sorry scene around him.

Here was the home they had shared for nearly three months, it was a farce really; if it hadn't been so sad he would have laughed out loud. The storm that looked like it was coming the previous day had obviously hit during the night bringing with it rain and from the looks of the tent's interior, half the bug population of the everglades.

In the thin morning light he could see that the interior of the tent was literally moving, as if it had taken on a life of its own. Unlike Jack he'd never been squeamish about bugs, or animals of any kind for that matter. Even the fat black scorpions that lived in the wood store at the construction site held no nightmares for him. In actual fact in some ways he actually preferred animals to people, they were more constant, you knew where you stood with them. Nevertheless the sight that confronted him was a revolting one and one that was likely to have Jack pissing his pants in cold terror.

Well good, he thought, it would serve the bastard right, perhaps he would even help matters along a little by putting one of the more juicy looking squatters in Jack's open mouth.

He looked around the tent for a likely candidate. It didn't take much looking, the entire insect Kingdom of the everglades seemed to have sent at least one representative to pay them a visit in the night, some species had sent entire delegations. He spotted a particularly horrible looking creature crawling up the side of the tent, lent forward and grabbed it. If you counted its feelers the beast must have measured five inches, it had a black carapace and when he turned it over he was rewarded by eight hairy black legs all working overtime on some obscure insectidal dance.

Holding his captive by the head and feelers he suspended it over Jack's open mouth, then started to slowly lower it inside. There was something about the look on Jack's face that made him hesitate, this was his friend and despite what was occurring between them he was still his friend. His arm jerked back from the brink in a spasm that sent the revolting creature flying across the tent into the far corner where it hit the side and dropped unharmed to the floor. It was still for a moment and then crawled off to join its brethren, apparently unworried by the whole experience.

In the meantime he made a decision, there was no work at the construction site that day and the ocean was out there waiting for him. Maybe after a dip and a dive things wouldn't seem so bad and he would regain his lost perspective, he knew from past experience the ocean could do that for him.

He took off his pants and grabbed a pair of swimming shorts, after he put them on he glanced round the tent looking for something. When he didn't see it he started to rummage round in the pile of clothes on his side of the tent and smiled as he put his hand on what he was after. He pulled the Hawaiian sling out from under the mess together with his weight belt and mask and carefully stepped over Jack before unzipping the doorway and leaving the tent.

The Hawaiian sling was a simple but effective device being composed of a cylinder of cork with a hole through the middle and a length of heavy duty catapult rubber fixed to the sides. The spear fitted through the hole and in the hands of a skilled hunter it was an effective weapon, capable of killing small fish from a distance of about two metres.

Standing beside the tiny tent, spear in one hand, mask in the other he looked every inch the hunter. Although not as well muscled as Jack he was much taller, nearly six foot four and bigger built. There was something about the way he stood that told any onlooker he was no push over, even at the tender age of twenty two. He was the kind of guy you could rely on in a tight spot, not reckless, cool headed, even on occasion cold and calculating.

Simon Shinerock

Ironically when it came to relationships he was just the opposite, his ego often turning him into a helpless emotional yo-yo.

The sight he met outside was a contradiction in terms, on the one hand it was most beautiful clear morning since they'd arrived. The air was fresh and clean, with for once, no trace of the oppressive humidity that usually made life in the Keys at this time of the year so tiring. There were a few small marshmallow clouds scudding across the sky creating a marvellous contrast of snow white against azure blue, a cool breeze ruffled his hair and caressed his skin.

The rest of the scene was chaos. All around him there was carnage, tents and awnings were scattered everywhere, there was debris and detritus of a human and natural kind ranging from branches of trees to an overturned Winnebago. There must have been the mother and father of all storms in the night and he hadn't even noticed. He felt oddly smug about the obvious disaster around him, it had passed him by.

Involuntarily he put his hand to his cheek and scratched. Immediately what had only been a mild irritation exploded into an unbearable itch, he'd been bitten and by the feel of it by something more potent than your everyday midge. He knew better than to give in to the urge to scratch the affected area hard. There was a much better solution and it was right in front of him; the ocean. Once he was in the water the bite would calm down and by the time he came out it would probably be virtually gone. He ran like a warrior past the other unfortunate campers, carrying the spear and sling in one hand and the weight belt and mask in the other, until he reached the shore. There he stopped and threw the sling on the ground.

He stared out over the water as he put on the belt and

adjusted it tightly round his middle. Experience and practice had taught him exactly how much weight to add so that he could dive deep without effort, yet still return safely to the surface before his lungs exploded. He could feel the white coral sand crunching beneath his feet, reminding him of the risk he was taking by going barefoot.

Long ago, the campsite had been part of the reef and the inert sand had been living coral. It was impossible to comprehend the billions of creatures whose bodies, piling up on one another had eventually breached the surface of the ocean to form new land. The Keys themselves were only there as a result of that ancient proliferation of life, and the process was still going on.

He knew the water was shallow for over five hundred metres, its floor made up of a base of jagged coral overlaid with marine organics and populated by a vast variety of creatures who had come to depend on the dead coral for their habitat. They existed in a relatively barren environment, protected from the ravages of the ocean by the living reef that now existed about two miles offshore. Two miles, not a great distance, tantalisingly close in fact but still too far for him to swim there and back in safety although he'd often thought of it.

He felt a little regretful, for although there was more than enough to keep him occupied in the shallows, he knew that the real delights were to be found out on the reef. He had been there once with Jack, They'd met up with some tourist who owned a small boat and wanted some company on a diving trip. He'd offered to lend them scuba equipment and was surprised when they admitted they'd never learned.

Nevertheless even skin diving the experience had been amazing. The reef was the most beautiful thing either of them had ever seen. There were living cliffs of pure colour populated by animals as exotic as the coral itself. So captivated were they by their surroundings, they were able to reach new depths and stay under longer than ever before.

He finished adjusting his rudimentary kit and snapped his attention back to the matter at hand. He bent down and picked up the sling, stood upright and strode purposefully into the still water.

III

Jack woke with a start. He knew right away where he was although everything else felt very hazy. The one thing he did remember though was that yesterday had been no ordinary day and its effects were far from over.

The first thing he realised was he was very stiff, in fact for a moment he thought someone had crept into the tent and tied him up, so difficult was it to move his reluctant limbs. Then he realised he was soaking wet, for some reason he'd gone to sleep still wearing his jeans and during the night the damp must have penetrated deep inside his body, leaving him chilled to the bone despite the warmth of the weather.

Sniffing the air he noticed the clammy humidity that had kept him wet in the night had gone. The air was dry and fresh, and the sunlight was already heating up the interior of the tent. He gradually began to test some gentle movements, reassured by the response albeit slow, that at least he wasn't paralysed. His neck ached, his back felt brittle, there was a stinging pain centred right at its base. He pulled his arms gingerly out from where they rested between his legs and wriggled them above his head. The shoulder joints creaked and popped like an old man's before bursting through the hole in the bag. He placed his hands on the ground and turned over fully onto his back, pushing down hard and forcing himself into a sitting position.

There was a sickening crunch underneath his left hand followed by the sensation of something that felt like warm custard erupting in his palm. Involuntarily he shifted his weight to his right hand and lifted up the left to examine what had occurred. There was a thick yellow substance spattered over the hand, the sight of which was so disgusting he nearly emptied the contents of his stomach onto the tent floor. Worse still there was something that looked like a knurled black twig caught up in the thick pus-like liquid, except twigs didn't usually twitch.

He looked down to where his hand had rested and saw the body of the creature he'd crushed. At the same time his eyes seemed to take in the interior of the tent for the first time. By now the heat of the day, amplified by the fabric of the tent had sent the population of bugs into a frenzy of activity. The whole floor seemed to be heaving with life. He hated bugs almost as much as he hated confined spaces, now he had more of both than he could stand. He twisted violently onto his front and scrabbled for the exit hardly noticing the zip flap was already open as he clawed his way through and out into the clean air.

It was as if the nausea that had built up inside him had been waiting patiently for him to get outside. Now he was in the open, he was no longer able to able to stop himself, he bent double and emptied the contents of his stomach onto the ground beside the tent. In fact there wasn't much inside him to throw up. What came up was mostly bile, leaving his throat burning but his stomach somehow cleansed and his head almost clear again. Memories of the previous day were still coming back, the voice inside his head was awake and full of enthusiasm to remind him of every weird detail, every stupid risk as it all flooded back.

Despite his discomfort and the traumatic events of the previous day, he felt renewed pangs of guilt, a feeling that was beginning to become uncomfortably familiar. He knew he would be feeling far worse than Tom would but it didn't matter, the guilt really gnawed at his guts, constantly reminding him of the way in which he was betraying his friend, or at least letting him down.

The voice in his head laughed at his discomfort, laughed loudly telling him not to be a fool, to stop whining and get on with his life, if Tom didn't like it then tough.

Why did something as beautiful as his love for Ruth have to have such negative consequences? He couldn't answer (*'bullshit'* said the voice), any more than he could carry on with the plans they'd made, or stop himself from going ahead with his new plan. The one which included Ruth but left Tom out in the cold. He stood upright and put his hand on the tent post for support. He needed to get out of his sodden clothes and go and find him, he needed to try and explain why things could never be the same. He had to put his cards on the table, whatever the consequences it had to be better than feeling like this.

'Fuck him,' said the voice and shut up in disgust.

His new-found resolve meant going back into the tent, something he was reluctant to do, although being out in the open again had diluted the terror enough for him to be able to at least rationalise the fear; after all, the bugs weren't dangerous or anything, it was just that he had a deep-seated revulsion for them.

In a way the events of yesterday had served to bring matters to a head. It had been obvious for some time things couldn't go on the way they were, something had to give and now it had. Steeling himself he pulled back

The Dark Lagoon

the tent flap and eased himself inside, taking care to sweep the floor below him with his sleeping bag so it was clear of bugs. He kept his spare clothes safe in a zipper compartment in his rucksack. From this he took out a pair of Bermudas and slipped them on. He saw that the Hawaiian sling was missing and guessed Tom had taken it along with his diving gear so it was obvious where he'd gone. He took his own mask and weight belt and climbed back out of the tent.

No matter what other issues weighed on his mind, the thought of the ocean raised his spirits. He looked around unmoved by the chaos around him on the site. He started walking towards the beach, picking up speed and strapping on his gear as he went.

Scanning the sparkling waters, he could see no sign of Tom. Directly in front of the campsite the beach ran into the ocean, the floor falling away gently and evenly for a long way, over quarter of a mile. A hundred metres out the water was still waist high allowing you to snorkel around, always knowing you would be in your depth.

Over to the far left however things were different. At the outer edge of the site there was a channel that ran into the heart of the Key. Along the channel stood the houses of Key Largo's wealthier inhabitants and outside most of them were moored impressive boats. Some of them looked very sad with barnacles clinging leprosly to their hulls way above the waterline, it was easy to see how their owners were more concerned with the prestige of having a boat than with the practicalities of looking after one. Nevertheless because of their size it was necessary for the channel to be wide enough, deep enough and long enough to accommodate them. Although he'd never before thought to explore the channel, today Jack found himself drawn there by an urge he couldn't explain or resist.

As he approached the edge of the channel he exhaled in short violent bursts, ridding his lungs of air until they threatened to collapse like a Hoover bag set to empty. Just as his chest felt like it would implode and before his body could override his brain by bringing on a fit of coughing to refill his tortured lungs, he started to breathe in. He didn't take great heaving gasps but relished the feeling of gradual relief as he slowly allowed the air back in. This process though slow would ensure the maximum possible uptake of oxygen. It would also mean that he would be able to stay under for up to five minutes without suffocating. The main danger came from the fact that by adopting this technique he was suppressing his body's natural reflex to breathe. He'd learned about it in a TV program about skin divers out in the Philippines, apparently they'd been known to pass out and die by staying down just that little bit too long.

He was standing waist high preparing to dive, aware of the salty water stinging his sun-hot skin. He took the plunge, feeling exhilarated and cleansed as his whole body became enveloped by the ocean and he entered another world. This new world, though silent and odourless, was incredibly tactile, as if the absence of sound and smell amplified his senses. Colours that looked washed out above the surface took on lustrous new hues, even the slow motion of his progress helped him see things in a way he never could on dry land.

He remembered the first dive they made when they arrived, he only made it down about ten feet before his ears started to hurt and his head began to ache. The dive probably only lasted about ten seconds but when he bobbed to the surface his lungs felt like they would burst. He remembered how hot it'd been on that day, hazy but hot. He remembered how, Tom had refused to cover up, ending up in the tent with sunstroke for three days, moaning in agony as he rubbed sticky aloe leaves into his blistered skin.

Then a local had showed them how to use a weight belt and how to equalise the pressure in their ears, allowing them to dive deeper. Experience lengthened the dives but it was only Jack who learned the breathing technique. He should have shared the secret with Tom but by then their relationship had gone past sharing.

After that first dive had come the gradual exploration of the waters in front of the campsite, the discovery of the lobster holes, the never learned technique of how to grab them without ending up with a handful of tentacles. Then the trip to the reef where he discovered wonders he would never be able to describe, colours so bright and so real they dazed his mind, creatures so exotic they had to inhabit a different universe to the one he lived in day to day.

It was on that trip that he really surprised himself and Tom. There was an outcrop of coral about ten metres beneath the surface, it was oval in shape but huge, like an enormous hollow pink flower. They saw a Jew-fish swim lazily into the centre, its easy movement disguising for a moment the sheer size of the beast. It looked like a dull coloured parrot fish at first, except when you realised the coral outcrop was at least twenty metres across, it was a giant.

Despite the stories they'd heard about divers being inadvertently sucked into the maws of monsters such as these, he couldn't resist the urge to follow it into its cave. Tom had set off after him but by the time they reached the mouth of the cave he had to return to the surface. Jack carried on bewitched by the moment, unheedful of the danger. It was another two minutes before he returned to the surface and he could still remember the look on Tom's face. It was jealousy that sat like a mask on his features and for that moment, what lay between them was dark and sinister.

Now he was an accomplished diver, good enough to stay with the best, so it was with ease and confidence that he glided through the water towards the channel. As he went he saw a multi coloured parrot fish swim by beside him. It slowed and looked at him inquisitively before carrying on its way.

He started to pursue the fish, knowing he wouldn't catch it but not caring. It stopped briefly at the edge of the precipice marking the channel, almost as if it was waiting to make sure he was following. The water in which he swam was only a couple of metres deep and was bright with sunlight. Over the edge the trench beckoned black and foreboding.

Some said that the trench was nearly forty metres deep, that it had been made specially to accommodate warships in the Second World War. Others said that was horseshit, in any event no-one claimed to have touched the bottom, although there was a rumour that at least one tourist had died trying. As he followed the Parrot Fish into the channel, the deeper he swam the darker it became, the absolute silence catching him by surprise. It was an attractive cocooned feeling, like he was somewhere safe and quiet where no-one and nothing could hurt him. He was still pursuing the fish when he began to feel sleepy, a dreamy floating sleepiness gently chiding him into submission; everything around him was black and still, the parrot fish had gone, Tom had gone, even Ruth had gone. Then he felt something tangible coming from below, tugging him down. He'd been lured into this place and now whatever it was trying to keep him there.

'*Get the fuck out of here*' screamed the voice.

Suddenly he was wide awake again, galvanised into action, adrenaline exploding into his system. But he was also disorientated, he didn't know which way was up and he his head was starting to spin, he was running out of oxygen.

His hands instinctively slipped down to the weight belt around his waist, fumbling against the buckle, unable to release the catch. He closed his eyes hard, forcing them shut with all his might, forcing back the darkness replacing it with pain, a pain on which he could focus and concentrate and out of which came light.

That light was Ruth, bursting into his brain like a beacon, scattering the shadows in her wake. He opened his eyes and now there really was a light, at least it seemed to him he could see one glinting in the distance. He struck out towards the silver sliver, gaining determination with every stroke. Soon he could see the real light above him and the edge of the channel. He touched the sides of the precipice and guided himself onto the regular ocean floor, bursting through the surface into the air with a whoop of exultation.

IV

The first thing he saw as the salt water ran from his eyes, standing no more than sixty metres away from him, was Tom. Tom's arms were stretched above his head and above him, suspended in the blue sunlit sky was a silver crescent moon.

Jack blinked uncomprehendingly, the moon had begun to move and gyrate as if it were a living thing. Then, to his horror it began to gush with blood, covering Tom's right arm, and dripping from his elbow into the ocean. He could hear Tom yelling and believing he was in danger, Jack started forcing his way through the water towards him.

Then the reality dawned, it wasn't a crescent moon that was suspended in the sky, but a silver fish on the end of a spear. Tom had somehow speared a three foot barracuda and was waving his prize above his head in triumph.

The waters of the Keys were generally safe, no sharks to speak of and few threats to worry the wary. The only large aggressive predator to be found in any numbers were barracuda. Even they would rarely attack a diver and then only if provoked. They were however attracted by the smell of blood, especially the smell of the blood of one of their own. For this reason it was entirely conceivable that soon the water would be alive with barracuda and Jack didn't want to be there if and when they arrived.

He couldn't believe how anyone could be so stupid as to spear a barracuda using a Hawaiian sling. Tom must have been literally on top of it when he made his shot. As it was the water around Tom was crimson with blood and Jack was sure it wouldn't be long before they were joined by a few more Barracuda, or even Sharks, intent on a free meal at their expense. These thoughts didn't even slow him down, as he gave a pretty convincing impression of running on water as he bounded towards the beach.

'See,' he could hear the voice saying as he ran. 'See what a schmuck you're worried about.'

'SHUT UP,' he yelled back. 'Why don't you just shut up?'

Seeing Jack's reaction and hearing him screaming "shut up" meaninglessly as he headed for the safety of the shore, made Tom realise the danger he'd put them in. He too started to head towards the beach, although more slowly and discreetly, being careful not to lose the fish that was still wriggling intermittently on the spear. By the time he reached the shore the barracuda had completely disembowelled itself. He didn't stop to talk to Jack or even to acknowledge him, simply carrying on until he found an abandoned plastic bucket lying on the ground. He took the bucket, returned to the shore, filled it with sea water and dropped the corpse into the receptacle as if it was a bream he'd just pulled out of the village pond.

He was standing admiring his catch, a broad grin on his ruddy freckled face just as Jack wandered over looking far from amused.

'What do you think of that then?' said Tom good-naturedly, as if to the world at large rather than to anyone in particular.

'I tell you what I think,' said Jack. 'I think you're a fucking nut case that's what I think, you could have got us both killed. How the fuck did you spear that thing anyway?'

The last thing Jack really wanted to do was start a fight but it was as if he couldn't help himself, as if he had no choice, somehow they seemed to be on a collision course and nothing seemed able to get them off it.

Tom was silent for a minute, he'd enjoyed the feeling of power he'd experienced when he speared the barracuda, but now the pleasure was melting away and the cause was standing there shouting at him.

'Where have you been?' he said, his voice calm but irritated, making direct eye contact for the first time.

The question hung in the air between them and for a moment threatened confrontation. Jack dropped his gaze first and looked pointedly at the fish. It was no good, he wouldn't be able to distract Tom from the issue, it was best just to fess up and get it over with.

'Look Tom, I'm sorry I didn't tell you where I was, it

was really bad of me, but honestly, things happened and there wasn't anything I could do.' Even as he said the words they sounded lame in his ears, pathetic really.

'Why are you explaining yourself to him?' Demanded his internal voice. *'He isn't your fucking mother.'*

Tom forgot the fish and gave his full attention to Jack, it wasn't that he really had been worried or anything but he did want to know what was going on. So, things had happened had they? Well, he wanted to know what those "things" were.

Jack felt oddly uncomfortable under Tom's inquisitive gaze. He'd intended to tell him all about his encounter with Wilbur, but now he wasn't sure. It was as if there was something unhealthy in that look, as if something voracious was awake in Tom, awake and eager to feed. Jack could feel the salt water from the ocean drying against his skin, stinging where he'd cut himself on the sharp coral and itching under his arms and between his legs.

It was ridiculous, Tom was after all entitled to know what had happened, yet still there was something telling him to be careful what he said. He decided to stall for time.

'I think we should go back to the tent, it's in a hell of a mess, full of bugs, I'll tell you what happened on the way.' Jack looked down at the bucket whose waters were now dark red, the barracuda curled up eel-like, its silver body already beginning to lose its sheen. Reflexively Tom stooped down to pick up the bucket and together they started to wander slowly back up to the tent.

'It must have been a hell of a storm last night!' Jack observed out loud. They both scanned the wreckage gradually being put right by the campers. Tom nodded agreement, still waiting for the story.

The Dark Lagoon

'It was weird really,' said Jack eventually, obviously having come to a decision. 'I was in the Winn Dixie and I met this old guy, he asked me for a game of racket ball, he seemed harmless so I went along with him.'

He quickly told the bones of what happened, leaving out the weird bits, for the moment at least. Instead he concentrated on the Van and how desirable it could have been, if it hadn't been such a wreck and they had been able to get the use of it. He was quite pleased at the way it was coming out, making it seem like he was still interested in their trip until he realised he was falling into the same old hypocritical trap. Why didn't he just come clean?

He was finished well before they even reached the tent, lapsing unconvincingly into silence. He was sure he wouldn't be believed, that Tom would spot the fact that he'd left things out, but he didn't, instead he took the tale at face value.

The truth was Tom was too wrapped up in his own concerns to be really interested in what Jack had been up too. He was in fact relieved that nothing really exciting or opportune had happened to him, if it had it would only have served to make him feel worse than he already did. No, he was glad nothing much happened and he didn't have to listen to some long tale of glamorous bullshit, showing how he'd missed out yet again.

As they approached the tent, their conversation finished, emotionally they were further apart than ever. The distance between them, already great had somehow grown in the night a great unbridgeable gulf.

V

At first they both assumed the short figure standing by the tent was just another camper, probably hoping to get some help from the two young English guys. There was something about the purposeful way he was standing that quickly destroyed this assumption. People who want favours have a submissive look to their body language, whereas this man looked nothing of the kind, his stance was too self assured, even arrogant to be there to beg a favour.

Although he'd never met Wilbur and had only heard the most superficial description of him, Tom knew straight away who he was. Jack was, surprisingly considering his better acquaintance with him, a little slower. Perhaps the traumas of the previous day had made him subconsciously wish him away; if they had it didn't work because there he was large as life and twice as ugly.

'Hey boys, I've been waiting for yer.' Wilbur's voice was full of bon homie.

The greeting was too familiar for Tom, he was in no mood to be buddies with some old tosser who was probably a pervert anyway, he gave Wilbur a look that was meant to signify contempt and ignored him completely.

Wilbur smiled his best shark's smile.

'You must be Tom, eh? Jack told me all about you, what have you got in the bucket?'

Tom was still pleased about the barracuda and was prepared to show it off to anyone who was interested, even this dried up old fart. He tilted the bucket in Wilbur's direction so he could get a good look, waited for the older man to take in the size and significance of the catch, then he said 'It's a barracuda, I speared it out on the reef.'

Wilbur sucked in his breath appreciatively before responding.

'That's a big sucker, no doubt about it, what do you intend to do with it?'

There was a note of humour in the small man's voice, Tom didn't like being teased or challenged and the question sounded like it was doing both. He stood upright in an attempt to dwarf Wilbur, intimidate him physically, then in a cold voice he said 'Eat it, what do you think I'm going to do with it, have it stuffed?'

Wilbur smiled again but this time there was no attempt to be engaging, his face showed the predator inside only too clearly.

'You know Kid, you might just be better off getting him stuffed, in any event if you decide to barbecue him, make sure you don't make any plans for afterwards.'

Wilbur paused to let the words sink in, then he carried on.

'Yer see the thing about barracuda is they're only edible when they're small, once they get big like this one, they get poisonous, anyone who eats this baby'll be attending his own personal last supper'.

Again there was a pause, Wilbur watched amused as Tom's shoulders slumped at the news. He also noticed how his mind opened up before him.

'Look guys,' He said, changing the pace of the encounter as expertly as ever. 'there's nothing I'd like better that to shoot the shit with you all day but see, the thing is there's work to do, so if you're ready I think we should be pushing on.'

Tom was nonplussed, on the one hand this guy had probably saved his life, because he almost certainly would have cooked and eaten the fish. On the other hand, here was a total stranger giving him orders like he was some kind of stupid school child. It was too much, so he just kept quiet. Eventually Jack broke the deadlock.

'What are you talking about Wilbur, things to do? What things?'

Wilbur's attention immediately re-focused onto Jack.

'The Van, what else, or do you want to live here forever? The Van needs to be cleaned out, fixed up inside, painted outside and the carburettor needs a rebuild.'

Tom's interest was re-awoken, here was the kind of challenge that appealed to him, he loved anything mechanical and was very curious to see the Van, which, if it was anything like Jack described, must be a real sight to see.

In the meantime Jack was staring at the sad looking tent. He had plenty of money saved from his two jobs to move into a motel but he needed the money for when Ruth arrived, the thought of another two weeks in the tent was an appalling one. In spite of his misgivings about Wilbur he was interested in taking another look at the Van and by the look of it so was Tom.

'OK, give us a minute to change and we'll take a look'.

It was Tom who spoke, making the decision for both of them; Jack was relieved, he knew that if it had been him who had agreed on their behalf there would have been another argument and more hell to pay.

Wilbur seemed pleased, he took a step back, opening his arms wide in a munificent gesture. 'Great, I'll let you get ready, see you over at the car park, don't be too long.'

He turned without another word and started to walk jauntily away. When he was out of earshot Jack said 'Are you sure you want to go along with this? I thought you were suspicious about Wilbur, didn't trust his motives?' He was deliberately questioning Tom's judgement, knowing full well that by doing so he would increase his resolve.

The voice inside his head thought this was another bad idea and had started questioning his sanity all over again.

Tom had already started to get into the tent, he was half in and half out but instead of climbing all the way in he jerked backward heaving the ground-sheet and all their stuff into the open. The bugs, clearly disturbed by this sudden change in habitat, jumped everywhere.

He watched them jumping, then turned to Jack and replied 'I don't trust him but we can't stay here any longer, anyway he's only a little old guy, what harm can he do to us? Stop worrying and help me with this.'

Jack nodded. 'OK whatever you say but let's just watch out, that's all.' Tom may have grunted a reply but it didn't matter, the dice had been rolled and whatever would happen would happen.

Twenty minutes later they were sitting in the Chevy on their way to Wilbur's house. So Jack had been wrong, the old buzzard must have gone back to the house and picked it up, didn't he ever sleep?

Being in the car reminded Jack of the previous day and he stayed quiet in the back. Tom, having chosen to sit up front as he knew he would, was chatting about this and that, asking questions like 'How old was the Van? What kind of engine did it have?' etc.

This was all trivial stuff to Jack who was more concerned with handling the feeling of dread that was forming in the pit of his stomach, warning him to get out of there while he still could. But he'd ignored all the other warnings so why should he take any notice of this one? There was no rational reason to leave, here they were for the first time since they'd arrived doing something together, something that could lead somewhere, why spoil it?

'Because if you don't, it's gonna spoil you,' answered the voice wearily. *'It's gonna spoil you good'.*

Jack was still having these thoughts when they turned off the freeway a few minutes later and started down a narrow winding side road. In less than a mile Wilbur was bringing them to a halt outside an unimpressive looking house beside which were parked an old Winnebago camper and an equally ageing speed boat. Also parked near the house was the Van. In the light it looked even more weird than it had done the night before except now it looked less dangerous. The rowing boat that formed its roof was really comical, looking as if the ocean had spat it into the sky during the storm and it'd landed on the Van's roof by accident.

Tom was entranced by the whole thing, this was exactly the kind of situation that would appeal to him. Jack saw him looking at the speed boat and was sure he was already planning to rebuild that too.

They exited the Chevy but rather than giving Tom a guided tour of the Van as he'd expected, Wilbur ushered them to the front door which he opened with a key, 'Maria' he yelled impatiently, 'Maria, come here, we have guests.'

There was a sound from across the room from where Jack guessed the kitchen would be but Maria didn't appear. There was enough time for him to take in the interior of the house which was as he expected decorated from the same era as the house in Miami. The fixtures and fittings looked less expensive, in keeping with the more modest accommodation but the flavour was the same. It was as if something had happened to Wilbur back then, like he'd retired and made sure everything was new, never intending to replace anything again. It made the place feel spooky, like it was a time capsule and they'd been somehow been sucked into it.

These thoughts were cut short by Maria's appearance. Jack didn't know what he'd been expecting, if indeed he'd been expecting anything. It certainly wasn't this young, attractive South American woman who gracefully entered the room with a genuine smile of surprise and welcome on her face. She looked no older than thirty, younger perhaps although the lines round her eyes said not. Was it unhappiness, or something else, something carefully masked but there nevertheless, fear perhaps?

Wilbur cleared his throat, getting ready to make the introductions. 'Maria this is Tom and Jack, they're over here from England. Boys, this is Maria, my wife.'

She was wearing a summer dress and round her small waist there was a floral apron, her hands were wet as if she'd been doing some dishes in the kitchen when they arrived. She smiled a warm smile and broke the silence.

'I'm pleased to meet you both, would you like a drink? Coffee? or would you like tea? We have tea.' Her voice was soft and slightly husky, she had a definite South American accent and her English was perfect.

Jack responded first. 'Yes, that would be great, coffee is fine for us, OK Tom?' Tom nodded dumbly, staring at Maria like he'd never seen a woman before. Maria glanced at Wilbur who signalled his approval and she disappeared back into the kitchen.

It was Wilbur who spoke next. 'Sit down boys, relax, we can talk for a while, get to know one another better.'

He motioned towards a corner settee which sat low to the ground, it was leather covered and the hide was faded and cracked in places. It looked none too comfortable either but they sat down anyway and waited for the coffee to arrive. It didn't take long, the aroma floating from the kitchen and filling the house with a superficial feeling of conviviality and warmth.

When Maria re-appeared she was holding a brightly coloured tray on which there were four large cups of steaming coffee. Beside these were a jug of cream, a stack of saucers and a plate of appetising looking chocolate biscuits. She lay the tray down on the large glass topped wicker coffee table in the middle of the room and proceeded to match each cup with a saucer. She handed the men a cup each and offered them biscuits before going back with the cream. When everyone was taken care of, she prepared her own drink and sat down quietly beside Wilbur. Jack and Tom thanked her, feeling more comfortable than they thought they could in the company of their new found benefactor. Eventually Wilbur broke the silence.

'You know Maria and I first met when I was driving that Van through Costa Rica.' He stopped and looked at the silent woman who flushed slightly, her eyes pleading him to stop. He didn't seem to notice.

'Yeah, when Maria and I met she was so poor she couldn't even afford a pair of everyday shoes, she was thin too. Out there in Costa Rica things are a lot different from here. They don't consider women have much of a value really, it's the sons that get all the breaks. In Maria's family they had eight kids, five daughters and three sons, Maria was the youngest which made her even less of an asset to the family. Chances are, if I hadn't come along she would have ended up being sold to one of the children's brothels in the local town.'

The Dark Lagoon

He paused here so everyone could appreciate what a generous person he really was, then he continued. 'she took me to see her parents and they let me take her, all they wanted was fifty dollars, can you imagine that, selling your own daughter for fifty bucks?

Maria got to her feet, face red, eyes blazing, she picked up the tray and walked out of the room.

'What's the matter?' Wilbur shouted after her. 'I married you didn't I?' Then he appeared to lose interest in his young wife and turned his attention back to the boys.

'Women! Can't live with 'em, can't live without 'em huh?' He spoke the cliché with genuine relish, clearly revelling in the trouble he was deliberately causing, finding it perversely funny. Deep down Jack could hear warning bells, he'd heard them from the beginning but they were getting louder all the time, turning into a hysterical cacophony in his head.

'OK guys, finish up, we have a lot of work to do and not much time to do it.' Wilbur made a show of tipping what was left of his coffee down his throat before placing the empty cup on the table and getting to his feet. Tom followed suit and pushed past Jack who appeared frozen in his seat as Wilbur walked past them and out the front door to the van.

As they left Jack turned towards the kitchen and saw Maria standing in the doorway, she was holding a tissue up to her right eye and he could see she'd been crying. He gave her a reassuring smile but wasn't sure if it came out right. She acknowledged him though, showing by her expression that she appreciated his concern. He hesitated a moment longer and then she'd gone from the doorway, leaving him feeling more uncomfortable than ever. Inside his feelings of antipathy towards Wilbur were beginning to crystallise, if things carried on as they were there was a confrontation coming.

VI

By the time Jack got outside Tom and Wilbur were already walking round the Van, apparently conducting some kind of survey into what needed to be done. Tom stopped in front of the back doors and took a firm hold of the handle. Jack felt a wave of panic as he remembered the last time those doors opened.

Something was telling him the rats had somehow got back into the Van, he knew it was ridiculous but the feeling was too strong. This time though it was going to be different, the rats would be bigger, stronger, they'd pull Tom into their domain and destroy him. He started to run, tried to shout a warning, a choked guttural sound coming from his throat. Although only a few feet lay between them, it was too late, he saw the doors first give slightly, then swing wide. Tom leaned forward, stopped for a second and disappeared, consumed by the open maw.

Reality returned with a bump as he ran into the open doors, the impact leaving him dazed, the start of a large red bump clearly visible in the centre of his forehead. Wilbur was laughing, smoke coming from his nose and mouth, the small black cheroot turned out of sight in his left hand. When he Looked into the Van he could see there were no giant rats, only Tom, who had already got the engine cover off and was peering down into the bay with a look of fixed and unshakeable concentration. Jack shook his head, as if the action would dislodge the fading images, it seemed to work. Suddenly he felt foolish, like a little child scared of its own shadow. He decided enough was enough and forced himself to concentrate on the matters at hand.

The others were also keen to get on with things and the rest of the day was spent in wholly down to earth pursuits, all connected with renovating the broken down van. First they made a list of all the materials they would need, including a part number for the carburettor kit; next they made a trip out to the local automobile hypermarket. When they returned it was just gone eleven and a natural division of labour took place. Tom was given all the technical and mechanical stuff, aided and advised by Wilbur who soon betrayed himself as knowing little or nothing of value on the subject of mechanics or engines.

Jack meanwhile was put in charge of painting. He went to work, starting with the boat and gradually working his way down. By the time he'd applied the off white undercoat it was mid-day and Maria appeared with hot coffee and sandwiches. They all worked hard, the work pulling them together however briefly, making Jack forget his earlier misgivings at least for a while.

After lunch he started the job of applying the top coat which they'd eventually agreed would be sky blue. Being a brush on rather than spray on job, the finish was never going to be perfect, given Jack's obvious lack of skill, aptitude and experience the final result was a lot better that expected. By the time he'd finished the Van looked quite respectable, provided you didn't get too close, although nothing would ever be able to disguise the oddness of the rowing boat roof.

Meanwhile Tom and Wilbur had to make two more trips to the auto parts shop to pick up various gaskets, washers and hoses they found were needed as the day went on. At one stage Jack poked his head in the Van and tried to ask questions about what they were doing, only to be told to shut up and get back to his own work. By the time he'd been finished for over half an hour he was getting irritated that no-one was bothering to come out and admire his handiwork.

Eventually he realised there would be no hurrying them up and he turned his attention to his own state. He was covered in sky blue paint, it was in his hair, his sandals, his shorts, all over his body in fact. Maria noticed the state he was in and invited him into the house to get cleaned up. He followed her into the house where she pointed out the bathroom door. The bathroom itself was full of Wilbur's shaving clutter plus an unreasonably large amount of men's toiletries. It was a small room with no window, only an inadequate looking air vent and there was an unpleasant swampy smell ingrained into the walls.

It struck him that there was no sign of any women's things in the bathroom and he wondered where Maria kept her toiletries, then it crossed his mind that perhaps Wilbur didn't allow her any. The thought sent a cold shudder through him despite the warmth of the steamy bathroom. There wasn't anything much he could do about his denim shorts but at least most of the dried paint had brushed out and he knew that after a few dips in the ocean the rest would disappear. By the time he re-emerged into the yard, he looked and felt fresh and clean, and seeing the Van looking as fresh and clean as he was made him feel quite proud of his day's work.

There was still no sign that the others had finished though. What if the engine wouldn't start? he wondered. What if the Van was really buggered mechanically and all their efforts had been for nothing? The idea really wound him up but he needn't have worried, a few seconds later the Van's engine burst into life with an energetic cackle that soon settled down to a sweet even idle. He walked round to the driver's door to find Wilbur sitting behind the wheel and Tom in the passenger seat, they were both smiling obviously delighted at the results of their labours. Jack tapped on the window, it came down slowly, the electric motor labouring with the effort.

'Not bad huh?' Wilbur said

He looked past Wilbur to where Tom was sitting, for once a look of real pleasure on his face.

'Listen you guys,' Jack said. 'Are you going to get out and take a look or what?'

They got out of the Van and made a show of walking round it, inspecting every panel, nodding here and shaking there. Eventually they assembled beside Jack about ten feet from the Van.

'Not bad, not bad at all,' said Wilbur.

'Yeah, it's great,' said Tom which for him was praise indeed.

'Well, it may not be great but it'll have to do, won't it?' Said Jack whose voice couldn't disguise his pride in the job.

Wilbur chose his moment to drop his next bombshell perfectly. 'If I can adjourn this self appreciation society for a minute,' he announced 'I think we have a deal to do, assuming that is you boys want to use this old junker, or perhaps you'd rather go back to that tent of yours.'

They looked at one another lamely, it suddenly dawning on them that maybe they should have carried out the negotiations before doing the work not after. Tom had gone red in the face, he wasn't pleased.

'OK' he said a little too loudly 'It's down to you Wilbur, how much do you want?'

Simon Shinerock

Wilbur rubbed his chin with his right hand, making a show of giving the matter careful thought. He reached into his pocket and pulled out a pack of cheroots, took one out, put it in his mouth and lit it, arrogantly blowing a plume of smoke over the two of them.

'Well, listen boys, I'm not a hard man and you have worked hard today, so I'm going to give you a break, you can have the Van for half what it's worth.' He paused at this point to give them time to fully appreciate the extent of his generosity. Tom's face relaxed a little as he started to think that maybe he'd been a little hasty in judging the old guy.

'fifteen hundred dollars, not a cent less mind you.'

The figure was ridiculous and Wilbur knew it. Jack just shook his head ruefully.

Tom on the other hand was outraged and indignant, he couldn't accept the hopelessness of their position. 'Look' he protested, waving at the van, whose shiny knew paint glinted back at him mockingly. 'This morning this piece of shit was worth less than three hundred dollars, now you want fifteen hundred, you suckered us, you're a cheating scum bag.'

Wilbur listened to this outburst with fatherly patience, when Tom was finished he asked him if he had anything else to say, he hadn't.

'You know Tom, I can see you're upset, so I'm gonna ignore what you just called me. You may even have a bit of a point, but the fact is she's worth fifteen hundred now. Put yourself in my position, would you take any less? I think not, see I ain't no charity. Anyway, the way I look at it you boys learned a good lesson here today and you owe me for it. So accept my terms and take the Van, or get out of here, the decision's yours.'

The Dark Lagoon

Tom looked like he was about to assault Wilbur.

Jack saw this although the old man seemed oblivious. He decided to intervene. 'Listen Wilbur, you don't mind if Tom and I discuss this for a moment on our own do you?'

Wilbur considered this request for a minute and then said 'Sure kid, whatever you want but make it fast.'

He turned on his heel and walked back into the house leaving them on their own with the Van, keys still in the ignition.

The resentful sullen look, which had become such a permanent feature lately, returned to Tom's face. Jack could see him staring at the ignition keys and knew exactly what he was thinking. They both really wanted the Van now, he knew that if he wasn't careful Tom would do something stupid and get them both locked up.

He knew Wilbur had ripped them off and he also knew that whatever he suggested Tom would disagree with it out of perversity. If on the other hand he didn't say something soon Tom would have a suggestion of his own and it would involve leaving three hundred dollars on the ground and using those keys dangling temptingly in the ignition, almost as if Wilbur was daring them to do it.

'I think we should tell him to stuff the Van and get out of here now.'

Jack managed to sound sincerely angry and hurt, his cheeks blazed *and there was something inside him that was genuinely convinced they should leave, leave right now and run, like he should have done right at the start, not even bother to collect their things just get out while they still could.*

It was too late for that now though, he had other ideas, he wanted the Van because it would get him out of the tent, he wanted it because it represented independence and he wanted it because somehow he felt like it already belonged to him. It was a crazy thought and Jack knew it, he shook his head trying to clear his mind, forcing himself to think straight. He'd decided to use the Van that evening to return to Miami and find a place for Ruth and him to stay when she arrived in two weeks. Now was the right time to fix things up, he had money and tomorrow he would have to return to work, there wouldn't be another chance to sort things out until the following Sunday and by then there would only be a week to go. His love for Ruth and the need he felt to see her again overrode all other considerations, what he thought of Wilbur, his relationship with Tom, the price of the Van, everything.

He turned abruptly on his heel as if to leave, held his breath and counted; for a moment he thought Tom wasn't going to take the bait but he needn't have worried. Tom wasn't in any mood to be dictated to by anyone else that day, specifically not by Jack Simons.

'Hold on just one minute,' Tom shouted, angry at being railroaded.

'I'm not sure about this. What are we going to do if we walk away? It's Sunday evening, we checked out the site, we have nowhere to go and you know as well as I do that the Van is worth the money anyway. It's typical of you, you drag us into a situation, make a pig's breakfast of it and then when things don't go your way you get all hot and bothered and throw a tantrum. Well I think we should play Wilbur at his own game, I don't think he even wants to sell the Van. You can see by the way he worked on it, it means a lot to him. I think he's in there right now laughing at the way he suckered us into working our butts off all day for nothing. Give him the money, we'll get it back in a few months in saved rent, that is if you intend to stay a few months.'

The Dark Lagoon

This last statement stung. The truth was the thought of being parted from Ruth again made his mind go blank. Deep down he'd already made his decision, Ruth's arrival would signal the end of their adventure and even if Jack hadn't fully admitted the fact to himself, Tom knew it and used it against him at every available opportunity.

Jack's face really was flushed now. He knew how much their friendship meant to Tom and how the thing with Ruth was making him bitter yet there wasn't anything even he could do about it.

'Don't change the subject,' he said, avoiding the real issue again. 'The point is, do we part with fifteen hundred dollars for this Van or leave? You say we can afford it but I don't think we can. If we give Wilbur that much money it will almost clean you out and leave me without enough to pay for a hotel for Ruth and there's no way that's going to happen.'

Tom snorted his contempt for this last remark although he knew what Jack said was right.

'So what's your suggestion then? Let's hear it.'

Jack spoke slowly. 'I suggest we offer Wilbur half the money now and half in a month's time. That way we get the Van, we stay liquid and who knows what will happen in the next month'.

Tom smiled, for a change Jack had come up with a sensible idea. 'There is one condition though; You have to agree we go to Miami tonight, it'll give us a chance to try out the Van properly and I can find a decent hotel for Ruth to stay in when she arrives, OK?'

Tom's eyes dimmed as Jack delivered this condition, the little bastard was going to stitch him up, leave him high and dry, he could feel it in his water. Now though wasn't the time to have it out, that could come later, for now he would go along with it. Besides, he liked the idea of going into Miami, if all Jack wanted was to find a love nest, that was his problem.

'Right, we go to Miami tonight, always assuming Wilbur goes for the deal that is.'

'Don't worry, he'll go for it, leave Wilbur to me.'

They walked over to the house together and knocked on the door, Wilbur appeared, in a bath robe, he looked affable enough, less sinister without his clothes on.

When it came to making the offer they were both surprised at how readily Wilbur agreed, seeming almost relieved they only wanted to pay half, as if he wanted to retain an interest in the Van. He made them sit down while he prepared the paperwork, the Van would stay in his name until the last payment was made, if they were late they would lose their deposit.

Neither of them liked the conditions, but having come this far they weren't prepared to back out and lacked the experience to negotiate better terms. Maria came in with more fresh coffee and chocolate biscuits. The curtains were drawn and the lights were low but despite the gloom bruises could be seen beginning to form below her right eye; Jack looked at Wilbur and the sight of him sent a chill through his whole body. It was time to sign up and get out and no mistake.

Once everything was eventually done and dusted and they both had a copy of the sales agreement, they stood up to shake hands. Jack was taken aback when the old man, still only wearing a bathrobe took his hand and pulled him into a fatherly embrace, the warmth of his body and smell of stale tobacco leaving him nauseous, gagging for air. When Wilbur finally let him go he had

The Dark Lagoon

something to say.

'You take care of yourself, eh boy? You know, you remind me a bit of the son I've always wanted but never had, crazy I know but there you are. Be careful in Miami, there are a lot of weird characters in the city.'

'That's a laugh coming from you,' thought Jack.

A stern note came into the old mans voice, all traces of sentimentality gone. 'Remember to pay your dues on time as well, I don't want to have to come looking for you.' Tom coughed nervously, distracting Wilbur and breaking the tension in the air. Wilbur looked at him and stuck out his hand. They shook and nodded at one another without saying a word. Then Wilbur was heading for the door and ushering them outside to where the Van still sat, its new paint gleaming in the fading light.

Chapter Two

I

It was just gone 8 p.m. by the time they left Wilbur's place, the light was fading fast and they had a good hour and a half's journey to Miami.

As they got under way, Jack concentrated on getting the feel of the Van. He was driving because Tom didn't have a licence; he was normally a fast, some would even say reckless, driver but now he was being careful, getting used to the Van's size and handling before using its power to the full. Within a few miles he was feeling at home behind the wheel, already able to judge accurately the its width to within an inch either side, able to sense how fast he could push it round corners before the tyres would start to squeal in protest. Everything felt good except the brakes which made an ominous graunching sound whenever he brought the Van to a sudden halt.

The night was balmy and warm, the air was still fresh from the storm, devoid of its usual sultry humidity. There was no need to try out the rather dubious looking air conditioner stuck through the Van's back window, instead they left their own windows half open and enjoyed the cool breeze rushing into the cabin as they cruised towards the city at a steady fifty five mph.

Jack found the driving relaxing, he could feel the tension of the last few days draining out of his body. He hadn't realised just how wound up he'd been. Ruth was the main cause but Wilbur was close behind. He had a sudden urge to tell Tom everything, tell him their trip was going to be

The Dark Lagoon

a disaster and admit it was all his fault, as if the act of admission would somehow grant him absolution. He also wanted to tell him all about what really happened with Wilbur, about the strange house, the school yard and his dream about the Island.

'Where did you get that necklace?'

Tom's enquiry broke his train of thought, confusing him. What necklace? He looked down and for the first time noticed the silver crescent moon hanging round his neck. He didn't have the foggiest clue where it came from or how it came to be there.

He took his right hand off the wheel and ran his fingers over the bright metal emblem. It was a solid piece of jewellery, no trashy hollow piece of tinsel this. Now he knew it was there he couldn't understand how he hadn't noticed it before, it felt really heavy. His hand felt round the back of the chain for the clasp but there was none, it was as if the chain had been forged as one piece, or grown around his neck of its own accord. He had a sudden vision of Onyx in the bar earlier, the look on his face just before all hell nearly broke loose; there had been something that held him back and now he thought he knew what it was.

Tom was still waiting for a reply when he realised that the Van had started to veer towards the centre of the highway. At first he thought Jack was trying to scare him, just in time he realised he wasn't, he was staring vacantly out into space, one hand still fingering the silver necklace, the other resting lightly on the wheel. He lunged over to the driver's side, it wasn't an elegant manoeuvre but it was effective, sending the Van careering back over towards the verge. His clumsiness had caused the heavy vehicle to tie itself up in knots, the chassis couldn't cope with the sudden change in direction and the back wheels had broken away in a vicious tail slide.

All the commotion jolted Jack back to his senses, he instinctively grabbed the wheel as the Van bucked and weaved from one side of the road to the other, on the edge of rolling. Somehow he managed to bring the tail slide under control, careful not to touch the throttle or the brakes, allowing the wayward energy to use itself up harmlessly. *Then it was over and neither of them could remember what had caused the crisis, the silver pendant fading guiltily back into obscurity.*

II

The rest of the journey was to prove uneventful. Jack concentrated on the job of driving the Van, determined not to suffer a repeat of his earlier lapse in concentration. Tom settled back into the passenger seat and dozed sullenly in and out of consciousness, bothered by dark images floating in front of his vision, some tauntingly familiar, others in an agony of torment.

The scenery gradually changed from lush vegetation interspersed with steaming swampland, to a more suburban, then urban landscape, not that either of them stopped to notice or appreciate their surroundings, being too pre-occupied with their own thoughts.

Although it was Sunday evening, not a busy time as a general rule, the highway was particularly quiet, allowing the Van to make uninterrupted progress towards central Miami. It was as if everyone had chosen to stay in that evening, perhaps put off travelling by the force of the previous night's storm. The road was a straight one, leading directly to the beach, which was where Jack hoped to find a small hotel for himself and Ruth. Nevertheless, it was necessary to pay attention to the signs to avoid taking

The Dark Lagoon

the wrong road at one of the many intersections they passed as they neared the city.

The closer they came the more agitated they both became. By now Tom was wide awake and feeling more resentful than ever. He didn't like the fact that it was Jack who was quite literally in the driver's seat, or that their mission that night was to make arrangements for the comfort of someone who at best he regarded as an interloper, at worst a straight rival. Jack on the other hand could feel the bad vibes coming from his friend, made clear by the extended silences and clipped conversation.

His feelings of guilt were reaching fever pitch. If he was honest he couldn't see himself waving goodbye to Ruth after two weeks and resuming his 'trip' with Tom. What he really wanted, but lacked the courage to face, was for Tom simply to go home. The trip they planned involving a carefree year of travelling, adventure and fun was conceived at a different time in their lives. If he failed to admit this to himself and allowed Ruth to return to England, he would risk losing her and he couldn't let that happen. Anyway, the trip would never be what they planned because he was no longer what he was, free and single. If he persisted in going on with it he would end up losing them both and he knew it.

Knowing something and being able to do something about it were not the same, so he continued to torment himself, putting off doing the right thing, which was to level with Tom and face the consequences now when they would be at their least serious.

It was in this frame of mind they eventually arrived in Miami Beach, neither in any mood to appreciate it. The last time they were in Miami was the day they arrived. Back then there had still been a remnant of optimism between them, excitement at what lay in front and a lingering sense of the great adventure of it all. It hadn't taken long for them to slip into their respective roles though, Jack as the guilty oppressed and Tom as the outraged oppressor. Perhaps if either of them had been able to level with the other, there wouldn't have been the fertile ground in which Proctor's seed of deceit and lies could take root and grow, but they couldn't.

The highway had turned from a dual to a single carriageway, they glimpsed the security lights of the skyscrapers of the financial district and for a while it looked like the road would take them there, but at the last moment it veered off towards the ocean.

Jack had chosen to drive straight to the beach because that was where Ruth's parents were going to be staying over Christmas, at the world-famous Eden Roc Hotel. He had to find a more modest establishment within walking distance of the Roc. By the time they arrived it was around ten and the streets were starting to get a little busier as fun seekers made their way to the many bars and discos that flourished along Miami's golden mile.

It wasn't hard to find the Roc. In fact it would have been nigh on impossible to miss, located as it was right between the beach and the highway, occupying one of the most valuable pieces of real estate in the United States. It wasn't the largest or the most glamorous of the five-star hotels on the beach but none of the modern towers would ever be able to take away its commanding position, or compete with its old world character. For this reason the more established and class conscious of the rich and famous still made it their business to stay there when they were in town. They rejected the greater splendour and better facilities of the newer hotels in favour of the less definable but more enviable cachet of the Roc.

The Dark Lagoon

At that precise moment though, Jack was less interested in the history of the golden mile than he was in finding a parking place close by and starting to search for a suitable place. He was starting to feel a little frantic, it'd been a busy stressful day and it was only now he realised how hungry and tired he was. The sooner he did what he'd come to do, the sooner they could find somewhere to eat and head back to the Keys.

As they drove along the golden mile, they couldn't help being struck with the glamour of the place. There were restaurants and clubs on either side of the street, all trying to outdo each other in tasteless kitsch and neon signs. It was all a facade of course, a superficial brightness covering up a seedier less attractive reality, the reality being it was all about getting the tourists' money and being none too subtle about it. Nonetheless to two young English students out in the world for the first time it all looked very impressive. The energy of the place was irresistible and they couldn't help feeling excited by it, the excitement helping to mask their differences, at least for a little while.

Before they knew it the impressive hotels and glitzy restaurants were giving way to more overtly seedy establishments. Motels and drinking clubs clearly in a different class, catering for a clientele with less discerning though no less demanding tastes. They started to notice a few tarty looking women loitering in the street, giving them encouraging glances as they drove slowly by, only to become haughty and rude when they failed to stop. At one point Jack thought he could see someone scurrying in the shadows of the back streets, following them. It was time to turn round and get out before something bad happened.

Turning away from the ocean, Jack noticed an eating

place called the 'Sub Mariner'. It was just a simple sandwich bar and take away but there was still an ubiquitous lurid blue neon screaming out incongruously above the door.

'Do you want to get something to eat?' he asked.

The question startled Tom. He looked at Jack through eyes that were clouded and dim, as if he'd been off on a journey of his own, to a place where storm clouds covered the sky and the lightning raged against the wind.

'Are you hungry or not?' Jack asked.

This time the question got through.

'Yeah, sure, why not?' Tom mumbled as Jack turned into the side street, having spotted a parking place between a Harley Davidson and a Malibu Classic. The Van still felt big but there was enough space and he was beginning to get used to its size. He surprised himself at how deftly he manoeuvred into the space, lining up parallel to the curb with only an inch separating the sills from the pavement. He turned off the lights, and took the key out of the ignition. The engine gave a small cough before it died and then there was silence.

He looked at himself and realised he was still wearing his old cut-off jeans, at least he was clean though, Tom on the other hand was still covered in dust and grease from his previous labours, between them they looked a pretty sorry state.

'We should get changed,' said Jack.

Tom nodded agreement and started to move out of his seat into the back of the Van.

When they emerged, Jack was wearing a clean pair of jeans, cowboy boots and a T-shirt, while Tom wore a denim shirt and chinos. If it wasn't for Tom's oil stained fingers, they would have been quite presentable, like any other young men out on the town looking for a good time.

The 'Sub Mariner' wasn't busy, there were a couple of slick-looking Mexican types standing at the bar drinking coffee and smoking and a slightly overweight though attractive blonde behind the counter. The blonde was dressed in a cross between a chef's outfit and a pirate's costume. They ordered two tuna subs and a couple of cokes to go and didn't have to wait long before the order appeared on the smooth blue counter. They paid separately, Tom being careful to show only a small amount of money, Jack however was less cautious, pulling out his entire bankroll and making no attempt to cover it up as he looked for a five dollar bill. Tom nudged him in the ribs but he didn't get the message.

Once they'd paid and were back in the Van eating the food, Tom turned to Jack 'Do you want to get us both killed or something?' he ranted.

'This is Miami Beach, they have more street crime here than almost anywhere else on earth and there you go flashing everything you've got for the whole world to see, why not just get a sign saying 'please rob me' and walk round with it on your back.'

Jack listened to the lecture, it was far from the first he'd received since they arrived and as always he was tempted to take the bait and argue back. This time though he bit his tongue 'OK, OK, I'm sorry, I'll be more careful in future, I wasn't thinking,' he said contritely.

Tom looked far from satisfied with this response, Jack wasn't taking the warning seriously, he considered delivering another tirade, thought better of it and went back to his food.

When they'd finished Tom took the packaging outside

and put it in a nearby trash can. He saw the two Mexican types hanging around, possibly attracted by Jack's exposed bank roll. He carefully avoided making eye contact and walked back to the van trying to look nonchalant and unhurried.

Immediately he was inside his manner changed completely.

'Get the hell out of here now,' he snapped the order as if he were the commanding officer in a pitched battle addressing a dull private. Jack didn't bother to enquire what the hurry was all about but turned the key, revving the one hundred and fifty horse power six to clear its throat. Whether the two locals really meant any harm they were never to know. Engaging drive Jack executed a screeching three point turn sending a curious local cat diving for cover as they made a conspicuous exit.

III

A moment later they were back on the main road and heading back towards the Eden Roc, resuming their search for a cheap, respectable hotel. Jack noticed a street he missed on the first pass, it shadowed the ocean and didn't look as bright and brassy as some of the others, it looked promising so he decided to check it out. As he hoped the street turned into a mixed residential district with some big old homes, interspersed with a selection of reasonable looking hotels. He chose the cheapest looking one, parked outside and left Tom sulking in the Van while he went in to negotiate with the bookings desk.

Out of Tom's company, he felt transformed, his eyes brightened, his face became more animated and his attitude sharpened. In no time the guy behind the desk had given him a rate on one of the best rooms in the house that he wouldn't have given his own mother. Jack smiled to himself as he left the hotel, feeling exhilarated as he always did after he used his unusual but totally natural talent for getting what he wanted from people. It was this talent that he always knew would ensure his success in later life. It was also what gave him such casual confidence in himself and led him to sometimes take stupid unnecessary risks. Deep down inside he felt invulnerable, if the worst came to the worst he believed he could talk his way out of anything.

When he emerged from the hotel he felt like a weight had been lifted from his shoulders, the city lights seemed brighter, and even the thought of dealing with Tom didn't seem so bad after all. There had to be a solution to the situation he was in, one where, like so often before, he could keep everyone happy and still get his own way.

When he opened the Van door he saw Tom had dozed off in the passenger seat, the effects of the long day finally having caught up with him. Jack still felt elated, although he could feel fatigue hovering not far away. It vaguely crossed his mind to wake Tom up and suggest a return to the less salubrious end of the strip to check out a few of the bars. On reflection he decided that wasn't a good idea. It was probably best to head on back to the Keys and sort out where they were going to stay, otherwise he could see them parked up at the side of the road and risking an unnecessary fine. Also he wasn't totally sure about the legality of his driving the Van. Wilbur had assured them the licence plate on the windshield was in effect a tax disc and insurance rolled into one but he would prefer not to have to rely on that being the case in the event of a brush with the local law.

So he climbed into the driver's seat once again and

Simon Shinerock

with growing familiarity piloted the Van back out onto the highway, retracing the route they'd taken earlier. It was now about midnight and the highway was once again relatively deserted, he soon lapsed off into his own thoughts, lulled by the gentle thrumming of the engine and images of Ruth.

He was jolted out of his reverie by a tugging on his right arm. At first he was confused by the way the steering suddenly appeared to take on a life of its own, sending the Van careering off towards the sidewalk in a near repeat of the earlier incident A shot of adrenaline startled his brain back to alert status. Tom had been trying to get his attention for a while, finally resorting to the tug when he failed to get a response. Now he saw Jack was paying attention he asked his question.

'Listen Jack, I was thinking that maybe I could drive the Van for a while, it's a straight road and there's no-one around. What do you say buddy? Pull over and let me give it a try.'

This was Tom trying to be at his most charming and obsequious but it came out sounding more like a veiled threat. Jack sucked in a breath, the request had caught him completely off guard. On the other hand why was he so surprised, he knew the guy well enough to know how much the situation of not being able to drive the Van must be bugging him, he also knew that in his own way Tom could be even more reckless than he.

'I don't think that's such a good idea,' Jack responded too quickly, too aggressively, he could hear the challenge in his own voice. In spite of knowing he was inviting confrontation he continued.

'Firstly you don't have a licence, secondly you have no experience with a vehicle this size and finally I don't think the highway out of Miami in the middle of the night is the right place to start.' Even as he spoke these words of wisdom and common sense he knew they would fall on deaf ears.

If he'd really wanted to put a stop to this hare-brained idea, he'd made a fatal mistake. The rules of engagement though unwritten were clear nevertheless. Whatever he said or did, Tom was bound to disagree. Therefore if he was going to stop him from driving the Van he would have needed to encourage him to go ahead, knowing his agreement would almost certainly cause a change of mind.

As it was it was too late. By dismissing the idea so firmly he may as well have pulled over there and then and handed over the Keys. He could actually feel Tom mentally digging in his heels. Tom's response was swift and predictable.

'Look, I paid for half this heap, I'm the one who's had to sit here while you make sure your girl friend is taken care of. Now, I want to drive the fucking Van, so pull over before I do it for you.'

He made a lunge at the wheel and the Van swerved dangerously for the third time.

Instead of doing the right thing and resisting, Jack nodded submissively. He slowed down and started looking for somewhere to pull over, it was the guilt again, it seemed to take all the fight out of him.

They were still in the suburbs of Miami, the road was wide and straight but there were plenty of places to stop. Jack noticed an empty bus stop coming up and indicated right, the brakes graunching ominously as he brought the Van to a halt under a large palm tree. Once at rest he let out a long sigh, suddenly feeling very tired. Despite his misgivings, he was relieved for someone else to do the driving. It shouldn't be too bad, after all the road went more or less straight back to the Keys. Granted Tom had no licence but then again he wasn't even sure if either of them were insured, the Van wasn't difficult to drive if you took it steady, thankfully it was an automatic so there was no gear shift to worry about. Maybe things would be OK after all.

But somewhere deep inside his head the voice made itself heard, it was weak and sickly sounding but the message was clear. Things wouldn't be all right, they were all wrong, all totally wrong.

'Move over then.' Tom was eager and excited, he sounded pent up, reckless.

'Just remember it's a Van not a sports car will you? All you have to do is keep on this road until we get back to the Keys'.

Having given this token warning, Jack climbed out of the driver's seat and into the back of the Van.

IV

It was a strange sensation, standing up in the Van. The interior of the rowing boat that served to extend its roof was pitch black and musty with the smell of old shag pile carpet and dust. *For a moment he thought he caught a whiff of something nasty lurking up there in the nooks and crannies of the boat. His head began to spin and his legs became unsteady, he put his hand out to support himself, grabbing at the air and ending up with a hand full of carpet. It came away with a tortured tearing sound, the ancient glue giving out at the same time as the dried and rotten hessian.*

There was no supernatural reason for his sudden loss of balance, it was just that Tom had slid over into the driver's seat and pulled straight back onto the highway. He was accelerating flat out and weaving in and out of the lanes like a man possessed. Jack managed to get a hand onto the back of the passenger seat and swing himself round into place, they were fast approaching a main intersection, the lights were red and there were three vehicles waiting patiently for the signal to go. Tom seemed to have lost his mind, either he didn't see the stationary vehicles or he intended to ram them, either way it looked like they were going to crash.

'Look out,' Jack managed to scream with no effect. He saw there was an empty right hand filter lane, it'd been obscured by the bright tail lights of the waiting cars. Tom had seen it though and was aiming the Van into the gap as if it was some kind of college hot rod. He obviously intended to get to the front of the small queue at all costs and presumably out-drag the other vehicles when the lights changed. As they entered the empty box the lights did change and the front row of the impromptu grid powered away unaware of the arrival of the Van. Tom found himself shut out as the three lanes became two, he tried to brake but he was going too fast, the already worn pads bit into the discs, letting out a nasty grinding sound as they bit into the tortured metal.

In the end he had no choice but turn off to the right, going away from the main highway and out towards suburban Miami. It would have been sensible for him to stop and turn around or let Jack take over. Sensible wasn't how he felt though, angry and embarrassed was how he felt. The incident at the traffic lights just made him worse, now he was determined to carry on, if for no other reason than to show that he could. There was no way he was going to ask for help, or indeed to accept any.

'Pull over and let me drive.'

Jack tried very hard to sound calm and reasonable, he knew if he lost his temper it would make the situation even worse and they would probably end up in a ditch somewhere. Tom either didn't hear or chose to ignore him. As it was they were fast leaving the highway behind, there were still street lamps but they emitted a subdued orange glow rather than the iridescent yellow of the highway lights. The street they were headed down was a main thoroughfare, leading into some nameless suburb which by the look of the large houses set well back from the road was an affluent one. They were still travelling too fast, but their speed was coming down as Tom gradually started to calm down.

Jack waited his moment before speaking again, this time he took a different tack. By now they were well away from the highway and had already passed a number of intersections at speed. The fact was they were lost.

'Why don't you pull into one of the side roads and we can look at the map and see where we are?'

He made sure his voice had an even reasonable tone, he waved behind him to where the map lay on the floor by his rucksack. By now the Van was going along at about thirty, Tom hesitated for a moment, then slowed further, making a right turn, driving up a dark street at no more than walking pace. There were no vehicles parked at the sides of the road, all the houses having private drives. In the Van's headlights it was possible to see the rows of well-kept trees and the carefully mown verge between the sidewalk and the road. This was definitely an affluent area, the kind of area where some of the residents would even now be rising from their beds, disturbed by the unexpected sound of a large vehicle cruising past their houses. Even now they may be at their bedroom windows, staring out into the gloom and seeing the odd looking

The Dark Lagoon

Van with a boat for a roof. Who would blame them for taking down the licence plate and even reporting the situation to the police? These were exactly the thoughts that were going through Jack's mind as they trickled along at a snail's pace, for all the world like a pair of burglars out to case a few joints.

For this reason Jack was keen to turn the Van round and get back to the highway as soon as possible. Tom on the other hand seemed preoccupied with other less practical issues. Anyone who saw him at that moment wouldn't be able to tell exactly what was the matter with him, they might think he was on drugs, certainly the staring eyes and vacant expression would seem to support this conclusion. Looking deeper into his eyes though, the observer might become unsure. *There was a heat coming from those eyes that spoke more of infection than addiction and sure enough there were small beads of sweat breaking out across his forehead.*

Fever or addiction, or something else again, something the casual observer would never recognise, it didn't really matter at that moment. When he finally turned to answer Jack's reasonable question, his face was contorted with rage and resentment. The sight of it made Jack gasp, despite their differences he had no idea Tom was capable of such a look, it was barely human and very scary.

For the second time since they left Wilbur, the voice which had remained muffled (or gagged) for so long began to make itself heard more clearly. 'There's something wrong here Jack,' it warned 'something very wrong, wrong wrong wrong........' but it tailed off into oblivion before it could tell him what to do.

So it was fear and self preservation that made him reach for the door handle to escape, but it was too late. Tom gunned the throttle and aimed the vehicle at the open driveway of a large house. Given his lack of practice it was a precise manoeuvre, he managed to avoid hitting the low stone wall that bordered the house's front garden by inches and brought the Van to a dead stop without ploughing into the garage immediately in front of them. Then he slammed the transmission into reverse and floored the throttle, simultaneously whirling the wheel hard left.

Despite being scared out of his wits, Jack couldn't help being impressed at the way the Van shot backwards, tyres screeching through the night, managing to avoid hitting anything, it was like being part of a stunt in a movie. Again Tom viciously applied the brakes throwing him back into his seat, then slammed the gear lever into drive, heading back towards the junction. When they got there he appeared to hesitate for the first time. The roads had been totally deserted but now as he stalled the Van halfway out into the road, they both saw a large truck bearing down on them.

Jack could see they had plenty of time to pull out before it smashed them to pieces provided Tom acted quickly. But by the time he managed to restart the Van and struggled with the transmission, precious seconds had ticked by, it was almost on them, sounding its horn but showing no sign of slowing down.

'Go! Go! Go! Fucking go' screamed Jack. It was all he could do, he was frozen to his seat.

This outburst brought Tom back to his senses, at least he finally managed to get the reluctant transmission to engage. The engine raced as the torque converter took up the slack, but instead of moving forwards, the Van shot backwards into the side street.

There was a loud bang and a scraping noise, then nothing. They looked at one another, shocked into silence.

'Swap places with me,' 'Tom's voice was panic-filled

and unstable. 'I don't have a licence or insurance, say it was you who was driving then it's just an accident.' Not bothering to wait for a reply, he got out of the Van and walked slowly round the back of the vehicle. No-one showed themselves, the silence was eerie, almost allowing him to convince himself that nothing had really happened.

Perhaps nothing had happened he thought, perhaps it was only an old trash can he'd hit, sending it careering into the trees somewhere, making a lot of noise about nothing. Yes, that was it, nothing had really happened at all, he could just get back inside the Van, in the passenger seat this time, and let Jack drive them home and everything would look a lot better in the morning.

V

'Hey buddy!' The words were low and thick, as if the speaker were talking through a mask.

'Hey buddy, you better get over here, don't make me come and find you.' The chill warning galvanised him into action, he took the last few steps down the side of the Van and looked behind.

There lying on its side in the street was a Harley Davidson motorcycle. Not the sort of chromed wonder ridden by off-duty executives, or the kind of customised fashion accessory favoured by the gay community, this was a serious biker's motorcycle, black, oily and mean. Not dissimilar to its owner who was standing on the grass verge beside his stricken steed. His jeans were badly ripped down the left side and there was a trickle of blood running down the exposed leg. He'd stopped talking to pull off his helmet which like the rest of his clothing was black.

Tom stared at the rider uncomprehendingly, he'd been

expecting a middle-class, middle-aged, middle American, not this; what he saw his mind dismissed and he ploughed on with his hastily conceived plan.

'Look, I'm really sorry about your bike, let me help you with it.' He started to pick up the bike so the rider could inspect the damage; it was heavy and awkward, during the last of these attempts it fell back to the floor with a sickening crunch. The rider was looking on with cool detachment, he appeared to have lost interest in the situation and was busy rolling a cigarette, or more likely from the size of the paper, a joint. After he'd satisfied himself with the size and weight of his smoke, he replaced his pouch and took out an old paraffin storm-proof lighter.

He held the loose orange flame to the tip of the joint, for that was what it was, and inhaled deeply. His face was highlighted clearly by the flame and the sight of it made Tom shudder. It was unshaven and there were wicked looking scars on both cheeks, the kind you only get from a cut-throat razor in a fight. In spite of what he saw, he carried on trying to talk his way out of trouble, digging a deeper hole with every word.

'There should be no problem here,' he babbled. 'The insurance will pay for any damage. Just one thing though, I don't have a licence so we've got to say my buddy was driving, OK?'

The rider seemed to find this idea quite amusing, in any event his face broke into a crooked smile. Then he said 'Listen bro. you're not from round here are you?'

Tom shook his head.

'Good, I didn't think so. Well I'm gonna make this easy on you then. See I don't need you to have any insurance, or a licence, hell I lost my licence years ago.'

He laughed at his own joke this time, a guttural laugh

that ended in a coughing spasm. He looked at the half smoked spliff and shook his head. Tom in the meantime was also smiling hopefully.

'All me and my friends here want from you is compensation, that's all, just compensation. We'll take it in cash or body parts, it's up to you.'

From out of the shadows four more figures appeared. At the same time as the rest of the gang appeared, Jack, who'd been standing concealed, close to the Van, listening to Tom's exchange with the first biker now stepped into the open. He held his arms out, palms up in a gesture of conciliation. Everyone's attention now focusing on him.

'OK, why don't we try and cool this situation down a little? The bike's been damaged and we will pay for it, now how much do you want?'

The gang were closing in while he was talking, two of them bent over the fallen hog and wrestled it upright, Jack could see the head-lamp glass was broken but apart from that it looked intact. Certainly there were dents and scrapes but it would have been tough to tell when they were caused, the whole thing wasn't exactly in immaculate condition. He was starting to think in terms of a couple of hundred dollars being the size of it, all he had to do was persuade their new friends he was right, if only Tom didn't barge in first and get them both killed.

He felt something hot close around his throat, choking his words before they had a chance to form. Everyone was looking at him, waiting to hear what he had to say but the harder he tried to speak, the tighter it became, until he could hardly breathe, forced to remain impotently silent as the gang turned their attention back to Tom.

It was obvious that if they ran they would be quickly caught and probably run down. The odds of coming out on top in a fight were also just about nil but at least they could hope someone would wake up and call the cops. Two of the bikers had closed in on Tom and taken an arm each, he struggled violently but they were too strong. A third had his back to Jack but he recognised him immediately nonetheless.

It was Onyx, his jacket carried the lurid red emblem of the Heathens and even from the back you could see the tattooed smoothness of his bald pate. Jack started forward, the adrenaline pumping into his veins. At the same time Tom kicked out at Onyx, catching him squarely in the chest and sending him reeling backwards. Tom was strong and no coward, he was struggling valiantly with the two bozos who were holding him and for a moment it looked like he would break free. He shook one off and moved sideways, taking hold of the remaining Heathen and swung round, using him as an impromptu club to knock his partner to the ground.

Now was Jack's chance, there was only one of them in his way, if he could take him out and get to Tom, then together they might be able to hold off the rest long enough for help to arrive. To his horror, instead of moving forward he was rooted to the spot. His chance missed, his adversary was on him, placing a large gloved hand on his chest and pushing him viciously back into the side of the Van.

The thing around his neck was burning now, burning and squeezing, stopping him from crying out or doing anything to resist. The biker who pushed him into the side of the Van held him there with one arm, casually drawing back the other, giving him a symbolic punch in the stomach. It wasn't enough to hurt, or wind him, just enough to let him know he'd been hit. His attacker looked at him and smiled, revealing a broken set of crooked yellow teeth.

'You better rest where you are if you don't want to

end up like him.' As he said this he looked to where Tom was now losing his battle. Onyx had got to his feet and the other two had been joined by the original biker, together they easily overwhelmed him, the three lackey's holding him still while Onyx went to work with what looked like a short club.

Jack could feel tears of anger and frustration coming into his eyes as he watched helplessly as Tom received a horrific beating. Onyx was methodical and thorough, starting with his legs and working his way up, never hitting him hard enough so he would lose consciousness, or do irreparable damage. It seemed he was meant to be awake for what looked more like a ritual punishment beating than a spontaneous street fight. The assault seemed to go on forever, occasionally he caught Tom's eye and seemed to see an accusatory question there. Why didn't he come to his aid? It was a question that was to haunt Jack for years to come.

In reality the whole incident only lasted about three minutes. When it was over they left Tom lying in the road, badly beaten but in one piece, the only thing he was missing was his billfold containing all the money he had. Before disappearing back into the darkness, Onyx walked over to where Jack was still being held against the Van. He was still holding the blackjack he'd used on Tom, for a moment Jack thought it was his turn but he needn't have worried. The blackjack remained passively at Onyx's side, he wasn't going to use it any more that evening. Instead he just looked at Jack and winked. It was a conspiratorial sort wink, as if to say

'It's OK bro' you don't have to say anything, we both know we're all bro's together here, all batting on the same team.'

That look and that wink did more to freak him out

than any beating, it left him aching in a place that no punch or kick could ever reach, a place that felt injured beyond recovery.

Then they were gone and he could move and breathe again, although too late to help Tom who still lay unmoving on the ground in front of him. He was making a sort of squeaking noise, his hands up round his head, trying to protect himself, his body curled into the foetal position.

'It's all right Tom, it's me, Jack, we've got to get you to your feet, we've got to get you out of here'.

Gradually Jack coaxed him to his feet and helped him back to the Van. Although the beating had been a savage one and he was clearly in a lot of pain, no doubt suffering from shock as well, there didn't appear to have been any permanent harm done. In many ways this puzzled Jack, although he wasn't about to complain about it. It was strange though, why hadn't they done more damage, they were obviously used to real violence, so what held them back? And why hadn't they beaten him up and stolen his money as well? Even more perplexing, why had Onyx winked at him?

These questions were going to have to go unanswered, at least for the moment, right now he had more practical considerations. What was best to do, call the police? Take Tom to hospital? Or just get the hell out of there and back to the Keys. The thought of returning to the Keys with Tom in this condition didn't thrill him. He felt very guilty about not being able to stop the beating, but there was no getting away from the fact that he'd brought it on himself, it was only fluke that they hadn't both been murdered.

In everyone's interests it was now better if Tom went home, assuming that is he was fit enough to travel. He felt a steely resolve come over him but he wasn't going to tip his hand the way he did with the Van, no way, this time he would play it clever.

'Tom, do you want me to take you to the hospital?'

He'd started the Van and was already pulling out onto the main road, the street was still empty and quiet. Tom was awake now and looking at his battered face in the mirror, he reached behind for his rucksack, took out a towel and started to minister to himself, dabbing at his nose with the towel which he'd moistened with his own spit.

'I'm all right, I don't need the hospital, those guys weren't trying to damage me, they were working me over for fun, they took my money.'

He said this as if it were more important than if they'd stabbed him. Jack waited and then asked again.

'What do you want to do then? Shall we go back to the Keys, or report those guys to the police, what do you want to do?'

'Oh yeah,' Tom spat the words out sarcastically. 'Let's report them to the police shall we? What exactly are we going to tell them though? How I was driving without a licence, no insurance and backed into a member of a passing gang of Hell's Angels who we can't describe and don't know anything about? I don't think so somehow, just get us out of here.'

Jack drove in silence for about half an hour, grateful that Tom didn't appear to hold his cowardice against him. They rejoined the main highway and were by default heading back towards Key Largo. Tom's mood had lost its earlier aggression and he'd sunk into a depressive state.

He was thinking about his position, no money, beaten

up and nothing much to look forward to, he just wanted out, the whole trip had been a fiasco from start to finish. He decided he hated Americans, everything he'd done since he'd arrived turned to shit and to make things worse all Jack could think about was Ruth. He had a bad feeling that unless he got out now, next time he wouldn't get off so lightly. On the other hand why should he leave? Leaving would be an admission of failure. He would have failed to cope in a new environment and been defeated by the situation, it would be like admitting he was a loser. Worse still it would also be admitting that Jack was a winner, that he'd got the better of him, this was the most galling thought of all.

As if to give a voice to his depressive musings Jack began to rehearse the exact same arguments out loud.

'Whether you like it or not you're going to have to face up to the situation sooner or later. The fact is things aren't going that well for you on this trip, Tom. Let's be honest, we haven't been getting on too well and now this has happened, I will help you out if you want to carry on but if you want to go home I'll understand.'

Now that the subject of going home had been raised, Tom felt better able to consider it. Would leaving really be an admission of weakness, or would it really show strength of character, the courage to retreat when faced with insurmountable odds? He who fights and runs away, lives to fight another day, which was more than Jack had done although he wasn't going to say anything about it; in spite of their differences there were some lines you only ever crossed once. If he was going to leave or stay he would need Jack to help him, if in no other way than by lending him his air fare home.

Jack judged his next contribution perfectly.

The Dark Lagoon

'I think you should stay,' he said. 'A lot of people would give up in this position, who could blame them, but the right thing to do is stick it out. OK, it will be hard, no money and everything, but you have a job and if you come through this it can only make you a stronger person. It's a test, a challenge and you have to rise to it.'

Every word bit into Tom like a barracuda nibbling at his open guts. It was worse than being beaten up, here he was in the toughest situation of his life and Jack was preaching to him like they were talking about owning up to some schoolboy prank. His mind was made up, he was going to leave.

'I want to leave, I've had enough.'

The words came out bitter but guarded, he still needed Jack's help so he couldn't afford to upset him just yet.

'Will you lend me the money to get home? I'm broke.' Although this was what Jack wanted to hear, he was stunned for a moment by how easy it had all been. Again the guilt rose up in his chest and he felt nauseous. Nevertheless he wouldn't look a gift horse in the mouth, if Tom wanted to leave, now was as good a time as ever.

'OK, I'll give you the money for the ticket but you must go now, not in the morning, right now, make up your mind, if you want to go I'm turning round and we're going back to the airport.'

Tom was a little taken aback by this reaction but he couldn't be bothered to argue, in fact it was best, if he was going to leave, the sooner the better. Another thing dawned on him, he didn't like the guy sitting beside him, in fact he doubted he ever liked him, the sooner he could rid himself of his company the better.

'Turn round,' said Tom with finality. 'What are you waiting for?'

VI

So Jack turned around and headed back to Miami International Airport. The journey passed in silence, both young men lost in their own thoughts. When they arrived Jack tried to park the Van in the underground car park, forgetting about the extra height of the boat roof. There was a loud bang as the Van tried in vain to make it through the entrance. Still not aware of what was causing the problem, he tried again, this time more gently. Again the Van came to a halt, encountering firm resistance. He got out and immediately realised his mistake. He felt foolish as he backed out of the tight entrance. The damage was superficial but it was a stupid mistake. It made him feel a pang of remorse about Tom, after all it was the same kind of stupid mistake that landed him here, beaten and robbed, those were the breaks he supposed.

When they entered the terminal building Tom went straight to the men's room. He spent a good half hour in there. When he emerged he looked a lot better, he'd changed his clothes, cleaned himself up and re-packed his stuff. Apart from a few red marks on his face he looked like any other student out to see the world.

While Tom was cleaning himself up Jack was at the information desk checking out flight times and seat availability for London. Delta were flying at 3.30 am, in about an hour and a half's time. He'd purchased a non-refundable, non-transferable one way standby ticket for one hundred and eighty six dollars and was holding it in his hand when Tom came into view.

'You look a lot better,' he said, trying to seem positive but the words just sounded fake. Tom nodded dryly and stretched out a hand for the ticket.

The Dark Lagoon

'It leaves in an hour and a half, you have to check in now.'

Tom took the ticket. 'Thanks,' he said stiffly, almost formally, not holding eye contact. Jack felt the tension building up between them.

'It's now or never, tinkled the voice. 'You have to level with one another now, or it'll be too late. there's something wrong, Jack, something wrong wrong wrong.....'

Whether it was the noise of the planes taking off, or just all the people going about their businesses, minds focused, all those thoughts interfering with the message, Jack didn't seem to hear the warning. If he did hear it he ignored it, either way he just lost his last chance to save himself and Tom before the game really had a chance to begin.

'Jack, why don't you leave' Tom spoke the words calmly, politely but Jack could sense the underlying bitterness and resentment.

'If that's what you want then?'

The other nodded in confirmation

He was standing only a few feet from Tom yet neither of them appeared able to bridge the small gap and shake the other's hand. If they had, maybe in spite of the odds the rift between them could have been healed. As it was after a pregnant pause, Jack turned slowly on his heel and walked away.

Chapter Three

I

Even before Jack left the terminal building trouble was brewing. A short man standing in the shadows behind a cluster of public telephones watched him go. Whoever it was had been regarding the pair for some time, noting their negative body language with subtle appreciation. He was standing patiently, a plume of grey smoke rising steadily from the small black cheroot he held nonchalantly in his left hand.

Wilbur waited until he was sure Jack had left the building and was well on his way before starting out after Tom. He intercepted him just as he reached the Delta Airways check-in counter. At that time of night the counter was deserted save for a stewardess who, despite the application of a thick layer of make-up, looked decidedly the worse for lack of sleep. Tom strode up to the counter and dumped his rucksack down onto the moving scales, at the same time handing the jaded-looking woman his passport and ticket. He would normally have noticed the presence of someone close behind him, well inside the green line marking out where the next passenger should wait their turn. He didn't notice Wilbur though, his mind was too caught up with other more vexatious matters to be distracted by anything short of an earthquake.

It was the young woman who brought matters to a head.

'Will you be travelling together sir?' she enquired

Tom didn't understand the question, he just shook

his head, for a moment thinking, she must be talking about Jack; though how she could have known about him was a mystery.

'In that case sir could you please step back behind the green line.'

Her voice was monotonous, even robotic but she wasn't addressing Tom, she was looking over his right shoulder at someone who must have been standing right behind.

The young woman was looking irritated and perplexed, clearly whoever it was wasn't doing as they were told. In spite of his intense disinterest Tom found himself turning round and staring straight into Wilbur's smiling face.

'Hi kid! How're you doing?'

The enquiry sounded friendly and warm, as if Tom were a long lost friend (son?) and their meeting was a result of happy coincidence.

'I'm doing fine, what are you doing here?' he offered, and then as an afterthought, 'I haven't got the Van, Jack has.'

Wilbur looked unperturbed. 'Don't worry about the Van. Listen, we need to *talk*.'

Wilbur emphasised the word "talk" in a way that made it sound very conspiratorial and important. He motioned towards the shopping area, most of which was closed because of the time. He was trying to point out a coffee bar, appropriately called "The Coffee Bean", still open with a few passengers scattered around waiting for lost luggage or late flights. The idea was they should go there and *talk*.

'I'm sorry Wilbur, I'd like to but I can't, I have a plane to catch so I guess I'll see you around.'

Tom turned his back on Wilbur hoping the old man

would get the hint and disappear. The young woman behind the counter was looking positively flustered at this unscheduled interruption to normal service. By the look on her face you would have thought there was a long queue of impatient passengers and these two were fouling up the system.

Whatever Tom hoped, it soon became clear Wilbur was not going anywhere, not yet at least.

'OK kid, whatever you like; you probably wouldn't be interested in what I have to say anyway. After all why should you care if your so-called buddy had you beaten up and robbed just so's he could get rid of you in time for his chick to arrive. Yeah, you're probably right, better to leave things where they are than stir up a whole hornets' nest, am I right or am I right?'

He turned to go, stepping with forced precision behind the green line.

'Wait a minute.' Tom's voice was strained and urgent, it was as if his sanity was a fragile pane of glass and Wilbur had just thrown a brick through it. He looked at the booking clerk who was by now at the point of calling Security.

'I'm sorry about this, something's come up, do you mind if I take my ticket back for a moment.'

Trying her best to keep a professional demeanour she picked up the ticket and passport and handed them over.

'You do realise this is non-transferable sir, if you miss your check-in time you lose the ticket, you only have a few minutes to decide.'

Tom tried to look like he knew what he was doing.

'Thank you for letting me know, I'll be back in a minute. Don't let the plane go without me.'

The Dark Lagoon

He didn't wait to hear her protests but grabbed his rucksack and went after Wilbur who was already half way to "The Coffee Bean".

By the time he caught Wilbur up the older man was already at the bar ordering two expressos, he didn't bother to ask Tom whether he took coffee that way. When the barman handed him the two small cups he pushed a five dollar bill across the counter and walked over to a table in the far corner of the lounge by the window.

"The Coffee Bean" was comfortably laid out, someone had gone to a lot of trouble to avoid it feeling like the corner of a vast air terminal. The colour scheme was a rich velvety red mixed with dark brown woods, all the china was good quality and authentic looking; all in all it gave a better than average impression of real South American atmosphere.

Once they were seated and he'd lit yet another of his foul black cheroots Wilbur prepared to expound on what he'd said earlier. During this time something in Tom was putting two and two together, so when Wilbur reached into his jacket and produced a packet with some bills poking out of the end, he was only too eager to see what it contained. Wilbur tossed the packet across the table at him. Sure enough inside the packet was the exact amount of money he'd lost. Worse still, on examination he recognised quite a few of the bills, one in particular which he'd used to make a note of the phoney social security number he'd made up for the construction site.

'Where did you get this?' he demanded angrily.

Jack may have arranged the high-jack but that still didn't explain how Wilbur came to be holding his money.

Wilbur took a long draw on his cheroot and inhaled deeply, blowing out a billowing stream of smoke, causing

Tom to cough violently before he replied. 'Let's say I was worried about you two boys so I followed you, to keep an eye on my investment if you like. When I saw you getting into trouble with those hoodlums, I tailed them. You understand I would have stepped in if I was a bit younger but....'

'But what?' Tom interjected. 'But how the hell did you get my money back?'

'Steady son, be patient, I was getting to that part. See, I spotted the one who took the money, the one with the tattoo on his head. I followed him until we got to a nice piece of deserted highway and then, well let's just say there was a clash of personalities between a Chevy and a Harley and the Chevy won.'

Tom waited for more but Wilbur was all done, so he completed the story for him.

'So you ran that guy off the road, took back my money and he told you about Jack?'

Wilbur nodded. 'You got it in one, kid, it's a bad shake but them's the breaks eh? Them's the breaks.' Boy did that ring true! Tom had certainly been getting the breaks ever since he arrived in America, the trouble was they were all bad breaks.

This though, this was much worse; all thoughts of going back to England with his tail between his legs were banished from his head, driven out by a more basic emotion. He was being overwhelmed by the desire for revenge. He could feel it surging through his body, giving him back his strength and resolve. Revenge would be the ultimate purge for his jealousy of Jack and the ultimate punishment for his betrayal.

Wilbur, the cafe, even the terminal building itself seemed

The Dark Lagoon

to disappear as he was sucked deeper and deeper into a dark fantasy world of revenge. Jack thought he was so clever, thought he had everything worked out, Well he was in for an unpleasant surprise, that's for sure. It didn't matter to him how long it took, or what it cost, *he was going to take him down.*

'Now if I'm not mistaken.' Wilbur's voice smashed through the daydream, bold and encouraging. 'You look as if you'd rather get even than walk away. Can't say I blame you really, I know what I'd do if someone did that to me, there'd be a place in the glades tonight where the gators would be feasting, that's for sure.'

Tom's head jerked upright, not as a result of Wilbur's words, although they also made their mark, but as a result of a sharp itch on his right cheek. The sensation was so strong, at first he thought he'd been stung. Looking round, he could see no bug that could have caused the itch, then he remembered the bite he suffered the night before. It'd gone away but now it was back with a vengeance. He reached up involuntarily to scratch the bite; Wilbur's hand shot out and caught him by the wrist.

'That's not the only itch you want to scratch tonight, is it boy?' He'd drawn in close, still gripping the arm with a force that belied his age and stature. Their faces were only a few inches apart; Wilbur's voice had taken on an urgency, almost a fever, not dissimilar to the one now running through Tom's veins. Yesterday Tom would have shrunk away from this intimacy, he would have seen Wilbur as a crazed pervert. Perhaps that was what he truly was; tonight though he didn't pull back, he listened intently and the words filled his soul like the waters of the dark lagoon. During that moment he and Wilbur understood one another completely, each saw the naked desire that ruled them exposed in the other's eyes.

Wilbur released his grip on Tom's arm and sat back in his chair. The arm hovered indecisively for a moment before dropping back to its side, the urge to scratch had gone, replaced with the need to listen.

When he spoke, Wilbur's voice had lost its gruff aggression; it had again become concerned, almost fatherly.

'There comes a point in a person's life when they have to choose the path they want to travel. You've reached a time like that, Tom, and you're going to have to choose which way you go. Call it a cross-roads if you will.'

Here he moved closer once again, as if what he were about to say was strictly against the rules but he was going to say it anyway.

'Now I can advise you but ultimately the decision has got to be up to you.' Wilbur paused to let his words sink in, so Tom would be able to fully appreciate what was to follow.

'I don't know what you're talking about,' said Tom. A simple statement but it meant a lot. It could have meant "I don't know what you're talking about and I'm not interested in finding out," but it didn't. Behind the statement was a pleading curiosity, he was hooked; he really wanted to hear more. Wilbur nodded sympathetically, indicating he understood how he felt, then he continued.

'You see Tom, even though I'm retired really, I still do a little work now and again for a very powerful man. I saw him today and I have to say I mentioned you because you impressed me. He told me he wanted to meet you and sent me out to find you. So imagine how I felt when I found you here about to leave. If I hadn't reached you in time you would have left without even knowing that opportunity was knocking at your door.'

He stopped and took a sip of his expresso, it'd gone cold and he gave a small grimace of disgust, then he smiled.

The Dark Lagoon

'Sorry about that but at my age I can't take these late nights any more, I need all the help I can get just to keep awake. Now then, where was I?'

He was talking to himself really but Tom took the question literally and reminded him.

'You were saying you do some work for this powerful guy and that he wanted to meet me, why would he want to do that?'

'That's right' said Wilbur. 'His name is Rex Proctor.'

He said this as if mere mention of the name should be explanation enough, nevertheless he continued. 'Like many powerful men Mr. Proctor is always on the lookout for likely young men, men with ambition and talent that he can fit into his plans. I can't say exactly what he has in mind of course but I do think you should meet him. I feel sure he would be able to help you fix your little problem with Jack, for example.'

Tom was intrigued and flattered by this proposal. In addition whatever it was that burned inside him sensed that here was a real chance to get even with Jack. In spite of these feelings he was still cautious, he wanted to know more about this mysterious Mr. Proctor before he agreed to give up his plane ticket and go to meet him. He leaned over towards Wilbur.

'Tell me more about Proctor, where does he live? What does he do? When does he want to meet?'

Wilbur pulled back slightly under this barrage of questions; when he replied he sounded more formal, like he was coming to the take it or leave it part of the negotiations.

'These questions are understandable but I think Mr. Proctor should be the one to answer them. All can tell you is he lives on a private island about two hours from here and he wants to meet you now. It's make your mind up time, stay or go, it's up to you.'

Tom could see that he wasn't going to get any more out of Wilbur on the subject of Mr. Proctor so he tried another tack.

'If I decide to go,' he said, pointing to the packet of bills on the table. 'I get my money back, right?'

It was a trick question because he intended to take the money anyway, he just wanted to see what the rules of the game were.

Wilbur waved dismissively at the packet as if it were of no importance.

'Of course you can have your money, take it now.'

His tone of voice was condescending, indifferent, bored. It implied that maybe he'd made a mistake, maybe he was wasting his time. As if to confirm this thought he got up as if to leave.

Tom was left in the lurch; he hated being railroaded but was he prepared to watch Wilbur walk away without ever knowing what kind of offer this Mr. Proctor wanted to make him? To remind him of what'd happened and how he'd been betrayed by Jack, the bite on his cheek gave another twang of irritation. It was enough to tip the balance; he got up and followed Wilbur; the decision apparently made. As they walked past the Delta Airlines check-in desk he didn't even give the check-in clerk a second glance, or hear her frantic warning.

'Sir, Sir, Mr. Kidman Sir, we can't hold the flight any longer, you must check in now.'

The Dark Lagoon

II

Tom slept during the car journey from the airport to the small jetty where the launch was moored. He therefore wasn't aware of the scheduled stop they made along the way.

After Jack left the terminal building he'd intended to drive all the way back to Key Largo and park the Van outside Wilbur's house; if that is he could remember how to get there in the dark. As it turned out though he was too tired to make the journey. After only half an hour his eyes started to close; his mind seizing longer and longer periods of micro sleep, if he didn't pull over he risked a serious crash. He passed a number of potential stopping places, eventually though he chose the car park of a Friendlies restaurant about halfway between Miami and the Keys. He chose this particular car-park because it extended round the back of the restaurant where he wouldn't be seen from the road. Also, being a family restaurant it'd been closed for a good few hours. There was a good chance there would be no activity till morning unless he was unlucky enough to be rousted by a security patrol.

By the time Wilbur swung the Chevy into the Friendlies car park both Tom and Jack were fast asleep. He left the engine running and got out, returning a few moments later carrying something bright and silver in his left hand. Before he got back into the car he held the object up to the sky, the pendant glinting in the watery light, a perfect replica of the crescent moon.

In his dreams that night Jack imagined the dark hand rising up out of the Island in the mist and reaching for him. He wanted to run but there was nowhere to hide. The hand took him by the throat, its terrible fingers reaching right inside of him, *ripping and tearing, searching for something deep within. He felt them find what they were looking for and begin to withdraw, taking a special thing that belonged to him with them as they left. He tried to struggle but it was useless. Then it was over and he was left feeling like he'd been tricked out of something important, although even in the dream he began to forget what it was. Then the hand was gone and he was standing on the shores of the Island. It was deserted and barren but for the sound of a terrible laughter coming from its black heart. The laughter boomed and echoed all around and he knew it was meant for him. It became louder and more hysterical until it was joined by the elements themselves, first wind, then rain and finally lightning. As the elemental comedy reached its climax Jack collapsed face down on the beach, breathing in the sterile white sand and choking silently into welcome darkness. When he awoke he was in the Van, a new day was dawning and he didn't even realise what had been stolen from him in the night.*

If Wilbur hadn't woken him, Tom would probably have continued to sleep for many hours. He was exhausted beyond dreams. His mind had retreated to a place far away where it could recuperate, where it could rest and somehow make sense of the powerful emotions to which it had been so suddenly subjected. So when he was shaken rudely awake he felt like he was being dragged out of a deep dark hole. At first he didn't know where he was or what he was doing there. He looked at Wilbur through vacant unseeing eyes thinking it was Jack who was rousing him; that they were still in the tent at the Bella Vista. His vision gradually returned and with it recollection of all the events of the last few hours. The memories were like a jolt of electricity, bringing him sharply alert, his nerves still tingling and raw, denied the healing of natural sleep.

'Time for you and me to take a boat ride.' Wilbur sounded wide awake and happy; he'd already switched off the Chevy's lights and engine and was opening the

The Dark Lagoon

door. Tom looked through the windscreen out across the ocean. There was a faint reddish glow in the cloudless sky signifying the approaching dawn. He stretched out in his seat and yawned; the bite on his face was itching dully in the background. Without thinking he reached up with his right hand and scratched his stubble. The bite had caused a small yellow blister to form on his cheek, ruptured by his roving nails, an unpleasant cocktail of blood and yellowish pus was now creeping down his face.

He stepped out onto the gravel surface of the car park. It was really only a widening of the narrow road that led to the private jetty; There was only just enough room for the Chevy to turn round. At the far end was a small hut that looked like it'd weathered many a storm in its life. In front of him the old wooden jetty poked out beyond the land into the ocean. Tethered there, looking mean and moody in the half light of the dawn was the launch. Despite everything he couldn't help admiring the sleek lines of the vessel. At least thirty five feet long, its glistening black hull winked haughtily at him as it rose and fell on the gentle swell. Along its sides emblazoned in red gothic letters was the legend 'The Devil Rides Out'.

Wilbur was busying himself on board, checking the fuel supply before their journey, then pressing a button and waiting while a hydraulically controlled electric motor lowered the twin props into the water.

'Jump aboard and make yourself at home.' Wilbur was looking at Tom with a gleam of excitement in his eyes; a gleam that became a sparkle as he turned the ignition on and hit the starter. You could tell immediately from the engine's instant response that this was no mere workhorse. Here was a true thoroughbred; not built for mundane considerations, or even the rigours of racing; this boat had only one purpose in life, pure exhilaration; a purpose it fulfilled completely.

Simon Shinerock

Tom stepped from the jetty down onto the side of the launch and jumped onto the deck. There was individual seating for four at the front plus a semicircular bench at the rear. Everything was upholstered in magnolia leather which seemed unmarked and immaculate. He settled himself down in the passenger seat and watched while Wilbur cast off. For the first time in what seemed like forever he felt exhilarated and happy; looking forward to the journey; hoping it would be a long one; secretly planning to ask for a turn at the controls.

Then they were under way, slowly and gently at first, the engines holding a steady drone, growing more urgent as Wilbur gradually slid the chrome topped throttle forward. Suddenly the launch seemed to lift itself up, nose pointing skywards, until it seemed as if they were flying; literally bouncing off the crests of the small waves.

To his surprise Wilbur didn't object when Tom asked to take the controls. On the contrary he seemed pleased, encouraging him to go a little faster, let his hair down, afterall he said 'you only live once'. After the aggravation with Jack, this was the first time Tom could remember since they'd arrived when he felt really happy; no it went beyond happiness, what he felt was elation, as if he'd taken some kind of strong narcotic. In what seemed like a few bright seconds, although it was in fact nearly twenty minutes, Tom saw they were approaching a sea mist. Wilbur indicated that he would take over and Tom reluctantly swapped seats, slow to give up his new-found toy. Wilbur throttled back as they entered the mist, the engine's note dropping down an octave as if they found the new air somehow distasteful.

Tom found the mist had a soporific effect, his heartbeat returning quickly to normal, the excitement of the last few minutes replaced with a fatigue that re-activated the injuries he suffered during the beating. For the first time since getting on board he started to question what he was doing here but his mind had become as foggy as the mist around him, after a few moments he stopped trying to think, instead settling back into the plush leather seat and closing his eyes.

It seemed only seconds later that Wilbur was digging him in the ribs, his bruises sending out sharp messages that had him sitting bolt upright like a jack-in-the-box. In front of them about half a mile off was a small Island. Even from that distance, being a geologist, he could see there was something unusual about it. Islands in this region were all made of coral; therefore the beaches were always white sand. There was no known volcanic activity in the area that could explain what now lay before him. The beaches of this Island were black, like in the Canaries, created from volcanic ash. He turned round to see the strange mist receding behind them, then back to the Island where it was possible to make out a large colonial style house set in formal gardens standing back from the beach about three hundred metres. The sight was even more incongruous set against the otherwise bleak landscape which otherwise consisted of thick impenetrable scrubland, rising slowly towards the horizon. Quite ludicrously the whole scene reminded him of Sleeping Beauty's castle and he wondered what lay at the Island's inaccessible heart.

As these thoughts occurred to him, they were drawing ever closer. He could see a modest jetty jutting out into the ocean in front of the house towards which Wilbur was aiming the launch. Since leaving the mist he'd started to return to normal, his head was clearing and he'd lost the tiredness brought on by the vapours. In normal circumstances he prided himself on being a rational person, yet here he was faced with inconsistencies he couldn't explain. His usual logical approach seemed to have gone out of the window, as his head cleared further he couldn't believe where he was or how he'd got there.

Turning to Wilbur the thought crossed his mind to ask to be taken back to the mainland, if necessary to commandeer the launch, to end this charade before it went any further. As fast as the thought came, it was gone, forced out by a sudden stinging irritation on his left cheek. In a leap of prophetic insight he connected the itch on his face with his being where he was. He had no time to explore this strange connection, all his attention was suddenly pulled towards the enigmatic mansion on the beach.

By now they were alongside the jetty and Wilbur was barking out instructions, forcing him out of his reverie and back to the matter at hand. When the launch was securely moored they disembarked quickly and walked towards the beach. To their left and right everything was black sand and scrub, as though some huge tanker had spilled its poisonous cargo over the Island, killing everything except the hardiest weeds and leaving the very fabric of the land dark and polluted. In total contrast to this bleak vista, the mansion which lay ahead of them was neat, attractive and impressive.

The first sign they were nearing the grounds of the mansion was when the blackness of the beach gave way to a swathe of white coral sand about ten metres wide. Beyond the sand, gently sloping upwards towards the house was an immaculately kept English lawn bordered by evergreen hedges over two metres tall. This first lawn gave way to a second and a third, each being divided from the next by an ornamental rockery. The middle lawn was absolutely flat and had the look of a well cared for but unused tennis court, behind it the third lawn was divided into three sections. On the left hand side was an orchard containing a variety of apple, pear and plum. Tom could see they were all heavy with luscious fruit, the sight of which made his mouth water and his stomach rumble. To the right was a rose garden, its beds in full bloom, providing a splash of vivid pinks and yellows that gave the whole scene a stylish finishing touch. Between the two upper lawns was a stone sun terrace about twenty metres wide; in the middle of which there was an ornamental fountain with a cherub at its centre shooting crystal clear water from its mouth and hands.

The house itself looked like it'd been built in the Twenties. There was more than a touch of baroque extravagance about the marble pillars that flanked the terrace; giving the faint impression that you were entering a *Temple*. Behind the terrace enormous French doors flung wide, beyond which the interior of the house could be seen. It seemed to Tom that this was an impossible place, created by someone without respect for, or at least the need to abide by, the laws of nature. It was more like a painting than a real place; he felt like he was stepping through the looking glass into another world.

Coming towards them as they made their way towards the house was a tall slim man dressed in the manner of an American Ambassador, the razor sharp creases of his immaculate black designer suit clearly visible against the bright background. Having meandered round the tennis lawn, the path now took them to the wide steps leading to the terrace where their host was awaiting their arrival. Tom was in front, eager and curious to explore this strange new place but before he could break away he felt a tug on his arm as Wilbur indicated he should fall in behind him as they got to the steps. He obliged and therefore gained the terrace fractionally behind the older man.

Rex Proctor gave Wilbur a warm smile of recognition, the kind of look reserved for old and trusted friends who don't visit often enough. He stepped forward taking

Simon Shinerock

Wilbur's proffered hand with both of his.

'It's good to see you, old friend, and I see you've brought someone with you.'

Without waiting for a reply he turned to Tom and they shook hands formally.

'You must be Tom,' he said with certainty. 'The young Englishman, I'm so glad you could come; tell me what did you do to make such a strong impression on Wilbur? He has told me so much about you, he's normally such a cynic.' Proctor's grey eyes seemed to sparkle mischievously when he asked this question, as if he were gently teasing Wilbur or letting Tom into some kind of private joke.

Tom wasn't sure what to make of any of it, he hadn't been aware of any impression he'd made. He shrugged his shoulders, all he could say was 'I'm pleased to meet you too.' Even this came out wrong, his tone of voice sounding ungracious and peremptory. Thankfully Proctor didn't seem to notice, exuding bonhomie through his every gesture, he motioned the pair to follow him into the house.

Tom hung back for a moment, taking the time to glance round the veranda. He was finding it hard to reconcile the virtual perfection of his surroundings with the scene of desolation he encountered on the beach. Everywhere around the house things had the look of being absolutely right, chosen to be there, in full bloom, even the tone of the colours seemed to be almost too bright, too cheerful. Perhaps it was the exaggerated perfection of everything else that led his eyes to rest on the one thing in the garden that wasn't rosy. In the corner of the veranda, almost hidden from view by the shadow of the low stone wall were two small mounds erupting out of the stone paving. At first he couldn't make out what they were, so he wandered over towards them. As he got closer he noticed more of the mounds scattered round the veranda's outer edge. Some were blind like the first two but others had exploded through the stonework, exposing the underlying cause. He'd never seen anything so disgusting in all his life, the solid stone slabs had been lifted and distorted by an organism of revolting splendour. A fungus, its green and black trunks surrounded by pustular sacks that were splitting in the daylight, weeping a vile yellow custard onto the stone. He would have noticed more detail but the sight stopped him in his tracks, there was no way he was getting any closer to those things than necessary; he turned on his heel and walked quickly after Wilbur and his departed host.

When he got inside, the image of the mushrooms, for that was how he thought of them, was pushed out of his mind. The room he entered was the most magnificent he'd ever seen. The floor was laid with hand painted tiles of exquisite quality, each one a unique piece of art in its own right. Persian rugs, themselves so deep and luxurious they would have graced a Sultan's palace, had been placed carefully so as to divide up the large room into three distinctive areas. The first area was informal, being dominated by a large leather chesterfield settee flanked with matching easy chairs surrounding an ornate coffee table of hand carved ivory. The second was clearly meant for entertainment and dancing. There was a beautiful Bechstein grand piano and a polished mahogany bar, Tom could imagine cocktails being served by a uniformed waiter to groups of well heeled guests while Proctor performed the duties of an attentive host.

The last area could best be described as an office or, study, in that it had a desk and a bookcase as its central features, both of which were obviously antique. Like everything else he saw in the house they were clearly of great value. Wilbur and Proctor were waiting for him by the piano, chatting informally. When he arrived they stopped talking, Proctor looked at him apologetically.

'I couldn't help noticing what you were doing on the veranda. I'm afraid my Island isn't looking her best at present. Quite recently we suffered from a terrible ecological disaster, I wish you could have seen how beautiful things were before. I managed to save the house and garden but there are a few signs that it too was affected, I think you have noticed one of them.'

This frankness was very disarming, it caught Tom off guard and made him feel a little shitty about his earlier negative feelings. He was also curious about exactly what it was that caused the "ecological disaster" and to what species those mushrooms belonged.

'By the look of the beaches it must have been quite a disaster Mr. Proctor, what was it, an oil spillage?'

Proctor flinched slightly as if the mere thought of the disaster was painful too him. When he replied his voice seemed a little strained.

'I don't want to appear unforthcoming in any way but if you don't mind I'd rather not discuss that at present. It took a lot out of me and it will take a long time to put things right, I will put things right though, on that you have my word.'

Proctor seemed to have closed the subject and despite his curiosity Tom decided to back off for the moment.

'Now,' declared Proctor. 'I think it's time we had some breakfast.'

The words acted like a switch, turning on Tom's hunger, Proctor noticed his changed expression at the mention of food and laughed. He turned to Wilbur who was leaning against the piano.

The Dark Lagoon

'I can see that our guest is ravenous.'

With that he took Tom by the arm and led him out of the large impressive reception room with its tall ceiling and expensive features, through a smallish doorway at the back and into an inner hallway. The difference in style was incredible, from twentieth century colonial, it became third century Gothic in character. The corridor could easily have belonged to an early French chateau or medieval castle. It would have been forgivable to think you'd been transported back in time so big was the contrast. There was no natural light in the corridor, but spaced about every three metres or so were oil soaked torches. These gave off an orange and yellow light that flickered constantly, casting weird shadows which danced with a life of their own as they followed Proctor towards the kitchen.

Tom was beginning to wonder if any of this was even happening at all. Perhaps he was really on a 747 heading for Gatwick, sleeping restlessly after a bad aeroplane meal. Maybe he would wake up in a moment to find he'd thrown up in his sleep, maybe all over one of his fellow passengers. He pinched himself to test this theory but was only rewarded by the sharp pain of squeezed flesh. Well if he wasn't dreaming then somehow there had to be an explanation for what he was experiencing. Perhaps after breakfast all would be revealed.

These musings were interrupted as they came to a halt beside a low wooden door. Proctor produced a large key ring and selected a small key which he inserted in the lock. As the door creaked open it crossed Tom's mind that he was being led into a trap; behind the door there would be a set of steep winding stone steps leading to the dungeons; into which he would be thrown and left to rot. The door swung wide open allowing the morning light to spill into the corridor, immediately dispelling any demons hiding in the shadows. They walked through the opening into a large kitchen in the middle of which was a massive wooden table laden with the most mouth-watering assortment of food imaginable.

Maybe Proctor was expecting another twenty or so guests thought Tom as his eyes drifted over the plates of cold meat, seafood and exotic fruits. Any ideas about other guests disappeared when he saw the three place settings at the end of the table, in front of which were the only three chairs in the room.

A massive range held pride of place, flanked by a great oak drainer and a butler's sink. The whole kitchen was a cook's dream and there must have been a team of them hiding somewhere to have prepared this feast. If that was so then they cleared up perfectly before leaving, the whole place was spotless. On the left was an enormous Welsh dresser stocked with crockery and china ornaments. The kitchen had a double aspect with large French doors beside the dresser and at the far end, both overlooked a working garden complete with greenhouses, beds of different herbs and a vegetable patch.

Tom could only suspend his disbelief at the unlikely scene and take his seat beside Wilbur who was already tucking in with gusto. In the middle of the table there was a large coffee pot standing on a cast iron plate. Proctor stretched out and took the pot, filling Tom's earthenware mug with the hot steaming liquid. He offered cream and sugar, which Tom accepted, taking a tentative sip of the coffee, half expecting it to evaporate into nothingness along with the rest of this improbable illusion. Thankfully the coffee was real, it tasted as warm and welcoming as it looked. His head tingled slightly as he drank, his whole body relaxing; despite himself he was beginning to enjoy himself.

In spite of his warmer feelings, Tom ate sparingly, his hunger blunted by the strangeness of his surroundings, sticking to some honey cake and fruit salad in favour of the more exotic looking dishes. If anyone was disappointed by his poor performance, they gave no hint of it. While they were eating Proctor told an implausible tale of how the house had come to be so diverse and multifaceted; as unbelievable as it was, the story made the meal go swiftly and in what seemed no time they were ready to move on.

'I hope you enjoyed your breakfast' said Proctor when Tom had finished his second cup of coffee and his fork had been placed neatly by the side of his empty plate.

'It was great,' said Tom truthfully. The meal had left him totally revived, the aches and pains of his beating had magically disappeared, he felt fit to take on the world.

'Good,' said Proctor, 'I'm so glad you enjoyed it but now you must come, we have serious business to discuss.'

So saying he rose to leave. They returned to the first room, gravitating towards the study where Proctor seated himself behind the antique desk and indicated that Tom should take a seat in the leather visitor's chair opposite. Wilbur didn't sit, he was waiting for an invitation to do so but it didn't come.

'Wilbur, old friend,' said Proctor after a while. 'Would you mind leaving Tom and I alone for a few moments? Perhaps you would enjoy a walk in the grounds, I'm sure we won't be too long.'

Wilbur looked slightly contrite at his dismissal, whatever he felt, he kept it to himself though, casting a quizzical look at Tom before bowing graciously and making his exit. Tom assumed the look was to tell him to watch his manners while alone with Proctor, something he was well minded to do in any case. As for the bow, it was out of place from the usually boorish old man and made him seem faintly ridiculous.

When they were alone Proctor started by making small talk. He asked Tom about his background and ambitions. He skilfully opened up the young man, finding out what made him tick without having to pry or make him feel he was being interviewed. Nevertheless within twenty minutes or so Tom, normally a private character, had told Proctor everything about himself; including things about his relationship with his father he had never discussed with anyone else. He told him about his ambitions for the future and revealed his strengths and weaknesses. Proctor had put him at his ease to such an extent his guard dropped completely. Eventually this part of their meeting came to a natural close. Proctor, who had been resting back in his chair, chin on his right hand, listening attentively, leant forward and picked up an ornament from the desk. He turned the trinket over in his hand before speaking.

'Thank you Tom, you have told me a lot about yourself and given me everything I need to confirm that you are the person I am looking for.'

Tom flushed at this compliment, although he still had no idea why he was there.

Anticipating what must be on Tom's mind, Proctor continued. 'I think it's only fair as you have been so frank and open with me, that I should return the compliment and tell you why I have brought you here. After that I have a proposition to discuss I think will be of great interest to you.'

Again Proctor paused. After a few moments he got to his feet and walked round to the bookcase where he opened up the front to reveal a small but well stocked bar.

The Dark Lagoon

'I know it is still very early in the day but before I start I would like you to join me in a drink. Think of it as my gesture of goodwill, signifying whatever you decide, you and I will still be friends.'

He didn't wait for Tom to agree but turned and produced a crystal decanter containing an almost clear liquid. He removed the stop and poured a measure each into matching whisky glasses. He held each up to the light as if to check they were both at the same level before placing them back on the bar and pulling out a small oddly shaped bottle covered in dust and cobwebs. Tom thought it was black although he could also see the remains of what looked like a parchment label with faded writing on it. Proctor removed the cork from its top and carefully allowed two drops to fall into each glass. The liquid had a green tinge and looked similar in colour and consistency to olive oil, it left the drinks with a light gold hue not unlike ginger ale.

The ceremony complete Proctor returned the bottle and decanter to their original places and closed the bar. Holding the drinks he walked back to his seat, placing one before Tom. It was clear he intended to make a toast; Tom got the message and rose picking up his glass as he did so.

'To a long and successful association.'

Proctor lifted the glass to his lips and drank, throwing back his head as he did so, then placing the empty glass back on the desk his eyes urging Tom to do the same.

For a moment Tom hesitated, looking deeply into those eyes for the first time. In that instant the casual bonhomie, hail fellow well met suavity was stripped away. What he glimpsed were flames of naked desire, the hunger of a voracious predator. If he had obeyed his instincts then he would have run away, prepared to take his chances with the ocean rather than face those eyes. But once again the itch on his cheek flared to the surface, reminding him of Jack's treachery and his desire for revenge. He looked into glass and fancied he could see answers there, answers floating in the swirling gold liquid, forming the letters of words which even now were hiding in the corners of his conscious mind. He felt an overwhelming need to know what those words meant, to own them for himself.

As he drank it was as if their meaning became clear to him, clear and obvious, burning a path into his soul. The effect of the drink was overpowering. It didn't burn like a spirit, it wasn't sour like lemon or bitter like poison. Nevertheless it had him gasping for breath sitting down, his head spinning quicker than if it had been a combination of all these things. Proctor sat waiting, when Tom's head stopped spinning his mind remained open and exposed.

'Thank you for joining me in that,' said Proctor. 'I think we can continue now.' His voice took on an intensity that indicated they were going to get down to business.

'Earlier I said it would take a very long time to repair the damage done to my Island. Well, what I said was true. It is also true that I will need your help.'

Proctor continued

'At least I will need the help of someone of your calibre who agrees to my proposal, that is. Of course I don't expect help for nothing; you will be well rewarded for the part you play; you could even say I will make it possible for you to attain your heart's desire. You may have noticed this place is a little out of the ordinary. For this reason the person I am looking for has to himself be out of the ordinary. The kind of person prepared to do the kinds of things most people can't or won't do to achieve success. Someone of great ambition and determination, it is vital for me to be sure you are that kind of person.'

Proctor had in one masterstroke turned the tables on Tom, from being the one waiting for a proposition on which he was to pass judgement, suddenly everything had changed. He was being tested to see if he was worthy of a great opportunity, unless he did something about it fast it would be withdrawn. Tom's mind raced furiously to find the words he needed to convince Proctor of his worthiness but found none. Inwardly he cursed his awkwardness, his lack of fluency. If it had been Jack being made this offer he wouldn't have been tongue-tied, oh no, Jack would have known exactly what to say, he would have done the deal by now and be on his way to wealth and power. At that moment he hated Jack more than ever, he so wished he could strip him of all his sharpness and luck and possess them for himself.

As if he could read Tom's thoughts, *or control them,* Proctor chose this moment to break the deadlock. He took the ornament he'd been holding earlier and held it up to the light. Tom could see it was a silver chain with a crescent moon just like the one hanging round Jack's neck, the one that up to now he had completely forgotten.

'Did you know,' said Proctor half to himself, 'there are things that happen in this world that men can't explain, will never explain? Powers that go beyond explanation, do you believe that? It doesn't really matter whether you believe it or not, the fact is that such powers do exist, Tom, and they can be controlled. There is a high price to be paid for such power, let's see just how much you are prepared to pay. Imagine for a moment that this small trinket is in actuality a device of just such power, make this leap of faith with me, and believe it can absorb a person's energies good or bad, filter out exactly the parts of a human soul that its owner desires and render them usable for other purposes. I see by your face you think me mad, or that I am perhaps trying to trick you with a fairy tale; never mind though, humour me for just a few moments longer. What if for the past day this thing was worn by your friend Jack? The one who called himself your friend yet betrayed you so completely, first cuckolding you for his whore, then arranging for your humiliating and painful exit. What if during the hours it spent around his neck it was working hard, draining him of all the things set to make him a success in life, of all the things you want for yourself. Now they are within your grasp Tom, all you have to do is stretch out and take them.'

Tom was totally mesmerised by the tale, he had involuntarily moved forward snatching at the chain, not really knowing what he was doing but Proctor snatched the pendant out of his reach.

Proctor hadn't finished yet.

'Before you take it there is something you should know. There can be no sharing such a gift, either you have it or he does, no compromises. It is a harsh thing to take something so precious from someone who was once your friend. Do not do it lightly.'

Now Proctor was finished.

Outrageous and unlikely as it seemed the proposition had real meaning to Tom and he meant to give his answer in all earnestness. On the one hand it was abundantly clear that here was his opportunity to grasp success and power by the throat, to become what he had always dreamed of being. At the same time he would be paying Jack out for his treachery, which after all was what he wanted. So why did he hesitate? He hesitated because basically he was a decent human being and something fundamental within him rebelled against the proposition, it screamed caution, loathing the thought of committing

The Dark Lagoon

an act at least as bad as any done to him and probably by its coldness far worse. That wasn't all. As he looked once again into Proctor's eyes he saw more than the naked flames of desire, he caught a glimpse of the ravenous beast within and the sight chilled him to the core. He knew at that moment that to refuse this proposition was to invite death. In spite of his fear he was a brave man and would in ordinary circumstances have faced any danger, even death, if the cause was worth it but these were no ordinary circumstances.

The bite on his cheek flared red, sending waves of resentment and jealousy through his veins and in full knowledge of what he was doing, he held out his hand to accept Proctor's gift.

Chapter Four

I

Jack couldn't remember the last time he'd slept so deeply. It was like emerging from a very long, very dark tunnel. Once when he was eighteen he had a wisdom tooth removed under full anaesthetic, when he woke up despite his best efforts he couldn't move, it was like his mind was trapped inside an inert body, it was very scary. He heard the dentist talking to the nurse, felt the bib round his neck as blood mixed with sputum dribbled down his chin, yet he couldn't move a muscle nor utter a word. Gradually, slowly, feeling came back and he was able to get up but it took several hours before his strength fully returned.

It was the same this time, except there wasn't anything to account for the condition, which made it a lot more frightening than before. At first he thought he was paralysed completely, even his eyelids refused to open. He could hear a faint drone in the background; the highway, the musty, slightly mildewed smell of the Van reminded him of where he was. Then, slowly, feeling started to come back into his body. It was like his blood supply had been cut off and then suddenly turned back on again just before it was too late. He felt the blood rushing back, bringing with it both the power to move and the most excruciating pins and needles he'd ever felt. He had a sudden urge to break free, although he wasn't in chains, just lying flat on his back fully clothed on one of the benches in the back of the Van. The urge was accompanied by a spasm which started with his left arm, followed by the rest of his body. He must have looked like he was having some kind of fit,

The Dark Lagoon

the end result left him crumpled on the floor, sweating profusely but wide awake.

The thought crossed his mind that he may really have suffered some kind of epileptic fit. He'd seen people have petit mal and grand mal seizures while he was working as nursing auxiliary in a mental home saving the money for his trip. He was told they were caused by electrical disturbances in the brain. Certainly whatever it was he'd experienced seemed similar. For some reason though the thought that he may be sick didn't bother him, he had other things on his mind. If there was anything serious then no doubt it would happen again but a more likely explanation for the experience was the pressure and stress caused by Tom the previous day. The thought of Tom caused a pang of guilt, displacing other considerations. However he felt about his actions or motives was irrelevant now, what was done was done and the consequences would have to be faced. In the meantime though there were other more pressing issues to be dealt with.

It was Monday morning and if he wasn't already, unless he moved his ass he would be late for work. The Van had a clock in the dash showing the time was six thirty, thirty minutes to get to the construction site; he could just make it. The pressure of a full bladder forced him to delay further. Opening up the side door he climbed out and surveyed the empty car park, satisfied it was empty he relieved himself against one of the tyres. Afterwards he felt a lot better, although his throat was parched and sore, not just inside but outside too. He put a hand up to his neck and felt a tender band running all the way round, as if he'd been wearing a red hot chain.

There was no time to contemplate this anomaly; he had to get going. Once he was on the road, the steady drone of the tyres helped him to relax and he started to review the events of the previous day. Sending Tom back home was a hard thing to have done, he felt shitty, things hadn't worked out between them but he knew it was for the best. At the same time he felt elated at the thought of Ruth's arrival in a couple of weeks. With Tom out the picture they would be able to concentrate on one another, it was going to be fantastic, he was so excited at the thought of Ruth's arrival he didn't know how he was going to survive the wait.

There was still one niggle that managed to intrude, Wilbur Kohn. Now that Tom had gone and with Ruth arriving soon, it wouldn't be easy to find the rest of the money to pay for the Van. He'd planned to resign from the construction site and rely on his waiter's job at Danny's place but that didn't look possible now. He'd just have to work two jobs right up to the day before Ruth arrived, at least it would mean he wouldn't have any time to brood. It was a hard regime though. Before the Van he would get up in the morning and ride an old bicycle the two and a half miles to the site where he worked as an unskilled labourer from seven till four in the afternoon. Then he would ride back to the park covered in grime, stop at the pool and do a length fully clothed. Then he would ride to the tent, put on his waiters' clothes and pedal the two and a half miles in the other direction to the restaurant. He had to be at Danny's place by 5.30 p.m. if he wanted anything to eat before his shift started and he wouldn't be back at the tent before midnight.

At least now he had the Van he could drive to work he thought, as he turned into the site entrance. The 'Company' whoever they were, (he'd been told it was a consortium from Miami financed by drug money) were building a new shopping mall; it would be the biggest in the Keys which meant more jobs for local people so no-one really cared where the investment came from. The job was nearly 70% finished though you'd never guess it to look at the place, unless that is you were in the business. All the ground work had been done and the main structures were already up. It was now a question of plumbing in the services, completing internal finishing and laying out the car park.

Jack was in a gang with about five others; it varied a little day to day. The gang boss was called Charlie, a tall rangy man of about thirty five who looked more like forty, a result of heavy drinking and a life spent outside working in the sun. He was a good sort; he liked Jack recognising the fact that he wasn't really cut out to be a labourer, often giving him lighter work to do inside. Jack appreciated this although he knew if he wanted to he could outperform most of the others physically, there was no point in knocking himself out if he didn't have too though.

One day he was required to pitch in on a heavy detail and things hadn't gone so well. They were out in the quad behind the mall fixing long wooden posts into the ground ready to be set in concrete. As ever it was a hot day, a hundred degrees in the shade, as midday arrived the temperature soared even higher. This coupled to the fact that the quad was in direct sunlight and its walls were painted white meant the heat out in the open hit danger levels. Being a limey Jack was the only worker out without a hat. One minute he was holding a post in place while Charlie tapped it with a sledge, the next he was sitting in the shade with a wet towel round his shoulders and it was two hours later. According to Charlie he'd lost it completely, started talking nonsense, babbling deliriously, entertaining everyone with the worst case of sun stroke they'd seen in quite a while. He could easily have lost his job that day but Charlie had looked out for him, making sure he wasn't noticed by anyone important, since then there was a sort of unspoken bond of loyalty between them.

The site office was a large trailer situated in the middle of the car park around which all the workers were now congregating in groups. Jack brought the Van to a halt in a space opposite the trailer, no-one taking any notice of him or the Van despite its strange appearance. He got out and joined Charlie's gang who were busily talking and smoking just a few yards away.

Charlie nodded at him in acknowledgement as he joined the group, then continued to explain the day's detail. It sounded like heavy work, they would be laying out some large wooden beams at different locations around the car park. These would act as the perimeter wall for flower beds that would surround the car park's street-lamps. For once Jack was quite looking forward to the exertion which would provide a way of cleansing his mind of thoughts of Tom and stop him from feeling homesick for Ruth.

Charlie was in the middle of the briefing when the back window of the trailer opened suddenly. Through the gap a face appeared, it was huge, florid and perspiring with wide bloodshot eyes. It was the face of an escaped maniac; it was also the face of Carl the site boss-in-chief, a man seldom seen or heard and feared more for it.

'Hey Charlie,' the face called loudly, getting the attention of every man present. 'Hey Charlie, didn't you tell Jack?'

Charlie looked at Jack, then back at Carl, clearly confused by the question.

He replied quickly nonetheless.. 'No Carl, I haven't told Jack anything, why should I have told him something?'

Carl looked put out, as if his patience were being strained to the limit. 'Charlie, you mean you haven't told Jack he's got to hit the road?'

The Dark Lagoon

On hearing these words Charlie's jaw dropped open and he was silent, seemingly unable to respond.

Jack however had no such inhibition and spoke out impulsively. 'No Carl, Charlie didn't tell me anything.' His voice sounded indignant and a threatening hush descended on the site as all present waited for Carl's response.

Carl turned from Charlie to the young man and looked at him as if he were an unwelcome cockroach at a Christmas dinner.

'Well I'm telling you now,' he boomed.

The head disappeared as fast as it had appeared as he slammed the window shut and there was silence. Eventually Charlie spoke, he looked apologetic and ashamed but nevertheless he wasn't going to put his own job in jeopardy.

'I'm real sorry Jack but I'm afraid you're gonna have to do like Carl says and hit the road.'

Jack was bemused by all this; in a way he was relieved because it meant he no longer had the dilemma of whether to keep the two jobs going but he was also angry. There was no earthly reason why he should be dismissed at all and certainly not in this humiliating fashion. Others may be frightened of Carl but he was going to go into that trailer, pick up his final cheque and give the fat cocaine snorting bastard a piece of his mind.

Charlie must have caught a glimpse of recklessness in Jack's expression because he put a hand on his shoulder as if to steady him down

'Best to take things easy Jack; no sense doing anything stupid is there?'

Jack heard the advice, knew it was well meant and probably sensible but he ignored it anyway. He brushed the friendly hand aside and strode over to the trailer.

There were three aluminium steps up to the trailer door which opened inwards to the reception area. In this space was a drawing board with a plan of the site, to the right was a small kitchen and to the left was Carl's private office. There were a few men and women already in the trailer; Jack recognised a couple of them as Carl's heavies. They were meant to be security guards but everyone knew their main function was to keep the staff in check and make sure industrial relations never got "out of hand". They smirked at Jack as he walked in, having just witnessed his embarrassing dismissal. Jack ignored them and addressed himself to the dowdy looking woman smoking a cigarette while shuffling some papers over by the photocopier.

'Denise, I need to pick up my cheque.'

Denise turned from the copier, ash falling from her cigarette as she turned and looked at Jack suspiciously.

'You'll have to ask Carl about that, He's in his office but if I were you I'd come back in the morning he's in a real bad mood, you know what I mean.'

As she said this she made a gesture with her empty hand, making a pinch with her index finger and thumb, then raising them to her nostrils and taking two quick snorts. This warning wasn't lost on Jack who knew Carl was a coke head, everyone knew it. He half suspected a lot of the rumours were self publicity though; after all it must be easier to control a gang of potentially violent labourers if they think you're crazy on drugs most of the time.

Jack knew if he backed down now then Carl would hear of it, know he was intimidated and probably decide to hold out on him. If he was ever to get his money he had to act now.

'Thanks for the advice Denise but I think I'd rather sort things out now thanks.'

The woman took a draw of her cigarette and shrugged her shoulders.

'Suit yourself,' she said and turned back to the photocopier.

He stared at the closed door separating him from Carl's office. He was still angry but pragmatism was starting to creep into his thinking. If he was going to give the man a piece of his mind it was best to get the cheque in his hand first. He knocked on the flimsy door, waited a moment then knocked again. There was a short pause and then Carl's voice could be heard bellowing through the wall.

'Come in,' he commanded

Jack turned the handle, the door swung open and he went inside. Carl was sitting directly in front behind a desk that looked too large for the small office as did the man behind it. Even sitting you could see he was a big man, big in every way, tall, overweight with oversized features. He had frizzy light coloured hair which was already on the way out, his hands which looked the size of hams were spread out on the desk.

'What do you want? I thought I just fired you,' He said when he saw who it was interrupting his peace. Jack tried to sound passive and determined at the same time when he replied.

'Yes Mr. Gates, that's right you did but before I leave I thought I might pick up my cheque.'

Carl seemed to be waiting for Jack to continue and say some more, give him some ammunition to fire back and get rid of him. When there was nothing he had no choice but to consider the request. In some ways it would be a good thing to get rid of the kid today, he didn't want him turning up to collect his money when the people from Miami were there. They might think he'd failed to carry out instructions; no it was better to give him his cheque and tie things up nice and neat.

'OK kid, you can have your money.' He picked up the internal phone and spoke in a low tone to Denise. There was an awkward wait before the secretary came in with the cheque already filled in. She presented it to Carl for signature and walked out leaving the door open.. He checked the amount, signed the cheque and stretched out a hand to give it to Jack who took it and insolently checked the amount; it was $220, minimum wages for a week and it was correct.

So far everything had gone remarkably smoothly, so much so Jack couldn't resist a parting shot.

'Just one thing before I go Carl.'

Carl looked up from the desk where he'd started to shuffle some papers around officiously. He was a slow man as befitted his size so Jack had plenty of time to continue.

'I thought I'd say you could use a lesson in manners; we don't treat people like this in England, maybe because we are a bit more educated than you are over here, a little less ignorant.'

He felt the adrenaline begin to pump as he delivered this speech; his muscles tightened ready for flight rather than fight. At first he thought he was going to get away scot-free. Carl didn't appear to be reacting at all, then he noticed the big man's lower lip begin to shake. It was if this small tremor set off a chain reaction that slowly spread through the gigantic body gaining force and fury on the way. It was like watching the start of an earthquake.

The Dark Lagoon

Within a few seconds Carl's whole body was trembling and rocking, his face had turned puce; the desk seemed to be bouncing up and down on his knees. Without warning he erupted like a volcano, standing upright, throwing the desk onto its back and showing an unexpected agility and turn of speed as he leapt over the desk hands outstretched for the boy's throat. Jack, though stunned at the site boss's reaction, just managed to step back out of range in time.

As he put on this remarkable display of naked aggression, Carl was simultaneously shouting the names of his henchmen at the top of his voice. Jack just had time to see them grabbing pickaxe handles off the floor as he fled from the office to the relative safety of the Van. He didn't know how he managed to escape the trailer unharmed but once inside the Van, the impact of the situation hit him, fear turning his fingers to sticks of dough and his legs to jelly. First he couldn't get his hand in his pocket, then the key wouldn't come out, he was still struggling unsuccessfully to get the bloody thing into the ignition when the passenger door opened and Carl's huge head poked itself into the cabin. He still looked crazy but there was something restrained about his expression that immediately calmed Jack down. Carl pushed his way further inside, stopping short of getting in.

'I'm real sorry about what happened in there Jack. You've got to understand I've got an image to keep up round here. I respect you for speaking your mind but what you did was very foolish, I might have had to kill you, understand?'

Jack nodded co-operatively; he could see there was more.

'That's good. Now I want you to listen to this carefully. You better go now and don't come back. If I ever see you around here again there won't be a second chance, you understand me don't you?'

Jack nodded again. By now he'd stopped shaking long enough to get the key in the ignition, he turned it and breathed a sigh of relief when the straight six caught first time sounding a lot more defiant than he felt.

'I'll not be seeing you around then Jack.'

It was a statement of fact and Jack nodded in confirmation. Carl withdrew, standing back and watching with his thugs as the marked English boy piloted his Van out of the site car park and back onto the highway.

II

Jack drove towards Pennycamp park, a State nature reserve about eight miles up the road. He'd never been there before but often noticed the signs. Now, with nowhere else to go, the place just seemed to leap into his mind out of nowhere. Once at the park he drove along the main thoroughfare which would have ended in the main car park and visitors' centre. The last thing he wanted was to find himself in the middle of a busy tourist area so when he saw a narrow track off to his left he decided to follow it. The track meandered around for about half a mile, it was quite overgrown, as if it had seen little traffic for some time. Eventually it opened out into a parking lot near a small beach, bordered by a sea water pool, separated from the ocean by a man-made barrier. It had been intended as a safe play area for families and small children but had never really caught on, as a result it now offered the privacy and seclusion Jack felt he so badly needed. Once out of the Van he was able to stretch his legs and enjoy the sunshine and scenery for the first time since he'd arrived in the Keys, the feeling was great and he spent the rest of the day sunbathing on the beach and taking the occasional swim. By the time he had to get ready to leave for the restaurant he felt refreshed and ready to take on whatever challenges still lay ahead. He'd also made a decision. Unless he was forced to leave, he would spend the remaining two weeks left to him before Ruth arrived in this very spot, which already felt more like home than the campsite had done in three months.

He was whistling and singing as he guided the Van into an empty space in the staff parking area behind Danny's place. As he got out he could hear music coming from the kitchen; it was 'Hey Jude' by the Beatles, it was Charlene's favourite song.. He walked through the back entrance which led to the kitchen and sure enough there she was with her tape player going at a gentle volume, humming along to the music. As Jack walked by she stopped briefly to give him a dreamy smile.

Danny's place was a typical privately owned seafood diner. It specialised in Florida lobster tails and two types of clam chowder. Every evening there was an early bird special to drag in the extra customers. It offered fantastic value and usually attracted older people or single businessmen passing through. There was a cocktail happy hour between six and seven where you could have any cocktail you liked for a buck fifty. Jack looked forward to happy hour as he often got asked to do the bar duty if the owner was busy. He enjoyed mixing up (and occasionally tasting) the drinks as well as chatting to the early evening drinkers, many of whom came back just to see the amusing English barman. He learned how to turn on the charm just enough to rake in maximum tips. Most of the time though he just looked after his station, concentrating on entertaining and serving his guests.

He quickly established that being from England, or more to the point having an English accent, gave him an edge when competing for the highest tips. This combined with his ability to act the extrovert on demand meant he usually ended up with a lot more dollars at the end of the night than the other servers. The wages were almost incidental, about twenty nine dollars a night; it was the tips where the real money was. On a good night he could take home anything up to an additional hundred and seventy dollars. He tried to conceal his success from his fellow workers but it was no good, they only had to look at the cash left behind at the tables he served to see what was happening. After a few weeks his station began to mysteriously shrink, he got the message and toned things down a little, after all there was no sense in becoming a victim of his own success.

That evening as usual, he started by making himself something to eat from the buffet left outside the kitchen for that purpose. One day he promised himself a lobster, although he suspected this would have to wait till it was time to quit. He was eating his soup when the head waitress Rhoda walked over to the table. They exchanged hellos as usual but Jack could sense there was something else she wanted to say. She was shifting uncomfortably from foot to foot, looking over his head avoiding any form of eye contact. This went on for some time until he finally decided to help her out.

'Rhoda, do you have something to say to me, or are you demonstrating some kind of new dance?'

In spite of herself Rhoda laughed out loud. She was a slim woman with a good figure and a handsome though not a pretty face. She wore a lot of makeup, which actually had the reverse of the intended effect and made her look older than her thirty six years. The smile shed the years instantly, revealing a warm person with a good heart. You could see that whatever it was she needed to talk to

Jack about was causing genuine distress. Eventually though her jaw stiffened, as if she'd finally come to terms with what she had to do.

'I've got to talk to you Jack. There's been a change of plan. You see there's this other waitress; Eileen. She used to work here last season and we thought she wasn't coming back. The thing is though she is coming back and she has children Jack, you know what I'm trying to say don't you?'

After the morning's fun and games he had a fair idea what she was driving at. At this stage though he wasn't going to let on, if she had news for him she'd have to deliver it herself, he was damned if he was going to do the job for her. Rhoda looked at him pleadingly but seeing he wasn't going to help her out she continued.

'There's been complaints too Jack. From the kitchen. They say they can't read your writing, on Friday there were two dinners sent back because of it.'

At this Jack could contain himself no longer

'That's crap Rhoda and you know it. Those dinners were sent back because the kitchen got it wrong, not me. My writing may be untidy but it's as readable as anyone else's, readable enough to get me a degree, never mind hold down a waiter's job. Get to the point Rhoda, am I fired or what?'

The middle aged woman's shoulders sagged at this outburst, for a moment he thought she would cry. This made him feel guilty, if he was being fired, it wasn't Rhoda's decision, she liked him and clearly hated having to give him the news.

'I'm afraid you are Jack. I'm sorry, if it means anything, me and the other girls think it's a real shame.' She paused and put a hand into her apron, pulling out an envelope which she offered to him.

'Here take it, it's not much but maybe it will help a little.'

Now it was his turn to feel bad. OK he was being fired but these women, they really needed to work, they were working mothers most of them, barely living above subsistence. For them to make a collection for him they must have been really upset. A young waiter getting canned was hardly an earth shattering event; it happened all the time without inspiring this kind of reaction.

He was upset at the news but again his natural reaction was to roll with the punches. What had angered him at the site was the humiliating way he was treated, here it was the opposite and he felt moved by the gesture.

'Look Rhoda, I appreciate what you and the others have done but I can't take your money, you work too hard for it. I've really enjoyed working here but perhaps it's time to move on. Anyhow, I was planning to leave in a couple of weeks, so not much harm done. Cheer up it could be a lot worse, I could be staying.'

He smiled and waved the envelope away. Rhoda looked relieved and forced the packet into his hands, bending down and kissing him on the cheek. As she came close Jack smelt her perfume for the first time, her breasts were close, he could hear her breathing shallow and fast, the warmth of her arousing him involuntarily. He knew that if he responded now they could part more than just good friends; the temptation to make a pass was strong, he remained still though, being careful not to encourage or offend until she pulled back and the moment passed.

He got up and took Rhoda's hand, shaking it gently. There was no point in hanging around. He had no pay to pick up and he didn't fancy another confrontation that day. He didn't even fancy saying his goodbyes to his other erstwhile colleagues; it seemed a bit futile somehow.

Some twist of fate had decreed that his era as a worker in the Keys had come to an end Who was he to resist? It was probably for the best anyway. As he went back through the kitchens no-one seemed to notice his leaving, even Charlene, humming to the tune of *'Let It Be'* paid him no attention as he walked past her, out of the back door, on his way to the Van.

III

The next two weeks passed Jack by as if they were a dream. A dream in which he was living on a desert island, spending his time swimming or reading or sunbathing, Rarely going anywhere or talking to anyone. He often forgot to eat and as a result lost weight, going down to less than 140 pounds for the first time since he was sixteen.

By the time Ruth was due to arrive he was so brown and skinny he was hardly recognisable. His hair had grown long, the extra weight pulling out the curls, framing his face and hiding the slightly gaunt look that gradually made its appearance, especially around his eyes.

During this time Jack made no attempt to contact Wilbur. He knew he should, he knew that as every day went by it would get more difficult to explain why he hadn't been in touch. Somehow though the days slipped by and although he kept meaning to call by and see him he never did. Eventually on the day Ruth and his parents were due to arrive he finally decided to telephone Wilbur. First thing in the morning he walked to the public pay-phone at the park's visitor centre to make the call. He looked in the phone book and sure enough there he was listed under W. Kohn 823457. Now he had the number, a great reluctance came over him. Maybe he should forget it, take the Van and go to Miami, Wilbur had probably forgotten about him anyway, he knew this wasn't true even as the thought occurred to him. No, *Wilbur was out there looking for him, he wanted his Van back and he wanted him back, he could feel it.*

There wasn't anything else for it. He would have to make the call and face the music. He'd spent so much time on his own lately; he was worried for the first time about his ability to communicate what he wanted to say. He rehearsed his argument in his head one more time. He would tell Wilbur his family were arriving for Christmas, thank him for all his help, then try and negotiate a discount off the Van. If Wilbur wouldn't play ball he had a fallback position all worked out. He would say he had decided to return to England in a few weeks with Ruth. Wilbur could keep the money and the Van in return for letting him use it until he left.

Feeling a little more prepared and therefore confident he made the call. The phone rang once, twice, three times, he began to hope there was no-one home but then there was a click and Wilbur's voice was grating into the ear-piece.

'Hello,' he challenged. 'Who is that?'

It wasn't much but it was enough to send Jack into a spasm of indecision. He tried desperately to recall his carefully thought out introduction to no avail. The silence was getting longer; he almost decided to hang up when Wilbur spoke again.

'Jack, is that you? If it's you Jack talk to me.'

There was no going back now,

'Yes Wilbur, it's me, I'm sorry I haven't been in touch,

things just got a little difficult that's all. I've still got the Van and it isn't damaged.'

So the conversation had begun. For a while it stayed on track as well. Wilbur let Jack talk, grunting gruffly at the appropriate moments. When he finished Jack even felt quite positive that he would go along with him. When it came, his actual reaction therefore was an even greater shock.

'Jack, I've listened to you,' Wilbur's voice was low and threatening. 'Now you're going to listen to me. You're in real trouble Jack. Not with me, not for taking the Van. I'm talking about real trouble. Your friend Tom, he's put you into something so bad I can't even tell you about it. I can help you though but you've got to do exactly what I say.'

Wilbur paused to make sure he still had the boy's attention. Jack was bemused by what he heard; his first reaction being to assume Wilbur had flipped. He wanted to shout him down, insist the nonsense stopped but he knew Wilbur well enough by now to know if he did that they would end up having a massive argument; so he waited to see what would come next.

'I don't know if I told you this before, but I have a son, he's about your age, good looking kid. Shame is we fell out, he got in trouble, just like you. I tried to help but he wouldn't let me, we ended up having a row, falling out; that was two years ago and I haven't seen him since. The thing is I don't want that to happen to you Jack, I want to protect you. You must come here now with the Van, you've got to tell your folks something's come up and you won't be able to see them, it's the only way I can help you. Are you listening to me Jack?'

Jack wasn't listening though, he'd heard enough. He'd

always suspected Wilbur was a kook and now he had absolute proof. The only question was, would Wilbur leave him alone when he rejected him? For he knew he must reject the absurd offer there and then. If he agreed to go to the house he would just get sucked further into Wilbur's paranoid fantasies, if he was going to break away, it was now or never.

'I'm listening to you but I don't understand what you're telling me. Before you try to explain, I don't want to understand either. My family are arriving soon and so is my fiancee. I don't know what's given you the impression that I would consider letting them down for anything but whatever it was it was wrong. I think it's better that we call it a day, I'm sorry about the Van but you can have it back in a few days, I won't run off with it. If you want to contact me you can leave a message at the Eden Roc Hotel, that's where my parents will be staying. If I don't hear from you I'll leave the Van at your house in about three weeks.'

There was silence at the other end of the line,

'Wilbur, are you still there?' said Jack.

But there was a silent click, he'd hung up, leaving Jack with an uneasy feeling that matters between them weren't settled yet.

'*Are you stupid? Why did you tell him about the Eden Roc?*' admonished the inner voice and for once Jack heard the criticism clearly and couldn't help agreeing.

There are some feelings so strong they can drive out all others, on the way back to the Van his feeling of unease were gradually displaced by eager anticipation at the thought of Ruth's arrival. He spent the rest of the morning sun bathing and swimming as usual, looking in astonishment at his virtually black stomach and smiling

The Dark Lagoon

at the thought of her face when she saw him. At about three thirty he started to clean up the Van, making everything as neat and tidy as possible. He'd even bought a can of air freshener especially for the purpose, it was called 'Ocean Breeze' and he sprayed it liberally into all the Van's nooks and crannies. Satisfied he'd made a good job he got ready himself, putting on his best jeans and a short sleeved blue silk shirt. He looked at himself in the Van's mirror, no zits, that was good, very brown that was OK too. He looked closer and noticed the strain round his eyes. Oh well no-one's going to notice that, he thought. Then he saw the ring of white scar tissue round his neck, what the hell was that? He'd never noticed it before, then he remembered the burning he felt round his neck on the day he arrived at Pennycamp Park. It was a mystery, that's what it was, something strange to talk about with Ruth and his parents. This thought reminded him he had to get to the airport. It was only four thirty and there was still plenty of time but he wasn't taking any chances with being late.

A few minutes later the Van pulled out onto the highway heading for the airport. He arrived over an hour before the plane touched down which meant he had to wait the best part of another hour before Ruth and his parents emerged through the Customs gate. He didn't mind though, now he was so close to being united with Ruth time seemed to have speeded up. He was euphoric, if there had been an earthquake, or a bomb, he probably wouldn't even have noticed. When eventually Ruth did appear it was like walking into a waking dream as they ran into each other's arms, kissing shamelessly in front of the anonymous crowds.

That night was the most amazing of his life. He felt just a little ashamed he paid so little attention to his parents especially since they'd travelled such a long way to see him. They didn't seem to mind though, leaving the young lovers to enjoy each other's company. After dinner at the 'Roc' Jack and Ruth retired to their hotel where they spent the night catching up on the time they had missed away from one another. In the morning they got up late, he'd promised to show Ruth the town, so they dressed and went downstairs for breakfast, after which they left the hotel and went to where Jack had parked the Van. It was gone.

Without having to guess he knew what had happened. Wilbur had come along in the night and stolen it back. For some reason he couldn't care less, it was only an old Van and compared to what he had with Ruth it was an insignificant triviality. She seemed more upset about its disappearance than he did, after he told her all about Wilbur though, she changed her mind and the subject.

Wilbur and the Van behind them, the pair went off hand in hand towards the Eden Roc to meet his parents. The four of them spent Christmas together, Jack's parents returning to England on Boxing Day, leaving the young couple another three weeks to spend alone as they wished. It was a magical time for both of them with only one sinister incident interfering with their happiness.

They 'd left Miami and gone to Fort Lauderdale, it was easy finding a small hotel; the season was over so they had the usually busy place virtually to themselves. One day Jack decided he would like to try surfing, he'd been watching the surfers for a few days and it looked fantastic. The waves seemed manageable and the hotelier's son lent him a board.

When he and Ruth wandered down to the beach one sunny afternoon there was no portent to warn them of impending catastrophe, no sign to read that could have stopped them in their tracks. Unless it was the fact that

The Dark Lagoon

for some reason there were no other surfers out that day, but as they were mostly local lads and it was a weekday they were probably still at school or work. Ruth waited on the beach as Jack paddled the board out to the breakers that started about fifty metres off shore. He found they were a lot bigger and more challenging close up, nevertheless he was soon engrossed in the challenge of getting through the surf and out beyond the break where he could plan his first attempt at riding a wave.

Perhaps it was the physical challenge that distracted him so he neither heard Ruth's warning shouts, nor noticed the dark clouds rolling in with the ocean mist until it was too late. From being faced with waves the size of a man in sunny calm conditions, he suddenly found himself in the middle of a thick mist, unable even to see the shore, the wind howling around him, whipping the ocean into a frenzy of destruction. What he faced now were no longer small hills of water but vast angry mountains. The first one he managed to paddle up the front of, hoping there would be a respite on the other side but what he faced was an even larger wall of water swollen to breaking point. Somehow he kept his head and kept paddling, reaching the crest as the massive wave was about to break. He managed to push the board through the white water at the top, virtually surfing down its back into an ominous dark sink. As he reached the bottom and looked up, there was the biggest wave he'd ever seen in his life towering over thirty feet above him. He couldn't help gasping in amazement and fear; pausing for a split second a he did so. By the time he resumed his paddling it was too late to reach the top before the colossus broke and it was too late to dive under hoping he could hold his breath until he reached the other side.

The thought that the surf board now presented a real and present danger raced through his mind. If he was to have any chance of survival he must try and fling the board as far away from himself as possible. Luckily there was no leash attaching the board to his ankle, if there had have been he would have been in even worse trouble. His next thought was to use the technique he learned diving to hold his breath; he was going to need every last second. Summoning up every last ounce of self control he possessed, he continued to paddle up the wave while exhaling in short bursts, by the time he started to inhale he was nearly at the top and the wave had begun to fall beyond the vertical. He just had enough time to glimpse the ocean beyond before the wave collapsed on top of him.......it was clear and flat.

He remembered being pummelled against the ocean floor and held there for what seemed like an age. Then as if it had tired of trying to crush him to death, the wave grabbed hold of his body, spinning it round and round like a two year old child on some insane fairground ride. This pounding continued until his lungs felt like they would burst. He'd tried to stay in the foetal position, making himself as small a target as possible for rocks and debris, now in desperation he stretched out, not really knowing if his legs were pointing up or down. Miraculously his feet touched bottom and he pushed off with all his remaining strength, bursting through the surface close to the shore but still caught up in a vicious rip tide. The first thing he saw was Ruth standing near to the ocean desperately looking for him, in her hands she held her rosary, when the storm hit and she'd realised Jack was in trouble she took it out to pray. It seemed her prayers were answered because although it was a fight, the worst was over; he managed to get back to shore and crawl up the beach on his hands and knees.

Ruth saw him immediately and started to help him up the beach. His whole body was shaking and even with her help he could only just stagger clear of the raging ocean before dropping to his knees and collapsing exhausted onto the sand. Even as the young lovers reached safety, the weather was clearing unnaturally fast, as if the ocean had made a personal attack on Jack and now he had escaped there was no longer any point to the storm. The giant swell was calming down, the vicious wind dropping to a gentle breeze and the black clouds were dispersing, giving way to fluffy white candyfloss scudding across a perfect blue sky. Ruth began to shake, not with fear for herself but fear for her man. She looked at Jack with questions in her eyes. What had he done to excite such hate from the elements? Who was it that was behind these dark omens? She resolved to keep her questions to herself and to stand between Jack and whatever evil forces wanted to claim him.

Chapter Five

I

Tom was unhappy, he was sitting behind one of the most important desks in the Shapiro Corporation but he was still unhappy. He wasn't used to feeling this way and he didn't want to get used to it. Unfortunately there was no getting away from the facts, he'd messed up big time. Sure there were risks associated in trading commodities on the international markets, everyone knew that. There was also a line that a trader only crossed if he was prepared to risk everything, including his career and possibly his freedom as well. Somehow he'd inadvertently crossed that line and he still didn't know how it could have happened.

He'd hardly moved for almost thirty minutes, his almost legendary powers of concentration completely focused on his predicament, looking at all the possibilities, searching for a solution. It was the kind of ability that had on countless past occasions left his peers baffled and beaten as he pulled off yet another financial coup, developed yet another clever strategy where none seemed apparent. Quick minded, thorough, dedicated certainly, almost oriental in his inscrutability but not impulsive, so how on earth could he have made such a stupid mistake? There had to be an explanation, a way out.

His ego had never been small but success had allowed it to grow and mutate into an unpleasant arrogant thing that now almost completely controlled him. He no longer remembered how he had become successful or where he came from, he had long ago bought his own PR and saw himself as being in possession of invincible talent, limitless stamina, not a normal person at all and therefore not subject to a normal person's weaknesses, like fear, self doubt and most certainly not to panic. So why were his hands all clammy, why was his pulse racing as his stomach churned and his sphincter twitched treacherously? Maybe it was the meal he had last night, Indian food never agreed with him, or maybe it was something else he hadn't thought about, yes that was it, there was a conspiracy, he'd been set up, they were out to get him but he would out-smart them all just like always.

The phone rang and he leapt to his feet so quickly he smashed his right knee painfully into the desk top. Before he could stop himself he let out a strangled cry, a sound which contained as much frustration and anger as pain, but underlying everything else the sound was pitiful, the sound of a helpless baby, moaning for its mother from the deserted nest.

Startled as he was he knew he couldn't ignore the phone for long. Funny really, after all the phone wasn't his master, it was only a servant, there to do its master's bidding but now the servant was demanding attention, enjoying its moment of supremacy.

'Who is it Sonia?' He held the receiver to his right ear, he was damned if he knew how it got there. He was pleasantly surprised at how normal his voice sounded, perhaps it wasn't so bad, maybe he could sort things out after all.

'Is everything all right, Mr. Kidman? You sound upset.' Sonia Rubenstein had a great voice, it was sultry and low, it conjured up a heavenly body and a generous nature, there was depth in that voice, strength.

'Yes Sonia I'm fine, who is it?'

There was a pause while Sonia considered her boss's reply, there was something wrong all right she was sure of that, he'd been acting strangely all day, no outgoing calls, no coffee, something was going down and she was determined it wouldn't take her with it.

'OK then, there's a man on the phone who wants to talk to you, I asked which company he's from but he says you know him, if you ask me he sounds strange.'

Tom was beginning to regain his composure, he was also starting to get irritated.

'No one did ask you Sonia, now who is it?'

Sonia bit her lip, the bastard was definitely rattled but there was no point in pushing too hard, better to be patient and see how things developed, she'd seen traders go down before, she knew the signs and they were all there today, all pointing at Tom Arsewipe Kidman.

'He says his name is Proctor, Rex Proctor.'

For a moment he stood transfixed, as if the name alone had exerted a powerful force over him, poisoning his system, causing his stomach already acidic with stress to rise up against him in a stream of bile. He choked violently and for a moment thought he was going to be sick but the expected release didn't follow, leaving his throat burning and sore.

'Just tell him I'm in a meeting.' he rasped.

Sonia's usual killer instinct was temporarily replaced by real concern for her boss who seemed in genuine distress.

'OK I will, shall I get his number?'

Her question went unanswered, the line was dead but when she returned to the call to give the stranger the polite brush off he'd already disconnected.

Tom slumped behind his desk. What was happening? First his whole career turns to shit and then a ghost from

The Dark Lagoon

the past comes back to haunt him, what was happening? Rex Proctor, the last time he saw Proctor was four years ago and such was the effect of the meeting he'd blocked it from his memory ever since. But now the thin veil of self imposed amnesia was lifting and he was being forced to remember things which he still wanted to forget, things which didn't fall into his world of explainable materialism.

It was as if in this moment of truth the real Tom Kidman was also suddenly revealed, the real Tom Kidman still only twenty five, only a child. With all the trappings and responsibilities of success stripped away he was vulnerable again, susceptible to human weaknesses; fear of failure, fear of not fitting in, of being rejected and relegated to the status of an also ran; a nearly man along with all the other nearly men who nearly made it and didn't. There was no way he was going to let it happen, he would do anything to keep what he had, anything!

He'd never really been a user, not seriously, yes he'd taken cocaine before, mainly so that he didn't seem odd or prissy in front of his fashionable friends but being honest he'd never felt the need for the stuff. So it came as a surprise that now he was under real pressure there was a sudden yearning for the drug. He knew that if he took a snort he would feel better for a while and he also knew that the effects would be short lived. The urge to do it started to grow in him as he sat there, he hated wallowing in self pity and the cocaine would give him a boost so where was the harm? He reached into the top drawer of his desk and removed a small velvet pouch from which he removed a silver key, he took an involuntary look around the office before carefully locating the concealed lock beneath the desk base.

Inside the compartment there were a variety of articles, a computer disk, a few papers, some bearer bonds and a cheap plastic bag containing a small quantity of white powder. He didn't see himself as one of those pretentious climbers who no doubt kept their stuff in a specially designed expensive case along with a solid silver inlaid coke spoon, in fact the only reason he had a supply at all was it was sometimes rude not to. His hands were beginning to sweat as he poured the coke onto the desk, there was no risk of Sonia barging in and catching him because she had gone to lunch and no one else would dare come in unannounced. Somewhat clumsily he formed the powder into two jagged lines and hastily bent down and snorted first with one then the other nostril. The hit was immediate as usual, he felt a great surge of confidence and power flooded his mind, he took a deep breath and rose to his feet unable to comprehend what had bothered him earlier. There was a solution and he would find it, nothing could stand in his way and nothing would.

The brightness of his cocaine-affected vision distracted him from the fact that his office had begun to alter around him. The sophisticated lighting was set up to create a natural feel, not too bright and synthetic and not too dim and depressing - the ideal environment for the successful executive to function at peak efficiency - but something was absorbing the light, either that or somehow overshadowing it. In the corner of the room the heavy drapes were tied back from the windows; although they were never used their fullness was a testament to the affluence of their corporate owner, dark and opulent as they were they provided an ideal hiding place for a voyeur or a thief. It wasn't however any ordinary thief that concealed himself in the velvet folds.

The Dark Lagoon

II

He was starting to lose the initial rush of his fix but he'd never before experienced the pressure he was feeling in the back of his neck, it grew quickly until he could think about nothing else. It soon became clear that the pressure was not without purpose, which was to turn his attention away from his concerns and towards the changes taking place around him. His eyes were drawn towards the corner of the room and the heavy drapes which seemed themselves to be changing shape before him. He cast an involuntary eye upwards expecting the lights to have failed but no, they were still working, it was just that the light was unable to penetrate the deepening gloom coming from the drapes. The pressure in his head was still increasing, he was no longer aware of any further changes in the office, pain took away his vision. Just as it felt like his head must explode he lost consciousness.

Awakening, his first thought was the cocaine had been spiked, that bastard Raoul sold him bad stuff, he could have died. The pain had gone and his head felt clear again, so why was the office still so dim, why did he feel a presence in the room, although he couldn't see who it was he knew he wasn't alone.

Rex Proctor emerged from the drapes like an old time magician reappearing after performing a time-honoured illusion. He stood before Tom Kidman looking exactly the same as he had the last time they met.

'How are you, Tom? Its been a long time, I hope you didn't mind me dropping in on you like this but I phoned and your secretary said you were busy.'

Proctor's, presence brought back memories Tom had been suppressing for four years, memories he could no longer ignore.

'What do you want, Proctor? We did our deal, we have nothing left to discuss so why don't take yourself out of here and haunt someone else, I have important things to do.'

'So it would appear.' Proctor's expression remained impassive as he listened to Tom's greeting, but now it took on an air of concern mixed with patient understanding for the impoliteness of a friend in trouble.

'You don't understand, I'm here to help you, help straighten things out. Didn't I help before? I can do it again if you let me.'

Tom knew that no one could help him, the trouble he was in couldn't be hidden, it was only a matter of time, probably hours at most before he was found out and made to pay for his indiscretions. Yet he also knew that Proctor spoke the truth, he could help him if he said he could but like last time there would be a price and this time it would be even higher than selling out his best friend.

'What's the matter, Tom? You don't look glad to see me, I would have thought you would at least want to hear my proposition before you reject it and bravely face the music.'

Tom's voice was husky with anger and frustration, for years he'd been hiding from himself, trying to pretend that what he'd done wasn't anything, that it didn't happen, but now he could ignore it no longer.

'You made me betray my best friend, how can you say you're here to help, you are evil, a destroyer and I don't want any part of you or your bargains ever again.'

He felt power returning to his body and decision to his mind, he reached for the phone intent on calling security and having this ghoul thrown out of the building. As his hand closed around the receiver it was as if other hands were closing around his throat, he managed to hit the security button but by the time a voice came on the line it was too late, Proctor was back in control.

'Mr. Kidman, can I help you sir?'

It was Max Kopesky chief of daytime security. Tom wanted to tell him to get up there as fast as he could and to come armed but all he could manage was to say everything was OK, he he'd hit the security extension by mistake.

'Tom, I think you should be a little more respectful, after all without me you wouldn't be here, you would be a nothing, I created you remember?'

Tom's head was swimming again, Proctor's words burned him with the fire of guilt, they stung his soul and made his spirit writhe. Yet all Proctor said wasn't lies, there was an element of truth in the boast that made him feel sick to his stomach.

'You didn't create me, you create nothing, you are a blaspheming devil, you find people you want and feed off their weaknesses. All you really know how to do is hate and destroy.'

Proctor remained calm in the face of this tirade, unruffled and unprovoked, he waited a few moments as if considering matters.

'So ungrateful and so vindictive, you really don't deserve my help, but I will save you Tom whether you want me to or not, you are much too important to me to let you destroy yourself like this.'

Proctor stood back from the desk, opened his heavy coat and extended his arms bat-like, eyes opening wide, black as night.

A dazzling light filled Tom's head and he reeled

backwards falling heavily against the wall and collapsing to the ground with a sickening thud. As he lay there memories began to replay in his head. The visions carried on, replaying over and over again in his head, changing subtly with each re-run. Proctor was metamorphosing from the demon who caused him to double-cross his best friend into his saviour and patron. The man whose kindly guidance had enabled him to uncover Jack Simons' treacherous plot before it could be put into effect, the mentor who'd selflessly taught him everything he knew and enabled him to become the success he was today. And now, just as that hard earned and well deserved success was about to be cruelly torn from him, who should arrive but Rex Proctor ready to lend him help once again. And what had he done to repay this selfless being? He'd rejected him, poured scorn on his offer of help. Tom felt enormous pain as he realised the hurt he must have caused this sage gentleman. Yet there he still was waiting patiently with the hand of friendship still outstretched.

Tom was sorry for the way he'd behaved but was determined not to make it any worse by dithering any further, he reached up and took the outstretched hand of Rex Proctor. As their hands met a split second moment of indecision came upon him, his flesh crept at the cold touch and the hairs on the back of his neck stood on end. He wanted to pull away but when he looked up into those dark eyes the moment passed and he allowed the demon to help him back to his feet.

Once he was again seated behind his desk he felt a lot better. All the agony and fear of earlier on had melted away. He no longer worried about being found out, or losing his job and going to jail because he knew now it wouldn't happen. The man in front of him would see to that. He sank back into the leather clad executive chair and relaxed because everything was going to be all right.

The Dark Lagoon

'So, Tom, tell me all about your problem.'

Proctor's voice was matter of fact, the voice of a professional used to sorting out his clients' little problems.

Tom started to tell the whole story, how he had opened positions across all world markets using company money to back his global domination strategy.

'It was perfect, nothing could go wrong, we were going to make a fortune, I still don't know what happened. The bitch of it is it's the first time I've ever exposed the company to these kind of losses. It should not have happened.'

He went into detail, explaining how, with the advance information at his disposal he should have known before any big price changes hit the market, he should have been able to close his position, reverse out of the situation and still come out with a profit. But something did go wrong, someone screwed up, or more likely set him up. His screen just didn't register the massive collapse in oil prices when the surprise break up of the cartel was announced. He somehow didn't see the whole board turn red until at least half an hour later by which time it was too late to close the positions and the company was effectively bust. Within minutes someone would work out what had happened and he would be taken away by security. Thousands of people would probably lose their jobs and he would go to prison as well as going down in history as the trader who bankrupted the Shapiro Corporation, one of the richest merchant banks in the world.

When he'd finished, Proctor rubbed his chin thoughtfully before making his reply.

'So, you still haven't closed those positions eh?'

Tom looked at his Reuters screen, which was still a sea of red and getting redder by the minute before replying.

'So what? All that's happening is the company is losing even more money it doesn't have, what's your point?'

'Patience, patience, before I explain my point we must discuss some finer points of our arrangement.'

'I don't know what you mean, if you can help me, just do it, you can have anything you want.'

'Good, I knew you would see sense. I will happily help you out of your embarrassing predicament and all I want in return is a small gift.'

Tom was immediately on guard, even in his altered state there was something he found disturbing about Proctor. The initial feelings of relief and trust that had swept over him were still there but not as strong now. This was OK though, Proctor was talking Tom's language, he wanted something that Tom had so there was a deal to be done.

Tom's eyes narrowed before he replied. 'Name it, you can have anything you want. My car, my house, hell you can anything except my wife, or my soul.'

These last words brought a strange expression to Proctor's face; a greedy look with a trace of hunger, they caused his lips to curl into a predatory smile as he threw back his head and laughed a great hysterical belly laugh. For the time being he'd forgotten Tom and their bargaining, he was alone with his own private joke.

'What's so funny?' Tom asked eventually when Proctor's laughter finally started to subside.

'Nothing, nothing at all. It's just the idea of me wanting your soul. Of course I don't want your soul, why should I want it?'

'No reason,' said Tom. He sensed this whole act was part of the negotiating process, designed to throw him off

The Dark Lagoon

his guard and cause him to give away concessions on whatever it was Proctor really wanted. 'But now we're on the subject, what do you want?'

'Well now,' said Proctor. 'That seems to be the problem doesn't it? You see there is nothing you have that I really do want, so you will just have to write me an open cheque, just in case you happen by something that does interest me.'

Tom didn't like the sound of this idea, neither did he understand it; true, as of today he was broke and worse but if Proctor really could fix things he would be wealthy again. What did the man mean by 'something of interest' anyway?

'Just hang on a minute, if I agree to giving you an open cheque, undated, then you could just wait until you felt like it and clean me out, leave me with nothing.'

Again Proctor's face creased into a smile, only this time no laughter followed.

'Don't worry about your money, that's not what I want. There are far more precious things in the world than that. In fact as I am a fair and sporting man I will allow you to name one more thing you wish to protect and I will not ask for it. One and only one, anything else I ask for is mine, agreed? What I want is for you to give me anything you have, if and when I ask for it. I will only ask for one thing and it will not be any of your precious materialistic possessions.'

Tom sat and thought about the proposition. It was clearly a trick but what did he have to lose? If he said no he would lose everything anyway and end up in jail. So what if he promised to give something away in the future? As things currently stood he didn't have a future and spooky as he was Proctor had already said he didn't want his soul, or the soul of his wife, nothing else he could think of meant that much to him, if Proctor wanted it he didn't care. Still, he needed time to think.

'OK, say I go for it, so what are you going to do about getting me out of this mess?'

Proctor's face lit up in a triumphant smile mixed with genuine pleasure, he nodded slowly before replying.

'That's more like it but hold your horses, first things first, if we have a deal we must seal it, make it official as it were.'

Once again warning bells went off in Tom's head. Proctor was too eager to clinch the deal, there was something he had missed but what was it? The effect of Proctor's spell was really starting to wear off now, although he was still far from his normal self.

Then the answer came to him and the realisation of what he had nearly done made him break out in a cold sweat. Proctor wanted some kind of favour from him, he wasn't interested in anything Tom currently had, or would have in the future. No, the game was now very clear, Proctor was aiming high, he wanted Tom to set up Shapiro and scoop the pool for himself. Despite his predicament and the things he'd done in the past, he wasn't prepared to sell out the corporation to this madman. He would rather end up penniless and in jail, perhaps that's what he deserved anyway. Feeling sure that once he told Proctor it was no dice the offer of help would disappear, he prepared to play his last card.

'Look, if you want me to promise to do you some kind of favour in the future that would mean betraying the people I work with you can forget it. I would rather go down than make that kind of deal.'

Proctor raised one eyebrow and looked pensively back at him, no longer smiling triumphantly but rather considering this new position. Tom knew he'd worked out the game and help was now only an impossible dream. Proctor's right hand moved to his chin which he was stroking carefully. After what a long time he spoke. His voice slow and deliberate, a serious weary voice, the voice of defeat.

'Very well, my offer still stands but I grow tired of this facade, we either do business right now or I leave you to your fate, which is it to be?'

Tom could see, feel and smell victory. He'd worked out Proctor's little game and now he had the chance to get off the hook without paying the price, if indeed his strange visitor could deliver the goods. Feeling stronger and more confident, more like his old self, he got to his feet and lent across the desk with his arm outstretched.

'It's a deal.' he said.

III

Instead of grasping the outstretched hand, Proctor side-stepped it. His momentum carried Tom forwards, out of control, before he could regain his balance Proctor grabbed him by the wrist. There was a blur of movement as Proctor produced a blade and slashed at Tom's exposed flesh. Without pause he twisted Tom's wounded arm with great force until the cut was facing down towards the desk where a parchment contract had appeared, Tom's blood dripping copiously onto its yellowing surface. Suddenly Proctor released his hold, took hold of Tom's thumb and brought it down hard into the small pool of red liquid, leaving behind a bloody but perfect imprint.

'We have a deal then.' said Proctor.

He released Tom, threw back his head and laughed aloud once again, the sound chilling, heartless, terrible. In a state of shock but free once more Tom turned and opened his desk drawer, took out a new white handkerchief and wound it mechanically around his wrist. As he turned he saw the Reuters screen out of the corner of his eye. At first he couldn't believe his eyes, what he saw made him forget the cut and everything else; the screen was a sea of black, his position had reversed so quickly he was not only out of trouble, according to the screen he'd just pulled off the biggest trading coup in market history.

'Did you see that? Did you see that?!' he yelled euphorically, looking for the saviour he no longer needed but there was no-one there, just an empty office. He was alone.

IV

He sat there for a long time holding his hurt wrist, replaying the last few minutes in his head. It all felt like a dream to him and if it hadn't been for the cut he would have convinced himself it was a dream. Closing his eyes so tight it hurt, he tried to make sense of what had occurred. There had to be a rational explanation. Eventually it dawned on him it had to be the bad coke; yes that was it, the coke had caused him to hallucinate and imagine Proctor, the contract, everything. He began to feel better, to feel his racing pulse returning to normal as he relaxed in the knowledge he was out of trouble, home free.

He opened his eyes confidently, the room seeming too bright after the enforced darkness. Instantly he felt uneasy, looking down slowly, reluctantly, hoping all the while there would be nothing there; his eyes fell on to the desk and there it was, a yellow parchment with his thumbprint clearly marked in his own blood.

Not wanting to, but unable to stop himself, he picked up the contract and read. The words had been written by hand using a quill pen and in an ink the colour of mildew. The parchment itself stank of rot and decay, this is what it said.

In return for services fully rendered, I the undersigned Tom Kidman do grant to Rex Proctor without condition or reservation, in full and final settlement, my first born daughter on her sixteenth birthday .
φσλκφγφπγεγρφ;σλγφ;λσγοφ
σδφγ σδφγ φγκλυωε;μ,ϖξο

There were a lot of other characters on the contract written in Cyrillic which he couldn't understand but beside his own imprint there was a symbol which was both clearly recognisable and disturbingly familiar. Right beside the bloody seal glowing stark silver out of the yellowing parchment was the sign of a crescent moon. The sight of the symbol sent him into a shivering fit as the full weight and enormity of what he'd done came home to him. A feeling of creeping despair gnawed at his throat, clawing at his guts, trying to steal his breath before it left his body.

Deep down inside he knew what would happen next, it was like he was being forced to act in a play the plot of which led to a destruction he was powerless to prevent. With a clammy hand he reached for the phone and called home, the bright enthusiasm in Ellen's voice when she picked up the phone serving only to tighten the noose of despair around his neck.

'Listen Ellen I must talk to you.' His voice came out husky and thick.

There was a pause as if Ellen was trying to recognise the alien voice on the other end of the line, she knew it was Tom and yet somehow he didn't sound the same any more. But there was something else on her mind that overrode any normal concerns she may have had for her husband's welfare. She was excited, actually she was bubbling over with excitement. Today it was she who had the important news, and nothing would be allowed to get in its way or dull its beauty.

'No Tom, I've got to talk to you. In fact I was about to call you I've got wonderful news, Wonderful news!' The words rang in his head like the bells of Notre Dame, he wanted to tell her to stop, that there'd had been a mistake, as if withholding the news would change the outcome. He couldn't stop her though and no power on earth could stop the tragedy that was about to unfold.

Ellen's voice broke the useless sterility of his repentance.

'We're going to have a baby! A baby, Tom! After all these years its really happened, we're going to have a baby girl.'

Book Three

Chapter One

I

On June 7th 1992, Oxford Street's routine frenzy of buses, taxis and tourists was heightened by an oppressive humidity created by one of the hottest summers on record. Only a soul unharmed by life could remain undisturbed in such an inhospitable environment, much less have the irreverence to pass through oblivious to their surroundings.

Such a soul was Samantha Kidman as she walked along completely absorbed by the delectable challenge of eating a toffee apple without covering herself in sticky goo. She was thinking about one of her favourite pastimes, shopping for new clothes; after all a young lady of thirteen already has an image to keep up. Ordinarily it just wouldn't be cool to indulge publicly in the act of toffee apple consumption, today however it didn't matter, she was miles from home and blissfully anonymous in the crowd.

Sam wasn't someone who had learned to dwell on life's improbabilities and so she was wholly unprepared for what was about to happen. Little did she guess that in the next few moments death would touch her cheek and whisper softly in her ear. Later there would be times when death seemed far from the worst terror in life and she would wonder what lay behind his gossamer veil.

The Dark Lagoon

II

Ben Ellman hadn't always been a lowlife. At school he'd been quite bright. His teachers were encouraged by the way he seemed to apply himself in class, a trait he would carry forward into work. The trouble wasn't what he did at work, but why he did it. Truthfully working to Ben was just a way of making the day pass more quickly, what he lacked was ambition and motivation. It was the same with sex, he liked women well enough, just couldn't be bothered with relationships; too much commitment, too much hassle.

From an early stage he'd gravitated towards the dregs of society, sharing their outlook and their appreciation of cheap booze and soft drugs. It wasn't long before regular work lost its relevance to him and for a while he seemed to merge painlessly into an alternative society.

To Ben, Eddie Miller had always seemed a kindred spirit, just like him. there was however one significant difference, somewhere along the line Eddie made the connection between his life style and his livelihood. By dealing he achieved self respect, as well as money and power, particularly over people like Ben, whom he came to regard as commodities. Sad cases, definitely not like him.

This metamorphosis went unnoticed by Ben who was caught entirely by surprise when one day Eddie told him there would be no more "freebies". After all he'd always paid his way, even if it was only by running Eddie's errands. Hell, they were friends, weren't they? He tried to explain he'd been a bit out of it lately but he could change. Eddie wasn't interested though, he'd made up his mind you needed to be ruthless in this life if you wanted to survive, no room for passengers. It was funny how casting his one time friend aside made him feel stronger, like he had control over his own life, like he knew what he was doing.

At first his new found status confused Ben, it presented too many possibilities. The chance to reform, to change his life, find a good woman, settle down and be normal. These were never really serious options though, it was already too late for that.

The day he snatched the purse there was no plan, if he'd been told about the incident a few days earlier, he would have laughed, after all he wasn't capable of such a decisively violent act was he?

So it was that Ben Ellman became an unwitting bit player in a drama of which he himself would never even be aware. His ill considered and blundering attack on the expensively dressed American tourist may even have succeeded, given the apathy with which such incidents are normally met in central London. Certainly if he hadn't panicked and run blindly up the main street blundering into the dense crowd, he could have slipped anonymously away before attracting any attention. As it was, the act of escape itself proved to be his undoing.

III

There is a critical point in the act of swallowing where food passes briefly over the wind-pipe. Normally this presents no danger as the body is cleverly set up to make sure the right path is taken. However as anyone who has laughed at the wrong moment at a dinner party will confirm, the results of any mis-direction can be catastrophic. Of course this would be true even where some dainty morsel is concerned, but far more so when the mouthful consists of a sticky mixture of hard

The Dark Lagoon

caramelised toffee and crisp green apple.

It was at the exact moment of swallowing that Samantha was struck hard on the back by a panic stricken Ben Ellman and the result was both catastrophic and instantaneous, as she was thrown to the ground at the same time as the offending piece of toffee apple caught fast in her wind-pipe.

In the general confusion no one seemed to notice the young girl laying on the sidewalk making small choking noises. Eventually a middle-aged gent carrying a black attaché case stopped to see what was the matter. He knelt down and turned her over, revealing a face which had already turned a ghastly shade of blue. Realising he was out of his depth this good Samaritan stood up and started shouting for help. Within seconds quite a crowd had gathered round and were quickly engaged in a lively discussion as to what could be the matter and what should be done.

'Drugs,' announced a rather senior looking individual. 'You can tell by the eyes you know' and sure enough it was true, her eyes had started to roll around in her head and she was beginning to foam at the mouth.

'Probably has Aids,' added another busy body who picked up on the earlier comment. 'They get it from sharing needles you know.'

While this was going on she was dying, slowly but surely slipping away, while those around her discussed the politics of social deprivation.

Ben Ellman wasn't aware of the drama taking place behind him. All he was concerned with was getting away. Fate however had decreed a different outcome. In his panic Ben had turned into a dead end street, the sort whose sole purpose is to allow commercial deliveries and collections.

Dating back to Victorian times it was narrow and dingy, more suited to a horse and cart than a van or lorry. There were some trash cans by the rear door of 'Jeans City', beyond which the alley curved sharply to the left ending in an impassable sixteen foot high brick wall.

Ignorant of what lay ahead, Ben careered up the street, coming to an abrupt halt as he hit something solid and unyielding around the corner. Already disorientated, the impact winded him and for a moment he couldn't work out what'd happened. He looked up and found himself staring into the piercing blue eyes of a tall stranger who'd taken him by the left wrist which he held in a grip of iron. Without a word the man began to walk quickly back toward the main road, dragging Ben along as if he were no more than a rag doll, to where a sizeable crowd of people were gathering around the stricken Samantha.

On the way they passed two policemen walking slowly but purposefully towards the incident, one speaking intermittently into his two-way radio. Without breaking stride the stranger pushed his unfortunate charge in their direction. Ben's face plus the purloined bag he still held under his right arm spoke louder than words. The surprised officers appeared put out by this unforeseen turn of events, taking some time to get organised enough to deal with their sudden prisoner. Had Ben been a little quicker witted he could easily have taken the opportunity to escape. As it was he just stood their fatalistically like a rabbit caught in the headlights of an oncoming truck. By the time they'd finally taken him into custody and were ready to question the public spirited citizen who'd delivered him, Proctor was long gone.

The crowd seemed to sense his arrival and parted respectfully to let him through. By the time he was at her side Samantha had stopped choking and was lying serenely still, like Snow White after biting the witch's poisoned apple.

Although her body lay unmoving, her spirit was free and soaring, experiencing joy no living person can ever know. She saw a brightness in the far distance, moving nearer, drawing her into itself, but she wasn't afraid, there was love radiating from it. She started to realise there were shapes and sounds within the brightness, laughter, people talking, calling to her. Then something changed, the indistinct shapes were becoming familiar, real. She was spellbound; before her she saw her beloved Tyler, but that couldn't be, Tyler was dead, put down four years ago, a broken shadow of his happy bouncing younger days. Yet here he was better than ever, barking for all he was worth and wagging his tail, as pleased to see her as she was to see him. Beyond Tyler there was another wonderful surprise, Aunt Ellen, her favourite aunt who had died so suddenly and tragically of cancer. Ellen looked radiant, ageless, she was smiling peacefully, walking towards Sam with her arms outstretched in welcome.

Just as Sam felt like she could stretch out and touch them she was aware of something else, behind her. Reluctantly she turned round and saw herself, at least her old self lying on the pavement. Over her there was a dark cloud, emanating hate, envy and spite, pulling her back with irresistible force. She felt her senses starting to reel, managing only to turn around in time to glimpse the brightness receding and with it a silent Tyler, whose tail had stopped wagging and Ellen whose face was suddenly lined with sadness. As she opened her eyes the first thing she saw was the face of the devil staring straight into her soul.

Displaying an owner's confidence the stranger knelt down and drew Samantha into his arms. He looked carefully into her sightless eyes, as if expecting to see something important there. Then he unceremoniously turned her over, placed her across his knee and gave her a hefty thump on the back. The offending apple was sent flying towards the ground, closely followed by the entire contents of her stomach. The manoeuvre did however have the desired effect, as the girl regained consciousness in a paroxysm of coughing.

'My name is Rex Proctor, we haven't been formally introduced.' It was the voice rather than the words which stopped Samantha from screaming and enabled her to get a grip on herself and sure enough, as she looked the face changed and became normal, even kindly. She tried weakly to get to her feet, then collapsed as her legs turned to jelly. The stranger caught her easily.

'I'd take it steady if I were you, you've had a nasty shock.'

The man before her had a hard but not unpleasant face, his voice was deep with a gravelly quality which hinted at authority. He had the face of a man who kept his head in a crisis, but more than anything else, it was his eyes that commanded attention, they were eyes which concealed secrets. Although it was hard to tell for sure he appeared to be about forty, despite the warm spring weather he wore a dark full length gabardine overcoat and around his neck there hung a silver pendant in the shape of a crescent moon..

'Can you walk?' he demanded.

'I think so,' she replied.

'Then I think we should go somewhere and get you a cup of tea. Come with me.'

Normally Samantha wouldn't have dreamed of going off with a strange man but under the circumstances she made an exception, after all he had just saved her life, so she reasoned it was unlikely he meant her harm. It would

The Dark Lagoon

be good to sit down away from the crowd with a hot drink and under the circumstances it would be impolite to refuse. So she allowed herself to be led away by the stranger, leaning heavily on his arm as together they headed towards a small Italian cafe just two blocks away.

The tired looking middle aged waitress escorted them to a table for two at the back of the cafe, handed them a menu each and with a business-like smile left them to chose their pleasure. The cafe was virtually empty, it was three thirty on a Wednesday, too early for the influx of exhausted afternoon shoppers and late enough to have missed the lunch-time rush. The only other customers were a couple of young lovers engaged in an intimate exchange on the other side of the room. To all intents and purposes they were alone.

Having ordered a sweet milky tea for the girl and a black coffee for himself, the man waited while she started to regain her equanimity. Eventually she broke the silence.

'What happened to me back there?' she asked.

Before he could answer the waitress reappeared with the drinks which she placed on the table and enquired if there was anything else. He shook his head dismissively, returning his attention to the girl.

'Drink first, questions later,' he said.

There was something in his tone which caused Samantha to forget her curiosity and to do as she was told. While she drank he waited patiently, watching her with those disturbing secrets-filled eyes. When he saw the colour begin to return to her cheeks he answered the question.

'You were unlucky enough to be in the way of some lowlife on the run after snatching a bag. You were knocked to the ground and were very nearly the world's first toffee apple fatality.'

Caught off guard by the humour, Samantha started to giggle, to make matters worse he proceeded to give a fairly convincing impression of what death by toffee apple must look like. The giggle exploded into helpless laughter threatening to cause her to collapse for the second time that day.

Eventually, sides aching, she regained her composure. Proctor looked a lot happier, like he'd won an important victory.

'Well Sam, I guess you'll be fine now. OK!'

She was suddenly on guard

'How did you know my name?' she demanded.

Far from looking annoyed at her suspicious tone Proctor looked positively pleased. He reached over and pointed to her left arm. Around her wrist she wore a solid silver identity bracelet.

'Elementary my dear Samantha.' He replied.

'Sorry,' she said blushing with embarrassment. 'That wasn't very gracious was it? I should be thanking you for saving my life, not acting like you're the bogey man or something.'

Proctor's face registered no offence.

'Think nothing of it,' he said graciously, then teasingly 'This sort of thing is always happening to me, why only last week I saved a bus-load of orphans from certain death you know.'

'I'm serious,' she said looking offended. 'I owe you my life.'

'Well I guess in a funny sort of way that makes you my

The Dark Lagoon

responsibility then, doesn't it?'

There was something about the way he said this that sent a shiver up her spine.

'Why should you be responsible for me?' she asked.

He looked at her for a long moment before replying.

'Because without me you wouldn't exist and so in a way I have become your creator, haven't I?'

Rex Proctor's face smiled as he said this but his eyes were full of secrets.

There was a few moments' silence, she didn't want to tell the stranger anything about herself any more but then found her tongue betraying her. She explained how she was on vacation with her parents and today she'd persuaded them to allow her to go shopping alone, they would be furious if they ever found out what happened. She told him she was an only child and used to being independent, travelling around the financial centres of the world, with her father's job.

Proctor listened attentively until she'd told him everything he wanted to know. Then he reached into the inside pocket of his coat and produced a leather pouch, from which he took a shiny object and laid it on the table in front of them

'Take this and wear it.' he commanded.

The shiny object turned out to be a crescent moon on a silver chain. An exact replica of the one he himself wore. Without question she found herself fastening the token around her own neck. Satisfied with the result, he removed a five pound note from his pocket which he placed on the table for the waitress, then Rex Proctor rose to his feet.

'I must go,' he said.

'Of course.' she replied.

Proctor nodded his approval giving her one final enigmatic look before turning on his heel and disappearing into the street without a backward glance.

Samantha was left on her own. The jaded waitress returned with a trolley loaded with a tempting variety of cakes and pastries, instantly reminding her of how hungry she was. She chose a wonderful looking chocolate eclair and all thoughts of the day's trauma were driven away as she enjoyed a moment of shameless self indulgence.

Once finished she asked for the bill, it was then she noticed the money on the table. She called the waitress over and very honestly handed over the money.

'I'm afraid the people before me must have left this money by mistake,' she said.

The waitress looked at her as if she must be mad.

'No, this is the money your father left you to pay the bill.'

'My father? What are you talking about, my father isn't here, I came in alone.' But Samantha didn't have time to ask any more questions as the waitress had already gone on her busy way. So, slightly puzzled, but glad to be feeling better, she left the cafe, the crescent moon hanging unnoticed around her neck.

Chapter Two

I

Tom Kidman lay reclined on the luxurious sun lounger, body glistening with sun tan oil, long drink resting on the small table at his side. The years had treated him kindly, he'd spent a lot of time working out and it showed, leaving him with the body of a younger man. He looked the epitome of the successful executive taking a few well earned vacation days, a picture of contentment and relaxation. In truth he was frustrated, angry and - somewhere beneath both these emotions - just plain scared.

The glamorous sunglasses with their iridescent blue lenses added considerably to the illusion of his allure attracting more than a few admiring glances from the many young bikini-clad girls who walked past in a steady stream. These admiring glances would have soon withered and died had the lookers been able to see into the eyes behind the glasses. There was no flirtatiousness in those eyes, no light-hearted repartee, they were dull, lifeless, the eyes of a geriatric or a burnt out alcoholic. No; any young girl who looked deeply into Tom Kidman's eyes would soon forget any thought of secret trysts and romance, she would turn her face away and find another subject for her daydreams.

As he lay there, unaware of the attention he was getting, he pondered on how he got himself into this situation in the first place. He had sixteen years to plan for this day, sixteen years to make sure that nothing went wrong, that he would be in control. Control! Huh, that was a joke! The word bit into his mind accusingly. All his working life he'd exerted control over others, he'd controlled a multi billion dollar merchant bank, exerted pressure and influence over politicians, held his own with the richest and most powerful people on the planet and yet he couldn't even control his own wife and daughter when it mattered most.

It was only three days ago that Ellen had sprung her "wonderful surprise", three days, it felt more like three years to him now. Three days and nights where he'd gotten no sleep, where his mind had raced through every possibility to regain control and re-establish his long laid plan but in the end, nothing. He'd drawn a blank and here he was waiting for something awful to happen without a clue as to how he was going to stop it.

When Ellen told him about the surprise cruise she'd arranged for Samantha's sixteenth birthday, at first he'd brushed the idea aside. Pressure of work, other commitments, these were the weapons he always used to avoid doing anything he didn't want to do. This time though Ellen had outflanked him, he remembered how she'd listened patiently while he came out with his excuses and the promise to make it up to her. The clever smile should have tipped him off that she had something different up her sleeve this time.

It was as if the issue of the cruise was a catalyst that brought to the fore all Ellen's deeply hidden frustrations, it became a symbol for all the things she wanted to change in their marriage. In the row that followed she took him right to the edge, to the edge but not over it. Tom loved Ellen, he was in fact utterly devoted to her and whatever the consequences he wouldn't risk losing her. Except that is when it came to protecting their daughter. Throughout the argument there were many occasions when he yearned to tell Ellen why they couldn't go on the cruise but the words just wouldn't come. Every time he tried, he heard a caricature of his own voice, full of sarcasm, mocking him.

'Oh, by the way, dear, the reason we can't go on that surprise cruise you arranged is because sixteen years ago I made a pact with the Devil and sold our unborn daughter's soul. Oh yes. I planned to spend the day of Samantha's birthday in a windowless room with one arm handcuffed to her and the other holding an AK 47 assault rifle just in case the bastard tries to collect.'

Nope, it didn't matter how many times he thought it through, there was just no way he could tell her. Even if he had found a way, it wouldn't have done any good, all he would have achieved would have been to convince his wife he was a lunatic, a fact she had probably suspected all these years anyhow. The result would have either been her having him committed, or more likely, in her insisting on an even longer holiday as he obviously needed the rest. Then again perhaps he was insane, insanity seemed like a far more rational explanation than what he took to be the truth. In a way, given the pressure he was under at the time, who could blame him for conjuring up an imaginary devil or two. It was just his guilty subconscious trying in vain to punish him for his stupidity, refusing to accept the fact that he'd manage to avoid paying the piper.

At least that was what Dr. Brian Mulvane, his analyst had been trying to persuade him for the past sixteen years. There were times when he had even bought into the idea for a while. Then the nightmares would return with their same dark images, mist, water, a monstrous hand and he would go back to Mulvane and begin all over. As the years passed the periods during which he remained convinced of the unreality of his anxieties grew longer, while the relapses grew shorter and less intense. His long laid plans to protect his daughter remained intact although he became less and less convinced of their necessity. But

when Ellen had sprung her surprise it had been like a
light bulb going off in his head. He suddenly saw things
as they really were. He realised how he'd yet again allowed
himself to be duped, let his guard slip, Proctor was still
toying with him, somewhere out there he was waiting
and laughing.

Finally the decision was taken out of his hands
completely. Samantha herself became involved, siding with
her mother; they insisted that if he wouldn't come they
would go alone. He could hardly forbid the trip without
offering an explanation so he was left with no choice but
to go helplessly along with it.

These musings had been going on relentlessly ever since
they got on the boat, the closer it got to Samantha's
birthday the worse they got, now with only a few hours
to go his mind was threatening to cave in completely.
This last thought suddenly entered his consciousness with
a sickening clarity which threatened to tip him over the
edge into real insanity. If it had been his own well-being
that was at stake he probably would have embraced
madness willingly. After all it was he who was responsible
for this whole mess, his greed, his arrogance that had put
his only daughter in a danger he now saw as far worse
than death itself.

This last thought exploded in his head like a mortar.
Death was the one way to cheat the Devil. Perhaps it was
a sin to take a life, any life, infinitely more so when it is
the life you love the most; but is not such a murder justified
when it is committed in the name of pure love? The agony
of this idea began to boil and bubble inside him. If he
were to do such a thing his life would also be over, he
knew that, every moment spent after that act would be
pure suffering, hell on earth.

So why should he not suffer? He deserved to suffer

and if his suffering would get Samantha off the hook then so be it, bring on the demons. Except the demons didn't appear to want him, or care whether he suffered or not, they were out there laughing at him and his weakness, knowing he hadn't the courage to destroy nor to protect their prey.

II

While his tortured mind continued to wallow fuzzily in self pity, shame and fear, he was actually doing nothing to protect Samantha at all. At that very moment she was wandering around the ship, uninformed, unprepared and unaware of the great danger that threatened her. If only her father could have taken off his glasses and looked out for a second instead of focusing inwards, perhaps he would have seen a way of turning the tables, better still if he could have freed his spirit maybe he would have been able to see the spell that lingered around him still and shake free of it. Perhaps the answer was closer at hand than he knew.

A thought struck him like a hammer blow, exploding in his head like a bell bringing pain and clarity in a simultaneous shock that nearly sent him reeling from his sun-bed. The only way to save Samantha was to right the terrible wrong he'd done to Jack. Where had this thought come from? How had it managed to steal its way into his head like a thief in the shadows? Jack Simmons was the last person on his mind right now and he'd no business cropping up, not when Tom needed all his energy for Samantha.

'*Remember what you did.*' The thought had a voice, a gentle but insistent voice. '*He was your best friend and you betrayed him, this is pay back time.*'

No! Tom almost screamed the word out loud, he felt a rush of blood to his cheeks, his forehead broke out in tiny beads of sweat and his hands were clammy against the fabric of the lounger. Guilt can be a destructive emotion and guilt which had been held back for years came flooding in to his mind and there was nothing he could do to stop it.

His hands were shaking now and the sweat was rolling down his cheeks as the full force of these emotions hit. Then Tom Kidman did something he hadn't done for over thirty years, he burst out crying. This was no muffled snivel either, no stiff upper lip, eyes filling up slowly, followed by a hasty retreat to the men's room. He had no time to think of his image, or to worry about embarrassment, his whole body just went into one heaving spasm of grief. The sobs were coming out of him so loud and hard he could hardly catch his breath, there was no stopping it now, finally the piper had arrived and he wanted to be paid in full.

Anyone able to rise above that ship and look down would have been able to see the mist surrounding him. A mist which had the sole purpose of clouding his mind and preventing him from thinking straight so that its originator could proceed with his long laid plan without interference. It wasn't after all a difficult trick to play, most men are weak and susceptible, if you know which buttons to push. Sometimes successful powerful men like Tom are more susceptible than most, they have so many buttons to chose from.

III

The boat on which they were sailing was called the 'Queen Charlotte'. She was a majestic vessel, to her crew however

The Dark Lagoon

she was regarded as a lucky ship and was known simply as 'The Queen'. They were steaming gently through an untroubled ocean about thirty nautical miles off the coast of Key West, the people who lived there unaware of the stately guest passing by. As far as they were concerned the ocean represented either a source of income, or leisure, or both. Most were aware of the activities of the DEA and the coast-guard in their attempts to block what was the most used drug smuggling lane in the Atlantic. The islanders were often rewarded when a gentle stroll along the beach turned up a bale or two of uncut marijuana, thrown overboard by a panicking crew of a drug ship trying to avoid capture. This booty was known locally as seaweed and was just one of the perks of life on the Keys.

No such baggage was likely to fall from the Queen Charlotte as she followed unknowing in the wake of the smugglers. She carried a cargo more precious than any drug, wealthy privileged humans guarded and protected by a dedicated crew, led by one of the most experienced seamen in the merchant fleet.

Captain Melvin Olroyd Simms stood on the bridge and stared pensively out across the ocean. He was dressed in his summer uniform of white and gold; as usual he wore his cap slightly tilted to the right and stood with his feet wide apart, his hands clasped firmly behind his back. He wasn't a tall man, about five six but he had a straight bearing with a rugged though mainly unlined complexion. He was slim and wiry, his appearance giving a lie to his fifty six years. Forty of those years had been spent at sea but never in his career had his job involved less seamanship. For although he stood on his bridge, the master of all he surveyed, the truth was the ship ran without him. Unless there was an emergency.

The real master was his number two, a man called Christopher Walpole. Chris was sixteen years his junior and had only seven years of real experience at sea but he did know computers. Apparently being the master of a modern vessel meant you had to be a boffin not a sailor. Chris of course wasn't on the bridge, there was no need, he spent his time in the control room, the communications nerve centre of the ship from which he could monitor and adjust all her vital functions.

Mel's job was much more one of PR. Keeping the rich guests happy, eating with them, answering their questions, organising and attending social events. Mel knew he was good at such things, which was why the company had chosen to keep him on when most of his peers had long since been forced into retirement. It was also true that he preferred the idea of being a glorified camp host to the idea of retirement and leaving the fleet altogether. Nevertheless, he missed the pressure and responsibility of true command, it was in his blood. One day, of course, he would have to retire and it was on that eventuality that his mind presently ruminated. In truth he knew he could never quit the sea. If he tried he would end up an alcoholic within months and dead soon after. As the Master of such an important ship, he was well paid and should have had enough money to retire tomorrow, go to the South Seas and buy a good schooner, live out his life in the way he always wanted. The truth was he was nearly broke, two wives, six children and two expensive divorces had seen to that, so he needed to work for at least another four years if he was to have any chance of realising his dream.

When he sat at the head of his table in the evening, making polite conversation with those lucky passengers invited to sit with him, he couldn't help feeling a little jealous of their wealth and the freedom it could bring. He tried to resist the idea that they were somehow less worthy than he, less deserving of riches, usually he succeeded, but late at night as he tossed and turned in his bunk those dark thoughts would resurface and steal a little piece of his mind.

The Queen Charlotte really was an impressive boat, six decks, eight restaurants, three swimming pools, including one indoor pool of Olympic size. She had a magnificent ballroom large enough to house all eight hundred of her passengers in comfort. There were sixty state rooms as well as seven different classes of cabin to cater for the pockets of all her guests, from the fabulously wealthy to the merely well off. There was also accommodation, albeit more modest for the crew who numbered as many souls again. It was a tribute to the slick organisation and management skills of the ships officers that so many crew could go about their vital business in such an unobtrusive manner. Most of the guests would have been astounded at their number, being aware only of the waiters and orderlies who saw to their needs and wants. This illusion was made possible by the complex network of corridors, passages and hatches built into the infrastructure, enabling the crew to move around without arousing the interest or even the awareness of those not meant to see the working side of life at sea.

Of course the existence of these discreet routes around the ship naturally gave rise to the possibility of them being used for more clandestine purposes. There was the time the Queen Charlotte had been privately chartered by an Arab sheikh and his entourage. On that occasion thieves had used the network to gain access to the royal suite, steal an undisclosed quantity of priceless gems and escape undetected. The profuse apologies of the directors weren't enough to prevent the sheikh demanding to be set ashore at the nearest port. Later there were rumours that he had bought a cruise liner of his own and was spending millions to make sure its security passed muster during family holidays.

IV

Ellen Kidman sat before the dressing table in her cabin carefully brushing her blonde hair. She'd already applied a little makeup after completing her usual thorough skin cleansing routine. Her rounded face was glowing with cosmetic beauty, there was no doubt she was an attractive woman and one who had looked after herself in mind and body. It was very early to be getting ready for dinner but tonight was special for three reasons. First it was the night of the Gala Ball, an event for which this cruise was justly famous. Everyone, including crew, would don fancy dress and the guests would sit down to a rapacious feast after which they would rock the night away to the sounds of one of the most exciting bands on the planet. Secondly it was the night of Samantha's sixteenth birthday and lastly she'd met an intriguing boy that very day. Ellen couldn't contain her curiosity any longer, smiling she turned to Sam and just asked her outright.

'So tell me, what is his name?'

Samantha screwed up her face and hunched her shoulders in a most unalluring way before answering. As Ellen watched her daughter's embarrassed response, she thought of how much her little girl had grown up. Even to seeing her now, dressed in cut off jeans, no make up, her dark blonde hair tied back tomboy fashion, she couldn't disguise the fact she was a beauty. She was taller than her mother and her figure was a little less rounded but it retained a sensuous quality of which Sam herself appeared to be unaware. Although Sam went to a mixed college and had many friends, including boys, none of these had led to any romance as far as Ellen could tell. Now however she recognised in Sam the signs of the smitten, she remembered those feelings well and fondly. Her little girl was on the brink of womanhood and her mother was both excited and scared for her.

There was the merest shake of the head.

'You mean you didn't ask his name? Well what did he look like then?'

Samantha had started this conversation but now she didn't know how to continue with it. She got on well with her mother, they had the sort of rapport which had always allowed them to communicate, even over difficult issues like bad school reports but now it was like there was a barrier between them. She wanted to tell her about the boy, she was flushed and excited by the meeting, nothing had really happened but she couldn't shake the feeling she'd done something naughty, something private, even a little dangerous.

She'd been walking along the promenade on the upper deck, something she had taken to do in the afternoons as a way of clearing her head after lunch. The food on the ship was wonderful, they had everything you could possibly want and Samantha wasn't shy when it came to food which she enjoyed thoroughly. This holiday was special in that she was also allowed wine with her meal, an even bigger reason for a refreshing walk. It wasn't the first time she'd drunk enough wine to become tipsy though. There were adult parties at home from the age of twelve when she would sneak a drink with some friends and spend the evening giggling and silly, normally waking up the next morning with a fuzzy head, not feeling like going to school at all. This was different, it was like she was being invited to join a club, one she had wanted to know about for a long time and now the invitation had come she felt nervous and a little reticent about accepting.

These thoughts occupied her mind sufficiently for her

not to have noticed how the deck was so unusually deserted. Normally there were half a dozen or so other promenaders up there with her, one or two older couples and often a pair of young lovers, plus the keep fit fanatics circulating endlessly dressed in their sweaty jogging pants. She'd already made several friends of her own age on the ship but they weren't invited on these walks which she regarded as her own.

Today there had been no-one to disturb her thoughts at all. The emptiness, had she noticed it, gave the deck a slightly eerie quality, especially as the ship steamed gently into a slowly drifting sea mist. As the mist thickened even Samantha saw the change and realised her solitude. It occurred to her whimsically that she could be all alone, that the whole ship could be deserted and that she could be a spirit, doomed to wander the empty decks forever like the ghostly crew of the Marie Celeste. Then emerging out of the *mist, forming from it*, there came another. At first she was startled, her pulse quickened, she stepped backwards involuntarily and into the railings that stood between her and the water below. The figure was now in full view and it stepped forward with surprising, disturbing speed.

'Gotcha.'

The voice had been a friendly one and belonged to a boy who must have been only a year or two older than herself. His hands were holding her gently but firmly by the shoulders and he was looking into her eyes in a way that made her head spin even more than the wine at lunch-time. Nevertheless, she wasn't used to being handled with such familiarity by a total stranger, however well-meaning. She tried hard to regain her composure and found herself floundering, those dark eyes just held her gaze and she couldn't break free. Just at the point where

The Dark Lagoon

intrigue would have turned to fear, the youth released her and stepped away.

Standing there with the mist swirling around his head he looked more like an apparition than a person. He was dressed in black, the style of his clothes slightly old fashioned with an oddly Gothic quality. He was slim and tall with straight features and unusually pale skin. There was something vaguely familiar about the line of his hair and the curl of his mouth and those eyes, she was sure she had seen those eyes before.

'Thanks, but you know I wasn't going to fall.' she scolded.

He looked down at the deck and then upwards tilting his head slightly out to sea.

'I know, I'm sorry, I hope you forgive me.'

His gallantry made her feel mean and ungrateful.

'Look I'm the one who should be sorry, you were only trying to help.'

It was getting colder as the mist grew thicker and Sam gave a shiver, rubbing her shoulders where his hands had been.

The boy had walked over to the railings and was looking out across the water.

'Don't you think the mist is beautiful?' he said.

Now he mentioned it she did think the mist beautiful, it gave an ethereal quality to everything it touched, the ocean, the ship, the boy; as though they had escaped the normal confines of time and space and were embarking on a journey to a land where no-one else had ever been.

Looking up, she saw a light in the sky. The sun had begun to set lending an incandescent glow to the heavens, mixing reds and yellows with the mist, creating monstrous shapes which appeared and disappeared in front of her. It was not the sunlight that caught her eye but something silver, ghostlike, as she continued to look the mist rolled away to reveal the perfect shape of a crescent moon. Looking down at the waves, on the far horizon, she thought for a second she could see land, an imagined island with the waves lapping gently on its distant shores. Then in a second the vision was gone as quickly as the mist itself had gone. There was no crescent moon, no mysterious island in the deserted ocean and when she looked back on deck, no dark haired boy with piercing eyes, she was all alone.

'Mum, it wasn't anything really, we hardly said hello, I don't even remember what he looked like, it was just that...' her voice trailed off. 'Oh I don't know...'

Her cheeks were bright red now and she looked as if she were about to cry. A look of concern came into Ellen's eyes but quickly vanished as Samantha burst into laughter. Then they were both laughing, Samantha came towards Ellen, sat down and gave her a warm hug.

' Mum, I'm a real idiot, aren't I?'

'No, you're not an idiot, darling, just a young girl who's fast becoming a young woman. I don't know who it was you met today, but he's one lucky boy to have you take an interest in him, you never know, perhaps you'll see him again this evening.'

'Yes, perhaps I will.'

Samantha had walked over to the cabin porthole and was staring out to sea wistfully. A long way away, beyond the horizon there was a mist forming.

The Dark Lagoon

V

During the rest of the early evening Tom finally pulled himself together and made his way down to the cabin. Thankfully neither Sam nor Ellen noticed his red eyes, although Ellen did ask him if he was OK. He passed his quietness off as being a case of a little too much sun and rich food and proceeded to dress for the Gala Ball. He didn't realise it himself but he was still under the influence of an unseen force, his mind was still an unfocused blur, unable to make or even face decisions. He went about his ablutions in a mechanical resigned sort of way, vaguely aware there were other priorities he should be attending to but unable to comprehend what they were.

When they were finally ready and entered the main state-room of the suite together, they were no longer an ordinary American family but something far more exotic. Tom had been persuaded to dress as a slightly ageing Superman, the famous uniform looked a bit out of character on a red head but the overall effect was suitably impressive. Ellen was dressed as Wendy from Peter Pan, this choice was widely regarded by Tom and others as a cop-out allowing Ellen to maintain a sense of decorum while those around her made fools of themselves. Nevertheless, a clever choice of dress, combined with a liberal sprinkling of Pixie dust, added to the illusion of a story book character and no-one who saw her would have doubted that Ellen was in fancy dress. Samantha had chosen the most daring costume of all, she was dressed in the style of a Greek Goddess and if anyone had asked her who she was she would have replied 'Echo', the fateful love of Narcissus. The costume seemed to release for the first time Samantha's full beauty, the radiance of her youth combining with the exotic finery to dazzling effect. When Tom saw her, the sight almost took his breath away, even in spite of his befuddled state.

'You look absolutely lovely, darling,' he said with real pride and not a little emotion.

'You look fantastic too, don't forget I want a dance later on, will you?' she said.

'You better believe it, I want to be seen with the best looking girl at the ball don't I?' He shot a glance at Ellen who also looked ravishing and quickly added, 'and the best looking woman too'

He put his arms round Ellen and drew her towards him, even after all these years she could still affect him. He felt the fullness of her figure beneath the skimpy dress and placed his lips over hers and felt their warmth, they were soft and inviting, Ellen pulled away, and scolded him.

'Hey, you'll have Peter Pan after you if you don't watch out'

His mind was now at rest once more, something had intervened to give him some peace. He no longer worried about Rex Proctor or the night ahead because his memory had been temporarily wiped clean of the deal he'd done and the significance of this night to them all. For the moment at least he was happy and proud, happier than he could remember and prouder than any man on earth. Still in this mood he took his ladies' arms and led them upstairs to the ball.

If there was ever a night to help a person forget their troubles then this was it. The whole ship seemed to have been bedecked with decorations to complement the mood of the evening and the appearance of the guests. There were some people who had taken a conservative approach but they seemed to be in the minority. Most seemed to have thrown caution to the winds and gone overboard in their choice of costume. There was much competition between the guests as to whose outfits were most lavish, complex, or just plain outlandish. It was interesting to note how many had chosen to arrive wearing masks and to realise that the masked guests were the ones who were making the most noise and calling the most attention to themselves.

At sea it is a fact that food is always seen as more important than on dry land. Sailors spend so much time away from their loved ones they need some substitute for physical love and affection. Food can be the nearest thing to the erotic if it is prepared and presented well. If the ingredients are also amongst the finest the world has to offer then the result can provide a veritable orgy of delights. So it was that night, the twenty three chefs overseen by one Monsieur Claude Berbier, late of the Salon De Paris and reputedly one of the world's culinary masters, had truly surpassed themselves.

In the middle of the Grand Salon there stood an icy fortress, an exact replica of the Sleeping Beauty's Palace in Disneyland. Around the fortress were arrayed the buffet tables containing an endless variety of delicacies. The many waiters and attendants, all dressed as palace guards of various ranks were kept more than busy discreetly replenishing the tables. There was an equal number of wine waiters darting here and there carrying silver platters laden with exotic cocktails in keeping with the style and atmosphere of the occasion. The ship's master, Melvin Oldroyd Simms, had also entered into the full spirit of the occasion in more ways than one. Firstly he was authentically dressed as Napoleon Bonaparte and secondly he was already more than three parts to the wind on Jamaica rum before the evening had begun.

Of all the duties he had to perform, this was the one

he looked forward to the least. It was enough that he had
to attend to the trivial desires and fancies of his pampered
guests instead of running the ship but at least most of the
time he could do so with a little dignity. It was just too
much to expect him to dress up and make an imbecile of
himself as well; why didn't they go the whole way and
shackle him into the stocks and let the guests and crew
pelt him with rotten fruit?

The rum couldn't completely take away the feelings of
indignation and resentment he felt but it did help. What
helped more was seeing Chris dressed as the funky chicken,
a persona he seemed to adopt with ease. Mel half thought
of suggesting he should take up wearing the costume full
time it suited him so much. There were so many guests
and crew milling about and the atmosphere was so highly
charged that even the grumpy Captain couldn't help
feeling a little exhilarated, although he would never have
admitted it to anyone.

Another advantage of this evening was that the
unofficial rules provided that no member of the officers
party need tell anyone what costume they intended to
wear in advance. As a result there was a pleasant
anonymity about the affair that allowed the Captain to
move around without his usual contingent of sycophants
and hangers on. He was standing on the dais at the far
end of the salon in front of a magnificent panoramic
window which gave a spectacular view of the star filled
night sky. He surveyed the company and listened to the
animated conversation and laughter and decided that
maybe things weren't so bad after all. To make matters
even better he had just caught the eye of one of his more
intriguing passengers, a middle aged but glamorous woman
called Mary Swain. Rumour had it she'd already seen off
two husbands, both wealthy and was on the lookout for
number three. Normally Mel would have given her a wide

birth but in his present condition he found the prospect of her company extremely attractive. Also there was no doubting she was a fine-looking woman, particularly now, dressed as she was in a fabulously ornate ball-gown dating from a similar era to his own costume. Making his way towards her, he took her outstretched hand and kissed it formally.

'Josephine I presume?' he quipped wittily, let down only by the slight slur in his voice.

'But of course,' she replied, amused and pleased by such an uninhibited advance from a man whom she'd previously written off as attractive but hopelessly stuffy; perhaps tonight was going to be an interesting one after all.

There certainly was magic in the air that evening, even if it wasn't all white. The atmosphere in the ballroom instantly captivated Samantha as she entered the throng. she'd never seen so many people gathered together, all laughing and talking at once. The sound mingled with the background music and the gentle rhythm of the boat as it continued its silent progress through the empty ocean, making Sam feel light-headed with excitement. Her parents also seemed very happy, this pleased her as they had appeared tense lately, especially her father. He'd never been a relaxed person but since they had got on the boat she thought he was going to have a breakdown or something. Now it was lovely to see him whispering into her mother's ear as if they were young lovers again just out of high school. Her mother had in fact been a prom queen in her day and as Samantha looked at her now she realised what a beauty she was, the realisation made her feel proud and sad at the same time although she didn't know why.

Turning her attention away from her obviously distracted parents, she surveyed the room looking for any of her newly made friends. At first it was difficult to make anyone out at all, or even to distinguish the people and their outlandish costumes from the decorations and glitter that bedecked the salon. Gradually though her eyes became accustomed to the sight and she recognised some of the people. She saw the gallant but usually stuffy Captain engaged in what looked like a very cosy chat with that awful man eater Mary Swain. She giggled to herself as she had visions of Mary dragging the poor Captain back to her cabin later on in the evening. There were some others she recognised but no-one she wanted to talk to. She was just starting to get a little disappointed when out of the corner of her eye she noticed a tall dark figure standing alone by the far wall, facing out the window, looking out to sea. He was dressed all in black and though his face was hidden and she had only met him once before, she immediately recognised the slim build and enigmatic stance of the boy with no name.

For reasons she didn't understand her stomach decided to take the opportunity of doing a back flip, leaving her reeling, head spinning, not sure if she was going to faint or throw up. She managed to pull herself together and make her way slowly to the exit. As she reached the doorway she felt a hand on her shoulder, the touch was both gentle and firm and its effect was to immediately calm her errant stomach and clear her head. She remained still for what seemed like ages but was in fact only a few seconds, when she finally did turn round the face that confronted he was smiling shyly, eyes cast slightly downwards.

'I'm sorry if I startled you.' said the youth.

She could now see that close up he was wearing an ancient Greek style costume, less ornate than her own and disguised by its uniform black but unmistakable nonetheless. She returned his shy smile without looking directly into his eyes.

'Don't be sorry, it wasn't you who startled me,' she lied. 'It was just all the noise and the lights in here suddenly went to my head and I needed to get out for a moment.'

He seemed pleased with this answer and let his hand slide down off her shoulder taking her by the arm. This act of familiarity would normally have unnerved Sam but there was something in the gentle way he did it that allayed her fears, she allowed the boy with no name to lead her out of the ballroom and onto the terrace.

When they'd reached the balcony he let her go, she put her hands on the railings and took a long deep breath and exhaled slowly. The night air was truly a heady cocktail, here she was on her sixteenth birthday, standing on the deck of a wonderful ship in the company of a mysterious boy whose name she didn't know. The night seemed full of promise and time hung motionless waiting for a signal to begin its never ending journey towards nothingness.

'I'm Samantha Kidman I don't know your name,' she said finally.

The boy wasn't listening, he seemed preoccupied, this irritated Sam who suddenly felt foolish, her cheeks burned red with embarrassment and she turned abruptly to go.

'Don't go, Samantha Kidman,' said the boy.

Sam turned, face flushed.

'I thought you weren't listening to me' she said uselessly.

'I heard every word you said, its just that I had something on my mind for a moment but it's gone now. My name is Simon, should I call you Sam, Samantha, or perhaps Echo would be better.'

He'd worked out who she was, that surprised her, she didn't think anyone would guess.

'How did you know who I'm meant to be?' she asked.

'Oh, that's pretty simple, you see I'm meant to be Narcissus, so I could hardly fail to recognise you could I?'

It didn't make sense really and somehow it didn't have to. For the first time in her life she realised she was more than just flirting with a boy, she'd flirted before and she knew it was more than that. This was quite different, like what he said really meant something, without being heavy or complicated. She realised that, after only such a short time, she felt happy in his presence. Looking at her watch, she couldn't believe it said 9.30 p.m., surely they had just left the ballroom and yet that had been over an hour ago! The other guests were sitting down to dinner and most were nearly finished, the band was beginning to set up and the waiters were running around clearing the tables and preparing the dance floor.

They'd missed their dinner but it didn't matter to Sam, as far as she was concerned, Echo and Narcissus were happy with their own company. She may not have needed food to sustain her but the music when it came called powerfully, he felt her need, without a word he took her by the hand and they walked into the ballroom. They were the first couple on to the floor, the music was still only the haunting strains of a background classical quartet but it didn't matter; no-one seemed to notice or even pay attention to the beautiful young couple swaying to and fro so captivated by one another.

In the meantime Melvin and Mary had been getting on famously as well. Mary was good company and she expertly encouraged the shy Captain out of his shell, helped by regular top-ups from the bar of course. Not that he

The Dark Lagoon

needed much encouragement he'd been holding himself in close check for too long, virtually forgotten the last time he had been with a woman, he did know it'd been too long. There was something about the way she smelled, the way she seemed to pay such close attention to every word he said that made him feel ten feet tall. It also had another equally powerful effect on him, it really turned him on. He could feel his erection contained in the tight white breeches and faintly wondered if the bulge had been noticed by anyone else. One thing was for sure, Mary had noticed. When they were dancing he could feel her pressed up against him, there was no doubting that she felt how hard he was, or that she had deliberately moved closer, rocking gently against him in a way that made his body ache with desire. After that dance she became much more familiar than before, resting her hand on his thigh while they were talking and even giving him a familiar squeeze a little too close to his crotch to be misinterpreted.

Then just after 11.30 p.m., Mary came over faint, she complained of a terrible headache, made her excuses to the other guests at their table, smiled apologetically at him and started to make her way outside and back towards her cabin. His first thought was one of total frustration. He should have been feeling sorry for the poor woman but all he could think about was how let down he felt. He hadn't realised how frustrated he'd become and made a mental note never to go through such a long period of celibacy again. In the meantime he wasn't ready to admit defeat.

The prospect of going back to his cabin alone and probably succumbing to the need to masturbate on his own was a desolate one, he couldn't ignore his situation though, he was so horny, if he didn't get his rocks off he was likely to explode. Almost without realising what he was doing he had got to his feet started walking towards the exit. He didn't stop to say his goodnights, despite the many greetings he received as he made his way across the crowded room. Many of the guests and crew must have wondered what had got into their Captain that night, except those who had seen his tryst with Mary and observed her departure, they may have known more than the Captain himself about his destination and duties that night.

As he reached the entrance to the stairwell that led to the guests' cabins, a sudden panic seized him when he realised he didn't know the number of her cabin. Then to his relief he remembered that while they were talking she mentioned the problems she'd been having with her bath; he'd offered to see to it that the issue was dealt with in the morning, her cabin number was on a napkin in his inside pocket. He stopped in the middle of the corridor and leant against the wall, sure enough there it was, a little ragged but still legible, the number was 723. That meant he was in the right part of the ship and that her cabin was down one level and a few metres to port. Relieved he replaced the tissue in his pocket, frightened that he may forget his destination on the way and started to walk towards the next stairway.

When he finally reached the door to number 723, he had to get the tissue out of his pocket one last time to check he was really at the right place. This time though the tissue was rolled between his fingers and cast into the dark corner of the passageway. The Captain's ardour had cooled slightly now that he was confronted with the practical hurdle of knocking on the door. What would he say? perhaps she was ill after all, or worse perhaps he had misinterpreted her interest and she was only teasing him, leading him on with no real intention of following it through. His forehead was getting moist and his hands clammy as the possible embarrassing outcomes played themselves out before him. By the third one he'd completely lost his bottle and his motivation to go on. Just as he turned to leave, the door opened of its own accord, Mary Swain stood before him wearing a medium length chiffon nighty, the smell of her newly brushed hair and peppermint breath changed him instantly, he was hard again, the aching desire greater than ever.

Mary appeared to recognise and understand his predicament and so spared him further need to speak by taking him by both hands and pulling him into the cabin, closing the door with a well aimed kick. In one flowing movement she slid down his body, her hands working expertly on the fastenings of his breeches. He stood in electrified wonder as they fell to his knees. She took his cock in both hands squeezing hard, the sharp pain forcing him to control himself, then she ran her tongue down the shaft to his balls which she cradled briefly in her soft wet mouth. His moan of pleasure signalled her to rise, helping him free of his pants on the way. Once erect she kissed him passionately then pulled away and walked towards the bedroom. He watched her go, remembering the soft feel of her breasts beneath the negligee, savouring the feeling, before removing the rest of his clothes and following after.

VI

Much later, Captain Melvin Oldroyd Simms couldn't remember whether it was before or after he'd slid into Mary Swain he was interrupted by the huge bang that rocked the Queen Charlotte to her gunwales. Either way he was sure that penetration did take place and in spite of what transpired after, nothing could shake the pleasure of the memory from his mind.

The bang was followed by a brief moment of silence in which Mel and many others tried to convince themselves nothing had happened. Then came the after shock and the ship lurched heavily to starboard sending guests, crew and cargo reeling across floors, down stairs and corridors and in a few cases over the side into the ocean. Considering his situation the Captain reacted quickly and coolly to the crisis. There was no question of fumbling apologies, nor was there any need for any, Mary realised what her new man had to do and was equally keen that he get on and do it.

He made his way to the cabin phone and using his personal code called the bridge. Jensen Cartwright had drawn the short straw that night and was in command of the bridge, what should have been a frustrating but uneventful watch was now turning into the most exciting day in a seafaring career that was to span nearly half a century.

'What the hell is going on up there Jensen?' barked the Captain.

'Don't know sir,' came the reply.

'We should be trawling deep water, no climate, just this damned mist.'

'What mist man, what are you talking about?' snapped the Captain.

There was a slight pause as the Jensen assimilated the response, then he replied.

'About twenty minutes ago sir, it came out of nowhere, a thick sea mist, didn't seem like anything to worry about at the time and then this.'

Melvin thought for a moment, he had to make up his mind quickly as to what to do. The sirens were already sounding the alert and the guests and crew should even now be gathering at the lifeboat stations, the question was did he give the order to abandon ship or not?

'Do you have a damage report Jensen?'

'Not yet sir but we're working on it, the instruments don't show anything but it feels like we hit some kind of reef or something.'

'OK stand by then I'm coming up.'

He shot one last glance at Mary who was standing a few feet away listening to everything, grabbed his clothes as best he could and ran naked from the cabin.

The decision not to abandon ship was a close call and one that earned Melvin Simms the respect of his peers and the gratitude of his company. It was a close run thing and in the end he had to go up against Chris Walpole who felt it was right to take to the lifeboats. Had they done so the storm that followed would have no doubt claimed the lives of many on board as well as resulting in the loss of the finest and most valuable ship in the fleet. In the end the whole thing passed off with relatively little trauma; true there was the issue of a fifteen foot gash in the hull, cause unknown and the mysterious disappearance of the young American girl. Despite attempts to find the boy she'd been seen with no-one turned up and no-one of that description was registered on muster the ship's. Her parents were naturally distraught, particularly the father who appeared to blame himself for what happened. In the end though nothing could be done, despite an extensive search over the next few days hampered by the thick fog and appalling weather conditions. An open verdict was recorded at the hearing with the girl being listed as "missing at sea presumed dead".

Chapter Three

I

For almost a month after the incident on the Queen
Charlotte, Tom was like a dead man walking. He couldn't
comfort his wife or even communicate with her. It was as
if the loss of Samantha had turned him into some kind of
zombie. Ellen was herself distraught and suffered badly
from her husband's reaction. At first she was convinced
their daughter had been abducted and that they would
eventually be contacted with a ransom demand. It was
the kind of arrogant under stress reaction that came from
being part of America's elite and untouchable super rich.
As the days unfolded into weeks and still they heard
nothing, she came to accept her daughter was dead.
Murdered by her abductors for some reason she couldn't
understand.

The police were very efficient and helpful at first, after
all it wouldn't do to upset a family like the Kidmans by
being unfeeling or overly pessimistic. It was Ellen not Tom
who kept in daily contact with the detective in charge of
the investigation. She would ask him how things were
going, he would tell her about all the new lines of enquiry
they were pursuing and reassure her that 'if those bastards
were out there, they would be found and brought to
justice'. Gradually these updates became shorter and less
sincere, eventually they started to double back on
themselves. She'd heard it all before and realised they were
just going through the motions, the police and everyone
else had given up.

Thank goodness for her friends. Never had a woman

needed the support of her friends more. Ellen's circle had always been tight, they shared so much in common. They came from the same kind of wealthy established American families, they went to the same schools, studied for the same degrees and most importantly, married the same kind of husbands. She had already experienced the profound comfort her exclusive group could provide but always up to now in the role of a comforter rather than the comforted.

As they all grew older there were more setbacks to contend with. The previous year Kelly-Ann had to have a breast removed so they all had a girls only party, got drunk and giggled at the prosthetic device she'd been given to wear. There had been other tragedies over the years. Children seemed to account for a lot of them, sickness, drugs, even runaways, one or other of her friends had been through it. Health, children and their husbands' jobs, these were the catalysts that seemed able to upset their otherwise serene lives and they'd developed a very effective system of dealing with them when they happened.

They seemed to rise to the challenge of helping one of their own with real enthusiasm. Never a day went by when there wouldn't be something to divert her from her grief, a tennis tournament, a bridge competition or a ladies' golf day. She accepted these invitations gratefully, they were the only thing that stopped her going crazy, like Tom.

She'd known for a while that he was on the edge. Even if no-one else noticed, she recognised the signs. Even before the cruise he'd become even more obsessive than usual, particularly when it came to Samantha. He didn't seem to realise she was nearly a fully grown woman who needed to be given more freedom and independence. Instead he seemed intent on smothering her with overprotection. When he was home, the poor kid was never allowed out the house, sometimes he wouldn't even let her out of his sight. If he was behaving as strangely at work then it wouldn't be long before people began to gossip, he was already at a "dangerous age". In merchant banking, once you were no longer believed to be safe hands you were finished. That's why she thought the cruise would be such a good idea. It would be an opportunity for Tom to see how his daughter had grown up, to give her some social freedom in a secure environment, one where she could come to no harm.

'Ha!' she thought. 'No harm. That was a joke, she couldn't have put her in more danger if she had forced her to play chicken blindfolded on the freeway.'

When he showed no interest in getting in touch with the office and explaining what happened, it was she who had to make the call. Don Shapiro seemed very understanding and sympathetic, sincerely so. He told her not to worry, if there was anything at all, she must call. He told her to tell Tom not to worry about the office, they could all get by just fine without him. The next day a huge bouquet arrived with a card, she was very touched, she even shed a little tear.

A week later an official looking letter arrived by recorded mail. It was from the company's attorneys. Tom wouldn't open it, she felt a bit unsure, wondering briefly if she should wait until her husband was better but eventually curiosity and apprehension got the better of her and she opened it. The language was flowery, as well as precise and legalistic, the point was clear. He'd been suspended on full pay, the bank was sorry about what happened but it owed a duty to its shareholders. So, Sonia was to have a new boss if she didn't have one already.

'Well,' she thought. 'Maybe it's all for the best.' If times were happier they could have taken some time out together. Samantha could have stayed with friends and they could have gone away somewhere to be alone and repair their damaged marriage. Somewhere warm and secluded like a tropical island.

As time dragged on and Tom got no better any thoughts she had of things being for the best faded away, replaced with a hard edged cynicism mixed with a sharp instinct for self preservation. At least if he could have returned to work he would have had something to take his mind off their loss. He would have been out from under her feet. These thoughts made her feel guilty but the guilt didn't make them go away. If anything they made her more selfish and cool, even though she new he felt her coolness and was badly hurt by it.

In her mind she had a fixed image of how a good wife should be acting in a situation like this. Her stereotype bore the pain of loss in a quiet caring way, she was a rock, a bottomless well of love from which her family could draw comfort, putting her own feelings last and drawing strength from her own unselfishness. Unfortunately she could no more live up to her stereotype than she could live in a small suburban house on the unfashionable outskirts of town. She knew her limitations very well and the knowledge made her even colder, even harder.

If he hadn't announced he was leaving she probably would have left him soon anyway. He tried to explain what he was doing but to be honest she didn't really listen. She thought, 'He may pretend to himself he's off to find Samantha but they both knew the real truth. He was running away, he couldn't handle what had happened, he had let it destroy his career and ruin their marriage.' Oh yes, she made all the right noises, even helping him pack and kissing him tearfully goodbye, but deep down she knew it was the end, she was going to have to start out over again.

Tom was oblivious to the metamorphosis his wife was undergoing. If he had realised, the knowledge would definitely have finished him. He really loved Ellen and believed she loved him, which, in her way, she did. The only thing was, her way had a lot of caveats attached to it, most of which he broke when he lost his job and started behaving crazy. Luckily he was too lost in self pity and guilt to notice what was happening to his marriage. Of course it wasn't just losing Samantha that was making him so dysfunctional. There were other factors at work as well.

These other factors weren't the kind his new analyst recognised. At least not for what they were, real. He nodded and sucked on his pen top, knowingly, thinking he understood how his delusional patient was creating imaginary demons to rationalise the loss of his daughter. These big city types were all the same, control freaks to a man. He swore that every overpaid city executive thought the whole world and its affairs revolved around their silly necks. Still what he thought hardly mattered, his job was to sit and listen, listen and sit and above all keep sending out those fat bills at the end of the month. Danny Sugarman thought neuroses were God's way of saying 'Danny, you're a good boy and as a reward I'm going to let you live off the rich Goyim, you have my permission to suck them dry.'

Mind you there were times when Tom Kidman had him rattled. There was something strange about this one, he looked like a man with a disease. (He was in fact in perfect physical health, Danny always insisted his patients take a full physical examination before starting therapy, after all the last thing he needed was to be sitting for an hour in a stuffy room with someone who had something catching). He really thought he may have a live one for the first time in his career, someone with a clinically diagnosable, if not treatable, condition. If he did it was his chance to get himself some respect, why if he played his cards right he could even get a new syndrome named after him. 'Sugarman's syndrome', yup, it had a good ring to it.

He'd just suggested hypnotism as the next step to the treatment when Kidman stopped coming. He was so upset he called him at home, something he made it a rule never to do. All he got was some stuck up bitch who he assumed was Kidman's wife telling him he'd gone a long trip and no-one knew when he was going to be back. Oh well he thought, the mad bastard probably wasn't that special anyway. That evening he sent his final bill to the Kidman residence and made it a really big one to make up for the disappointment.

II

The idea he must do something took shape only slowly in Tom's tortured mind. There were a lot of tangled weeds in there to choke the seed of decision before it could firmly take root. Some seeds are hardy though, they can live in the most cruel environments and there was one seed of hope in his mind that just wouldn't die. This thought hadn't anything directly to do with Samantha but with Jack Simons. A voice he'd rejected for so long he'd forgotten it existed was finally making itself heard and it was telling him to go and see Jack. It was as if he was suffering from a fever, caused by a virus which had laid dormant in his system for years and Jack somehow held the antidote. If he was ever to be well again, to stand any chance of even looking for Samantha, never mind about getting her back, then he would have to go and see Jack.

Chapter Four

I

Jack woke up feeling the first signs of depression washing over him. They were symptoms with which he'd become only too familiar over the years. It was five o'clock in the morning but already sunlight filled the room, the cheap curtains losing their pathetic attempt to keep out the intrusive rays. He lay there in a sweat of frustration, wanting to get up and pee but too lost in his own grey world of shadows and self pity to get out of bed.

It would be unfair to say his life was all bad though. Being married to Ruth had its compensations; their life together was a rich one in many ways. During the time that separated his depressions he would feel almost happy, almost fulfilled. He kept telling himself how lucky he was, how much he had to thank God for. He was healthy, his wife loved him and he loved her. They had three beautiful healthy children, even money wasn't a big problem; so why did he always end up the same way, lying in bed feeling like the biggest failure in the world.

Every time it happened he would slip into a deeper depression than the time before, it was an illness the doctors said; a curse more like. It was only having Ruth around that made life bearable. It was only her patience and optimism that had kept him sane over the years. There were countless times when, out of desperation he had seriously contemplated walking away from everything but Ruth's, inner strength stopped him.

It hadn't always been this way. There was a time when

his self confidence was a wonder to behold, when he coveted nothing, feared nothing. That was a long time ago though, it was almost as if he were a different person then, more complete somehow. The reality of life had taught him he couldn't rely on himself, whenever he trusted his judgement he regretted it, whenever he made a decision that affected his family it was the wrong one. It seemed the harder he worked, the more energy he put into his work, the less he was rewarded. Some unseen dealer had marked the deck and was dealing his cards off the bottom.

If he was going to be totally honest with himself it wasn't all bad luck either. Somehow he'd never been able to really deliver the goods. The flare and self confidence that so marked out his earlier years had deserted him. Without it he was like a crippled athlete; he could remember what it was like to perform but could no longer do the job. It wasn't from want of trying either but the harder he tried, the worse it was and the more frustrated he became. He was missing some vital component that defined what he was, without it he was a pale shadow of what he was meant to be.

There was no doubting the curse would have destroyed him long ago if it weren't for Ruth. Left to his own devices, he would have allowed himself to be consumed by jealousy, frustration and resentment. He would have lost his love of life completely and succumbed to the dark side of his nature, the side that even now kept him awake, preventing him from finding peace. The reason for his salvation, thus far, was lying beside him, her breathing, as with so much else about her, was calm and reassuring.

Why Ruth had stuck by him all these years he would never know. That wasn't true; actually he did know, she stayed because she really loved him. It was why she loved him he couldn't understand, he had let her down so many times. What he did know was it was only her strength and belief that gave him reason to carry on. There was no pity in her love, pity would have killed him; no demands and no disappointment. She just believed in him pure and simple. It was Ruth's ability to make the worse disappointments seem OK that enabled him to keep his self respect, to keep hoping, to keep trying. He still really wanted to live up to her love, but it was getting more and more difficult. Every time he suffered another episode of depression, he could feel himself being sucked into an ever deeper, darker vortex of hate, from which eventually, even Ruth wouldn't be able to rescue him.

II

It all started after they came back from Florida together. The three weeks they spent there were like a dream to him now. They were so wrapped up in one another, nothing bad could ever have come between them. Their happiness burned so brightly it either destroyed, disguised or, at the least, held at bay whatever evil eye had been cast upon him. He remembered arriving back so full of hopes and ambitions; Where were they now? What had he been able to achieve over the years?

At first he wasn't easily discouraged. Ironically, in the beginning it was always he who would brush aside failure or bad luck, gently chiding Ruth, telling her to have faith, not to worry.

His plan was simple, begin in sales, move into management, then start his own business and make a fortune.

Everything went more or less according to plan as far as the first hurdle anyway.

The Dark Lagoon

Admittedly, the interviews should have given him a clue to what lay in store; he didn't read the signs though.

He expected all the companies he applied to be falling over themselves to get him.

As it turned out the first two were less than enthusiastic. Both were computer manufacturers; at the first he seemed to clash badly with the sales manager, no matter what he said the guy would take it the wrong way. He wrote that one off to bad luck.

The second company said his degree was inappropriate and that he wasn't numerate enough for the job. This concerned him a bit more so he changed his approach slightly and chose an office equipment manufacturer for his third attempt.

He was offered the job. The interview lasted all day, he was grilled by three different managers but he got there in the end. The name of the company was Butler and Walker. They weren't as glamorous as the computer companies but they were well established and regarded as one of the "big boys". Jack was reassured when Derek the sales manager showed him the board on which the salespeople marked the value of their sales. It was clear that some of them were earning good money, at least the same or more as could be earned selling computers. Derek assured him the company ran a superb graduate training program, he winked knowingly at the end of the interview saying it was a much easier market than computers and with better commissions.

The interview was a close run thing, if his eventual boss and team leader Roger Williams had arrived on time and in the mood for an interview, he may not even have been nodded through. As it turned out though, he and Roger seemed to have an immediate affinity. Roger was a naturally intuitive salesman; he could sniff out deals in places other salesman wouldn't even think of. He worked long and hard to get Jack off the ground, they became friends, he even ended up as the best man at Jack and Ruth's wedding. It was no good though; nothing worked consistently for Jack. Inevitably he eventually failed to meet target three months in a row, meaning automatic dismissal. Roger tried to win him a reprieve, even putting his own job on the line but the company wouldn't budge and so they both left.

Roger got him his next job in recruitment, the company was a young one but expanding fast. They specialised in providing software engineers and programmers on a contract basis. There was big money to be earned; passengers weren't tolerated. Despite Roger quickly establishing himself as their top producer, they wouldn't keep Jack who seemed either hopelessly unlucky or just plain hopeless. He had survived at Butler and Walker for nine months; ITP only kept him for five.

After he lost the job at ITP he spent a couple of years doing the circuit of the second rate companies. Sometimes he would last longer than others but it would always end up the same. He would fail to meet his targets and get the sack. The only thing that amazed him more than his poor performance in those days was the gullibility and stupidity of the companies who took him on. You'd think they'd be able to learn from other people's mistakes and give him a wide birth.

In the end he ran out of road, there wasn't an unlimited number of companies prepared to pay a guarantee, eventually he was faced with commission only or looking for another field of endeavour. Never lacking in bravery he had a go at selling insurance on a commission only basis. This went the same way as all the other failed attempts with the added twist that he managed to alienate

The Dark Lagoon

most of his friends and family in the process.

It was after the insurance debacle that Ruth insisted they talk about other things he could do. She was pregnant with their second child at the time. In a few weeks she would have to give up her job in the solicitors' office. She was justly worried about how they would survive without her wages if he didn't get a regular job. This was a particularly painful memory, he knew Ruth would never say anything but she secretly wanted to give up her job and look after the children full time. She wasn't lazy or afraid to break with tradition, she was just that kind of person. He felt horribly guilty at having let her down so he agreed to look for a less risky job for a while.

He had still not totally given up though, promising himself another try at the big time as soon as she returned to work.

The baby was born and Ruth returned to work. Over the years somehow there was never a right moment for him to give selling another try. He eventually admitted to himself that he was scared to go back to it. Then Ruth was pregnant again and it was pointless worrying about it any more. He was doing a milk round at the time, bringing home more money than ever before. When Ruth left on maternity leave he was offered another round. For once things seemed to be going their way, it was hard work but the money made it worth it. For the first time they were able to put something aside for the future, he even harboured the secret hope that they could start their own business in time.

When Ruth returned to work this time he was determined to make things work out. He put his head down and worked all the hours God sent to save money. At the end of a year he was exhausted and almost relieved when the dairy announced it would be closing. Apparently milkmen were an anachronism, a thing of the past; he had to find something else. Between them they'd saved over twenty thousand pounds, enough to see them through comfortably until he found himself a steady job. He didn't want that though. Ruth never was a business woman; she was the first to admit to it, when they met she utterly believed that it would be Jack who could be left to make all the practical business decisions. Now she found herself being brought into a situation she felt ill equipped to deal with.

Conscious of his past failures he wanted Ruth to fully participate in the decision to go it alone. He wanted her to help him choose a business and to work in it with him. This proved to be a misguided strategy, she thought safety first, he wanted to take risks but lacked the judgement to evaluate them. Between them they decided to compromise and chose a franchise, at least that way they would get some back up and support, they wouldn't have to reinvent the wheel.

It was an unmitigated disaster. Because they had chosen a franchise the bank agreed to extend their mortgage and lend them an additional twenty thousand. Looking back at it why they chose an American ice cream franchise he would never know. As it was two miserable years of no summer were enough to see them go under. To make matters worse the year after there was a brilliant summer, they had to watch as the business they had struggled so hard to establish took off with its new owners who had bought it for a song.

Ruth went back to the solicitors' office and Jack got a job in an export warehouse working for a childhood friend. He felt totally burnt out, a shell of a person. It was at this point his fragile self respect finally crumbled away and he had his first real bout of depression. It wasn't something he could easily come to terms with. He really didn't believe in mental illness, at least not when it came to him. It felt more physical, like there was something dark sucking at his mind, taking away his will to go on. During that first episode he lost his ability to communicate with everyone including Ruth. He would have lost his job again but there was an insurance policy at the company that paid three quarters of his wages.

He refused to go to the doctor at first. It was only when his boss, still a friend, sent him home, telling him he would have to go or the insurance wouldn't pay that he agreed. The doctor examined him and prescribed anti-depressants, but he went to the chemists to get the prescription and threw the pills straight in the waste-bin. Something inside him said they wouldn't help, that whatever it was that ailed him couldn't be treated with pills. After three weeks he went back to the doctor who seemed concerned he hadn't improved so referred him to a clinical psychologist.

Somewhat surprisingly there followed a series of tests that revealed he was lacking some kind of enzyme. The specialist was quite excited; said she'd never come across a similar case. Apparently this enzyme was normally produced in the brain. Although it had never been directly connected to any particular bodily function, there had been experiments on rats. These showed that, where it was removed, the animals became listless, often refusing to eat, even starving themselves to death. She said there was some research being done into producing a synthetic version but that in the meantime no treatment existed. She recommended he seek the help of a psycho-analyst and take up yoga. This last suggestion helped to save him for a long time.

After the meeting with the specialist he decided that if he was going to pull himself out of his depression he needed something to give him back his self respect. This realisation was the first step to his recovery. He managed to talk to Ruth about it; she had been worried out of her mind; using all her powers to bring him back to himself but to no avail. She would have agreed to almost anything he wanted at that stage. If he'd said they were taking the children and going to live on the African plains, she would have gone along with it if it meant he got well again.

As it turned out, she needn't have worried. His way out of the black hole was purely a physical one. If there was something missing in his brain that stopped him performing, there was no such handicap with his body. He decided to take up martial arts. He felt the discipline would help him resist the urge to succumb to his darker thoughts. So he joined a local karate dojo.

At the dojo he met a remarkable man, an Irishman recently returned from Japan. His name was Shamus Rouanne; he'd studied for fifteen years in a monastery, learning the innermost secrets of the most deadly and demanding of all the Japanese fighting styles. Over the weeks he observed Shamus becoming more and more impressed with what he saw. Then one evening Shamus invited him for a drink, apparently he'd found an empty building and wanted Jack to become the first pupil at their own Dojo.

Unknown to the two men the pub was a known haunt for an especially violent West Indian street gang specialising in the usual pursuits of drug trafficking, extortion and prostitution. Jack and Shamus stuck out like sore thumbs amongst the locals, they were taken for cops and the decision was taken to deal with them.

When the group of Rastas started to move closer to their table, neither man reacted. There were eight in the gang headed up by an ugly looking piece of work with a hair lip and biceps the size of Jack's thighs. They weren't kidding around either, There were no warnings or chit chat; they hardly even bothered to provoke a fight. Jack saw hair lip pulling out a switch, suddenly he could smell the jerk sauce mixed with Marijuana coming from their sweating bodies; almost taste the danger they were in but it was too late, seconds later all hell broke loose.

Although clearly the leader, Hair-lip wasn't the one to start the fight, he stood back from the action like a general commanding his troops from a safe distance. From the smile on his face he obviously didn't count on a long campaign, expecting the two ineffectual white men to be easy meat for his battle hardened soldiers. The look changed so fast it was comical when first one then another black man went down, then they were falling like shallow rooted trees in a cyclone.

The speed with which Shamus moved was amazing, almost supernatural. He was tall but not particularly heavy; nonetheless he was able to put down these larger opponents with consummate ease. Soon it was only Hair-lip who remained standing, still holding the switch, which no longer seemed threatening, more like a toy in the hand of a naughty regretful child. The leader looked round in disbelief at his vanquished troops groaning or unconscious around him; then back at Shamus. Despite being the victor, there was no gloating in his eyes, no overstuffed pride. Here was a true hero, shunning glory, someone who sincerely believed in what he preached

III

Jack saw salvation in Shamus, a man without worldly riches who seemed to have achieved true self esteem. He followed him willingly, throwing himself into his studies and sticking rigorously to a punishing program of training. Others quickly joined them, some better than others. Over the years the new Dojo grew beyond even Shamus's expectations, achieving a cult status in the world of martial arts. Its charismatic leader became a guru to whom other European masters would turn for advice and guidance. Jack was happy to see this success, down the years he kept training and his special relationship with Shamus, being recognised by others as having been there from the start. Despite his growing physical prowess, he shunned combat. He wouldn't compete, or even spar using full contact. Shamus never pushed him on the issue, respecting his decision. The truth was he couldn't do it, the same malaise that dogged his business life destroyed his effectiveness as a fighter. Every time he'd tried the hands that were so deadly in the gym lost their power, his punches became gentle taps, his legs went to jelly under him. He kept training though; kept punishing himself, working ever harder in an attempt to exorcise the demon that possessed him.

Ruth allowed his fanatical devotion to training to continue knowing the alternative was to lose him completely. Nevertheless it put a big strain on their home life. What with his job in the warehouse and training, he never had enough time for her and the children. It was all too often she who ended up neglected. Despite his devotions though he could never fully exorcise the demons that haunted him. He could keep them at bay for long periods but then they would always re-surface, ever stronger, ever more voracious.

Eventually he took to fighting them alone, going to desolate places and living like a hermit for sometimes weeks at a time, punishing his body mercilessly. Often training for up to ten hours a day, returning to the hut or cabin where he was staying too exhausted even to sleep or eat. Ruth hated these periods when he would be away, coming to dread them, fearing that one day he would leave and never return. In her own way she tried everything to help him fight his demons but she was aware of their growing power, how every battle was harder than the last. She began to see a time when even their combined strength wouldn't be enough. She could see her beautiful Jack being torn from her forever into the dark twilight world of the creatures that stalked him.

Then suddenly, a few weeks ago the storm clouds disappeared, it was as if he'd been given another chance, been born again. After so many years of disappointment and struggle they hardly dared to hope that it would be permanent this time; that he'd finally overcome the darkness. As he lay in bed, dripping with sweat he knew they were right to be sceptical. He remembered the wave that nearly killed him all those years ago in Florida, it was coming for him now only this time there would be no escape.

He turned and looked at Ruth, following the curve of her body as it slipped beneath the bed cover. He loved her so much; loved his children; loved their home; even loved their animals. Yet it wasn't enough to save him any more. He felt like a fake person. Ruth hadn't got what she truly deserved; the kids only had half a father. If they were ever in trouble would he be able to protect them? He knew the answer was no and the knowledge burned like acid. He also knew that if he left them they would be devastated. It was what had kept him there all this time. The thought of their pain was what made him fight the darkness and he would fight it again, only this time he knew he would fail.

His deteriorating mood was suddenly interrupted by the telephone. By now it was six o'clock in the morning, Ruth and the kids were still fast asleep; the house was quiet. The ringing pieced through his self pity, deflecting him from his dark introspection but it would stop if he ignored it and he could return to his morbid pondering.

The ringing wouldn't stop though it continued persistently.

Between every ring he thought, 'It'll stop now, whoever it is will give up now.'

Then it would ring again. It must have been at least three minutes before he finally eased himself out of bed, intrigued in spite of himself by the determined caller. The house's single phone lived in the kitchen so he had to put on a robe and walk downstairs before answering it. He went deliberately slowly, all the way daring the caller to hang up. By the time he reached the phone it must have been going for five minutes, he looked at it, mesmerised by the sound which longer seemed to be coming from the phone but from somewhere deep inside himself.

Would he answer it? Dare he answer it?

A voice, loud and strident shouted no. It challenged him to pick up the phone, mocked him for his weakness laughed out loud at his pathetic impotence. His right hand crept out, furtively caressing the receiver as if it were something potentially lethal.

Death; was death such a terrifying prospect? What was so attractive about his life anyway? Perhaps he should give death a try. Maybe he'd like it.

He picked up the receiver and held it up to his ear listening but all he heard was silence.

The seconds ticked by, then a voice thick with fatigue spoke his name.

'Jack, is that you? If it is speak to me; it's Tom, Tom Kidman, I have to talk to you.'

IV

The sound of Tom's voice acted like some kind of trigger in his mind, like someone had let off a firework in his head. He saw a blinding flash, heard a deafening explosion, the concussion throwing him backwards across the faded floor. The receiver was left dangling by its curly plastic cord, Tom's voice barely audible like static from a cheap radio.

He came to disorientated, head aching, vision swimming in and out of focus, settling eventually on the telephone receiver still swaying back and forth inches off the floor. Then he remembered Tom Kidman his bête noir.

They'd been college friends, both starting out with big ambitions, the difference was Tom had actually gone on to achieve his. He'd followed his meteoric rise to the top with interest at first, then awe and finally bitter irony. It wasn't that he was jealous exactly, more that Tom's success served to highlight his own failure. Perhaps that was the reason he'd never got back in contact. For a few years he hoped Tom would call, when he never did, Jack just assumed he didn't want to be associated with a loser and who could blame him.

He was calling now though. Jack struggled to his feet and picked up the receiver.

'Tom, are you still there?'

He could hear his voice trembling as he said the words. Indeed he felt cold, although the room was warm and his whole body was shaking.

'I'm here Jack. I need to talk to you, it's important.'

'Where are you?'

Jack expected to be told he was calling from a plush office somewhere in a different time zone. That would explain the odd hour for the call.

'I'm right outside your house buddy. Right outside; I've been here since three this morning, calling you every ten minutes or so. If you don't mind I'd like to come in.'

Despite his surprise and confusion Jack didn't hesitate.

'Come in? Of course you can come in, hang on a minute.'

He placed the receiver on the work surface, somehow fearful that if he put it down properly and ended the call, Tom would disappear with the connection like a mirage in the dessert. He ran to the front door and opened it, the cool morning breeze clearing his head; even though it was July, this was England after all. Sure enough there, parked across the street was a Mercedes limousine. The passenger door was open and he watched as his old friend stepped out and walked his way.

He wore a beautifully tailored tan cashmere coat which hid most of an equally exquisite Italian suit, more obvious were the expensive designer shoes he wore on his feet. The subtlety of his clothes was contradicted by his red hair, still his outstanding feature, glowing like an admittedly diminished beacon in the watery morning sunshine. Jack felt a peculiar smugness wash over him at the sight of the thinning hair as he thought of his own fulsome though greying mop. He was suddenly self conscious about the way he looked; unshaven, wearing a shabby dressing gown, teeth unbrushed, sleep still in his eyes.

'Follow me into the kitchen, Tom, make yourself at home a second; I'm going to go upstairs and get dressed. Make some tea, you'll see where everything is.'

The Dark Lagoon

It was all he could say before, trying to stop himself from breaking into a run, he hastily made his exit. When he entered their bedroom, Ruth was still lying under the covers, as he walked in she rolled over and propped herself up on an elbow.

'What's going on Jack? Is there someone downstairs?' She said sleepily.

He went over to the bed and sat down beside his wife. He put an arm on her shoulder, taking a moment to admire how fine she looked after all these years, even first thing in the morning.

'It's OK, we have a visitor, though you'll never believe who. Tom Kidman and he's arrived in the biggest car you've ever seen. He's in the kitchen now, I told him to make himself some tea.'

Ruth looked troubled. Not the kind of look Jack would have expected. There was a protective note in her voice when she next spoke, all traces of tiredness gone.

'What does he want Jack. We haven't seen or heard of him for so long.'

She was silent but he could see she wanted to say more, he nodded encouragingly.

'I've never talked about this with you, never thought I would have to but.....' Again silence, he was confused by her reaction, feeling under pressure to get ready and go back to their unexpected guest.

'But what? Darling. I don't know what you're talking about.'

Her expression changed. She'd come to a decision; whatever it was she was going to say could wait. The situation was the situation; it was better to find out what Tom wanted before saying more.

'Oh, nothing really, Just promise you'll be careful when you talk to Tom, there's just something about him I'm not sure about.'

He didn't have time to consider the strangeness of these words. He kissed his wife on the forehead in a gesture of affectionate reassurance and left for the bathroom. He shaved unusually carefully, making sure not to nick himself or leave any telltale stubble. He washed himself thoroughly, then washed his hair and towelled it dry. He was still brushing his teeth as he re-entered his bedroom and opened the wardrobe. Moments later he was fully dressed and on his way back downstairs. As he went, Ruth was sitting up in bed watching him pensively.

When he walked into the kitchen Tom was sitting at the table with two steaming mugs of tea in front of him. He looked at Jack with searching eyes, taking in his slightly greying hair and the impressive leanness of his body,

'I didn't give you any sugar, is that OK?' He said.

Jack sat on the chair opposite and nodded his head, at the same time he reached over and took the mug. They both drank, studying one another as they did so. Eventually it was Tom who started to talk. He began with niceties, enquiring after Ruth and the kids, about Jack's job etc. but it was clear he wasn't there for a social chat. After a while he stopped in his tracks and got to his feet, clearly in distress.

'I'm sorry Jack,' he declared. 'I'm making a terrible job of this like I knew I would.'

He paused, summoning up the resolve to continue.

'I haven't come all this way after such a long time to shoot the shit with you, Jack. The truth is we're not even friends any more; I don't even know if we were ever friends.

The Dark Lagoon

We haven't spoken for over twenty years. I've done things to you; things you can't even imagine. It would have been better if I'd strangled you in your sleep than do what I've done. I don't even really know why I'm here, except that I had to come. When you hear what I've got to say you're going to think I'm mad but I'm not. I'm going to convince you I'm telling the truth and when I've finished you're going to hate me. I can't stay long though, I must go soon... must try and find....'

His voice tailed off and he collapsed back into the chair, head slumped forward in his hands sobbing.

Here was real irony. When Jack woke up this morning he was depressed to the point of suicide or worse because of his utter failure to achieve material success. Tom arrives like a ghost from his past; he has wealth, recognition, everything Jack wants. Is he happy? No, he ends up with his head in his hands sobbing like a baby. Maybe it should make him feel better but it doesn't; it's like someone or something was making fun of him, trying to make his life seem worthless and shallow as well as meaningless and confused.

One thing was for sure though, whatever had driven Tom to travel across the Atlantic wasn't sentimentality, it wasn't a reunion of old buddies he wanted. It was something scary that motivated him.

In spite of himself Jack couldn't help feeling pity for his one-time friend. His natural urge to protect was still intact at least. He waited while the other man regained his composure, then he spoke.

'Look old buddy, you and me seem to still share at least one thing in common. We're both in the shit, maybe for different reasons but that's where we are. Look, no promises eh; I don't know if I can help you, I don't even

Simon Shinerock

know if I want to but if it'll do any good I'll listen.'

Tom sat upright; his jaw stiffened.

'OK; that's better than I deserve. Before I start though You've got to promise to listen all the way to the end without interrupting.'

Jack nodded his agreement to this request.

He started slowly, almost stopping on several occasions, half hoping he would be interrupted in spite of the promise; there was no interruption though, instead Jack remained silent and attentive. When he finally came to the crucial point where he would have to admit his total betrayal he faltered, lacking the resolve to continue. The first sobs escaped in short gasps in spite of his efforts to keep them in, then he was crying like a child, crying for his betrayal of Jack, crying for himself but most of all he was crying for his lost daughter.

Jack was so taken aback by this outburst, he temporarily forgot his own problems, desiring only to somehow console his old friend but not knowing what to say. As usual though he tried his best, stretching over and placing his hands comfortingly onto the others.

'I don't know what happened back then to make you feel like this now, I don't know what kind of trouble you're in to have made you come and find me after all these years but I do know this. For years I've envied you; I've envied your success and your achievements because as you can see, I've achieved nothing.'

Here he paused, gathering his strength

'The reason I'm telling you these things is because the one thing I have learned is how to come to terms with frustration and pain, you could say I'm an expert at it. Sometimes shit happens and no matter how clever you are you can't stop it.'

Again he paused; this was hard; just like everything else he tried to do, he bit his lip hard, the salty taste of his own blood filling his mouth.

'So I'm not going to make you any false promises old buddy, if you still want me to I will listen and if I can help then I will.'

It was the best he could do. Sadly inadequate he knew, but the best he could do anyway.

Tom seemed to calm himself down, Jack could feel the shaking subside and removed his hands. Tom's eyes were still red rimmed and puffy but now there was a steely determination in them.

'I'm sorry' he said simply.

Then in a steady voice that sounded flat and drained he told the rest of his story.

V

As he listened Jack found the answers to many questions that'd plagued him for so long. It was like having a cancer removed from a vital organ, the tumour was no longer there but its removal left him weak and powerless to recover. He could feel the frustrated impotent anger building up in him, anger that wasn't directed against Tom. No, he could see how the poor bastard had been tricked and played for a sucker all the way along; they both had. His anger was directed at the source of their mutual misery. Proctor was the cause of all this and he was sure that somewhere on that impossible Island he was laughing at them both.

Simon Shinerock

They stood staring at one another for what seemed like ages, appreciating the other's misery, unable to be of any help or comfort. Then just as Jack felt he could stand it no more Tom began to speak again.

'I know there's nothing I can do about the past Jack, what's done is done. There is something I can do about the future though.'

Saying this he reached into his coat and withdrew a letter sized brown envelope. It bulged as if it contained something more than paper, he placed it quickly on the table in front of them as if frightened it would burn his fingers. Jack watched in fascination as Tom gingerly opened the small package and tipped the contents out in front of them. Whatever it was caught the morning sun as it cascaded onto the table, sending reflections flashing into their eyes.

The crescent moon attached to a silver chain, stirred emotions in Jack so old he could hardly recognise them. He felt light headed and put a hand on the table to steady himself. His neck began to itch, when he reached up to scratch himself with his free hand he was amazed to feel the impression of an old scar. Tom looked on in amazement as the thin line around Jack's neck appeared from nowhere, turning quickly from white to livid red.

'Pick it up Jack, it's the thing Proctor used to rob you. I've worn it for over twenty years without even knowing it was there. When Sam was taken I thought I would die. I can't describe what I went through, it was like a fever, it went on for three days. Ellen says I was delirious, ranting and raving like a madman. The doctors found nothing wrong with me Jack but when it was over this thing was there round my neck. It must have been there all along, it's the source of his power Jack; I know it is. If you put it on maybe it will give you back what you lost because I'll tell you one thing, I haven't got it any more...'

The Dark Lagoon

Jack wasn't listening, long forgotten nightmares were flashing through his head, a dark hand reached out for him from across a distant ocean. He could hear a voice speaking words of despair inside his mind, telling him the awful truth, this wasn't his friend sitting before him; this was his betrayer. He wasn't there to make amends but to finish off the job he'd started. There was no escape, said the voice. No escape but at least there could be revenge.

He got up from the table, walking deliberately to where several plastic handles poked out of an oak block. Withdrawing a bread knife he turned and faced his betrayer a murderous look in his eyes. Tom was transfixed; perhaps he too was being held by a power neither of them could understand or control; a power that was forcing them to act out the final scene of an unwritten tragedy.

Jack advanced slowly, the veins on his temple pulsating grotesquely green. When he reached his victim he took him by the hair, forcing back his head, exposing the vulnerable flesh of the neck. The hand that held the knife moved swiftly, placing the instrument like a violinist's bow ready to play a long note, deep and deadly. You could almost hear a band playing in the background, getting nearer, ever louder as demonic musicians approached the climax of their black symphony.

Before he could make the final deadly lunge that would have preceded his own suicide something happened to save them both.

Ruth had come downstairs unnoticed just as Tom emptied the pendant onto the table. She watched as Jack took the knife, at first recoiling in horror as she realised what he was going to do. She ran to the table picked up the silver chain and with fingers that felt amazingly steady she placed the chain round Jack's neck. She looked for the clasp to secure it but there was no clasp; the chain ended with unbroken silver links. She hesitated for a moment, indecision threatening to overcome her; then she thrust the two ends together. The effect sent her reeling backwards as the pendant gave off some kind of powerful energy as the ends fused together round her husband's neck.

It was like connecting all the plug leads to a racing car, then giving it full throttle from cold after years of running on one cylinder. Jack thought his brain would explode. He'd existed two dimensionally for so long he couldn't deal with the colour and depth that suddenly overwhelmed him. He dropped the knife harmlessly to the floor and opened his arms wide in exultation, throwing back his head and laughing as the tears rolled freely down his face.

Tom had also regained his senses, the last vestiges of the infection that had contaminated his blood for so long had finally out of his system. He knew he would never again feel a power that belonged to another but it didn't matter, he would learn to be happy with his own gifts.

Even though he was himself again Jack knew the game was far from over. He could see agony written into Tom's face. Proctor wasn't worried whether he had his life back or not; why should he be? ....After all, he had what he wanted........ Samantha,..... she was the prize and while she was in his grasp Proctor was still the winner, but not if he could help it. He made himself a solemn promise, even if it meant confronting the devil in the fiery halls of hell itself, he would hunt Proctor down and destroy him.

Tom saw the anger flare up in Jack's expression and turned away in shame, what he saw troubled him more.

'Ruth'

She was lying still on the floor.

Jack turned at the mention of his wife's name, all other thoughts instantly driven out of his mind. He went

The Dark Lagoon

to her side cradling her in his arms, tears running down his cheeks. Everything he regained would be hollow and barren if he couldn't share it with the woman meant more to him than life itself. His worst fears proved unfounded as her eyelids fluttered then opened, then blinked shut as his tears wet her face.

She smiled and reached up to him, putting her arms around his neck, kissing him full on the lips. It felt as if it were the first time they'd kissed in over twenty years. She realised that the man holding her in his arms was the man she once knew. He was much more than the man with whom she'd lived all these long years. That man was a two dimensional shadow, a shell creature deserving pity only, yet she'd loved him as if he were whole. Now the shadow was gone forever; after all this time her man had come back to her.

In their joy they'd forgotten about Tom who now appeared a haggard figure, shaken physically, mentally diminished in a way that no designer suit could ever hide. He'd watched their reunion with satisfaction and anguish; what was it that had brought him here? A desire to get help or a compulsion to atone for his sins? He knew now there could be no help, if Samantha was to be saved he would have to face the terror on his own. He knew there would be no atonement either; what he had done could never be forgiven. Believing he was still invisible to the lovers he turned to leave. Samantha was still in the hands of the beast and he was impatient to face his doom.

Before he reached the door Jack stopped him in his tracks, his voice was clear and strong.

'Wait. I'm coming with you.'

The words unfroze his heart; yet how could he take Jack with him now? Hadn't he already done enough to ruin his life. No; he would have to go alone.

'Thanks Jack but this is one journey I was meant to take alone. You've already given me more than I deserve after what I've done. Stay here with Ruth, forget about me Jack.'

'I said I'm coming with you.' Now there was an irresistible authority in Jack's voice that stopped once again.

'Wait there for me Tom,' he commanded. 'I have to speak to Ruth alone.'

VI

Jack looked into Ruth's questioning eyes seeing fear and wonder in her gaze. Without a word he took her by the hand and led her out of the kitchen, up the stairs and into their bedroom. He lay her down on their bed and gently made love to her in a way that explained more than words ever could. When they 'd finished, snuggling close to one another under the warm covers he explained why he had to leave. She listened and at the end it was she who was in tears. Tears of happiness mingling with tears of sorrow; after all these years was she to lose her man on the very day he returned to her? Yet there was something in his words that compelled her to understand, something in his voice that made her see the necessity of his actions.

They kissed for a long time, snuggling up once again until after a while he sensed she was asleep. He gently untangled himself and got up to pack. When he was ready he walked back to where Ruth was lying, her breathing regular and low, her face peaceful. He bent down, his lips brushing her cheek, her brow furrowed slightly and she gave out a small sigh. Jack stood up picked up his bag, turned and walked to the door. He looked back at his

The Dark Lagoon

sleeping wife and thought how lucky he was to have her, how much more she was worth than all the money and power in the world. Then he entered the children's rooms and kissed them one by one; when he finished he went back downstairs to where Tom was still waiting and followed his old friend to the waiting limousine.

Chapter Five

I

The first thing Samantha saw when she opened her eyes was Simon's face looking down at her. She had no idea how long she'd lain on the white coral beach but it was long enough for her clothes to have dried completely. The sand was warm; it smelt good; like sea salt and coriander. At first she didn't remember what happened, just smiled back at the boy comfortable under his gaze, feeling happy although vaguely, in the back of her mind she wondered why.

He reached out his hand and she took it. She felt gentleness in his grasp; it was almost, though not quite a caress, pulling her to her feet with unexpected strength. They faced one another holding hands; their eyes locked together, each studying the other. Gradually her mind cleared and she started to remember, thoughts coming like hazy waves out of a foggy sea; small at first, then bigger until they came crashing into her mind with a violence that left her sobbing uncontrollably in his arms. The Queen Charlotte, her parents, they were all gone. She pulled away and looked out across the calm deserted ocean, her anguish seeming to melt into the gentle summer breeze.

'Where are my parents?' she said at last.

His face took on a sombre look as he replied. 'When the ship went down we were thrown overboard. I don't know how it happened but I found you unconscious in the water. I tried to get us to one of the lifeboats but I guess they didn't see us in the fog. If I hadn't found something for us to cling on to we would have drowned. I saw one of those inflatable dinghies floating close by, by the time I hauled us in the other boats had disappeared. We drifted for a day and a night before we reached this Island. The weather started to get bad again and then we hit some kind of reef. The dinghy was holed badly, I only just managed to get us out. I thought you were going to die.'

His tight expression began to fall apart

'I'm so sorry,' he said, voice choked with emotion.

'I don't know whether your parents escaped. We're all alone here and I thought I'd lost you.'

His vulnerability helped to make her strong. If he'd tried to take charge, act the protector; then she would certainly have caved in. She could see he needed her as much as she needed him, except he had already done so much. He'd saved her life at least twice and somehow guided them to this Island. She couldn't help fearing for her parents but the practical side of her was saying they had to think about the here and now. If they didn't find food and shelter soon they would end up dying of thirst or exposure and everything else would no longer matter.

'You saved my life,' she said pulling away slightly and touching his cheek; it was hot, feverish. She had a sudden urge to kiss him on the lips, not a kiss of gratitude but a proper grown-up kiss. She wondered where such a kiss would lead but instead she put a hand to his forehead. Sure enough he was burning up.

'You're not well, we must get you out of the sun.'

Her words broke the spell between them and he nodded. She could see the fever in his eyes now. It was frightening the speed with which it was taking hold. They had no time to lose, now it was Sam who put her arm round Simon, offering him support as together they made their way up the beach towards the cover of the trees. Although it was less than a hundred metres, by the time they reached cover he was delirious and Sam, herself still weak and frail could no longer support his weight. She just managed to lay him down beside a tall palm, out of the sunlight that was growing in intensity as every minute passed.

She didn't want to leave him, not only because she feared for his safety but also because she was scared to explore the strange Island on her own. There wasn't anything else for it though; unless she found them some water they would both die. She tried to explain but he didn't hear her, he was moaning incoherently on the ground, strange mutterings she didn't understand. She kissed him on his forehead, wishing she had some cool water to sponge the fever away. There would be no relief here though, it was up to her to save them both.

Without a better plan she decided follow the line of the trees around the Island. If she headed inland at this stage there was a good chance she would get lost. In spite of her situation she couldn't help feeling awe-struck at her surroundings. If a person had to die there was no more idyllic a place on earth to do it. Although young she was well travelled and educated. She'd seen more than her fair share of impressive places but this was different. This place was so beautiful it was almost surreal, like something out of a fantasy. It was real enough though; of that there could be no doubt; just as her growing thirst was real and the fever draining Simon of his life's force was also real.

These practical considerations forced her to concentrate. She picked up her pace slightly, conscious of the needs to get a move on and conserve energy. She walked to the water's edge where it felt cooler and the sand was harder packed and easier to walk on, suddenly aware of just how tired and hungry she was. She'd only been walking for about half an hour but it already seemed as if she'd been trekking along the hot deserted beach forever. The vista remained the same; blue sky, empty ocean and the line of tall palms giving way to the mystery of the Island's interior.

Just as she was beginning to lose her resolve, in the distance she heard something out of the ordinary. The noise was only just audible over the gentle lapping of the small waves on the beach. At first she wasn't even sure if the new noise was real or her imagination. It sounded like tubular bells being played rhythmically in perfect key but without a melody. No, it wasn't the sound of music at all but a melodious rushing sound. Whatever it was, it was familiar and for no reason she could put her finger on it caused new hope to stir in her chest. The sound drew her on, curiosity overcoming exhaustion and despair.

The vista in front of her was changing, she realised the beach was coming to an end, giving way to a sand spit which reached out far into the ocean. The tree line also ended with the beach, the last few palms bravely venturing out further onto the sand than their fellows completing the barrier which separated where she stood from what was clearly another part of the Island. What lay on the other side of the spit she couldn't tell but she could hear the rushing noise getting ever louder as she approached. Desperation mixed with curiosity drove her on in the vain hope she would find something beyond the spit to save them both.

II

The spit was only about three hundred yards away when she spotted the anomaly. At first she thought it was her eyes playing tricks on her. The air above the spit seemed to be shimmering. She closed her eyes tight, counted slowly up to ten and opened them; it was still there, faint but unmistakable, a delicate membrane translucent in the sunlight forming a disturbing barrier between her part of the Island and the next. She started to shiver, a sudden urge to run away almost overwhelming her; to run away from this strange desolate place, run until she found her parents and her normal life, or fell exhausted onto the sand.

The thought of what might happen if she gave way to despair wasn't what made her fight it, of what might come crawling out of the sea while she lay exhausted and defenceless on the sand never crossed her mind. It was the thought of Simon that made her take herself in hand and force her fears to the back of her mind. He was still back there waiting for her to return, he'd saved her life and now it was her turn to save his. She had to carry on no matter what and if she was going to die on this Island then death wouldn't win easily; he would have to fight hard for his prize, she would struggle to the last. Forcing tiredness, fatigue and hunger to the back of her mind she walked, impatiently towards the sand spit.

As she grew nearer the barrier she half expected the anomaly to disappear like a mirage. She remembered what it was like when she first skied in the French Alps. Going through the clouds, seeing their substance melt away to mist as she approached. Unlike the alpine clouds, the barrier was apparently no illusion. If anything the closer she came the more substance it took on. By now she should

The Dark Lagoon

have been able to see clearly beyond the barrier, instead all that was visible was a dull haze, even the colour of the sky beyond was impossible to determine. The sand spit itself also seemed to be changing as she approached. From a distance it seemed to be a simple continuation of the beach, albeit in a different direction. She was still about a hundred yards away when it dawned on her the spit had sides.

Up to then her plan had been a simple one, walk right up to the spit, find a path through the trees and find out what lay on the other side of the Island. The noise she heard earlier had also taken shape in her mind, she was convinced it was the sound of running water. Fresh water meant hope of food, hope for her and hope for Simon. Now she was becoming perplexed once again. The enigma of the shimmering barrier was intriguing but of much less practical significance than the possibility she wouldn't be able to climb the sides of the spit. If this were the case her only option would be to try and find a way through by forcing her way into the Island's interior. She cast an eye up the beach to the line of palms standing like soldiers at the sand's edge. If the forest was as thick here as it was back where she left Simon then she would probably be lost within a few feet of entering it. There had to be a way up onto the spit and she would have to find it.

As she suspected, by the time she actually reached the spit, the sides had grown well beyond her stature. Any thoughts she may have entertained about scrambling up them were abandoned when she saw how smooth and steep they were. Although it looked like a sand spit from a distance, now she was up close, Samantha realised it was after all not a natural phenomena at all. It must have been made out of some kind of local sandstone using a method she couldn't even guess at. Perhaps there used to be two tribes who lived on the Island and were constantly

Simon Shinerock

at war, maybe one of them built the barrier to prevent whoever it was on the other side from invading.

She reached out and touched the surface of what she still thought of as the spit. It was rougher than it looked, the thin covering of beach sand giving way to something else with sharp ridges and needle like points. Anyone trying to rush these defences was going to end up sorry, if she was going to get to the top she would have to find an easier way.

She took a few steps back from the spit noticing an area about halfway between the ocean and the palms where there was a darker coloured band slashed neatly into the side of the wall. It didn't look like an opening exactly but at least it was something different. She walked towards the dark swath feeling more apprehensive with every step. There was something wrong about this whole place, something she should have recognised straight away. The short hairs on the nape of her neck were beginning to rise and deep down in her subconscious childhood warnings about the bogeyman were surfacing. Perhaps it was all a dream, yes, that was it, this was all an illusion She was really lying sick and delirious in her bed, being ministered to by her mother while her father argued with the Captain about getting a helicopter to fly her to hospital. Her eyes were tight shut, she was pinching herself furiously and for a moment she thought she could hear her mother's voice. She opened her eyes but all she saw was the harsh reality of the sand spit and the dark band which seemed to draw her closer, daring her to test its secrets.

Feeling powerless to resist whatever force it was that had brought her there, she took the few steps separating her and the dark band. Sure enough as she approached she could see that carved in the stone face were a series of small bumps, no more than that. The bumps were arranged straight up the face and could have no other function than that of a ladder. Perhaps they used to be bigger and had been eroded by the action of the waves over hundreds of years, she didn't think so, they were just big enough for their purpose and after all why waste energy making them any bigger than they had to be?

She took hold of the first bump, finding it surprisingly hard to get safe purchase, still very aware of the danger potential of the rock should she lose her grip. She couldn't afford to get hurt, there was no-one around who would come to her rescue. She proceeded slowly and carefully, only moving upwards once she had properly found her balance and had a firm grip on the next rung. It seemed to a long time to reach the summit about nine feet above her. The sun beat down on her shoulders telling her the time was approaching midday and reminding her of how hungry and thirsty she was. Just before the top she nearly fell, her right hand broke its hold, her elbow crashing into the rock with a sickening thud.

Despite the pain she managed to cling on with her remaining hand long enough to regain a safe purchase. The effort left her shaking and exhausted, her elbow throbbing, her head reeling and her left hand dripping blood from the stubs of its torn and broken nails. In spite of this setback she was nearly at the top, she'd made the last rung and emerged onto the parapet that ran along the top of the spit.

Her new vantage point was like being on the ramparts of some kind of medieval castle. Her attention was now entirely taken up by what she saw, at least what she thought she saw because it had to be an illusion. Hanging there in the air a few feet in front of her, weaving its way seamlessly between the palms was the shimmering heat haze she had seen from the beach. This close though it was apparent this was no heat haze, it was more like more like a prism. Samantha found herself gazing into it an

infinite number of angles, possibilities opening and closing
with every move she made. She stretched out her hand
and pushed it into the prism, gasping in wonder as it
disappeared, something knew and multifaceted taking its
place. Involuntarily she snatched her hand back as if it
had been dipped in scolding water. When she realised she
was unharmed she became bolder, this time immersing
her complete arm up to the shoulder in the strangeness.

All the while this was going on, she could hear what
was now the unmistakable rush of running water just
beyond the barrier. Simon's image flashed through her
mind and she realised that while she delayed, he was
probably either dying of thirst or fever, or perhaps
something far worse.

That did it, she had to suspend her wonder and
disbelief. The important thing, the only important thing
was to get Simon what he needed and get back to him as
soon as possible. Although she had a feeling it would take
a whole lot more than fresh water to cure his ills. She
took a step back, trying one last time to divine what was
on the other side, but the light just danced and curved in
front of her eyes showing teasing glimpses of unending
possibilities. Taking a deep breath to brace herself, muscles
tightening to anticipate the worse she stepped forward
into the prism.

For an instant she noticed a strange tingling sensation,
then suddenly she was through the barrier and out the
other side. It was as if her worst fears were realised, there
was no foothold to gain a purchase. She seemed to hang
momentarily in the air, not quite long enough to take in
her new surroundings. Then she was tumbling head first
down a grassy bank, coming to rest in a heap at the
bottom; the fall cushioned by the thick carpet of leaves
that covered the floor of the rain forest. The ocean was
still to her left, she could hear the sound of waves breaking

gently on the shore but she could no longer see them. In front of her was the source of the noise she'd heard on the other side. A small energetic babbling brook, its waters glinting in the sunlight that filtered down from the canopy of leaves that formed the ceiling of the forest. The gradient down to the ocean was a steep one, the waters bouncing and cascading off rocks which sent out crystalline reflections of rainbow light.

Samantha got to her feet filled with amazement. Yet there was something compelling and substantial about her new surroundings that made them somehow more real than the deserted shore she'd left behind. Surely in a place like this she would find food to go with the water that was so abundantly available, although how she was going to get either back to Simon hadn't yet occurred to her. She decided to follow the course of the stream upwards and see where it led. At least that way she could safely explore the Island's core without the fear of getting lost. She glanced behind her, marking the spot where she'd emerged from the prism. It was still there shimmering reassuringly, giving her confidence she would be able to retrace her steps when the time came.

In her excitement she'd forgotten her own hunger and thirst. Now as she contemplated setting out on the next leg of her journey her own needs resurfaced. The stream looked fresh and clean. She looked down at her self, the walk had served to add sweat to the salt that covered her clothes and body, she was beginning to itch all over. In front of her the bank of the stream fell away gently for about four feet, breaking up into a series of medium sized rocks which offered a safe way down to the water. Stepping gingerly in case the bank or the rocks should be unstable, Samantha made her way down. The bed was deceptively steep, closer in the waters were running even faster than it seemed from above, the noise they made an effervescent chattering. *Ting ping dink plink?* it seemed to question her enthusiastically in a language she half thought she could understand.

Maybe the pleasant chit chat would suddenly change to a belligerent roar if she dared step into the waters, she thought, then feeling ridiculous plunged a toe into the water. It felt fresh and alive, a little colder than expected but under the circumstances she wasn't going to complain. Just below where she stood the waters cascaded off a small ledge and tumbled freely for a few feet into a clear pool. The pool looked quite deep, deep enough for what Samantha had in mind anyway. In a trice she removed her dress, hesitating for the merest of moments before discarding her underwear as well. Naked she looked around self consciously, aware of the strangeness and danger of her surroundings.

There wasn't anything in what she saw to be afraid of, no rustling in the trees, no furtive eyes staring at her from above. She neatly folded her clothes and placed them on a rock above the pool, if she felt any misgivings these were now put aside as she plunged into the sparkling cool waters. The feeling was wonderful, the pool was bigger than it looked. Samantha dived beneath the surface and opened her eyes, the water didn't sting, it just carried all her tiredness and fatigue clean away. Opening her mouth she drank and the taste of the water was pure and fresh.

She was so carried away with the experience, she lost track of time. She could have been in the pool a minute or an hour before the thought of leaving occurred to her. Here she was actually enjoying herself while Simon lay on the hot beach waiting for her return. Her cheeks flushed guiltily at the image and she quickly pulled herself from the pool, returning to the rock where she left her clothes; they were gone.

The Dark Lagoon

Her heart skipped a beat, she looked around wildly, half expecting to see some painted savage brandishing a spear topped with her clothes, running towards her. There was no savage though, only the noise of the forest around her. Did she hear the sound of a rotten branch crunching under someone's foot, or were her ears starting to play tricks on her? Away from the stream visibility was limited by the foliage to a matter of a few yards. It would have been easy for a voyeur to have sneaked out of the trees and taken her things without her noticing. Equally it was possible that the thief wasn't a person but an animal, this thought gave her little comfort, only serving to remind her she was naked in a strange jungle.

Irrespective of who or what had taken her clothes, the fact remained they were gone and she must decide what to do. If she tried to return now she would have accomplished nothing, if she carried on there was a chance that something would turn up to help herself and Simon.

Warily she climbed the bank and began to make her way upstream, often casting a glance left and right, occasionally looking behind in case her mysterious stalker should decide to appear. She couldn't help being thrilled by her surroundings, they were so exotic, so beautiful. As she walked her ears became more accustomed to the noises coming from the forest and her eyes to the phenomenal range of colours burgeoning around her. The sound of the stream began to fade into a background, overlaid by a myriad of bird songs, some high and lyrical, others low and moody. The effect was intoxicating. Occasionally she caught glimpses of multi coloured birds perched in the trees at the edge of the forest. They didn't seem to be afraid and regarded her much as she regarded them with wide curious eyes.

After she'd been walking for about fifteen minutes the

shock of losing her clothes had entirely worn off. She was held rapt by her surroundings, even her own nakedness caused her no concern. The stream had begun to narrow slightly and its course to steepen,, then the bed veered off sharply to the left while a path of sorts opened up to the right forming a cross-roads. What should she do? Attempt to follow the stream, which seemed to be becoming impossibly steep, or take the path?

The path was the obvious choice, it was wider, flatter, easier. Looking at it carefully though Samantha decided she didn't think it'd been used lately, there were no tracks, the ground was washed smooth by rain and from what she could already see there were places where the path was blocked by fallen branches and other debris. The thought that the path was disused somehow cheered her up. She knew she should be looking for signs of human habitation because people would mean rescue, but somehow she felt reluctant to share this place with anyone but Simon; for a while at least. It would be the path then. Decision made, within a few seconds she was leaving the stream behind and walking into the heart of an unknown jungle.

III

Away from the stream, the light from the canopy was all there was to break up the shadows. It made the forest seem a more sultry, secret place though by no means an unpleasant one. To start with there were none of the discomfort associated with natural rain forests, like mosquitoes and other biting insects, or the incessant dripping as condensation caused by intense humidity finds its way down to the forest floor, or the ever present smell of rot and decay. None of these things were present in

The Dark Lagoon

this rain forest; it had the colour, the mystery and the romance but somehow all the real world nastiness had been either removed or left out. Samantha didn't notice these things, all she knew was she liked the place, it was seductive, warm, dreamy. By the time the path opened out into a clearing about thirty minutes later, the forest had gone a long way to stealing her heart.

The clearing wasn't large, perhaps thirty metres at its widest. The earth floor was hard packed and mostly flat except where it was broken by the occasional large tree root protruding through the surface like the body of an ancient gnarled sea serpent. It was darker than the surrounding forest, dominated by a huge tree that stood at its far right hand end. The tree was the size of a mature Canadian redwood, its trunk bisected by an opening large enough to drive through in a family car. It stretched skywards without branches for at least sixty feet, almost as high as the rest of the canopy. Then the branches appeared; themselves with girths as large as the largest of the other trees. The sight of it started Samantha's heart racing in a way that none of the strange happenings since the wreck had succeeded in doing. There was something about the tree; its size, its strength, that suggested majesty, promised safety and shelter.

Feeling bold she entered the clearing and was immediately struck by how much like a great hall it felt. The boughs of the tree stretching out like the beams of some ancient fortress, its leaves providing total seclusion. There was enough light filtering into the clearing for her see how neatly the forest came to a halt at its edge; holding back from encroaching into its space. Then she noticed a faint smell of wood smoke. Smoke meant a fire and a fire almost certainly meant people and the chance of rescue. She made her way towards the smell, across the clearing to the tree.

As she got closer she saw the opening in the tree was like an archway, its roots seemed to emerge from the ground and then criss-cross one another to form amazingly intricate designs. Underneath the arch she realised one half of the trunk was solid while the other was hollow. To be exact at first glance it seemed to be solid like its twin but closer examination revealed a gap at the far left hand end. The gap was about three feet wide, easily enough for her to walk through. The urge to do was irresistible, so strong it made her head spin. What she found inside was a cross between a passageway and a spiral staircase. Someone had painstakingly, lovingly, carved footholds into the hard wood allowing the nimble and the brave to climb upwards from within the tree.

She began to climb, quickly losing track of how far she'd come. Eventually the footholds came to an end at a platform. In order to reach the platform she would have to give up her perch and pull herself up, if she failed she would fall into the stairwell. Taking a deep breath she allowed her body to fall forwards, her hands reaching out for some purchase on the platform. To her relief she managed to get a firm hold but now she was stretched, straining to keep her balance. There was no way back, if she didn't act quickly her fingers would weaken and she would fall.

Closing her eyes she allowed her legs to swing free, at the same time pulling herself up to the platform, accomplishing the manoeuvre with surprising ease. Once she'd satisfied herself she was safe, she looked down to see there was a much easier way up. dangling just above where her head had been was a rope, its clear purpose to allow safe access to the platform. She made a firm mental note to use it on her way back down.

She was standing on the smoothed surface of a giant

The Dark Lagoon

branch that acted like an aerial gangway. The gangway was flanked by rope rails leading to the doorway of a tree-house, although the word seemed inadequate to describe the structure which confronted her. It looked more like one of those log cabins settlers used to make in America's Old West. Captivated she walked towards the door, looking for a knocker or a bell, any way of announcing her arrival to whoever lived within. There wasn't anything so she had to resort to rapping on the hard surface of the door with her bare knuckles. She waited a few moments, listening intently for any sound, when she heard none she waited a few moments longer to make sure and then knocked again, this time a little harder. There was still no response from inside yet she had to be absolutely sure before she tried the door. Summoning up all her courage she called out in as loud a voice as she could muster.

'Hello. Is there anybody at home?' Her voice rang out clear as a bell, so loud she startled herself. Still there was no reply.

The door was a heavy one, it had no handle and no lock so she lent against it. It took all her strength but eventually the door started to swing open, stiff and creaky, like it hadn't been used for a long time. Samantha felt relieved and let down. Relieved because she wouldn't have to meet strange people in her naked state and let down because she was now sure she would find no-one to help her inside. Nevertheless what she saw when she entered the tree house immediately raised her spirits. The interior was light and airy, there was a fireplace at the far corner and a balcony ran along the left hand side. There were various pieces of furniture dotted around of which a large sideboard particularly caught her eye. Off to the right there was a recess which looked as if it were the sleeping area. Closer investigation revealed two comfortable looking hammocks hanging side by side.

Simon Shinerock

She made her way onto the balcony. It was wide with sturdy wooden rails. The sensation of being part of the forest was overwhelming. The tree-house was at least sixty feet off the ground, from where she stood it felt like she could stretch out and touch the very tops of the surrounding trees, or even walk along the roof of the forest itself. Breathless she went back inside reminding herself she was not on a sightseeing tour. There was serious business to be done. The house had to contain something that would help Simon.

She didn't really know what she was looking for but when she saw the water skins lying on what could only be the kitchen table she knew she'd found it. This was only her first useful discovery. In the sleeping area she found a beautifully made wardrobe which contained some clothes made of animal skins. To her delight the first outfit she tried on fitted her perfectly, the soft skins feeling delightfully sensual against her body. She didn't take the time to examine the rest, a growing sense of urgency goading her to return to her stricken friend as soon as possible. On her way out she made her last and most important find. Sitting on the large sideboard was a solitary brown bottle, its colour was similar enough to the wood to make an effective disguise.

Samantha would have overlooked it completely if the glass hadn't picked up a stray reflection from the setting sun. The sun was setting, that meant Simon had been on his own for much longer than she'd realised, she had to hurry back to him before the night drew in.

She picked up the bottle pausing long enough to read the faded label which announced the legend

DOCTOR PROCTOR'S FAMOUS CURATIVE
100% successful in the treatment of warts, gangrene,

ill humour
tumour, foot rot, ulcers, gout, fevers of the mind and
body as well
as most other common ailments suffered by man:
USE SPARINGLY

However bad it looked Samantha felt that in her position beggars couldn't be choosers so she crammed the bottle inside her new jacket and headed back towards the door. She could afford only one more stop no matter what wonders the forest revealed and that was to fill the water skin from the stream. She hoped against hope it would be sound because if it leaked Simon was as good as dead.

IV

She used the rope to gain access to the stairwell, practically jumping from foothold to foothold, emerging from beneath the arch and running across the clearing, hastily re-tracing her steps back to the stream. It seemed a much shorter journey on the way back, interrupted only by a stop to drink from the stream and fill the water skin. Then it was a headlong race against time. If night were to fall before she got back she wouldn't find him and he would die. She hardly even paused at the prism, simply plunging through to the other side as if it were something she'd done all her life. Once on the parapet she leapt the distance to the beach, keeping her feet, searching round for her own footprints in the sand. The setting sun was a bright red orb on the horizon just above the ocean, throwing out rays of rose tinted light lending a rose hue to the white sand. Samantha didn't have time to notice, she was already following her own tracks as fast as her legs would carry her.

Simon Shinerock

By the time she reached the point where she'd left Simon the sun had finally set. All that remained was the warm afterglow, itself fading quickly to be replaced by watery light from a newly risen crescent moon. The line of palms had become an unbroken wall of shadows as she made her way up the beach. Her footprints, barely visible now were all she had to guide her back to the place she'd left him lying already feverish beneath the shade of a palm.

To her utter relief he was still where she'd left him. His face was a ghastly white in the moonlight, for a moment she really thought he must be dead and she burst into tears. Then she saw the faintest of movements from his chest. it was enough to rekindle hope in her heart. Moving closer to the sick boy she knelt on the sand in front of him and placed a hand on his forehead. He was cold, terribly cold but she could feel his weak breath on her fingers. His lips were all caked and cracked, the sight of them reminded her of the water bottle.

It was all she could do to keep her hands steady enough to remove the top as she poured a few drops into his partly open mouth. He responded to the moisture by letting out a low brittle moan but his eyes remained closed. She introduced a little more of the life giving liquid. This time he began to choke. At first Samantha thought he would wake, not so, the gagging became gradually weaker, fading away.

He lay there still and white, just as she imagined a corpse would look lying in a funeral parlour, waiting for grieving relatives to pay their last respects. She took his cold hand trying to find a pulse, after a few moments she thought she found one only it was so faint it was difficult to be sure. Nevertheless if there was even the faintest chance he was alive there had to be something else she could do to help him. As if it heard her cry for help the brown bottle inside her jacket, which up to now had been forgotten, came floating gallantly, if a little too eagerly to the surface.

Samantha suddenly realised the bottle was in her left hand although she couldn't remember how it got there. Now it was there she couldn't believe she'd forgotten it until then. Even in her predicament though there was something about the bold promises made on the label that seemed too good to be true; no it was more than that, they seemed like some kind of trick. On the other hand, what did it really matter at this point if the bottle did contain quack medicine? Simon would die, but he was going to die anyway if she didn't do something.

Having satisfied herself there really was no alternative course of action she acted swiftly. The bottle's cap was made of solid glass with a round top and a tapered end that was inserted into the neck. It was a tight fit, at first she thought she would have to break the bottle open risking losing the contents, then suddenly the bottle top started to work loose. Samantha was in no way ready for the foul smell which wafted up from the opening, it nearly made her retch and immediately caused her to have second thoughts about administering the contents.

Surely anything that smelt so foul must be poison. She had no idea how long the bottle had remained in the tree house undisturbed before she came on the scene. It might have been years for all she knew and whatever was in the bottle may not have improved with age. Whatever it was smelt like a sewer contaminated with sulphur and perhaps the carcasses of a few animals to boot. None of this changed the situation in any way. Her choice remained exactly the same, administer the poison and perhaps see Simon die of its effects or watch him die anyway. At least if she gave him the medicine there was a chance it would work, although after smelling it she really didn't give that possibility much credence at all.

Well, the label said 'use sparingly' and that was what she intended to do, use very sparingly indeed. She put the bottle top back in her jacket so she could use one hand to steady herself, then she knelt down and bent over Simon. Suddenly she wished it'd come supplied with one of those droplet dispensers, the mouth of the bottle seemed awfully big. She decided to have a dry run before doing the deed for real.

She held the bottle up to the crescent moon to try and see how full it was but nothing was revealed through the brown glass. She could feel the contents sloshing around though, finally she tipped the bottle very carefully until the tiniest of drops appeared at the rim, hung there for a moment indecisively and then fell to the white sand. By the lazy way it fell, stretching out all the way and by the tail it left on the bottle's rim, Samantha could see the liquid was thick, almost syrupy in texture.

As it dropped on to the white sand it seemed a golden colour although she couldn't be sure in the thin moonlight. As she looked it sank into the sand, a few seconds later all traces of the liquid had disappeared. Feeling like she had now taken all precautions open to her, Samantha felt ready to try the medicine on Simon. As she knelt back down though, one last thought occurred to her. She could test the potion on herself first. The idea terrified her, no matter how much she wanted to save Simon, she was incapable of tasting the disgusting stuff herself.

Two drops. That was the dose she decided on. If he seemed no worse then she would give him another two drops and carry on until he either appeared to improve or.... she didn't want to consider the "or", not at that moment anyway. She looked at his pale face one more time, his skin had turned almost transparent. Her chest heaved as she stifled a sob, she couldn't afford to indulge her feelings now, she had to stay focused. Placing the bottle as close to his mouth as possible to make sure the two drops reached their mark, she started to tip it up. Once again the gold liquid (she had decided it was gold) formed in a small droplet on the rim. This time she allowed it to grow a little larger before shaking her wrist to send it falling towards its target. She had judged it right, exactly two drops breaking free one after the other, falling into the dark gap between Simon's lips.

V

What astonished her was how unbelievably fast the medicine took effect. It was less than ten seconds before he gave a little cough, then opened his eyes, reached forward and kissed her fully on the lips. Before she realised it she was kissing him back, his lips tasting sweet as she shared the curative that had worked like magic to bring him back to her.

After a little while Simon released her and lay down, he was smiling although there was also a puzzled expression creeping slowly across his face. Finally he spoke.

'You look cute, where did you get that dress?'

Considering what they'd been through, the question was so silly and put in such a matter of fact way that Samantha couldn't help laughing. He looked confused and a little embarrassed. With difficulty she stopped giggling, held her breath for a moment and then just as she was about to speak, off she went again. This happened three times before Simon joined in himself, unable to resist the power of her amusement. They laughed together until

Samantha was holding her stomach begging him to stop. He seemed to be totally revived, the colour was back in his cheeks, it was hard to believe that just a few moments ago he was at death's door.

'There's so much I want to tell you,' she said. 'Only I'm scared you won't believe me.'

He looked at her reassuringly.

'It wouldn't matter to me what you said. As far as I'm concerned I'm just lucky to be here, happy to be here with you. You saved my life.'

He sounded so sincere she couldn't help feeling better herself but she still didn't know how to explain the fantastic things that she'd discovered on the Island. Instead she had another idea.

'Can you walk?' she asked

He looked a bit surprised by the question as if he wasn't really sure of the answer. Slowly he got to his feet, stretching out his arms and kicking out with his legs to check everything was in working order.

'It's quite amazing, I feel great. I know I should feel lousy but I don't, I feel great.'

'That's good,' she said. 'Then unless you want to spend the night here you can follow me and I can show you what happened instead of telling you.'

With that she started to retrace her steps along the beach towards the spit. She looked back after a few yards to make sure he was following. He was, so she carried on, fighting back the thought that everything she remembered was a figment of her imagination.

The Dark Lagoon

VI

She needn't have worried, even in the moonlight the prism could be seen as before hovering above spit like a mystical doorway to another world. He started to ask questions when he saw the prism but she stopped him in his tracks saying he would get all the answers he needed in a few minutes. In this way they passed through the barrier together and followed her footsteps back to the clearing and up into the tree-house. Simon seemed held in silent astonishment, Samantha supposed he had no more questions, knowing full well there were no answers to explain what he was seeing. That night they slept side by side in the hammocks.

Samantha didn't remember her dream and when she awoke had no recollection of the dark hand reaching up out of the mist to engulf her.

The next day they spent surprisingly little time discussing the strangeness of their new home, concentrating instead on more practical considerations like exploring their surroundings and finding a source of food. This last consideration was the most pressing. Although they now had more than enough fresh water for their needs, they were both very hungry not having eaten for nearly two days. A careful examination of the house revealed there were no supplies hidden away, the only thing they could do was to go into the forest and forage for a living. He in the meantime had changed into one of the outfits in the house, Samantha thought he looked kind of cute, a sort of more refined version of how she imagined Huckleberry Finn.

One discovery they did make in the house was a small cracked mirror which had been left standing in the corner, there was also an assortment of knives and other cutlery in the sideboard drawer. In any event he found a knife sharp enough to shave with. When he finished he took the blade, which was about four inches long, and tucked it into the belt of his tunic.

They went into the forest together, being careful to get their bearings so they didn't lose their way. Their mission was more successful than they could have hoped. The forest abounded with small game and there was an abundance of fruit trees, many of which were strange but most looked safe to eat. When they returned to the tree-house they brought back a varied selection from which they managed to prepare a decent meal. The subject of rescue just didn't come up, Samantha had a vague feeling that maybe they should be doing something like building a beacon on the beach to attract passing ships but somehow there always seemed to be something else to do that was more pressing and more interesting.

By the third day he'd started to hunt for meat while Samantha had worked out how the stove worked on the open fire. All thoughts of other people or of rescue had gone completely, they'd become totally engrossed in one another and their idyllic surroundings.

It was an entire lunar cycle before they became lovers. When it finally happened the act seemed so natural to Samantha she hardly even paused on its significance. Her life had changed, it was the Island and Simon that now occupied her thoughts, the Island and Simon were the only things that mattered in her new life.

VII

The day after it happened Proctor sprung his trap. That evening Simon asked her to walk back with him to the beach where they'd arrived. It would be the first time they'd ventured out of the forest since the first night. Simon was always insistent they didn't stray too far from the tree house, he said there was no point in tempting fate when they had everything they needed right there. So his request surprised her a little but she was happy to walk with him anywhere he wanted, he was her first and only love.

By the time they reached the spot the crescent moon was high in the western sky, overshadowing the myriad of stars that seemed somehow brighter on the beach than in the forest. They'd walked the whole way hand in hand in silence.

When they arrived he swung her round to face him, looking deeply into her eyes, probing for any doubts of reservations. All he saw was trust and naiveté, that was good, that was very good indeed.

'Samantha,' he said and waited.

Eventually she saw the troubled look in his eyes and responded.

'What is it, what's troubling you?'

His gaze seemed to penetrate her soul.

'Samantha,' he said again. 'You know I love you don't you?'

The question surprised her. 'Of course I know, I love you too'

He looked sad.

'I don't think you understand,' he said. 'I love you more than life itself which is why it's so difficult for me to tell you what I must tell you.'

It was Samantha's turn to look troubled.

Simon Shinerock

'You can tell me anything my darling, anything at all, it won't make any difference. I love you.'

He let go of her arms and turned away as if trying to hide the tears that were welling up in his eyes.

She was beginning to get frightened. She'd never seen him like this before, whatever it was on his mind was tearing him apart. She reached out and put her arms gently on his shoulders.

'Tell me,' she said reassuringly. 'Tell me what's bothering you and I can help, I promise, I can help'

He wheeled around suddenly and took her in his arms, kissing her hard on the mouth. The kiss felt almost desperate and only served to increase her anxiety. When they came apart he held her once again in that terrible fixed stare and started to speak.

'Do you remember,' he began, 'when you were thirteen a man you never met before saved your life?'

The question jogged something in the back of Samantha's mind, a connection long unmade fell into place.

'Doctor Proctor's famous curative,' she exclaimed. 'Rex Proctor, that was the name of the man who saved my life.'

'That's right,' he said. 'And my name is Simon Proctor, Rex Proctor was my father. It was no accident he was there to save you Samantha. It wouldn't have mattered what danger or misfortune befell you, he would always have been there for you.'

'No questions,' he said putting two fingers to her lips that had already formed into the shape of incredulity.

'Listen. My father is gone now but he was friends with your father. You are a special person Sam, just like he was a special person. You were chosen from birth to save this Island that he built. If the ship hadn't gone down it was going to be your father who was going to explain everything to you. Now I feel so inadequate, it's all gone wrong.'

'I don't understand,' she said. 'What do you mean, I was chosen at birth? How could your father have made this Island? What am I supposed to do to save it? I don't understand any of this, you're frightening me.'

Samantha's eyes were so wide they looked like shining saucers.

'There are strange things that happen in this world, Sam. Things that are hard to explain and harder to understand. This Island, my father and in a way, you yourself are all such things. What I can tell you is that it's already too late for him and if you won't help then it will be too late for me and the Island; everything of value will be lost forever and we don't have much time.'

She burst into tears and he gathered her to him and let her weep like the child she still was, her head nestling into his shoulder. When her sobs had slowed down a little he drew back.

'What do you mean too late for you?' she entreated.

Her eyes imploring him to tell her this was all some kind of silly test, none of it was true; they could go back now and carry on the way they were. Something in the way he looked said this wouldn't be so, he was serious, more deadly serious than she knew.

His expression changed and he looked thoughtful and sad, as if it was just too difficult for him to explain.

'All I can tell you is that this Island is dying and only you can save it.'

He paused and then added in a much lower voice, 'and if the Island dies, then I'm afraid my darling that I die with it.'

She could hardly believe her ears but the words still devastated her. The thought of losing Simon, of their Island being destroyed was unthinkable. He was saying there was something she could do to prevent these things from happening, whatever it was she would do it, no matter what the cost to her. She didn't have the chance to voice this decision before he spoke again.

'I don't want you to say anything until I've shown you what it is we're dealing with, come with me.'

With that he took her hand and led her up the beach to a path she'd never noticed before and together they walked towards the Island's rotting heart.

VIII

The palm forest on this part of the Island was very different to what she had come to think of as their forest. Nevertheless even in the moonlight she could see it was equally beautiful and full of delights. Therefore she couldn't believe her eyes when the sounds of wildlife started to die away and the foliage began to thin, showing signs of decay and rot.

A few hundred yards further on and the place they were in had become a sick caricature, barely recognisable as belonging to the same Island she'd come to trust and love. She was heartbroken, everything was sick, dead or dying; she realised that whatever the cause the sickness was spreading, Simon was right about that; if something wasn't done then the Island would die, of that she was now certain.

A few hundred yards further on and the forest had all but disappeared, giving way to barren ground that looked like it was itself suffering from the sickness. Here and there she could see pale mounds erupting from the earth like some kind of deadly contagion; she made a mental note to make sure she didn't end up treading in one by mistake. She had a feeling that anyone who came into contact with one of those mounds wouldn't remain healthy for very long.

Then finally she saw it. Or rather first she smelt it, then she saw it. The smell was identical to the medicine in Doctor Proctor's bottle only ten times as strong. She didn't have to speculate as to where it came from though, in the distance like a spectre emerging from a nightmare she caught her first glimpse of the black fetid waters of the dark lagoon.

They walked to within a few feet of the water' edge before he stopped.

'I wanted you to see everything before you decide. If you go ahead with your destiny it must be from your own free will, I will not try to force you or even to persuade you should you decide you cannot shoulder the burden.'

This time he looked away from Samantha and up towards the crescent moon, her eyes followed his and for the first time in three years she became aware of the pendant that still hung around her neck.

'That's right my darling, it is the moon that calls you. You wear the sign around your neck, you are the one.'

His voice rose an octave. Was there just a hint of madness there? If there was she didn't hear it. All she heard was the boy she loved, all she saw was the silver crescent moon, and her destiny mingling together in the waters of the dark lagoon.

'You see it don't you?' he said, unable to hide the excitement in his words.

'You see what you have to do, it is the only way. Only if you bathe in these waters can the Island be restored to what it once was, only your goodness, your purity, can purge the evil infecting this place and rid us all of the sickness forever.'

His voice faltered as if just saying the words had drained him of all his energy. Indeed his face had once again taken on the ghastly pallid complexion she first saw on the beach. Her heart almost leapt out of her chest when she it.

'Simon.' She said his name, taking comfort in the word.

Then she asked the thing she needed to know before she made her decision.

'Simon. If I do this thing, what will happen to me?'

The trap snapped shut

He turned away from her. If he hadn't she may have seen the deep shadows that suddenly formed in the hollow recesses of his cheeks, at how his nose seemed to take on a more sinuous hue. She may have noticed these things but the probability was she wouldn't because love is blind and true love is blinder still.

The chances were it was far too late for Samantha to see Simon Proctor for what he really was, he had done his job too well. Nevertheless he could feel his disguise beginning to slip and he intended to take no stupid chances now, not when after so many long years of planning and scheming, victory was almost within his grasp.

'I'm sorry my darling but I can't bear to look you in the eye. I'm scared if you see me you won't make your decision for the right reasons and that would be more dangerous than anything you will face in those dark waters. You see if you enter the lagoon with doubt in your heart then it will consume

The Dark Lagoon

you and everything will have been for nothing. The Island will crumble, I will die and the world will have lost its finest jewel. But if you put your doubts aside, if you believe in me and trust what I am telling you then you can survive and it will be the waters themselves that will be destroyed.

You see now why it must be your decision and why I can say no more. If you are to do this thing, it must be out of sincere love and above all the act must come of your own free will.'

His crucial closing speech delivered, Proctor regained his composure, re-established control over his disguise and turned to face the infatuated young girl. He was struck with how truly innocent she looked, her innocence multiplying her beauty by some unimaginable factor. The sight pleased him, it pleased him very much, everything was going to work out just fine, just fine and dandy. Whatever he really felt, his face betrayed none of it. All Samantha saw was the deep concern and despair of a young boy in love.

In her mind there wasn't really much for her to think about. The facts were simple. Fate had chosen her to play an important role, win lose or draw she would do her best to live up to it. She felt an inner power she had never experienced before, it gave her the strength to do what it was that had to be done. She was now the one who gathered Simon in her arms, reassuring him with soft words of love, kissing the tears from his cheeks, promising to come back to him.

She really didn't have any reservations. Her mind was clear and focused, the dark lagoon had even lost its terror, to her it was now just a filthy pool waiting to be cleansed.

One final kiss and the deed would be done. Her lips lingered against his a few seconds longer, then she swung him round so her back was to the lagoon and his face was picked out by the moon light.

'Don't be scared for me. I'm happy to do this thing. I will

Simon Shinerock

come back to you and we will be together forever, you just wait and see.'

Samantha didn't wait for a reply but let go of his hands and turned to face the fetid pool pausing only for a barely discernible moment before walking boldly towards the water's edge.

Book Four

Chapter One

Reconciliation

I

Tom's limo was waiting for them outside the house, its engine running. The driver was an African American and even seated you could see he was a big man. The way his cropped hair brushed the headlining and his neck seemed to be straining to burst out of his formal white shirt, even the sheer amount of space occupied by his shoulders were all clues to his size and implied strength.

Seated though, Rufus Cole could not do his physique full justice. At college, despite weighing two hundred and thirty pounds then, (and a lot more now) he was agile enough to win a Yale scholarship on his basketball abilities alone. If he'd wanted to he could have become an all American football player but such trivialities never really appealed to him. Instead he entered the Marines straight out of college as a regular soldier, (he heard the chance of seeing "real" action was greater that way). In his ten years as a marine he undertook several covert operations in South America and the more troubled Arab states. By the time he was honourably discharged he'd risen to the rank of platoon sergeant and acquired a reputation for being both cool headed and ruthless.

His reputation made him a prize catch for the select group of international agencies specialising in protection, (both passive and proactive) for their rich powerful clientele. It was through one of these agencies that he met Tom Kidman. Tom didn't know what to expect, when he went to their plush down town offices, certainly not the well-spoken individual he was introduced to. They were alone both seated comfortably, drinks on the coffee table in front of them. They sat in silence for a long time, Tom couldn't help noticing how relaxed the man was, cool, prepared to wait patiently until the other was ready. In the end his first question came out unprepared, it was so unexpected he surprised himself.

'Do you believe in the Devil, Mr. Cole?' He asked.

Instead of being taken aback by such a strange enquiry, Rufus looked unsurprised, as if this was exactly the kind of question he was used to answering. He put down the drink he held in his right hand and leant forward.

'Well, Mr. Kidman' he said, his voice creamy and low. 'That depends what you mean by the Devil.'

Tom shrugged his shoulders and coughed nervously, unable to explain further. The big black man's eyes narrowed, there wasn't a hint of frivolity about his expression.

'Well,' he continued. 'If you mean do I believe in some dude with horns and a tail wandering around hell with a pitchfork then the answer's no.'

Tom's shoulders slouched forward at the inevitable reply; this was going to be impossible, it had been a mistake to come, he suddenly felt claustrophobic despite the airiness of their surroundings, he wanted to leave.

'If however you mean do I believe in supernatural evil, then the answer is maybe.'

He felt a buzz of excitement when he heard the rest of the reply. He was worried that whoever he chose to accompany him on his mission would think he was crazy. This answer though held out a small hope but he needed to be sure.

'What do you mean by supernatural evil, Mr. Cole'

Rufus's eyes went blank, Tom was sure he wasn't going to answer the question, eventually though he broke into a disarming smile.

'Well, if we're going to talk personal Mr. Kidman, I think we should at least be on first name terms. I'm Rufus, it's Tom isn't it?'

He finished the question and leaned forward his hand outstretched. The two men had already shaken hands when they were introduced but that was different. Then they were strangers, now they were on the verge of something more.

'Sure Rufus. You can call me Tom' said the rich white man as he responded to the big Negro's friendly gesture.

'OK Tom, now we know one another a little better I can answer your question.'

He went on to describe some of the atrocities he'd witnessed during his time as a marine commando. The stories made Tom feel sick to his stomach, he found it hard to believe that any human being was capable of abusing his fellow man is such horrifying ways. By the time Rufus was finished over half an hour had passed.

'So you see, when you ask me if I believe in the Devil, I have to say I have seen things transcend human evil. I've formed the opinion that some of the people I've been sent out to kill have been the instruments of a force I don't understand. If you want to call it the Devil, well then I think that's as good a word as any other.'

He paused for a second, smiled and added.

'So if you're looking for a fellow kook as your body guard I guess I'm your man.'

II

Rufus kept mostly quiet while Tom told him about Samantha's abduction. He occasionally interrupted to ask questions about times and places but mostly he just nodded encouragement. Despite the fact that Tom trusted this man, there were some things he couldn't tell him, like the pact he made for instance. Nevertheless by the end Rufus was in no doubt that what they were dealing with wasn't the instrument of some supernatural force but the force itself.

When Tom finished Rufus let out a low whistle.

'Well, that's some story, the parts you told me that is. I think there's more to all this that you don't want to say. That's OK though maybe you'll decide to fill me in another time. If you do you know where you can reach me.'

He smiled a bland smile and got up to leave. Tom panicked at the thought of being left alone to repeat the whole sorry process with someone else.

'Wait, don't go,' he begged, oblivious to the tears that had started to well up in the corners of his eyes.

'What do you want from me?'

Rufus stopped and looked at Tom.

'I want it all Tom. If I'm going to go with you on this trip you have to tell me everything, sorry, it's all or nothing.'

'All right, I'll tell you.'

The words came out in a choking rasp but at least Rufus sat back down and looked attentive.

He went ahead, slowly at first, filling in all the gaps. It

was the first time he'd told another human being about his fall. It was the first time he'd admitted his sins even to himself. When he finished he felt like a great weight had been partially lifted from his shoulders. He wouldn't have protested if Rufus had got up to leave this time but he didn't. Instead he looked levelly at Tom before saying.

'I don't think you stood any kind of a chance against the thing you were up against. For what it's worth I think I would have ended up the same way. It's bad though, there's no denying.'

Then came a moment of indecision, it was only slight but it was there. Perhaps Rufus Cole was searching his own soul, asking himself whether he really needed this much action.

' I must be mad but you can count me in.'

III

'This is Rufus Cole' Tom said to Jack as they got into the limo. 'He'll be going with us all the way.'

It took twenty minutes to get to the airport. When they arrived Rufus dropped them at the departure lounge and went to return the limo to the hire company. Jack hadn't flown in a long time, he was astounded at how busy the place was as he followed Tom to the first class check-in counter, the only one without a queue. A few moments later they were being ushered through to the exclusive first class lounge.

Jack was amazed by the complimentary champagne and hors-d'oeuvres on offer from immaculately presented hostesses, whose sole job was to make sure the exclusive user's of this facility went for nothing. Dotted around the lounge he noticed there were a number of computers giving direct access to the Internet. So, this is what I've been missing all these years, he thought, as he settled back into one of the beautifully made leather armchairs and poured himself a fresh coffee.

The flight held more of the same revelations. If he thought the departure lounge was extravagant, he quickly realised it paled by comparison to the opulence of the first class cabin. This was just the kind of thing that only the day before would have seen him seething with resentment. Today though things were different, the world had moved on. Today he was restored to what he was. No, to more than what he was. He didn't any longer need to feel jealous or frustrated by the material success of others, neither was he taken in by it. Jack's vision was clear, clearer than it had ever been and the clarity of his vision gave him the power to see things for what they really were.

During the flight he and Tom talked. They talked in a way they'd never been able to, even when at college. The competition was over, they no longer needed to prove anything to one another. By the time they touched down they'd made peace with one another, each accepting the other's weaknesses, their friendship strong enough to bring about reconciliation. Whatever else, they were both sure of one thing, going up against Proctor united would be hard, disunited it would be an act of suicide.

IV

The first thing to hit them as they emerged from Miami International airport was the searing heat. It was hot when they arrived the last time but not like this. Whereas before the humidity was like hitting a brick wall, now there was almost no moisture in the air. Vaguely Jack remembered reading something about a drought in Florida. Apparently it was the worst since records begun. There was the usual talk of global warming, changing weather patterns and melting ice caps, he'd read it all before. Miami had always been known as a green State though you'd never guess it looking at the brown scrubby grass and the trees withering in the shimmering heat. Things weren't good, there was a sickness at work here and they all knew it.

Waiting for them as they emerged from the air conditioned terminal building was an air conditioned pickup. The Chrysler Typhoon had a pretty pathetic load area, it also rode so low if you attempted to take it anywhere other than a smooth highway you would almost certainly wreck the undercarriage. It did however have two redeeming qualities. Firstly it had a king cab conversion which meant it could seat four adults. Secondly it had a four point two litre, six cylinder high output turbo charged engine. This was capable of propelling it from nought to sixty miles per hour in five seconds. Whatever else was going to happen they weren't going to fail for lack of a fast set of wheels.

Jack smiled when he saw the black pickup with its huge chrome wheels and blacked out windows. Rufus smiled as well because he was going to drive the beast.

They were all relieved to get out of the heat. Tom rode shotgun while Jack shared the back seat with their minimal luggage. It had just gone midday and they had an hour and a half's journey in front of them to Key Largo. Although they hadn't discussed it they both knew where they were headed. It was obvious really. As neither man had the slightest idea of the location of Proctor's Island, they had to find the one man who they knew did - Wilbur Kohn, they had to go to Wilbur's house. The only problem was the last time they saw Wilbur was twenty years ago and he was in his sixties then. There was no guarantee he would still be alive, never mind living in the same house. As long a shot as it was, it was their only shot and they had to take it.

The journey from the airport on the interstate highway was a more familiar one. They noticed some changes, a new diner here, an old building missing or abandoned there, but in the main things were as they remembered them. The most startling difference though was the appearance of the flora. Everywhere what had been lush green was either brown or grey. Many of the trees were without leaves completely, their trunks bare, either dead or dying. Locally they blamed acid rain. In the newspapers there were regular articles putting forward various politically correct hypotheses. Privately many eminent scientists were baffled, clueless and worried.

It had just gone three when they reached the twenty mile bridge that acted as the gateway to the Keys. At this time of year the roads weren't busy, it was too early in the season for the tourists, even in better times the weather in June was just too hot. They had therefore made good time, so overshooting the turning to Wilbur's place was no great setback. In fact Jack was fascinated when they passed the Winn Dixie where he first met Wilbur. They were both even more interested when Rufus pulled into the shopping mall where they'd worked as labourers all those years ago.

The place was barely recognisable. Of course it had been finished years ago. Though far from becoming a thriving modern retail centre, it looked deserted, scruffy and past its sell by date. The world certainly had moved on thought Jack. The place must have been superseded almost before it was open, people opting for huge air conditioned indoor malls with everything under one roof. This place was neither large enough to compete with the malls head on nor pretty enough to be quaint. It fell between two stools and fell on its face because of it.

The car park was virtually deserted, many of the shops on the outer perimeter were boarded up. Jack guessed correctly that the second tier of units were long since forsaken. There were a few still open though, they could see a souvenir shop, called "New Wave" and a fishing shop called "Fair Bait" proudly displaying a range of cheap looking rods and lines.

These retailers looked like the last hardy animals to survive a long drought. The difference was the rains were never going to return to the "Largoland Mall". Eventually the last of them would close their doors and the big city developers would get another bite at the cherry. That is if the weather changed and there was still a tourist trade worth catering for.

Rufus swung the pickup round in a wide arc, passing the place where the site office had once stood, where Jack had his showdown with the boss. As they drove by Jack may even have felt a slight tingling at the back of his neck, his new senses picking up the faint aura of that long forgotten confrontation, the echo of Carl's demented bellowing still hanging ghostlike in the scorched air.

A moment later and they were back on the highway, the mall was receding into the distance, its shabby sign the last thing to disappear from view. Tom asked Rufus to drive slowly, he didn't want to miss the turning a second time. On this part of the Key the highway was a wide dual carriageway with a large central reservation, big enough in places to provide a site for restaurants and other businesses. On their way back they passed the Bella Vista Park, it looked run down, perhaps even abandoned

The Dark Lagoon

like so many other places they saw. A few yards further on they passed Henry's bar.

Jack and Tom looked at one another simultaneously, each mirroring the other's expression of incredulity. Here was a place that'd bucked the local trend big time. As they remembered, Henry's was a shabby tasteless place long past its best even then. If they'd been asked to put money on it before they arrived they would both have gambled on the place having closed long ago. To the contrary what was now passing rapidly before their eyes was anything but closed.

Henry's had turned into a neon-lit edifice, a monument to tasteless hedonism. Set atop the roof of the building (which seemed to have grown considerably in size) was the largest most garish neon lit sign any of them had seen outside of downtown New York. It blazed out the legend "Henry's" in huge flickering red letters mesmerising onlookers to such an extent that local legend had it the sign alone was responsible for an increase in fatal road accidents.

The main sign was however only for starters. Once it had your attention, you were rewarded by a series of other images flashing out at random, ranging from the titillating to the blatantly profane. A naked dancer gyrating electronically, a fiend on a motorcycle holding aloft a decapitated pigs head. The degrading pièce de resistance was a complex image which, if it had come on for long enough, would have been recognisable as a variety of people and animals engaging in perverted sexual practices. As they drove by there was just enough time for them to note the two unsavoury looking bouncers at the entrance and the lines of Harleys that filled the car park.

In the end it was Rufus who expressed what all three men were thinking.

'Well I don't know about you guys, but that's one place I wouldn't go even if I was dying of thirst.'

Jack laughed, although his newly acquired sixth sense was telling him that before long they may have to visit Henry's for something a lot more dangerous than a bottle of Bud.

Tom nudged the big driver to remind him they had important business to attend to, he was too caught up with thoughts of Samantha to give consideration to other issues, serious or not. Jack was the only one who gave a passing glance at the Winn Dixie as they moved slowly by half a mile further on, trying to reach back into the past and remember what Wilbur looked like. The image that eventually came to him was of a thing with a man's body and a shark's face.

'Are you OK? you look like you've see a ghost,' said Tom who'd noticed his sudden change of expression.

'I'm fine' he replied. 'Don't worry about me, there's the turning.'

Sure enough there was the break in the central reservation and they could see the familiar left turn that led down to Wilbur's place. Rufus slowed the truck and swung gently into the left hand lane. The road was clear so he carried on, executing a fluid turn which took them away from the security of the highway and into an altogether more disturbing environment.

It was true to say the whole Key Largo had gone to pot in the past twenty years, but that wasn't anything compared with the deterioration and decay that seemed to have attacked the place they now found themselves. Within a few feet the narrow road became rutted and torn up. Creeping weeds seemed to reach out from the scrub land on both sides, their tendrils digging in to the crumbling tarmac, creating great bulbous mounds as they dived beneath the surface to emerge bigger and fatter a few yards later. The process was repeated again and again, making them look like a slow breed of serpent swimming through some nameless polluted sea.

As they made their way slowly down the decaying lane things got worse. The voracious roots were getting larger, protruding high enough in places to hit the underside of the truck and forcing Rufus to weave and turn just to make forward progress. Worse still the mounds of earth were being joined by less familiar substances, at least to Jack and Rufus. Tom however remembered seeing these festering yellow pustules once before, outside Rex Proctor's colonial mansion, erupting through the immaculate terraces like mushrooms through a soft tarmac driveway.

Just as it was becoming obvious they would have to stop the truck and either turn round or proceed on foot, they saw something up ahead that looked like it could be the house. It wasn't possible to say immediately because of the dense undergrowth, it was in roughly the right place though so the odds had to be good.

Any feelings of relief were choked by the sight of the place as they drew nearer. Rufus pulled into a small clearing about fifty yards before the building and parked the truck facing the road, ready to make a quick exit in either direction.

V

Tom was shaking his head a little too fast.

'No, no, no.' He spat the words out as if they were pieces of rotten fruit. 'No no no.'

The word quickly lost its meaning as Tom repeated it staccato fashion, increasing the volume with each repetition until he reached a hysterical crescendo that was little more than a scream.

There were no men in white coats to administer a sedative and put the distraught father in a nice safe straight jacket, so Rufus improvised. He moved so quickly the slap caught Tom completely by surprise. It was a blow hard enough to knock a smaller man unconscious and easily hard enough to have his brains bouncing back and forwards in his head. His eyes cleared slowly, vision refocusing after the shock of the blow. The madness was gone from them, at least for the time being, although unless they found Samantha soon Jack could see his old friend would succumb totally to the demons that pursued him.

In the heat of the crisis they were all distracted from the derelict house that sparked off the outburst. It was virtually falling down, the exterior walls were covered with creeping vegetation, the roof was a craggy mess, the woodwork bereft of paint, openly rotting in the dank air.

It was Jack who first noticed the light. At first he thought it wasn't anything, perhaps a stray sunbeam from the setting sun reflecting off a broken piece of mirror. No, reflections didn't give off a constant yellow light, which was what they could all see coming from first one, then from every window of the house.

'That is some kind of weird shit,' exclaimed Rufus.

Tom sucked in his breath and let it out in a low whistle of combination of relief and disbelief.

They got out of the truck and started walking towards the house, passing a few familiar relics on the way, the camper, the speed boat and last but not least the Van.

The Dark Lagoon

All these things were in an even worse state than the house, barely recognisable as what they were. The Van had been attacked by a rust bug that had left its body work full of gaping jagged holes. The weight of the rowing boat had clearly become too much for the weakened structure and its prow had dipped beneath the surface of the roof, looking as if it was going to collapse at any minute into the interior of the Van.

Jack shuddered as he passed it by, remembering the nest of rats, seeing bloodshot eyes and deadly teeth coming towards him out of the gloom. He shook his head and the image faded, the thought of what they were about to encounter driving it out.

He reached the door and stopped. Now it was his turn to experience the merest moment of indecision. What was he doing here? Should he knock on the door, or just break it down? his mind was slowing down, his brain turning to treacle inside his head, it was too much of an effort to think.

Jack stood there rooted to the spot. He was frozen, paralysed by a power coming from the house. If he could have turned round he would have seen that Rufus and Tom were similarly affected. The thought occurred to him that if he didn't do something fast they would all become like the Van, rotting human statues being eaten slowly by the foul inhabitants of this godforsaken wood. Even this thought was coming slower and slower as his brain gradually wound down like some cheap clockwork toy. The yellow light from the house was getting steadily brighter, seeming to escape the confines of the house and enveloping the three men in its strange ethereal glow.

Just as he was about to lose consciousness he felt something jabbing at him in the centre of his head. The pain made him wince, the yellow light in front of him was now dotted with white spots. The white spots were getting slowly larger, absorbing

*the yellow. As this battle raged in front of him he could feel
some of his mind freeing itself of the lethargy that gripped it.
He could feel the heat of the air, hear the crackle of electricity
and smell the odour of burning flesh. At the end, two red dots
appeared, hot coals of concentrated hate, staring into him with
a malevolence that made him feel physically sick. Then they
were gone and the silence was shattered by a broken cackle
coming from within the broken down house.*

'Hey Jack, what's'amatter? Door's open. Come on in,
it's been a long time.'

The voice was barely human yet it was also familiar,
somewhere in his past he'd heard the voice, or something
like it, before. Without checking to see if the others were
following, or still frozen where they stood, he leant against
the door. Its hinges groaned as if this were the first time
they'd been used for a long time, the door opened and he
went inside.

As he entered the living room, there was no trace of
the yellow light. What he saw was in stark contrast to the
rotting exterior. Everything was very much as he
remembered it. The furniture hadn't changed at all, there
was no sign that anything had been changed or even
suffered any wear over the years. Anything that is except
the man who sat staring at him, looking too old to be a
living thing.

'Jack,' said Wilbur from his wheelchair. 'I knew you'd
be back to see me one day, just couldn't keep away huh?'

He looked over Jack's shoulder noticing Tom and Rufus
who'd appeared looking ashen face and drained.

'You brought your friend,' the thing in the wheelchair
carried on. 'Tom isn't it?'

He didn't wait for a reply. 'And some muscle too, I
see.'

The thing made a rattling noise that Jack took to be laughter.

'Well as you can see boys I'm not exactly gonna leap out of this chair and rassle with yer so be civilised and sit down, tell me your news.'

Jack turned to Tom. He wanted to make sure the other man didn't want to do the talking. The look on Tom's face gave him the answer he needed, it was he who was going to have to ask the questions.

'We're not here to chew the fat with you, Wilbur. We're here because your friend Proctor has Tom's daughter and we want her back.'

Before he could continue Wilbur cut in, his voice just a little bit stronger than before.

'Well that's very noble of you boys, very noble indeed. I wish you a lot of fucking luck but I'm afraid I can't help you.'

Jack carried on undeterred. 'You mean "won't". You know what we want. We know because it was you who took Tom to the Island and that's where we're going. So it's up to you Wilbur, either you come with us to the Island or ...'

His voice trailed off. Or what? They killed him? Looking at the state of him, that might be doing him a favour. Killing him would do no good and a beating would probably kill him anyway.

Again the thing in the wheelchair rattled with laughter. 'What's the matter Jack. You were going to tell me what you were going to do if I don't tell you what you want. Well? What are you going to do? Kill me? Burn down my house?'

More rattling laughter. 'I'm disappointed in you, Jack,

I really am. I thought you were more creative than that.'

Its voice had changed again. This time it not only regained some more of its vitality, it also took on a familiar paternal tone. It was hard to say but the thing in the chair also seemed to have become a little more robust. When they first arrived it had been little more than a bag of bones held together by sagging grey flesh. Jack estimated Wilbur must have been in his eighties but the thing in the wheelchair looked far older, too old to be alive. It looked more like a caricature of age than the real thing. He couldn't help feeling that someone somewhere was sending them up, toying with them for amusement like a cat toys with its prey before the kill.

The thing in the chair carried on. 'You know I always had a soft spot for you Jack, I can see this thing has you really upset and anything that upsets you upsets me, it really does. So I tell you what I'm going to do. I'm going to take you to the Island. I know I shouldn't and I'll probably get into terrible trouble but for you Jack I'll do it.'

Jack didn't know what to say, he knew the thing in the chair was lying but they had no other choice than to go along with it, they had no other options.

'Well,' said the thing in the chair. It seemed to be getting younger by the minute now.

'You don't mind if I go to the bathroom and freshen up before we get started do you?'

No-one said anything, they just stared as the thing in the chair, that was rapidly starting to look like Wilbur, rolled passed them towards the bathroom door. It occurred to Jack that he was trying to escape but the thought was absurd for two reasons. First this thing was in a wheelchair and couldn't walk. Second there was, he remembered, no window in that room and therefore no means of escape. The feeling wouldn't go away though.

Five minutes later when Rufus broke down the bathroom door and found the empty wheelchair, somehow he wasn't even surprised.

'What are we going to do now?' Tom's question echoed round the room despairingly.

'You have to go to Henry's bar. That's where you'll find him, but if you go, be ready for a fight, be ready to kill, be ready to die.'

VI

Maria stood in the kitchen doorway, how long she'd been standing there they didn't know. She was stockier than they remembered, her hair was streaked with grey but otherwise she looked the same, not bad for a woman in her fifties. Her face though wore an expression of infinite sadness. The only time Jack had seen a face like that was in pictures of the victims of the Nazi Holocaust. It was impossible to say what torments Maria had been subjected to during her years with Wilbur, though one thing was certain, she'd come to the end of her tether.

By helping them she was crossing a line which could never be re-crossed. Win lose or draw, she'd thrown her lot in with these men against her husband. If they were destroyed then she would be destroyed along with them.

The four of them went outside where they were greeted by the setting sun and the rising crescent moon. The house, the road, everything was different. The were no more mounds of poisonous earth, no more roots chewing up the ground. The house itself had been restored to the condition they remembered twenty years before. The air was vibrating the fading sound of laughter.

Rufus shivered and spat on the ground, Tom looked like he was freezing cold despite the heat and Jack stared deep into the dusk.

Maria's voice shattered the silence.

'We have to hurry, there's not much time now, if we don't go it will be too late.'

'What do you mean, we?' said Jack.

'I'm coming too. Wilbur will know I've tried to help you and he'll kill me, at least if I come with you I may be able to help.'

Jack was touched at the sacrifice this woman had made for them and wanted to tell her so. Before he could say anything, Tom interrupted his train of thought.

'We don't have time to argue about this.'

The imperative in his voice was irresistible, Rufus was already opening the driver's door of the truck, by the time the others were inside the six cylinder turbo was already growling menacingly.

The drive back to Henry's fully demonstrated both the driver's ability and the truck's full potential. Keeping maximum acceleration in every gear as they rocketed down the narrow road, Rufus showed amazing control as he threw the unlikely looking hot rod into a perfectly controlled four wheel drift to re-join the highway. He repeated the exercise as they arrived in the car park of Henry's bar, bringing the truck to a halt a respectful distance from the lines of Harleys flanking the main entrance. Since the sun had gone down the place looked even more lurid and debauched than earlier.

The Dark Lagoon

They all saw the Heathen guarding the door, he was impossible to miss. They were parked about thirty metres away but even from that distance it was clear he was a big man, possibly as big as Rufus. He was white, shaven headed with a surfer's beard, the beard being the only thing that defined his neck, apart that is from the wicked looking scar that ran round his head where his neck should have been. It was like someone had decapitated him, removed a section of neck and sewed the head back on. He was staring at them through narrow hooded eyes, arms folded suspiciously across his chest.

'Only his mamma could love him,' quipped Rufus wryly. 'Yup, and look at the body language, that man has a lot of repressed hostility.'

Jack resisted the urge to burst out laughing and concentrated on the problem at hand.

'Rufus,' he commanded. 'Stay in the truck with Maria. Tom and I will try and get inside. Once we're in there leave it three minutes, then come in and get us.'

Rufus looked at Tom for confirmation, he got it.

'OK by me, boss.' He sounded a little too servile to be taken seriously but Jack ignored his harmless insubordination.

They got out, Jack taking the lead as they walked towards the entrance to the bar. By the time they arrived No-neck had been joined by one of his compadres. The new Heathen was a lot smaller and scrawnier, he had long dirty hair and a series of profane tattoos running up both bare arms. His face was long, lean and dirty, his top teeth protruding too far over his jaw giving him a feral rat-like appearance. The two of them were engaged in deep conversation and appeared not to have noticed the two strangers standing in front of them. As they were blocking the doorway, Jack had no choice but to get their attention.

'Excuse me, gentlemen,' he said. 'But me and my friend here would like to get by.'

No response. The two Heathens carried on talking as if they hadn't heard anything.

'I said me and my friend here would like to get by.' Jack raised his voice enough to smash through No-neck's conversation but was careful to keep the tone even and friendly.

It had the desired effect. No-neck looked up slowly from his smaller buddy down at Jack.

'Bikers only.' He spat the words out as if he were clearing his throat of an unwanted fly that'd been blown in by the wind, then he immediately resumed his conversation with Rat-boy.

Jack kept his cool, reaching out and placing a hand on No-neck's huge left arm just below the shoulder. He was careful to exert enough pressure to get his attention but not enough to cause pain. The big biker again swung his head in his direction. This time his eyes had narrowed to dangerous looking slits.

Jack leant forward in a gesture of confidentiality and whispered directly into the Heathen's ear.

'That's great, I understand and I agree with you. But you see, I'm a biker, and this here is my friend. I promised to take him to a great place for a drink. We've come a long way to be here and you wouldn't want me to let my friend down now would you?'

Having said his piece he released his grip on the man's arm and backed away a pace. For a moment No-neck seemed to be thinking, then his decision made his face

The Dark Lagoon

spread into a doughy grin. He stepped aside, motioning to Rat boy to do the same.

'OK brother. Have it your own way, go in, enjoy.'

Without returning the smile Jack went through the gap, pushed open the door and entered Henry's bar.

Even though Henry's had changed from the outside, nothing could have prepared them for what had happened to the inside of the bar. It was impossible they knew but somehow the interior seemed too big, Tardis-like. The only thing that hadn't changed was the position of the bar which lay directly in front of them. Between them and the bar were a series of raised round platforms surrounded by flashing coloured lights. Atop each of these platforms a naked girl writhed and gyrated to the pounding base of a heavy metal beat which seemed to emanate from the walls themselves. Their eyes drifted helplessly from platform to platform, scrutinising each dancer, comparing breast with breast, leg with leg.

Between the platforms were tables, mostly empty. It was easy to imagine the place later on, seething with leering Heathens, egging the dancers on to perform ever more obscene acts and joining in with obscenities of their own. There were more platforms set high up in the walls, accessed via a gallery running round the entire circumference of the bar. There were a few scantily clad waitresses moving quickly between the tables, serving the guests who had arrived early. Over by the bar a larger group congregated, in the middle of which stood Wilbur Kohn.

VII

Jack had counted at least fifteen Heathens before he saw Wilbur. He never doubted it was him although the face he was looking at couldn't have been more than thirty years old. The face was younger but the eyes were the same, cold and dead, a black cheroot dangling from the corner of his mouth. As their eyes met the music seemed to hush and Wilbur spoke.

'Good to see you Jack. Glad you could make it. I see that you and Tom approve of the surroundings eh?'

Jack tried to appear relaxed even though every muscle in his body was itching for action.

'I don't have time for small talk Wilbur. You know why we're here.'

His voice carried a steely authority that couldn't be ignored. He met the abomination's gaze full on, never wavering.

Eventually Wilbur looked down cowed. When he looked back up his face had aged. He was the "old" Wilbur Jack remembered from twenty years before.

'Jack, Jack,' he pleaded. 'It doesn't have to be this way. You know I always had a soft spot for you, you were like a son to me. You don't have to do this, you're wasting your time trying to help a loser. He's not your friend, he betrayed you and now he wants to welsh on a deal he made. Forget about him and join me. Join me and together we can live forever. Do it Jack and there'll be a hundred Toms and Samantha's, you'll see.'

It wasn't the words that captured Jack's attention. Wilbur exerted a power over him that went far deeper than words. He turned around and looked at Tom who seemed to have shrunk in size. No, it was more than that, he had withered. His face was covered in ugly looking warts as if the treachery in his soul had finally come to the surface and exposed him for what he was. Jack was revolted. He felt his stomach heave and he turned away. There was Wilbur surrounded by a bright light, extending his arms in friendship and forgiveness. How could he have been so wrong? how could he have allowed Tom to fool him? It didn't matter though because he had time to put things right.

'You know what you must do.'

Wilbur's words floated across the bar, their tone was sweet reason itself.

'Yes I know' Jack nodded and turned towards Tom.

Tom didn't even look human any more. His face looked like a rubber mask with no substance behind it. His features were exaggerated, grotesque. Jack assumed the attack stance that had become second nature to him during his years of training. He prepared to deliver a blow to the side of Tom's head that would rupture the main artery feeding his brain. He would be dead before he hit the floor.

The pounding base of heavy metal was now replaced with a rising chant coming from the Heathens who had gathered round with Wilbur at their centre. The words were foreign but their meaning was clear, to redeem himself he must strike Tom down. The world slowed down, he felt himself coiling up like a spring, compressing all the energy in his body into a small knot. He allowed that knot to grow and build until he could contain it no more. Then he released the full force of that compressed energy into his shoulder, catapulting his arm towards the side of Tom's head.

Somewhere between launching that fatal blow and it reaching its intended target something happened. A white light exploded in his head and he saw Ruth. She didn't say anything, she didn't have to, her presence alone was enough. In the light of her goodness he could see where the evil really was and how he was being duped into carrying out its will.

His fist came to rest harmlessly against the side of Tom's head, which to his relief had returned to normal, he looked at Jack questioningly.

Wilbur's face was changing again. This time though it was the real Wilbur that was finally revealing itself. The human facade was peeling back to reveal a black horror of unimaginable evil. The human eyes had gone now, replaced instead with two burning red coals. There was still enough of Wilbur left in the demon to allow it to speak with his voice.

'OK Jack, have it your own way. If you aren't with us, then as the saying goes, you're against us.'

The Wilbur demon turned to its Heathen cohorts and back to Jack.

'KILL THEM.' It screamed in a voice so inhuman it froze their hearts where they stood.

The Wilbur demon had began to advance on the two men, its red eyes engulfing them in their foul gaze. The Heathens were also advancing only more slowly, many of them were armed with weapons ranging from baseball bats to machetes and sawn off shotguns.

As the Wilbur demon came close, claws extended, it was clear it meant to dispatch Jack personally. One of the Heathens aimed a machete blow at Tom's head, the man's chest imploding just before he could strike as the pump action shotgun in Rufus's right hand cut him virtually clean in two.

The Dark Lagoon

Then as the Wilbur demon was almost upon him Jack was engulfed in a red haze of his own. Like the time he opened up the back of Wilbur's Van and was attacked by the giant mother rat protecting its mewling offspring. There was a pivotal moment where his mind could have given way to fear, it didn't.

The struggle that followed was more than just physical, although as the blood flowed from four deep wounds where the Wilbur demon's claws raked Jack's chest, it was clear there were to be mortal consequences.

While Jack fought the Wilbur demon, Rufus was using the pump action shotgun to good effect, cutting gang members down left and right, while using his free arm to fight off those who managed to make it in close. Tom too was giving a good account of himself. In the end though they couldn't hold out against such odds and the inevitable happened.

Tom was engaged hand to hand with a tall biker armed with a combat knife when another assailant came up behind him with a baseball bat. Rufus saw the move going down only he was too late to stop it. He would never be sure whether it was the odd sight of the biker's tattooed green head that caused him to hesitate for a fatal second, but by the time he'd swung his weapon around the baseball bat was tracing a wide arc, landing solidly in the small of Tom's back. A sickening crack split the air and he keeled over like a felled tree. Rufus managed to get off two rounds in quick succession, taking care of Onyx and the knife man before either realised what was happening.

He looked down in wonder at the reddened blade of the machete poking out from the middle of his chest. He had no sensation of pain, yet he knew straight away it was a mortal wound. He could already feel his strength begin to drain out of him. He knew in a moment his legs would start to wobble and his vision would begin to fade. He'd seen too many other men suffer similar injuries in action not to know the score. If he was to have any chance of taking revenge on his killer he would have to act quickly.

Summoning up every ounce of the considerable determination and guts he possessed, Rufus Cole reached behind him and found the hilt of the blade. His attacker was too shocked or stupid to try and stop him, instead he relinquished his grip on the machete and watched in dumb amazement as the huge black man pulled the blade out of his body. The look turned to horror as in one fluid almost balletic action, Rufus whirled round, arm outstretched, beheading his erstwhile opponent in one uninterrupted movement. This was to be Rufus Cole's last act on earth, after carrying out the execution, he crashed forwards against the bleeding torso of his killer and rolled onto his back, eyes vacant, staring blankly at the ceiling.

As Jack held the Wilbur demon by its fibrous wrists, their eyes locked in a battle of wills, the ground seemed to open up beneath their feet. They fell for what seemed like an eternity. One moment the demon had the upper hand, the next Jack could feel himself gaining control, forcing its arms apart ready to seize it by the throat and wring its corrupted neck. He could feel its hot sulphurous breath against his face as they fell ever deeper into the pit. The air became thicker, choked with smoke from fires burning not so far below. He cast his eyes downwards and thought he saw the gates of hell itself opening to greet them.

But he was possessed of a supernatural power of his own. It was as if all the powers he should have had during the years he spent as a loser had come back to him all at once. The heat was becoming unbearable, he could feel his skin begin to crackle and burn, smell his own flesh start to cook as they entered the flames. Still his heart remained true, he refused to succumb to the fear that waited patiently for a sign of weakness so it could enter him and eat his mind. The claws of the demon started to grow in his grasp, stretching out, enveloping him in their frightful embrace, then they enfolded him, ready at last to do their awful work.

For a split second Jack knew it was over. He'd fought valiantly but in the end how could any man overcome such malice, such evil? But in his moment of defeat, for the second time Ruth was there. This time though she appeared in a point of light at the centre of the darkness. The light was so small, at first he questioned its existence. Whether out of hope or desperation he focused on that point of light, giving it his total concentration. He could still feel the agony of the flames licking at his body through the dark but he was also aware that the point of light had begun to grow. Ruth was now clearly recognisable at its centre, her smiling face full of faith, her mouth framing a single word.

'Believe.'

He did believe, and his belief shattered the black tomb in which he had been incarcerated.

Suddenly he was standing on the wooden floor of Henry's, the building was on fire, smoke choked the air and Jack's hands were truly round the throat of the demon. Only it was no longer the demon, it was Wilbur who Jack held in his hands, watching as the red light faded from his eyes. It wasn't necessary for him to wrestle with his conscience about whether or not he should choke the thing he held. In front of his eyes its body was disintegrating, this time ageing way past the point it had been in the wheelchair. The skin of its face first fell in on itself, then holes appeared through which Jack could see grey flesh and white bone. Horrified he dropped the dying thing to the floor where it collapsed in on itself, sending up a cloud of dust which was all that was left of Wilbur Kohn.

He didn't have time to ponder the horrors of what he'd seen and felt. He looked himself over quickly and saw that apart from the four wicked cuts on his chest he was unscathed. Large pieces of burning masonry were raining down around him and he knew if he didn't get out he too would be turned to dust, forced to share eternity with the abomination he'd just helped to destroy. He looked around and his eyes fell first on Tom who was lying on the floor a few paces to his left and then to Rufus who was nearer the exit. There was a large pool of blood surrounding Rufus and he could see even from where he stood that he was dead. Tom on the other hand was moving, wasting no more time he crossed the distance between them in two strides, dodging fiery debris as he went. Not stopping to listen to what his friend was saying he grabbed him under the arms and started dragging him towards the door.

They only just made it. Jack had managed to put only a few metres between them and the bar when the roof gave way and came crashing down on whoever remained inside. The burning building sent flames up towards the crescent moon, wooden beams rending and splitting, sparks flying, seeming to touch the sky.

Jack looked down at Tom who was fully conscious looking calmly back up at him.

'I think my back's broken, Jack, I can't move my legs.'

Tom made this announcement so casually, at first the meaning was lost on Jack who looked back at him quizzically.

Tom waited for his friend's eyes to clear.

'I can't walk Jack,' he said flatly. 'You're going to have to carry me to the truck.'

The Dark Lagoon

Finally Jack seemed to get the picture, his face contorting with grief, tears welling up in his eyes.

'Save it Jack,' chided Tom. 'I think you did something good in there. I think we still have a chance. Don't worry about me, I guess in a way I've got what I deserve, forget me, we have to find Samantha before it's too late......'

He didn't finish the sentence, he didn't have too, they both thought what he wouldn't say.

'If it's not too late already.'

Jack realised his friend was right, he couldn't afford to indulge himself in sentimentality, there wasn't time, instead he started to drag him towards the truck. When they finally got there he managed to heave him upright and with Tom's help to arrange him in the passenger seat. He went round the other side and got in. The keys were still in the ignition and the engine was running.

'Is he dead?'

The question was so unexpected both men yelled in surprise. With everything that had happened they had forgotten about Maria. She'd watched every thing from where she still sat in the back of the truck.

'Yes, Maria, he is dead,' said Jack, delivering the news as if he was reporting a tragedy and chastising himself for his stupidity.

'I thought he was,' she said half wistfully. 'I suppose you want to go to the Island now?'

Tom turned round at this, his useless legs almost causing him to collapse forward as he did so. He just managed to save himself by grabbing the back of the seat.

'You mean you know how to get to the Island?' he said incredulously.

'You've known all along? Why didn't you tell us back at the house, you could have saved.....' He gestured at the carnage that was left of Henry's bar, 'All this.'

Maria sniffed as if she were fighting back tears.

'If I had told you back there you would never have come here. You would never have destroyed Wilbur and I would never be free. You don't know what it's like to have lived with someone, something,' she corrected herself, 'Like that for all this time.'

Despite the seriousness and possible consequences of her deception, neither man could deny she had good cause for what she did. Anyway that was the past and nothing could be done about it. In front of them was the future and she knew how to get to the Island.

'Wilbur had a launch, I know where he kept it, the position of the Island is on the launch. It's not far from here but before we go I suggest we go back to my house first, it's virtually on the way anyhow.'

'The wheelchair' said Tom. 'We can use the wheelchair now can't we?'

He looked forlornly at Jack who just nodded as he gunned the truck out of Henry's car park and back onto the highway.

VIII

In the moonlight the black launch seemed to bob up and down on an oily sea, its name "The Devil Rides Out" blazing out into the night. It was a daunting prospect to pilot this unholy vessel into unknown seas but it was a prospect that neither man could avoid.

'We can take it from here,' said Tom to Maria. 'I know how to handle the launch, you take the truck.'

He paused. 'And Maria, thanks.'

The middle-aged woman looked pale and wistful, for a moment Tom wasn't sure if she'd heard him.

'I'm coming with you,' she said. 'I've lived over half my life with a beast and I'm not missing my chance to destroy its master.'

Before Tom could protest further Jack interjected.

'We might need her, with you in your condition; anyway I think she has a right to come if she wants to.'

Tom shrugged his shoulders. Jack got out and set up the wheelchair helping Tom in and pushing him the short distance to the launch, and manhandling him into the cockpit. Maria was right behind, casting off and stepping nimbly onto the rear bench.

'Jack,' said Tom. 'I know how to handle one of these things, if you can help me into the driver's seat I think I can do it.'

'OK old buddy,' he said and heaved Tom over into the pilot's seat.

Tom looked impotently at the controls.

No key, no fucking key. An arm reached over his shoulder dangling a set of keys in front of him.

'I think you might need these' said Maria. 'He always kept a spare set under the rear bench, I guess that was one thing he didn't lie about.'

Tom took the keys and quickly located the ignition. Seconds later the launch's powerful engines burst into life, thrumming impatiently in the background.

'The co-ordinates are written down on a piece of paper in the glove compartment.' Maria yet again came to the rescue.

This time it was Jack who located the compartment and read out the co-ordinates to Tom who seemed to know what they meant. He looked at the dials in front of him for a second, then gunned the launch directly out to sea.

IX

In the event the co-ordinates were hardly necessary. In the first place the Island seemed to be directly in the path of the crescent moon and in the second place the launch seemed to know where it was going without any input from Tom at all. Once or twice he tried to steer off course, only to find a few moments later the stern of the launch had come round on its own, the prow pointing directly into the moon. After a few attempts he stopped bothering. After all everyone seemed to want to get to the same place, if for different reasons, so why fight it?

Everything seemed to be going so smoothly, too smoothly. The sea was calm, there was a gentle breeze blowing. It was almost as if the ocean itself was lulling them into a false sense of security, encouraging them to be unwary, to drop their guard just enough, *just enough*.

Up ahead a mist was forming, it was Tom who saw it first, he shook his head realising he'd been sleeping with his eyes open. He turned and looked at Jack who saw it too. They could hear Maria praying softly in the back.

'I've been through this mist before,' said Tom. 'The Island's just on the other side, we're nearly there.'

The Dark Lagoon

As if to emphasise the irony of this last remark the launch entered the outer edges of the mist. As it did so the engines died leaving them to drift on helplessly.

'Spoke too soon I guess,' said Tom ruefully as he hit the starter button again and again to no avail; the engines just turned over uselessly.

Tom asked Jack to check the fuel lines which he did, they were OK, there wasn't anything to explain why the engines had died and by now they had drifted into the heart of the mist. They could barely see one another, never mind what was up ahead, all they could hear was the lapping of the ocean against the launch's hull and a barely audible high pitched ringing that seemed to be coming out of the mist itself.

The ringing grew quickly, drowning out the sound of the water, drowning out the sound of each other's voices. It grew until it was like a creature inside their heads, gnawing, foraging excitedly at its new hosts.

'Maria'

Maria nearly jumped out of her skin when she heard her name spoken by a voice she had believed and prayed she would never hear again.

'Maria. You know you've been a bad girl, a very bad girl. And you know what happens to bad girls don't you? You know what happens to bad girls who disobey their husbands. Who betray their husbands to men who would see them destroyed, who would see them dead and turned to dust.'

The voice, which had started in a whisper ended in a roar that made her head feel like it was about to explode.

'Please,' she pleaded. 'Please don't, I didn't mean to.... I mean I didn't think....'

'Save it,' said Wilbur's voice from inside her head. 'I

don't want to hear. The important thing is you're sorry. You are sorry aren't you Maria?'

The noise inside Maria's head rose in pitch, the pain it brought with it threatened to send her overboard as she reeled backwards hands clasped uselessly over her ears.

'Yes, yes I'm sorry, I'm sorry' she shrieked.

'I didn't hear you' said the voice. 'Say it again but louder this time so I can hear you.'

The noise had become pure agony.

'I'm sorry,' she yelled it out so loud she thought her lungs would burst. Suddenly the noise stopped, at least for her.

'Good,' chuckled the Wilbur voice. 'That's very good indeed. You know, Maria, all couples have their differences but that's no reason why they should split up. You see I think that marriage is for life, my dear.'

The Wilbur voice paused here to laugh at its own joke before continuing.

'Well I'm afraid we have no more time for reconciliation, perhaps later? Right now I have something I want you to do.'

She tried to fight the force which had invaded her, she tried to fight it with all her might but it was no good. The Wilbur voice had taken complete control of her body, all she could do was look on aghast as she picked up one of the heavy oars and got ready to strike.

Jack turned round just in time to see Maria swinging the oar at his head. His reflexes weren't enough to save him completely, the oar struck him a glancing blow that sent him reeling across the boat and into Tom who was knocked to the floor by the impact. His head was just

The Dark Lagoon

starting to clear in time to see Maria standing above them bringing the heavy wooden oar down onto his face. Instinctively he put out his arm to fend off the blow. Anyone without his training would have seen their arm broken in two. As it was Jack could feel the bone crack as the oar rained down on him. One more like that and he too would be incapacitated and at the mercy of whatever forces dwelled in the mist.

Her eyes glowed with small red coals as she gathered herself to deliver the coup de grâce. Her arms reached behind her head, showing unnatural strength she arched her back, pulling her arms up above her head as she did so. For a moment Jack saw her there, framed against the moonlight, an expression of pure agony on her face, the deadly oar extending into the sky.

Before she could deliver the blow her chest exploded in a ball of red fire. The force of the explosion lifting her clean off her feet, sending her flying over the side, becoming ever brighter as she flew, lighting up the mist like some sort of cursed human beacon. Then she was gone, there was no splash, no scream, she just disappeared into the mist as if she'd never existed.

The high pitched ringing stopped. Jack looked down to where Tom was holding the smoking gun. He'd seen the flare pistol under the dash and used it without thinking. Now he seemed horrified by what he'd done, dropping the pistol hand shaking uncontrollably.

'God forgive me, God forgive me, what have I done?'

He kept saying the words as if he expected God to reply at any second.

Jack pulled himself painfully to his feet, nursing his injured arm as he did so. Next he pulled his friend upright and sat him back in the driver's seat.

'Listen Tom,' he said. 'There wasn't anything else you could do. For what it's worth, I don't think there was anything either of us could have done to save her and I think she knew it. There's no point in you going to pieces now, we're going to need everything we've got if we're going to stand any chance against Proctor.'

Tom was crying tears of pain and frustration.

'Stand any chance? What do you mean, stand any chance? We're stranded out here, we can't even reach the Island.'

Jack sounded tired when he made his reply. Sounded it and felt it, more tired than he had ever felt in his life. 'Try the starter, Tom, I think you'll find it's working now.'

Sure enough, when Tom pushed the button the launch's engines burst impatiently into life as if to say 'What's the matter, why the delay? Let's get going.'

In silence the two friends watched as 'The Devil Rides Out' brought herself about and accelerated into the mist like a bat out of hell. Seconds later they emerged into the clear moonlight, Rex Proctor's Island directly in front of them.

Chapter Two

I

One second they could see the Island dead ahead, the next it disappeared behind a huge pumping swell that came out of nowhere. Suddenly there was no time for Jack or Tom to brood on Maria's fate, or the horrors that lay ahead. They were both fully occupied in trying to stop themselves from being tossed from the small vessel into an ocean which had become a seething cauldron of anger.

The roaring wind sharpened and deepened the swell, creating gigantic foam topped waves, the first of which was about to come smashing down on top of them. Awestruck the two men braced themselves for the impact, involuntarily shutting their eyes as they did so. When nothing happened they opened their eyes to a calm ocean, no hurricane blowing, no gigantic waves crashing down, just a flat calm as the launch throttled back entering the shelter of a idyllic looking bay.

Whatever terrible force controlled the Island was sending them a message.

'Just testing you boys,' it was saying. 'Just wanted to make sure you were still awake, wouldn't want you to go to sleep and miss all the fun, now would we?'

'What the hell was that?' Tom demanded as he tried to haul himself upright. His legs like useless lumps of meat, dead and heavy. It was no consolation but, denied exercise, in the months to come they would wither to a shadow of their former selves and tasks like this one would become ironically easy.

Jack lent his friend a hand, grabbing him under the armpits and hauling him up onto the seat.

'I don't know but if I'm not wrong it won't be long before we find out.'

He motioned towards the small jetty jutting out from the fast approaching beach. At that same moment the launch veered off wildly to the right away from the jetty. Tom grabbed the wheel, relieved to find the controls were responding normally again.

'Looks like we're meant to do the rest ourselves,' he muttered wryly to himself as he steered the boat back round, giving the throttle a vicious pull as they approached their mooring sending the launch's nose skyward and Jack, who had stood up ready to grab hold and tie on, tumbling onto the back seat.

'Sorry about that,' Tom apologised. 'I couldn't resist it. I should have warned you but I wanted to surprise....,' he struggled for the right word '"it", I suppose.'

Jack picked himself up, a smile on his face.

'That's OK no harm done, maybe we can give "it" a few more surprises yet.'

With that he took the rope from the launch and jumped out onto the jetty. He tied her on to the metal ring that was conveniently to hand and jumped back in for Tom's chair. Once he'd set the chair up and made sure the brake was firmly applied he turned to the task of getting Tom out of the boat. Despite the calm sea there was a slight swell, not enough to unbalance him normally but too much to allow him to cope easily with the larger man as well.

He tried putting an arm round Tom and dragging him

The Dark Lagoon

along but there wasn't enough leverage, they just collapsed in a heap before they even started. In the end there was no alternative but to throw him over his shoulder in a fireman's lift. Jack's legs wobbled under the weight but held, he managed to get to the side of the boat and deposit Tom onto the jetty where he sat balancing himself with his arms.

'Sorry about that. I guess I'm not used to my new condition yet.'

Tom's eyes clouded as he reflected briefly on his own personal tragedy

'That's no problem, old buddy, now let's get you into that chair and get going.'

Jack looked up at the crescent moon and down at his watch. Time was moving on, soon it would be midnight and he had a feeling if they didn't find Samantha before then they would never find her.

Suddenly the ground shook violently. It wasn't like the warning tremors that come before an earthquake, just one huge shudder accompanied by a loud rending sound. As if some abominable creature had been released from its Stygian pit to hunt them down.

Looking down towards the beach there was nothing to explain the quake. The Island looked the same, white sand running up to a thick barrier of palms. They shivered despite the warmth of the night air and Jack went back to his task of getting Tom into the chair. Once he was securely in place Jack started pushing on towards the beach with a growing sense of urgency. The wooden jetty came to an end at the white sand which from a distance had looked flat and smooth.

Close up it was a lot deeper; Jack's heart sinking with the wheels of the chair. Pushing the thirty or so yards to the trees wasn't going to be easy. He put his back behind the task but all he succeeded in doing was to drive the wheels deeper into the soft sand. After no more that two minutes he was covered in sweat and they hadn't moved more than three feet away from the jetty.

'I'll have to get out,' Tom said as he threw himself out of the chair onto the sand.

'You take the chair up the beach to the trees and I'll pull myself up there and meet you.'

Jack could see there was no arguing with him, it was the only way they would reach the hopefully firmer ground of the palm forest. He'd swung the chair around and started to drag it up the beach when he saw the first of the creatures emerge from the sand over to their left.

II

At first he wasn't sure if it was his imagination playing tricks on him, or if the creature was real. After all it'd been an unusual sort of day and he could be forgiven for conjuring up the odd nightmare or two couldn't he? But no, as he looked again it stretched skywards out of the sand, back arched, revealing its gaping black maw and he was absolutely convinced of its reality.

Although it was still about thirty feet away, he guessed the body was about two feet in length, it looked like a gigantic version of the maggots he used to use when he went fishing as a young boy. He always remembered his father taking him into a bait shop and the owner taking the lid off a huge black plastic dustbin full of the squirming creatures. The owner would plunge his arms into the heaving mass right up to the shoulders, laughing at him as he did so.

The Dark Lagoon

For years he suffered a recurrent nightmare featuring the bait shop owner and that plastic dustbin. Instead of pulling his arms out, hands full of maggots, a big grin still on his face, the grin faded while his arms were still submerged. First the grin was replaced by a grimace, then a look of terror as he pulled wildly trying to get his arms out of the bucket. As he pulled the creatures in the dustbin were pulling back, trying to drag him into the bin with them. With a last desperate effort he would tear himself free, except when he stood upright his arms were gone, replaced with grisly stumps, white bone showing through the tattered remains of his shirt, dozens of the filthy white maggots hanging onto pieces of loose flesh with small razor like teeth.

It was as if a creature from his childhood nightmare had been somehow plucked from his brain, magnified a hundred times and incarnated here on the beach. He turned to Tom who was also fixated on a different spot off to their right. Jack could see the sand trembling, then a mound appearing, ballooning out before bursting like an infected boil, yellow pus spilling over the white sand. Another of the creatures, this one streaked with red throbbing veins emerged from the crater and started to wriggle and squirm its way towards them.

After the second creature appeared the beach turned into a war zone, craters were appearing everywhere. More and more of the creatures emerging, their white bodies, some with livid varicose veins, wriggling towards them, gaping black maws full of wicked looking razor like teeth open in anticipation.

Neither man needed to spell out the danger they were in. It was Tom who spoke first.

'You have to leave me here Jack and make for the trees. I don't matter now; Samantha is here somewhere and you have to find her!'

Jack was trying to think, he hardly heard Tom's desperate plea.

'Go on!' Tom shouted the words out. 'GO!'

Jack kept hold of the chair and ignoring Tom turned towards the palms and started sprinting as fast as his burden would allow him. He had to dodge several of the mounds as he went, one of them burst within a few feet of his right leg, spraying it with thick yellow pus. He didn't look down, if he had done he would have seen the creature leaping from the crater, jaws snapping hungrily together inches from his calf.

He didn't look back, just concentrating on reaching the trees, praying there would be no more mounds erupting in the forest. As he got closer he could make out a path heading directly into the Island's interior, seeing no other way through the tightly packed palms he made for the opening. Thankfully the path seemed firm and uninfected.

He was twenty yards or more into the forest, the moonlight almost entirely gone, in virtually total darkness, when he remembered Tom. What fever was it that gripped his mind so hard as to cause him to forget so easily? He left the chair where it stood and raced back down the path, stumbling and nearly falling over unseen roots and fallen branches as he ran.

When he hit the opening he saw Tom had made it nearly a third of the way up the beach before the creatures had surrounded him. He could see they were closing in, inexorably tightening the circle they'd formed around him. A few of the larger, bolder creatures had broken away and were already moving in for the kill. If he was to have any chance of performing a rescue, he would have to act with lightening speed.

The Dark Lagoon

His pulse raced, adrenaline flooding into his system, a red veil descending before his eyes. The creatures may have held a special horror for the old Jack but this new Jack gave them hardly a care as he came charging down the beach yelling and screaming like a demented dervish.

Even taking into account the power sapping effect of the sand, the slope of the beach enabled him to get up to a good speed before he broke through the circle of carnivorous maggots, kicking one creature several feet into the air as he did so. He was still sprinting as he reached Tom who lay powerlessly watching as the largest boldest creature went to work on his left shoe. If he didn't act quickly Tom would be forced to watch as these maggots from hell first devoured his useless legs and then started on the rest of him. As it was Jack aimed a mighty kick which connected with full force with the creature's eyeless face. The result was to sever its jaws and about three rings of its body, sending them flying into the air in a cascade of grey liquid.

He ploughed on, reaching the jetty in a few more strides. What he wanted was the remaining oar from the launch. He found it tucked into the side of the boat, picked it up and, wielding it over his head like a claymore, came charging back up the beach. Even though it had only taken a few seconds to retrieve the oar, by the time he reached Tom the creatures were all over him. The crippled man was putting up a brave show, using his bare fists to hammer as many of the little bastards as he could, as the mutilated bodies scattered around him testified.

He was however, going down fast. One of the creatures had already taken off a sizeable chunk of his left foot, it had retreated a few paces away from its victim and was casually chewing on its gory prize. Another of the maggots was crawling up his leg, seemingly disinterested in the meat of his thighs, set on what it could smell between his legs.

Jack didn't hesitate this time, even for a split second. He waded in among the maggots, quickly dispatching the one trying to get at Tom's private parts along with its kindred who were hanging on to various parts of his body. He used the oar wherever possible and where not, his feet and fists. The red haze became deeper until all he could see was blood and the bodies of his victims. When his vision began to return to normal, what he saw both shocked and amazed him. Strewn all around were the mangled bodies of the maggots, not one had survived his onslaught. As for Tom, he lay on the sand face down, bleeding from a dozen wounds. For a moment Jack thought maybe his rescue attempt had been in vain. He knelt down and gently turned him over, relieved to hear a soft moan as he did so.

On closer inspection most of his wounds were superficial. The only serious injury was to his foot, pieces of bone sticking out at odd angles, a great flap of skin all that was left of where the toes should have been. He'd lost a lot of blood, he needed to get to a hospital and soon.

During the fight Jack hadn't been aware of having suffered any injuries. It therefore came as a surprise to discover that he too had been bitten in at least six places. He would survive though. For the first time he was starting to get an impression of the enemy they faced. Up to now he had no concept of what Proctor was, or the extent of his power. Wilbur was the only face he could put to the enemy until now, but slowly another image was forming, pulsating in his mind, an image that made his blood run cold in his veins. What next he wondered and even in his wondering he knew the answer. He had to go onwards into the Island's interior, only there would they find the answers they needed. Somehow he had to get Tom up the beach and back into that chair.

III

While Jack was pondering what lay ahead, Tom was slipping into a semi-delirious state. He'd been close to the edge when he set out to find Jack, after meeting his old friend again the realities of the journey brought him back to some kind of normality. Even when his back was broken he remained resolute, but now the sense of purpose that had driven him so far was beginning to break up, melting like a thin layer of ice on a sunny autumn day.

The attack of the maggots was the last straw, it wasn't just the physical injuries, his mind had become unhinged. The only thing he remained able to focus on was Samantha. He was going to get his little girl; she'd been taken away from him but he was going to get her back.

He couldn't feel himself being dragged up the beach, or help as his friend struggled to get him into the wheelchair. He was oblivious to the deep ruts as Jack pushed the chair along the path that led to the dark lagoon, and to the roots that threatened to tip the whole thing up as they progressed slowly through the forest. He couldn't hear Jack panting and gasping with the effort of his labours, he wasn't aware of the gash to his forehead, or the blood running down his face and into his mouth, when the chair finally hit an obstruction big enough to spill him out onto the infected ground. The only cogent image he had left in his tortured brain was that of Samantha, his beautiful Samantha.

Daddy had come a long way to find her, he was coming to get her, to take her home before the bad man could hurt her.

As they emerged from the forest into the clearing his eyes were rolling convulsively, spittle hanging in spidery strands from his bottom lip. His psychoanalyst would have had no hesitation in pronouncing him crazy as a loon.

IV

As soon as they entered the clearing he woke up snapping into total consciousness like the Christmas lights in Oxford Street when the power goes on. He saw his daughter standing in front of him; radiant, more beautiful than he could ever remember. The sight galvanised him into action so fast he left Jack standing stunned in his wake.

'Samantha! Samantha!' he called hysterically. 'I'm here, daddy's here, I've come to take you home.'

He called out her name, great tears of relief running down his face as he wheeled furiously towards her oblivious to his surroundings.

When they emerged from the dying forest Jack had been almost done in from the effort of pushing Tom and the chair through the soft sand. The last part of the journey reminded him of a scene from Snow White where she ran through the forest, roots and branches coming alive, reaching out to trip her up. It had been the same for them, the ground itself seemed to be alive and hostile, doing its uttermost to ensure they never reached their destination. But now as he looked out over the vastness of the dark lagoon he knew they had reached it nonetheless. From where he stood he saw Samantha; but unlike Tom he also saw Rex Proctor standing there like some unspeakable spectral bridegroom at a satanic wedding.

Tom had almost reached her now, still shouting out her name.

'Samantha! Samantha! It's Daddy, it's Daddy, I've come to take you home.'

Her heart leapt when she heard her father's voice. She'd been about to take the plunge when she heard him calling to her. At first she thought it must be an illusion, how could it be him? How could he be there? Hearing him calling to her, real or not was enough to make her pause and turn around. What she saw upset her more than all the things she'd been through since the ship went down.

In her mind's eye her father was a tall strong man, perhaps a little harsh at times but someone resolute she could always rely on, lean on if necessary. The sight of him in a wheel chair covered in blood, clothes tattered, the sound of his voice thick with unsteady emotion shook her to the core. She was seized with an overwhelming urge to go to him, to take him in her arms and comfort him, to tell him that she was there, that everything was going to be all right.

'Samantha,' this time it was Simon's voice that stopped her in her tracks.

He was still standing there a few feet away, just the sight of him reassured her that everything would be OK.

'Samantha, your father is here. He has come to see you do the thing you know must be done. He has suffered so much to be here, he will be so proud.' The voice was silky, persuasive, irresistible.

'Don't listen to him,' Tom's voice rang out like a bell in the night air, all traces of insanity gone. Now was his chance to face the evil that'd haunted him for so long, now was his opportunity to snatch his daughter back from the jaws of the death.

'He's a monster, Sam, don't listen to anything he says, it's all lies. Whatever it is he is asking you to do, don't do it, it will destroy you and make him strong again. You have to believe me, darling, you've been tricked, I've been tricked, we all have.'

Samantha couldn't believe what her father was saying. What was he talking about, "tricked"? Who was a monster, Simon? What he was saying didn't make any sense, yet why would he say these things if they weren't true? She was deeply troubled, until now there had been no doubt, no hesitation clouding her resolve but now.... She looked from her father whose wheelchair had come to a halt about ten yards away to Simon who was almost close enough for her to reach out and touch. As their eyes met she knew he hadn't tricked her, she knew without him having to say anything that everything he had told her was the truth, she didn't even need him to explain what was happening to have her faith restored.

Tom saw the problem and so did Jack. One moment there were questions in her eyes, then she looked at Proctor and the questions vanished.

'What do you see when you look at him Sam?' Jack shot the question out before Tom had a chance to say any more.

She looked at him with wide enquiring eyes.

'Who are you?' she asked.

'I'm a friend, a friend whose come a long way to be here, Sam, a very long way and it's been a difficult journey. I'm here because your father and I were once friends, too. Now we're here we want you to come with us, we want you to come home. I can see you have something else on your mind, Sam, so I ask you again, what do you see when you look at him.'

Jack looked at Proctor and back at Samantha.

The girl pondered the question and the answer.

'I don't know why you're asking me that question but what I see when I look at him is the boy I love, the boy who saved my life and whose father saved my life. I see someone who has given me a mission meant for me alone, one that no matter what the cost I cannot avoid'

Jack looked again at Proctor, what he saw was a tall man in his forties dressed in black, a leering grin spreading over his hooded features. What he saw and what Samantha saw were totally different.

Summoning up all his strength Jack broke the spell Proctor was working on him and spoke again.

'Sam. I know this is hard for you. It's hard for me too. We all have images of the ones we love, when they turn out not to be what we thought they were it can tear us apart, believe me I know. But you must look at him again, look harder and deeper this time, you have to look past the veneer to what's underneath. What you will see will make you cry, it may even destroy you but you have to do it. If you don't it won't only be you who pays the price it will be everyone you love, everything you care about.'

His impassioned plea penetrated everywhere and everything except Samantha's heart. That was shielded and impenetrable, kept inaccessible by the black hand that enfolded it. Jack could see he'd failed, tears of anger ran down his face and once again the red veil started to fall before his eyes.

' How touching, both of you,' Proctor spoke the words quietly. 'You're wasting your breath you know. She can't hear you anymore.'

Proctor's voice cut through the night air like a knife through Tom's heart. But Jack wasn't interested in words anymore. The time for words had passed. He leapt at Proctor with the speed and ferocity of a cheetah but even as he closed the gap between them, fast as he was he wasn't fast enough. His enhanced perceptions registered the change starting even before his eyes confirmed them.

What he and Tom had seen when they entered the clearing was a middle aged man, what Samantha saw as she stood on the edge of the dark lagoon was a slim youth, but what was emerging now was the real Rex Proctor. The human shell was cracking and breaking like an eggshell revealing a creature blacker than the night, its form shifting shapelessly in the breeze.

Jack felt his throat constrict violently, his heroic effort ended before it begun. The whole thing had been a hoax, a charade put on by Proctor to heighten the drama of his victory. He saw all this as he felt all his old weakness return with overwhelming force. It was as if he was a terminal cancer patient who'd been enjoying a few brief days of remission before the end and that end had finally arrived.

'What a waste,' he thought. 'What a terrible waste,' as he sank to his knees before the black apparition. Everything had been for nothing; they'd lost.

V

Out of the trees on the far side of the dark lagoon a figure emerged dressed in white. The sight of her drew everyone's attention, especially Jack's.

'Ruth,' he managed to gasp through the pin-sized hole his throat had become.

Proctor had reformed himself and for the first time wore a puzzled expression. Up to now things had gone largely as planned. In truth the two men had put up more of a fight than he would have predicted but still he'd never felt under threat. The arrival of this woman was unexpected though. Not that it made any difference one way or the other though. Nothing could stop his plan from succeeding now, or his destiny from being fulfilled. What did it matter if one human more or less witnessed his triumph?

Chapter Three

I

When Ruth was awoken by Tom's unexpected arrival at the house she'd seen the effect he'd had on Jack and was elated. In all the time they'd been together they'd never talked about what happened when they were younger but she always knew those days somehow held the clue to her husband's depression, a depression that she felt as acutely as him.

Her ability to feel the emotions of others had caused her much pain and joy since she was a child. She'd always been able to see through a person's facade to what was underneath which meant she'd always faced a clear choice between good and evil in a way that few others ever would, simply because she could see the difference between the two so clearly.

After they'd made love that night Ruth asked Jack to tell her what was going on. At first he refused, wanting to shield her but when she insisted, he realised she had a right to know and told her everything he knew. She wanted to go with them but he would not agree and there was no time to argue so instead she followed them in secret.

Nothing on earth could have prepared her for what she would have to do; except the conversation she had with Maria in the back of the truck while the men fought for their lives in Henry's bar.

Maria had recognised Ruth's character for what it was straightaway. Having lived so long with evil she'd became very aware of its opposite and Ruth's goodness shined out of her like a beacon. Maria took the biggest gamble of her life in the back of that truck, she put her absolute trust in a woman she'd only just met. She told her everything she knew about Proctor, his nature and his plans. Ruth therefore became the only person on earth outside the closed circle of his followers who knew the full extent of his ambitions and the full depth of his evil. In that moment she assumed a mantle of responsibility which went beyond herself, beyond Jack and the children, and out to the whole of mankind.

She rented a boat and arrived at the Island before the others, making her way to the centre and watching from the trees as Simon and Samantha entered the clearing. She knew what Proctor wanted Samantha to do and why he wanted her to do it. What she planned wasn't suggested to her by Maria, it came from within herself. She was still in hiding when Jack and Tom emerged. Her heart nearly broke as she watched the pain and humiliation the monster was dealing out to the man she loved but she held her resolve, waiting for the right moment. Seconds later that moment was upon her.

The woman paused to look at the group gathered on the far bank, if they'd been close enough they would have seen her eyes shining brightly with inspired purpose. What she was about to do she would do out of love, pity, and courage without thought for herself or any guarantee as to the outcome. She gave Jack one final glance and smiled her warm generous smile before plunging of her own free will into the dark lagoon.

II

One moment Ruth's silhouette was in sharp outline against the night sky, hair streaming in the breeze, the next she was gone, absorbed by the black waters without even a splash to mark her going.

Proctor watched this spectacle intently. When it was over he turned back towards the others and laughed out loud. It was the laugh of a demon, all pretence stripped away, it was the laugh of a demon rejoicing in his evil work, feeling no threat from this woman's selfless act.

Jack wished he were dead, it would have been better for him if Proctor had killed him. At least that way he wouldn't have had to watch as the love of his life threw herself away in such a noble but useless act of sacrifice. Tom sat impotently watching as his daughter continued on her path of self destruction. Samantha seemed not to have noticed Ruth's demise, she was totally bewitched.

Suddenly the still waters of the dark lagoon rippled unexpectedly.

At first a gentle eddy lapped against the swollen banks. There was a pause as if the waters themselves were drawing breath. In the dead calm the silver crescent moon could be seen reflected in their mirror smooth surface. Then the ground shook, only this time it wasn't Proctor but another power that caused the movement. The ground stopped shaking and for a moment it seemed that would be the end of it. Perhaps Ruth's goodness had caused a little mild indigestion, a few burps and that was all, or was it?

Samantha had frozen where she stood, there was something happening at the centre of the lagoon. It was as if someone was dropping pebbles one after another into the water. Ripples were forming and with each ripple the darkness in the water was fading. It was hard to detect at first but after a little while the change was undeniable. The waters were clearing faster and faster, their texture changing from thick and viscous to light and fluid, in a few more seconds they would be as clear as any mountain stream. Then in the centre of the crystal lagoon a lone figure broke the surface.

For over a thousand years things had gone Proctor's way. For over a thousand years he'd fed mercilessly off of humankind without resistance or failure, now finally was it over? There truly was no power on earth that could stand against him and yet was he now to be felled, beaten by the very thing through which he had sought to gain his salvation, human goodness? It would not, could not be, he would not allow it. This woman may have thwarted him but the outcome could still be the same, what difference which human made the change, it was made, that was all that mattered. The dark lagoon was gone and he was free to build once more.

III

Before she took the plunge Ruth had no idea whether her action would thwart Proctor's plans or fulfil them, resulting in her own destruction. She knew she had to do something, couldn't just look on helplessly while the Demon destroyed them all. In a way she felt as if she'd been born to do this thing, that she was in some way fulfilling her destiny. There was no terror, no hesitation or holding back. When she gave herself, she gave herself completely and it was perhaps this selfless purity that saved her.

At first it had been awful, it was like the lagoon was a malevolent life force trying to absorb her. She could feel the darkness invading her mind, filling every crack and crevice with its putrescence and corruption. She did not resist but allowed herself to be defiled, used as a vessel, taking all the evil, all the hate the lagoon contained and giving it a new home in her heart.

If the blackness had been allowed to mingle with her own essence she would have been destroyed instantly. Somehow though she was able to confine it to a part of her she never even suspected existed. There was a partition in her soul where the blackness could remain without infecting the rest of her. There was so much though, so many half lives of pure evil. Yet her compassion for these disembodied and divided souls had no end, she allowed herself to absorb more and more until she had taken all the lagoon could give her. When it was over she felt an energy no human had ever felt for more than a millisecond before succumbing to its power but it could not touch her.

She swam to the shore and saw her husband standing there beside his friend, rooted to the spot. She saw Samantha standing waiting beside the lagoon, her expression blank and lifeless. She saw the monster responsible for all the evil the lagoon had harboured standing like a spider whose web had caught three juicy flies, trying to make up its mind which one it would suck dry first. So distracted was it by its musings she was out of the water and only ten feet away before it noticed her.

She felt its attempt to subjugate her to its will like a battering ram against the gateway of her mind. For the first time she too felt terror as she experienced the horror of an evil so pure, so concentrated it, threatened to send her mad. She could feel the darkness within her bursting to break free and something else as well, something that shaded even the Demon's power, the incredible magnetic pull of the silver crescent moon.

The Dark Lagoon

Rex Proctor watched with mounting confusion as the woman raised her arms in defiance of his will. Her hands glowed with an aura so black they gleamed against the night sky. To his astonishment he felt a foreign power invade his being, forcing him to raise his arms in a powerless salute to the crescent moon his hands radiating a light so white it was the alpha to the omega of the shining blackness.

They faced one another forming an archway with their bodies, arms outstretched, the crescent moon blazing at the apex. In perfect unison twin beams of light, one black, the other white burst forth from the vessels that contained them arcing upwards, colliding across the face of the silver moon. Ruth released the darkness she had absorbed in the dark lagoon and the demon was forced to return all the goodness it had stolen during a thousand years of stealing. As the last traces of darkness left her body, the black aura disappeared and Ruth became herself once more.

At the same time the white light coming from Proctor was also exhausted and his hold over the others broken. His human shell disintegrated and the shapeless Demon grew before them, rising up in fury like a demonic storm cloud, terrible black hands reaching out to engulf them.

Before the Demon could seize its prey, it let out the most agonising scream that human ears have ever heard. The thing that was Proctor was starting to rotate, hands held skywards, faster and faster, becoming a vortex of blackness with two burning coals at its centre. A vicious wind rose around them, its banshee wail merging with the Demon's scream, the vortex expanded and contracted before streaming upwards towards the moon in a chromium beam of blackness. Then it was over and the humans stood alone.

VI

'The Island's disintegrating. We must get out of here,' shouted Ruth above the growing storm.

Sure enough the ground was beginning to shake convulsively, trees could be heard crashing down in the forest and great geysers were shooting out of the lagoon.

'Come on,' said Jack. 'We've got to get back to the launch, follow me.'

'No Jack,' Ruth's voice could only just be heard above the howling storm. 'The launch will be destroyed along with everything else that monster created. You have to follow me.'

And so they followed her, Jack pushing Tom's chair, Ruth leading a dazed Samantha by the hand, somehow managing to avoid the falling trees and gaping chasms which were opening up all around them. When they reached the shore they got in the boat and left without a backwards glance, lest by God's wrath they, like Lot's wife escaping Sodom and Gomorra, be turned into pillars of salt.

Epilogue

So in the end the Devil didn't get his prey. Jack returned to England where in the course of time he would become wildly successful, although not in such a brash, superficial way as may have been the case if his brush with the supernatural had never taken place. In many ways he felt he owed something to Proctor, without whom he would never have learned what was truly valuable in life. Material things would not rule him now, he knew there were things much more valuable and powerful in the world than money or possessions and he was a better person for the knowledge.

Tom stayed in America, eventually coming to terms with his injuries. He gave up his job with the bank, after all he'd made more than enough money and it was time to smell the roses. Ellen never told him how close she'd come to leaving him, how could she? He was so different now, so helpless. True she was worried that he would end up round the house all day, under her feet but she needn't have. He became absorbed with his old interests of geology and animals and after a while Ellen even started worrying that she hardly saw him at all.

Jack and Tom kept in touch, their friendship re-established, although it would never be quite the same. They would speak on the phone and visit once a year. Tom would never talk about the events in their past although Jack often wanted to. There was a distance between them caused by their experiences that could never be wholly bridged.

Three months after they returned from the Island it was confirmed that Samantha was going to have a baby.

Simon Shinerock

Five months later she gave birth to a healthy little boy whom she named Simon. Samantha asked Jack to be the boys God father, he agreed readily bringing his whole family over for the christening. Tom and Ellen said nothing although it did send a chill through both of them to hear the name. They soon forgot their misgivings though as Simon was a delightful child, intelligent and vivacious, his babyish charm, winning the hearts of all who came into contact with him.

The next few years seemed to fly by, there were no tragedies or triumphs to mark the passing of the years. It seemed the lives of all who had been marked by Proctor's hand had finally returned to the everyday humdrum world. Alas such is the way of life that lightening rarely fails to strike twice. It's as if the elements themselves recognise differences in people not apparent to science or even magic, differences that attract calamity no matter how fast the unlucky host may run, or how cleverly they may hide.

It was a tragedy when they lost Simon. It should have been the perfect family holiday. No-one could understand how such a small child managed to get out of his room while his mother slept, never mind about scale the waist-high railings and end up falling overboard. This was in the end what must have happened, either that or he was abducted in the night and somehow spirited away. All the passengers and crew were thoroughly investigated but to no avail. Despite an extensive search of the area no body was ever found. Of course the search was somewhat hampered by the odd sea mist that seemed to appear from nowhere, obscuring the crescent moon that hung motionlessly omnipotent, in the cloudless sky.

E.E. 'Doc' Smith's classic Lensman series

Triplanetary

The planets Arisia and Eddore were at war for control of the Universe. The battleground was a tiny backward planet in a remote galaxy called Earth!

Only a few Earthlings knew of the titanic struggle, and of the strange, decisive role they were to play in the war of the super-races.

ISBN 1899884 12 2

First Lensman

No human had ever landed on the hidden planet of Arisia. A mysterious space barrier turned back both men and ships. Then Samms of the Galactic Patrol got through—and came back with the Lens, the strange device which gave its wearer powers no man had ever possessed before.

ISBN 1899884 13 0

Galactic Patrol

The pirates of Boskone raided at will, menacing the whole of interstellar civilisation. Masterminded by a super-scientist, their fleets out-gunned even the mighty cruisers of the Galactic Patrol.

When Kim Kinnison of the Patrol found the secret Boskonian base, it was impregnable to outside attack. But a single infiltrator might penetrate its defenses—if he wanted to take on million-to-one odds!

ISBN 1899884 14 9

Gray Lensman

Somewhere among the galaxies was the stronghold of Boskone—a network of brilliant interplanetary criminals whose mania for conquest threatened the future of all civilisation.

But where?

Boskonian bases dotted the universe—shielded by gigantic thought-screens that defied penetration. It was up to Lensman Kin Kinnison, using his fantastic mental powers, to infiltrate the Boksonian strongholds and learn the location of the enemy's Grand Base—and smash it forever!

ISBN 1899884 15 7

Second Stage Lensman

Kim Kinnison had the incredible assignment of infiltrating the inner circle of Boskone. His job was to become a Boskonian in every gesture, thought and deed. He had to work himself up through the ranks of an alien enemy organisation, into the highest echelons of power—until it was he who would be issuing the orders that would destroy his own civilisation!

ISBN 1899884 16 5

Children of the Lens

It was beginning to look as though no one could prevent the annihilation of the civilised Universe. For a weird intelligence was directing the destruction of all civilisation from the icy depths of outer space.

Kin Kinnison of the Galactic Patrol was one of the few men who knew how near the end was. And in the last desperate stratagem to save the Universe from total destruction, he knew he had to use his children as bait for the evil powers of the hell-planet Ploor...

ISBN 1899884 21 1

Masters of the Vortex

A churning nuclear fireball, appearing out of nowhere, bringing utter destruction—and countless numbers of them were menacing planets throughout the Galaxy!

'Storm' Cloud, nucleonic genius, set out in his spaceship 'Vortex Blaster' to track and destroy the mysterious vortices—and embarked on a saga of adventure, discovery and conflict among the far stars.

ISBN 18899884 17 3 (Due out spring 1998)

**All titles are available from all good bookshops or by direct
mail from Macmillan Direct on**
01256 302699 (code 160)

**Cheques should be made payable to Macmillan Direct,
Houndmills, Basingstoke, Hampshire, RG21 6XS**
You can also contact us at our website—

WWW.Ripping-pub.co.uk

Ripping

HOBSON & CO

(PARANMORMAL INVESTIGATORS)

BY BRIAN HUGHES

On a dark and stormy night towards the end of the 19th century, amongst the collection of grimy Lancashire terraces known as Greyminster, a sinister meal once took place. The repast of two hoary geriatrics, the consequences of which would have far reaching effects, culminating a century later in the destruction of the known universe. Mrs Prune knew that the end was approaching. Something sinister was playing havoc with the arthritis in her right leg. She was also aware that there was absolutely nothing she could do to prevent it from happening. Only two men had the ability to accomplish that particular task. Unfortunately, one of them was a bone-idle, bigoted drunkard known as Jess Hobson, who would rather spend his evening down the Old Bull and Duck. And the other one was dead. Don't look now, but Armageddon has just arrived and it's got nasty, pointed teeth. A story of incredible and inventive imagination. Superbly illustrated by the author.

About the Book...

Unbeknown to Ripping Publishing, Hobson & Co began life as a Bulgarian soap opera. I skilfully recrafted the script, having stolen the characters and jokes from several episodes.

Actually none of this is true, but I bet it got Ripping going for a moment there! To be honest, Hobson & Co started out life as a script that I had originally planned on turning into a home video. Unfortunately, video cameras have a nasty habit of turning close friends into distant enemies. When it became apparent that nobody wanted to dress-up in stupid costumes, never one to let a good joke go to its rest in peace, I decided to adapt the screenplay as a novel. The rest is history.

ISBN 1 899884 11 4   £5.99

MERCER'S WHORE

BY J.K HADERACK

'Mercer raised the shield bearing the cross of Christa in his almost useless left arm as the cruel barbs of the demon's hooks attempted to rip at his flesh. Once more he struck with his broadsword and sparks flashed in the night as he struck the creature's heavy armour. His energy was all but spent; Mercer had never planned to meet his opponent in the dark of night. The demagogue should have been destroyed by the flames which devoured the temple. His parries were getting weaker and weaker, soon he would make a fatal mistake and that would be the end of it. It was then that Haye, his whore leapt up from the edge of the river and struck the demagogue with incredible strength and ferocity. It was as if she was possessed by the soul of Christa!'

The temple of cards conceals many dark secrets but, far beyond its warped and twisted wall, men whisper of the Slow Room which dilates time extending pleasure or pain infinitely.

But, for those who enter that room, there is sometimes a terrible price to be paid when human flesh is wagered upon the outcome of the barbaric combat ritual of Chain, Hook and Blade.

Facing Kum, the demonic Temple Guardian, many warriors have died in slow agony. But now, as clouds of war darken the land, a new challenger approaches from the East. His name is Mercer, a man who is perhaps the greatest horse-warrior of that age.

Yet, at the centre of it all is a woman who must finally stand between the forces of light and the powers of ultimate darkness. Her name is Haye but to others, she is known simply as Mercer's Whore.

ISBN 1899884 19 X   £5.99

MINDS OF THE EMPIRE
by WARREN JAMES PALMER

'For a moment Moss stood rooted to the spot staring down
the muzzle of the rifle pointed at his head. Then without
any conscious thought, pure power and anger surged
down his back from his head into his arm and then to his
hand. It felt as if his whole body was charged with a
million volts of pure energy, like some huge capacitor.
Where that power came from he couldn't say, it was as if
it came from the very roots of his soul. From head to toe
every hair on his body stood stock upright as if charged
with static electricity. Without even knowing the reason
why, he raised his hand and pointed at the guard with one
finger.'

By the year 2020 the United Nations World Defence
Force can finally guarantee the security of every nation on
the planet through the use of orbital laser battle stations.

That is until the day the Dyason arrived. The Dyason
are humanoid, but not from our star system. In a blitzkrieg
attack they wipe out the World Defence Force and within
days, force worldwide capitulation. except for a few
renegades, mankind is enslaved.

Out of the prison ghettos of London a new hero
emerges, a youth with exceptional mental powers. Minds
of the Empire follows Moss as he struggles to escape the
rubble of London and flee from both the Dyason and the
Resistance.

The first book in the Dyason series spans space, time
and legend in a fast moving adventure that keeps the
adrenaline pumping.

ISBN 1899884-00-9   £4.99

DOMINATOR

BY WARREN JAMES PALMER

Myrddin turned, looked the president in the eye and said, 'Yes Mr President, we have Excalibur. We have placed all our faith in one ancient vessel and a handful of new, untried fighter craft. Now it looks like this will be all we have, to face a brand new Dyason fleet. A fleet based on the same technology as we have ourselves. Don't you think we just might be putting all our eggs in one basket?'

Three years after the defeat of the occupying Dyason forces Earths survivors are slowly rebuilding a world devastated by war, safe in the belief that the ancient spacecraft found below Stonehenge will protect the planet. 'Excalibur' and her crew are a match for any new invasion fleet—or are they?

A reconnaissance team returns from the Dyason home world with news of a battle-cruiser equal in power to the 'Excalibur'. Known simply as the 'Dominator' the new Dyason battle-cruiser is the first prototype of a new fleet. Moss, the young telepath; Jenson, hero of the resistance; Myrddin the mysterious ancient and the beautiful Jennifer are gathered together for one more mission—destroy the Dominator!

Dominator is the second book in the 'Dyason' series and once more spans space, time and legend in a fast moving adventure that continues the cult saga.

ISBN—1899884 02 5   £5.99

THIRD PLAYER
BY WARREN JAMES PALMER

'Through a red haze of pain he just saw the shape of a huge beautiful bird with incredible graceful lines rise out of the hill where the abbey had stood only moments before. The bird of salvation was huge, dwarfing the combatants on the planets last battlefield. As the pincers closed about his body snuffing out his young life a smile touched his lips and the huge bird disappeared into the heavens with a triumphant roar.'

As the Dyason homeworld collapses into anarchy and chaos, a new threat is marching across the Galaxy. The Star-Web have but one purpose to their existence—The eradication of all humanoid forms of life!

The seer Dauphne and a few survivors from the agricultural world of Heligsion seek out Moss, Myrddin, Jennifer and Jenson as the saviours who will stop the self appointed Guardians of God.

The Star-Web see humanoids as vermin who destroy and pollute God's galactic Garden of Eden. It is their belief that for the humanoid races to achieve redemption for their sins, they must pay the ultimate penance—genocide!

Meanwhile, the clone Gulag and the ancient starship Dominator are trapped in an alien outpost called Extremity Station. Until now, Gulag has been the number one adversary of Moss and his team, but it will take the combined forces of all the Humanoid races to battle against extinction.

ISBN—1899884 08 4   £5.99

STARWEB

BY WARREN JAMES PALMER

'Myrddin stared out the creature who bore the resemblance of a human, but who's mind and soul belonged to another species entirely. He fought valiantly to maintain his mental shields, but knew in his heart he could not win. It was only a matter of time. And why couldn't he battle against this other mind? What was it that was so different about her as opposed to any other human, or even the Starweb? The answer was really quite simple, but one he had never even considered.

'You're not human, nor human-created!' He croaked aloud, desperately hoping the millions watching the drama unfold, would understand his words. 'You're completely alien! My God—you don't even belong in this universe!'

It is time for the humanoid races to pay for their sins. The Starweb has found Earth, the last planet still inhabited by the species. This time there will be no mistakes made, no second chance. With overwhelming force the Star Web attacks, determined to complete the genocide it began aeons ago. Moss, Gulag, Myrrdin, Jennifer, Jenson and Sandpiper are the last hope. The humanoid species has been eradicated from everywhere in the galaxy and Earth has only just begun to recover from the invasion and war with Dyason. The Starweb is a collective of sentient computers linked togethor like a galactic Internet. Can the Starweb be defeated? Can the human mind defeat sentient computers who believe God is on their side? One thing is for sure, necessity can make for strange bedfellows as enemies become allies in the first of this new exciting series!

Includes superb illustrations by Brian Hughes—author of 'Hobson & Co'.

ISBN—1899884 20 3   £5.99

Visit our Website for the latest in news, reviews and sample chapters!

From September 1997 the Ripping website will be open to everyone across the globe!

Visit our virtual bookshop and purchase copies of your favourite titles from not just the *Ripping* range of books, but the best of SF, adventure and sports books from a wide selection of other publishers!

WWW.Ripping-pub.co.uk